Bonnie Navarro
and
Louise M. Gouge

Instant Prairie Family
&
Cowboy to the Rescue

LOVE INSPIRED
INSPIRATIONAL ROMANCE

LOVE INSPIRED®
INSPIRATIONAL ROMANCE

ISBN-13: 978-1-335-97197-5

Instant Prairie Family & Cowboy to the Rescue

Copyright © 2021 by Harlequin Books S.A.

Instant Prairie Family
First published in 2012. This edition published in 2021.
Copyright © 2012 by Bonnie Navarro

Cowboy to the Rescue
First published in 2014. This edition published in 2021.
Copyright © 2014 by Louise M. Gouge

This edition published by arrangement with Harlequin Books S.A.

For questions and comments about the quality of this book,
please contact us at CustomerService@Harlequin.com.

Love Inspired
22 Adelaide St. West, 40th Floor
Toronto, Ontario M5H 4E3, Canada
www.Harlequin.com

Printed in U.S.A.

CONTENTS

Bonnie Navarro lives in Warrenville, IL. She and her husband will celebrate twenty-four years of marriage this year. They have four beautiful children, two still in high school and two college age. Cesar has often called their children Amerikicas—a mix of American and Incan. Bonnie works as a trained medical interpreter for a hospital close to home and when not at work, she is either reading, writing or knitting.

Books by Bonnie Navarro

Love Inspired Historical

Instant Prairie Family
Rescuing the Runaway Bride

Visit the Author Profile page at Harlequin.com.

INSTANT PRAIRIE FAMILY

Bonnie Navarro

"For I know the plans I have for you,"
declares the Lord, "plans to prosper you and
not to harm you, plans to give you hope and a future.
Then you will call on me and come and pray to me,
and I will listen to you."
—*Jeremiah* 29:11–12

My deepest thanks are due to my Savior and Lord.
May He receive all the glory for any thing
I might ever accomplish.

I would be remiss if I didn't give thanks
and honorable mention to:

Joanne, I blame you for empowering me
to believe that I could write a story someone else
would actually want to read. You said someday
you'd see me in print. Thanks for believing in me
even when I wasn't so convinced.

Betty, Dad, Martha and Terry.
You all took your time to read and
suggest corrections on different manuscripts.
I learned something from each one of you.

Cesar, Liz, CJ, Gaby and David—thank you for letting
Mom work on her book even when you wanted
dinner/to talk/clean clothes... I love you guys!

There are so many more who have helped me
on my journey to write—to each of you,
thank you and God bless.

Chapter One

❧

Harlan County, Nebraska, 1881

Will scooped up six-year-old Tommy and called to Willy over his shoulder, "It's time to go, son. The wagon is hitched and we need to leave so that we can get to the river before nightfall." Will had left detailed instructions with Jake, his nephew, about the care of the livestock and what Jake should be doing in the next three days. Now everything was ready for them to leave—everything except his oldest son. Willy had dragged his feet all morning, and Will was quickly losing his patience with his namesake.

"Are we going to go get the new Auntie Shelia?" Tommy asked, his little face full of excitement. His eyes were the same color as Caroline's had been—an expressive hazel that changed hues with her mood. Did the boy actually remember Auntie Shelia? No, that was impossible. Tommy was only three when Auntie Shelia had come to stay with them after her niece Caroline's death. She stayed six months before she declared the

West "too dangerous and uncivilized for anyone to hope to raise a respectable family."

"No, Tommy, not another aunt. She's our new house-keeper," Will corrected gently, trying to find the right words to explain. "Miss Stewart is coming to do the cooking and cleaning and help you and your brother with your studies. She will be like a grandmother to you but isn't related to you. She'll be our housekeeper. Do you understand?"

Will glanced out of the window impatiently, aware of the sun rising high in the horizon. It must be close to nine and they had a full day's ride to get to the river before dark. From the river it was only a little more than a two-hour ride and they would be in Twin Oaks with time to get cleaned up well before the train arrived tomorrow at noon.

Miss Stewart was due in on that train and he needed to be there. It wouldn't do to have his new housekeeper step off into the small prairie town and not have the family there to extend their welcome.

Will hadn't been all that set on the idea of bringing in a housekeeper when his mother had suggested it, but after several letters back and forth, he'd become convinced Miss Stewart was the perfect woman for the job. She was only one of a few dozen women who had replied to the ad his mother had placed in the *Christian Ladies' Journal* who seemed to want the job for the right reasons. Most of the others were only thinly veiled attempts to trap a husband. Miss Stewart wrote that she was ready to move on from her sister's home where she had lived for years, and that she wanted to settle in with a family who loved the Lord and where she could put her education and her gifts of cooking and cleaning to use.

Instead of answering his father, the boy yelled to his brother, leaving Will nearly deaf, "Hurry, we're going to go get our new house."

"Not *house,* Tommy," Willy snickered, finally sauntering down the stairs. At age nine he felt he knew all there was to know about life and delighted in informing his little brother. "Our new *housekeeper.* She'll probably take one look at this mess and make Pa take her right back to the train station." He sounded almost hopeful. Willy was right about one thing—their house wasn't likely to make a good impression. He and the boys would have to do their best to make up for that.

"Hey, that's enough. Now both of you head out to the wagon," Will ordered, setting Tommy back on the ground and glancing around his kitchen. The place had become messier as time went on. He had a bad habit of burning the oatmeal, and two skillets sat soaking in the sink were reminders of his lack in the culinary arts. One more thing Will had included in his instructions to Jake—make the place somewhat presentable before they arrived with the new housekeeper.

Will imagined a woman his mother's age. From what he had read in her letters, her character seemed to be above reproach, and that was his main interest—that, and how well she cooked. Hopefully Miss Stewart could teach his boys some table manners, as well.

Finally, Will and the boys were in the wagon, moving along toward the river. The sky seemed so big and far above the earth and stretched out in all directions without any hindrance. The prairie plants, just having started to grow again after the winter, danced at knee level and waved on the breeze that kept the sun from completely baking both man and beast. Will was grateful for his hat. There were no trees to offer shade on the large expanse of prairie until they came closer to the river.

As he drove, he took in the breathtaking scenery. His thoughts turned to how majestic God was, having formed all this with just a word. Will didn't need to be in church to be awestruck by God. Creation was enough to hold him spellbound and speechless. The boys asked questions and he took advantage of those opportunities to show them God's handiwork.

After a full day's drive and a good night's sleep by the river, Will headed into town, glad to be almost at his destination. He couldn't help but be impressed by the way the small town of Twin Oaks had grown from just five houses in the middle of nothing a few years ago to a small but bustling village. New settlers seemed to be arriving all the time. People were still taking advantage of the Homestead Act that President Lincoln had signed back in 1862. The same law Will and Mathew had taken advantage of ten years ago. Will found a spot in the shade of the train depot and tethered the horses to the hitching post.

Their first stop once they were in town was the barber. He wanted to impress Miss Stewart—not scare her off. The boys had not had a haircut in more than a year. He hadn't been very vigilant about combing out the snarls, either. Once everyone looked civilized again, the barber offered them each a piece of hard candy from a jar on his countertop.

Main Street was crowded—plenty of people waiting for goods and travelers off the incoming train. Back out on the street, he headed the boys toward the mercantile. Glancing at his pocket watch, he assured himself there was still time to pick up supplies before he needed to meet the train. Afterward, he could take the new housekeeper and his boys to lunch at the one and only hotel in Twin Oaks.

Standing in the doorway of the store brought back memories of his father's store back in Philadelphia with all its sights and sounds. His throat tightened and he was surprised as a wave of nostalgia caught him unexpectedly. He took in the sight of wares stacked on wooden shelving and in barrels on the floor. Would his boys ever see his father's store?

Pushing aside his sudden homesickness, he set to work, choosing supplies. Warning Tommy and Willy not to touch anything, he let them wander around to look at the toys and gadgets on display. Meanwhile, he bought some coffee, sugar and a few other cooking items women used to buy at his father's store. He didn't even know how to use most of them but figured maybe Miss Stewart would. He hadn't savored homemade baking since Mathew's wife, MaryAnn, had died. It would be a treat just to have someone who knew their way around a kitchen again. He would ask the new housekeeper if she had ever made raisin bread or bread pudding....

He picked up the small crate of raisins and made his final selections. At the counter, he greeted Josh, the owner.

"Good to see you again," Josh said, tallying up the purchases on a piece of paper and then entering the figure in his ledger. "I haven't seen you since you brought in your wheat last fall."

"Yeah. I like to stock up when I get out. It's more than a day's trip out and I wouldn't risk it in the winter," Will rejoined. He wasn't really in the mood to chat, but he didn't want to seem rude, either. "Town seems to be growing."

"It is. We're getting more people every year. Are you going to be staying in town overnight or are you headed back?"

"We'll be headed back." Will was used to keeping his life to himself, but Tommy had other ideas.

"We gotta take our auntie House back to our farm," the little tyke explained in his mixed-up way. The shopkeeper blinked at Tommy and scratched his head, but Tommy continued on without a break. "She's gonna be a grandma to me and keep the house nice. She's even gonna teach us stuff like how to be gent'men. She's gonna be really nice—not like our other auntie, who was mean and yelled all the time...."

"Tommy." Will was surprised at the last statement. Tommy couldn't possibly remember his great-aunt. He must have been parroting something he heard from his older brother, or his cousin. But, no, it wasn't likely Jake had said anything—the teenager wasn't the type to tell tales. If anything, Will wished he was more in the habit of speaking up for himself. Willy, like his brother, had no such problem.

What did Willy remember of his great-aunt? Will had been too busy trying to keep the farm afloat to pay much attention to how the woman treated the children. He was going to have to do a better job this time. He wanted his boys educated but not at the cost of their being mistreated.

Once again, doubts assailed him—was he doing the

right thing by letting a total stranger into his home? Maybe he and Jake could handle the boys on their own. But he'd given Miss Stewart his word, and she had packed up her whole life to come out to Nebraska. He had to at least give her a chance. Maybe he could let her stay for a few weeks while he watched how the boys reacted to her. Meanwhile, he'd pray about sending her back or having her stay. She might decide Nebraska wasn't right for her after all. She'd hardly be the first to feel that way. In the meantime, there was no sense in borrowing trouble.

After all, he had been praying for this since last spring. God directed Miss Stewart to answer his ad and she would be arriving within the hour. Obviously God's hand moved in this and had sent her here. Tommy and Willy needed a woman's influence in their upbringing.

With that thought in mind, he prayed for wisdom and headed the boys out of the mercantile and off to the train station. The sound of the locomotive whispered on the wind as it came closer to town. Its whistle announced its approach before it even came into view. In just a few minutes, Miss Stewart would step off the train, and Will would see how right he'd been to bring her to Nebraska.

Within a few minutes, Abigail Stewart would be arriving in the town that was to be her new home.

The prairie looked so different from the rolling hills of Ohio that had been her only home for all of her twenty-six years. Nebraska felt as if someone had taken a huge rolling pin and flattened everything, leaving only waving grasses and flowers. Even the trees were missing. But the colors were vibrant as Abby watched the world pass by, and she couldn't help hoping that they symbolized a bright, happy new life she'd have with the widowed Mrs. Hopkins and her children, free from Abby's domineering sister and her brother-in-law's inappropriate attentions.

How would she be able to recognize Mrs. Hopkins? She had never asked for a description before. She'd just assumed that she would be able to see something in the woman's eyes that would match the gentle spirit and spunk Abby inferred from her letters. Now she wished she'd asked for more details.

Abby glanced around the stuffy passenger compartment at the other passengers traveling with her these last few days. The loud Erving family spread throughout the car. Watching them, Abby couldn't help wondering what her own nieces, Megan and Hanna, were going to do now without Abby there to encourage them. They were beautiful girls, almost on the brink of womanhood. Would suitors begin to call on them soon? What sort of lives would they end up leading? And the rest? How would Harold get his studies done with Peter always bothering him? Would little Katie even remember Auntie Abby? The girls had promised to keep in touch, and Abby knew she would cherish their letters and the news they would share. She only hoped she'd have lots of good tidings to share by return post about her new home and the family she hoped would accept her as one of their own.

As the conductor opened the door to the car and called out, "Twin Oaks, Nebraska. Next stop," Abby stuck her knitting into her satchel. She checked under her seat, pulled her satchel strap up over her shoulder and hugged it close. It held her letters, coin purse and knitting. Her heart sped up as she saw the town come into view. It was small and somewhat rough, as Mrs. Hopkins had warned her, but it looked fresh and exciting to Abby as she hoped that maybe she would find a place to belong to here.

As the train bounced and lurched to a stop, Abby tried to stand and found herself tossed against the conductor. Mr. Galvan had proved to be kind, making the trip as comfortable as possible for everyone. He regaled them with stories about other trips and the fascinating people he'd met over the past three years working for the railroad. The stories were a little marred by the man's terrible memory for names, but were very entertaining all the same.

"Careful," he chuckled, "you don't want to get banged up right before you meet Mrs. Hooper."

"Mrs. Hopkins," Abby corrected softly, "and thank you for all your help."

"It's been a pleasure to assist you on your trip. If you ever need anything, you can always leave word with the train station. Maybe I'll look you up in a few months… see how you're faring with Mrs. Hoskills."

"Mrs. Hopkins," Abby corrected for a second time.

"Twin Oaks!" Mr. Galvan's voice boomed, cutting off their conversation. He moved past her and stepped to the door of the car so that he could assist the passengers while they disembarked.

Abby clutched the seat in front of her, waiting until the last lurch of the train, and then followed the rest of the passengers to the door. She wasn't sure if it was the jerky motion of the locomotive or—more likely—the nerves of meeting Mrs. Hopkins and embarking on this new adventure that had her stomach twisting. What a first impression that would make—to get sick just as she stepped off the train.

Taking in a slow, deep breath, she prayed silently that God would protect her and lead her to the right place. The smoky air from the train did little to settle her stomach, but her nerves calmed slightly as she closed her eyes and imagined God watching her step onto the wooden platform. It didn't manage to go quite as smoothly as she'd imagined. Between the noises, the smoke and the bright sun, she tripped, lurching forward.

A strong and calloused hand reached out and caught her upper arm and kept her from falling. She blinked, finding herself face-to-face with a stern frown chiseled into a bronzed face, piercing blue eyes focused on hers. His face was shadowed by his straw hat, as if shrouded in mystery.

"Careful, miss." His voice were low and gentle, surprisingly cultured for a man in ripped overalls, a faded black vest and a threadbare cotton shirt. He held a child in his other arm. The boy clung to his shoulders as the man stepped back and released Abby. Strangely, she felt drawn toward him. He made her feel safe.

"Thank—" Her words were cut off by the shrill of the train's whistle and the belching of smoke that followed. The man looked past her, obviously searching to find someone else. It shouldn't have bothered her to so quickly lose his attention, but he had seemed nice… sincere.

Now was not the time to consider her confusing feelings. She needed to look for Mrs. Hopkins. Maybe the woman would be waiting with a wagon over by the station so they could get Abby's luggage off the train and head home. Abby made her way through the throngs of people to the end where men were unloading the freight. Seeing her three chests set to the side, she sighed with relief. She turned to study the faces of the people rushing around her.

Suddenly she felt very small and alone. What would happen if she couldn't find Mrs. Hopkins? The thought had never even occurred to her until she stood watching the other passengers meeting with their families or heading off to the livery to procure transportation. Soon she was completely alone. Minutes passed, but there wasn't a woman nearby who could have been Mrs. Hopkins.

She took a seat on one of the benches and prayed, hoping Mrs. Hopkins would arrive before she concocted a backup plan. The sun shone bright and the air stifled her very breath. It was hotter here than it ever got back at home in May. Her stomach churned, reminding her that the last thing she had had to eat was a greasy sandwich of scrambled eggs and some unidentifiable meat she'd barely swallowed down at daybreak at a tiny train stop.

Where could Mrs. Hopkins be? Did something happen to keep her from coming? Abby tried to pray, but the thoughts all got jumbled up in her head.

Will waited while a large family with a passel of kids piled off the train. A few men and a pretty, young lady who needed some assistance disembarking followed. Maybe Miss Stewart was having trouble gathering her things or had difficulty with the jerky motion of the train's stop. Did she need aid to exit the train? Will hoped he hadn't hired someone who was too feeble to be able to carry out basic chores.

"Excuse me, sir. Could you tell me if there are any more passengers getting off at Twin Oaks?" he asked the conductor.

"No, sir. Everyone's disembarked," the man answered. "Is there someone you're looking for?"

"Our auntie House," Tommy replied before Will could get a word in edgewise.

"He means our new housekeeper." Willy offered the information before Will could intervene.

"Yeah, her. She's old like our other mean auntie, but she'll be nice 'cuz Pa's gonna pay her to be nice and teach us lots a'stuff like how to be gent'men." Tommy picked up the story, hanging off his father's neck precariously to peek into the train.

"I'll bet she saw the prairie and got off the train back in… What state is that where the prairie starts?" Willy questioned midsentence.

Taking control of the conversation before the boys told all of the family secrets, Will eyed the conductor again. "Are you sure Miss Stewart wasn't onboard? She should have been in her fifties. She was coming to fill a position of housekeeper and tutor for my children. She would have been coming from Ohio."

"Nope. The only woman traveling alone was Miss Stevens." The conductor's gaze followed the girl who had just tripped off the train, and he pointed toward her. "That's her. She was going to be a housekeeper, all right—but for a widow woman…" He looked deep in thought as if he was trying to remember something. "Mrs. Hopple or Hope."

"That young lady?" Will clarified.

"Yes, sir." The conductor looked Will over from head to toe through narrowed eyes. "You had better behave around that young lady. She's very special," he warned in spite of his obvious disadvantage in height and build. Will looked down on the smaller man and wondered wryly just exactly what the man thought he would be able to do if the situation arose.

There was no reason to upset him, though. "I don't doubt it," Will said in a pacifying tone. "I have no intentions of bothering anyone. I just came to look for my new housekeeper. Are you sure she wasn't on the train?"

"No, sir, I've been on the train since we headed out of Illinois three days ago. There was no other woman that came alone except for Miss Standish. I hope everything is all right with your new housekeeper. Maybe she will be on next week's train."

Will felt the stirring of annoyance, then something akin to anger. If Miss Stewart wasn't on the train, she had just made off with five dollars' worth of his hard-earned cash. He had sent her a ticket and asked her to let him know if there were any obstacles that would keep her from arriving on this train. There was plenty of time for her to have sent a letter or a wire. He knew that she hadn't because he'd checked both at the post office and at the mercantile for any messages before coming to the train depot.

"Thank you for your time." He barely remembered to be civil as embarrassment and frustration warred within him. What kind of fool must the conductor think he was?

"Let's go get something to eat." Will forced a pleasant tone even though he was simmering inside.

"But shouldn't we wait for Auntie House?" Tommy questioned innocently.

"She didn't come. She's just like all the rest of the

women. They won't live out here in the wilderness and let the Injuns scalp them. She won't come to live out here. Even our own mother didn't want to stay with us here." Willy shouted the last part and darted off, not paying attention to the wagons or horses on the dirt street.

"Willy! Wait, son! You can't go running—"

He caught up to Willy two blocks away. The boy was hunched over, hiding in an alleyway with his face in his hands. Just before Will reached him, he let out a sob.

"Willy." Will set Tommy down and pulled Willy into his arms, holding him tight. "I don't know why Miss Stewart didn't arrive when we expected her, but it's all going to work out. Maybe she wasn't the one God wanted taking care of you and Tommy. Or maybe she is, and she'll come on the next train."

Even as Will said the words, he realized he was too far behind with the farm chores to make the trip again in a week. He would have to leave some kind of message at the train station just in case. And if there was a next time, he certainly would not be bringing the boys with to have their expectations dashed to the ground.

"No one wants to live out here. Auntie Shelia said it and so did Ma. It's a savage land with savages running around with no clothes on, killing people. I'm glad she didn't come. She would have been mean just like Auntie Shelia. Women are just trouble. I'm glad we don't have any at the house." The boy straightened his shoulders and pulled away from his father.

Will wasn't sure exactly what he should do. Willy's speech just showed him how much he had failed his boys. His own mother was wonderful… It was a crying shame the boys hadn't had a chance yet to know a woman like her—kind, generous and loving. But how could he possibly convince his sons of that if the only women they had lived with were women who had made life miserable at home? Was it time to think of sending the boys back to Philadelphia to be raised where they could get an education and where his mother could instill some appreciation for women into them?

"I know it's hard to believe, but there are some women who are good and gentle. Like your grandma and my sisters, your aunts and then there's Mrs. Scotts. You like her...." The boys *did* like Mrs. Scotts, and the other women who attended their small church. But with the busy lives these farmers' wives led, there wasn't much time for visiting with neighbors. They only saw them for a little while at church the one Sunday a month they had services. And that short amount of time wasn't enough to really know anyone. Even Caroline had been pleasant enough to their neighbors for a few short hours at church each month. It was when they were home that her mood had changed.

He stood and took Tommy's hand in his right and Willy's in his left. "What d'ya say we go get something to eat now? We need to head back in an hour or so if we're going to get to the river before nightfall. Maybe we can bag that stag we saw last night."

Tommy happily started chattering about their trip back and what animal he wanted to hunt as they headed back down the main street to the hotel. Willy swiped at his face with his hands and then his nose with his sleeve before Will could produce a handkerchief.

"Where's your kerchief?" he asked.

"I forgot, Pa." Willy blew his nose soundly.

"I ain't got no kerchief, Pa," Tommy reminded him. "You were gonna give me one and then you forgot."

"Sorry, son. We'll get you a few at the house." At least he hoped that there were still some hankies somewhere in the house.

A few minutes later, Will and the boys sat at a table in the dining area of the hotel, perusing the menu. "Pa, what are you going to eat?" Tommy's questions never stopped. Without letting his father answer him, he launched into his own opinion of the food, what he wanted, and ended with another question. "Why don't you cook like this, Pa?"

"Well, son," Will hedged. "I guess some things I just haven't learned yet."

"Maybe our auntie House... I mean our Miss Auntie could do it better," Tommy reassured him.

"Don't you understand anything!" Willy yelled at his brother. "She's not coming!"

"But I want her to," Tommy whined. "I want someone to cook better than Pa and fix my clothes so we could go to the meeting with nice clothes like Jill."

"Boys!" Will exclaimed, glaring at his offspring. He gave a short lecture on the right way to behave in public. Even as he was speaking, he remembered his father saying something very similar when he was young. When both boys calmed down, he nodded approval.

The waitress came and took their order, smiling and teasing the boys before she left. Comfortably plump, the woman looked to be about Will's mother's age. "Maybe we can ask her if she wants to be our auntie... How do you call it again?" Tommy quizzed his brother when the waitress left.

Before Will could stop the conversation, Tommy

turned his attention to the door. Standing up in his chair, he grinned, pointing and then waving at someone who had entered. "There she is, Pa. That lady that you caught at the train. Maybe she'll be our—"

"Tomas, sit down and put your arm down!" Will was about to pick both boys up and take them to the wagon. It was downright embarrassing that he had come all this way for nothing, and now the boys were making a ruckus here.

"But she's here, Pa. She looks really nice," Tommy whispered this time, dropping back into his seat but still staring at someone behind Will.

"I'm sorry, miss," he could hear the waitress answering the woman. "We don't have any jobs here. There are hardly any customers except on the days the train comes through. Why don't you come in and have a bite to eat and maybe by then the lady you're waiting for will come by?"

Since his back was to the two women, Will wasn't able to see what happened next, but the expression on Tommy's face brightened. Before he could stop his son, the boy shot off his chair toward the stranger.

"Come sit with us, lady. You look nice. We need someone to teach us how to eat nice and not like a bunch of wild hogs."

Will turned in his chair and caught the surprised look on the woman's face. She quickly disguised it with a smile. "Well, hello to you, too, little man." She crouched down and looked into Tommy's eyes while she spoke.

Will was taken by her soft, sincere voice. She sounded as though she actually enjoyed talking to the little boy. Will opened his mouth to call Tommy back to the table, but the words died before reaching his lips when he saw the rapture on his son's face.

"I'm not a little man, I'm just a boy. My brother says I haf'ta be more'n eleven to be a man. He's gonna be a man soon 'cuz he's already nine," Tommy informed her, holding out eight fingers until she helped him lift one more.

"That's nine." She smiled, ruffling his hair.

"I just got my hair—"

"Tomas." Will didn't know what to do with his son. He seemed bound and determined to get the whole town laughing at his antics. "Leave the lady in peace and come back to the table."

"But, Pa, she don't have nobody to sit with and we could learn how to be gent'men if she were at the table," Tommy argued, taking hold of the woman's hand.

"Tomas, you need to heed your father, dear." Her melodic voice soothed some of Will's embarrassment, and her eyes sparkled with delight. She straightened back up and led Tommy to the table without withdrawing her hand from his.

Reluctantly, Tommy sat down and let her go, but as she turned to leave, she suddenly turned back to look closer at Will. "Oh, my! You're the one who—"

"Yeah," Tommy answered for his father, "he caught you at the train. You were gonna fall on your face."

"Yes, I was. I don't think I had a chance to thank you, sir."

"Don't mention it. I'm glad you didn't get hurt," Will mumbled uncomfortably. It had been years since he was in polite company.

"Can she eat with us, Pa? Please." Tommy pushed the issue.

"She probably wants some peace and quiet after her train ride, Tommy."

"Yeah, you talk too much," Willy whispered to his brother. Tommy's face fell and he bit his lower lip.

"I'd love to eat with you, young man. You're the most handsome gentleman who's ever invited me to sup with him. I'd be honored, but your pa might want to have you boys all to himself."

"It would be our pleasure to have your presence at our table," Will responded, belatedly standing in the presence of the lady as his mother had taught him. "Please, have a seat, if you'd like." Even as he stepped around to hold out the chair between Tommy and Willy and opposite his, he wondered what he was thinking. The young woman had just given him the perfect out and instead of taking it, he asked her to join them and endure his sons' antics. Maybe it was just the idea of talking to another adult or maybe it was the worried look she was trying hard to hide from the boys.

"Thank you again," she murmured. The waitress set a menu in front of her and soon returned with a glass of water for everyone.

"Well, my young friend." She smiled down at Tommy. "I don't believe we've been properly introduced. My name—"

"I'm Tommy," he interrupted, "and I'm six years old." He held out his hands and this time he had managed to get six digits to stand in the air.

"It's a pleasure to meet you, Master Tommy." She grinned and shook his hand as if he were a grown man.

"And you would be...?" She turned her attention on Willy.

Will did all he could not to stare at the young lady.

Her eyes were a mix of green and blue and she smiled genuinely at his son. Her blond hair had been pulled back into some sort of braids and then wrapped into a bun. With the jostling about of the train and the wind, little spirals had escaped, bouncing close to her diminutive ears.

She couldn't be more than eighteen. What person had sent her out on the train by herself? Didn't they know that the prairie was full of single men? Many hadn't had an opportunity to socialize with a lovely lady for months or even years. Where was her father or brother? What was she to do now that no one had shown up to the station? And who was so irresponsible to have a young lady like her come halfway across the continent and then not meet her train?

"He's my big brother. He always tells me what to do. He's sweet on Jill. So, what are you going to eat? Pa likes the chicken 'cuz we mostly eat venison and rabbit on the farm. I'm gett'n' the same thing 'cuz it's got potatoes in it. I think I like potatoes."

"That's very nice, Tommy, but you didn't tell me you brother's name."

"I told ya you talk too much," Willy muttered.

"I do not!" Tommy answered his brother with a glare.

"Do, too!"

"Do not!"

"Do, too!"

."Boys!" Barely keeping his voice low, Will intervened and frowned when he saw the young lady biting her lower lip. Was she trying not to laugh at the boys or trying not to show her discomfort? He had had almost all the humiliation that he could take for one day. "Behave yourselves."

His warning was understood and both boys lowered their eyes. "Forgive us, miss. We don't get to town very often and it seems we've left what few manners we have back home."

"Don't think another thing about it, sir. My nieces and nephews were always saying things without thinking them through first. I find your boys refreshing." She smiled reassuringly at both boys.

"Well, I should try to start the introductions again," Will stated, wondering why her smile made his stomach flutter just a bit. It must have been the hunger for his supper sending ripples though his middle. "I'm Will Hopkins and this is Willy." He pointed to his older son.

"It's a pleasure—" The young lady had turned to Willy, extending her hand to shake his, when she froze and turned stunned eyes back to Will. Willy stared at her strangely, his hand in the air.

"I… What did you say your surname was?" she asked in a choked voice.

"Hopkins, but around here we usually are very…" Her face had gone deathly white and she looked as if she was going to faint.

She looked too stunned for words, barely gathering herself together enough to speak. "I… Where is Mrs. Hopkins? Where is Francis?" she stuttered.

He hadn't heard anyone call him that in years—in fact, other than his mother, no one called him that at all. He could feel himself flush, and tried to talk over it. "I'm, um… My father was… I'm Francis, Francis William Hopkins. I go by Will most of the time."

"But you're not a widow!"

A widow? Why would anyone think he was—

"I thought… My mother's best friend was Frannie,

Francis…and if you…if you're… Why didn't you tell me who you were at the station? You just walked past me and left me there!" The confusion on her pretty face gave way to obvious anger.

"How'd you know my given name? What are you talking about?" Will asked, curious and accusing at the same time.

"Your ad."

"What ad?"

"The ad that you placed in the ladies' Christian monthly pamphlet," she explained. "I subscribe to it and in April of last year, there was an ad…" She pulled her satchel up onto her lap and started sorting through her things. Finally she pulled out a paper and handed it to him.

He only read the first few lines before he glanced back up to study the young woman again. It was the ad his mother had created to find him a housekeeper. The ad Miss Stewart had answered. But that meant… No, it couldn't be. This girl didn't look a day over twenty, and the letter he'd received had clearly stated that his new employee was in her fifties. The woman in front of him, who looked as if she might give in to tears at any moment, *couldn't* be Abigail Stewart.

"What's wrong, miss?" Tommy asked her, having come to stand next to her, his small hand on hers.

Will watched as some of the anger and frustration melted out of her expression as she looked down at his son. "I'm not quite sure of that myself, honey," she answered, pressing his hand with hers. "It's been a long trip and I have had a very taxing day. I was looking forward to meeting my new employer and her…*his* family. But this hasn't gone at all like I thought it would." She looked up from Tommy to glare at Will. "Especially the part where I was left alone on the train platform while your father walked away."

"You're…you're Miss Stewart?" Will said incredulously.

She straightened her back and tilted her chin up to look him straight in the eye. "Yes, I'm Abigail Stewart."

Any answer Will might have given was interrupted by Tommy's response. Throwing his arms around the woman's waist, he squeezed tight while yelling out, "You're our auntie House!"

Chapter Two

"Housekeeper, not Auntie anything," Willy hissed at his brother.

Abby didn't know how to respond to that, so she addressed their father. "I came all the way from Ohio just to be part of Mrs. Francis Hopkins's household. Now what am I going to do?" she asked out loud, not expecting an answer from him.

"But you're not old!" Willy burst out. Abby tried to focus on the boy, but her head felt clouded.

"That's right. You wrote you were fifty-eight." Will eyed her suspiciously.

"I did no such thing. I'm twenty-six, as I told you in my letter." How could he say something so strange? She had been a little uncomfortable when Mrs....er... Mr. Hopkins had asked her age, knowing that the posting had specifically requested a "mature" Christian woman, but she decided to be honest, deciding that if her honesty somehow lost her the opportunity to work for the family, it was because God was closing that door. When there had been no further mention of her age in the letters, she had assumed her new employer had decided that it wasn't important.

"Here, I'll show you." Mr. Hopkins reached into his worn denim shirt pocket and pulled out a pile of letters that even from a distance Abby recognized. Her heart sank. There was no doubt about it. She had been corresponding with *Mr.,* not *Mrs.* Hopkins.

He shuffled the papers and then scanned one, holding it out to her, his strong, calloused finger pointing to a paragraph. As she took it, she noticed that the page was watermarked and that the ink had run. Even Abby had to admit that the number she had written out did look like a fifty-eight.

"I'm sorry. It must have gotten wet. I *did* write that I'm twenty-six. I never intended to be dishonest or misleading."

"I believe you," he replied gruffly. "But I'm afraid that doesn't resolve the problem. I'm sorry if there was a miscommunication, Miss Stewart, but I was specifically looking for a, um…" He looked uncomfortable as he searched for the right wording. "A more mature woman. Someone closer to the age of my mother."

"Well, I'm not the age of your mother, but I can cook, clean and teach as well as anyone twice my age." Suddenly, staying here and keeping the job was important to her. If Mr. Hopkins withdrew his offer, where else could she go? She couldn't go back to Ohio. Emma and Palmer would never welcome her back, and if she went anywhere close by, they would make life impossible for her and anyone who was daring enough to help her. No. She had to find a way to stay out here in Nebraska. And since jobs for women in the area seemed to be scarce, her best chance was to convince Mr. Hopkins that she could be his housekeeper after all.

"I don't doubt your capacity, miss. It's just that on the farm it's just me, the boys and my nephew, Jake. It wouldn't be proper or right for us to have you out there with us, a single woman of your age. I'll take care of paying your passage back to Ohio and then you can be with your sister again." His words were meant to be reassuring but elicited the opposite effect.

"I can't go back," she whispered to herself. This was worse than not being picked up at the station. Before, she had wondered if something had interfered with Mrs. Hopkins's arrival, but now she knew she had been judged unwanted again.

"Why not? Did something happen to your sister?"

"My brother-in-law…" She almost spilled out everything but then remembered the boys listening. Straightening her back, she lifted her chin. "I can't. I'll have to look for work around here."

"I doubt there will be very much in the way of work for a decent woman." He studied her for a moment more and then shook his head. "Why did you even apply to come out on the frontier at your age? You should be looking to settle down and marry. Have a bunch of kids of your own."

He had no idea how she'd longed for that—a husband and children, a home of her own. But there had been no chance of that. No man in Ohio had any interest in a girl who wore her sister's old castoffs and was too busy minding her nieces and nephews and looking after the housekeeping to go to any social events. This was the only way for her to leave her sister's house—to find a job somewhere else. What would she do if that chance was taken away?

"I'm sure that once you get back to Ohio, some young man will be real glad to see that you've come back where you belong. And no doubt your family will be glad to have you home, too."

"I wish it were that simple," she answered. "I have lived with my sister and brother-in-law since my parents died when I was thirteen. My brother-in-law is very powerful… I can't go back now that I left against their wishes."

"So you disobeyed your sister and brother-in-law to come out here?"

"Yes. I came because…" She glanced at the boys and bit her lip. "I had to get away from Palmer—my brother-in-law. I didn't feel quite…safe living with him anymore," she finally finished, hoping he would understand what she had left unsaid. "But my sister, Emma, felt that I had a responsibility to stay and continue to take care of the house and the children. The day your last letter came to the house, Emma found it and I had to snatch it from her or I would never even have gotten the money or ticket. I ran all the way to my pastor's house, and he and his wife helped me get away. I even have a letter from Pastor Gibbons for you…or at least it was to be given to Mrs. Hopkins."

She reached down and once again sifted through the different letters until she found what she was looking for and handed it over to Mr. Hopkins. As she watched him unfold it, she felt dizzy. What if he still decided to send her back? What was she going to do?

"Have you made your choice?" The poor waitress was back, pad of paper in hand.

"Um…"

"Why don't you try the chicken like me?" Tommy prompted.

"Or she could try the steak that I'm gonna get," Willy suggested.

"I don't know," she answered honestly. She didn't really feel like eating anything and was afraid that food wouldn't stay in her churning stomach even if she could swallow past the huge lump of fear wedged in the middle of her throat. She took a sip of her water and willed it to stay down. "I guess I'm not really that hungry right now. It does all sound so good, but—"

"Don't worry about the money," Mr. Hopkins interrupted with a deep frown on his face, his eyes not even lifting for the first page of the letter. "I'll cover it. It's my fault, after all, that you've come all this way for nothing."

Suddenly Abby knew that she had to get outside and breathe some fresh air. Her stomach threatened revolt. Even with the letter from Pastor Gibbons in his hand, the man was going to refuse to hire her.

Without explaining anything to anyone, she bolted from the room, out the door and around the side of the building. She was almost to the back of the clapboard restaurant when she couldn't keep her stomach from emptying any longer. For the first time in her life, she wished she had died with her parents. What was to become of her? She was truly alone in this world—and in this strange and unfamiliar town. Back home, the sky had been high and the hills had surrounded her, but she had not known the immenseness of God's creation until she sat hour after hour and watched prairie grass wave to an endless clear sky. She was a small speck on a wide-open prairie and only God cared she even existed. No wonder King David had asked, What was man that God was mindful of him? She was as insignificant as a stalk of the prairie grass.

"Oh, God, What am I going to do now?" she cried. The sobs that racked her body were almost as painful as the retching. She leaned her forearms against the clapboard wall and hung her head between her elbows. She didn't even feel the coarseness of the building scratching her arms. Closing her eyes she prayed for a home. Somewhere to go where she could rest— where she could feel safe. She had traveled more than a thousand miles thinking she found a new home only to find it was the biggest mistake of her life.

Will sat staring at the spot the girl… Miss Stewart, had just vacated. He almost hoped that this was just a bad dream and he'd wake up any minute now to find that he was still camping down by the river on his way into Twin Oaks to pick up his new housekeeper. But Tommy's little hand pushing on his shoulder, trying to get him to pay attention to yet another barrage of questions, made him aware this was all too real. The new housekeeper was a young, beautiful girl who looked as if a stiff wind could carry her off. She wouldn't last a week on the frontier.

"Pa, where'd she go?" Tommy asked, his confusion making Will regret even more having started all this craziness. Surely he and Jake could handle the boys on their own just as they had done in the past. Maybe he would not plant in the western field he had cleared last month. He would still make a profit, though not as much as he had hoped. Still, that sounded better than adding more chaos and anxiety to his boys' lives.

"Pa!" Tommy's hand pounded harder and Will finally focused on his small son.

"I don't know where she went. Maybe she needed to get a breath of air." What did he know about women anymore? He'd been a failure at being a husband, and it had been more than ten years since he had seen his own mother or sisters.

"Um, sir?" The waitress was back again. This time she had two plates full of mashed potatoes, gravy, corn, chicken and broccoli. The third had a large steak and a baked potato with the same side vegetables. "I have your meals."

She set a plate in front of each of them and then leaned a little closer to him. "Is the young lady all right? Will she be joining you again?"

Will groaned and closed his eyes. That was the question, wasn't it? Would she be joining them on their trip back to the farm, or would he send her back to Ohio? The sliver of the letter he had been able to read stated the pastor's approval. According to the pastor, Miss Stewart was an upstanding Christian girl, well respected by the other members of the church where she had attended since she had been little. The pastor indicated that he had known her parents and wanted to make sure she was arriving to a Christian home where she would be protected and respected. It had confirmed what Will surmised about her from her letters.

The only problem was her age—how could he bring a young woman to live with them? True, they wouldn't be completely alone, thanks to Jake and the boys, but it still didn't seem proper. Yet it hardly seemed proper to abandon a young woman in a strange town, either.

"Oh...all right!" He gave in to his guilty conscience. He needed to go search her out and see what solution he could offer. It was getting later in the day and he still needed to be back to the river by nightfall. "Can you keep an eye on my boys for a minute?" he asked the waitress, wondering what he could possibly do to make this situation better for everyone.

"We'll be just fine here, right, boys? I remember when mine were this size." The waitress smiled at Tommy and Willy and then nodded to Will.

Maybe he could ask Mrs. Scotts to let Miss Stewart stay on their homestead. The Scotts were his closest neighbors, and Mrs. Scotts had always struck him as a kind woman. He played with that idea as he left the building and blinked in the afternoon sun. Once his eyes adjusted, he turned and followed the forlorn sound of someone sobbing. When he found her, she was leaning against the building, crying so hard she looked on the verge of collapse. She was the picture of distress and disillusionment. Knowing he had created this big mess, causing her so much misery, struck him like a sucker punch to his stomach.

He had prayed and sought God's guidance each step of the process that had brought her here. Mother had started everything when she suggested he advertize for a housekeeper last spring. Being that it was her idea, he'd asked his mother to write his ad and get it placed in a good Christian publication. Miss Stewart's copy was the first he had seen of the original ad. He never even dreamed she had used his given name—Francis, the name he had grown to hate as a boy growing up.

Miss Stewart was not the first person to think it a woman's name. How could it have gone so terribly wrong? Now the poor girl was in a strange place with no one to count on and nowhere to go.

God, I need a little help here, he prayed as he approached, wondering what he could possibly say.

"Um, Miss Stewart?"

She jerked around so quickly that she almost fell. Her pallid face looked as if she had powdered it with flour. Even her lips looked gray. Her red nose and red-rimmed eyes contrasted her lack of color.

She spun away from him just as quickly and her stomach heaved again, although she brought nothing up. A sob escaped her throat and ripped his heart in half. He stepped closer. Supporting her elbows with his hands, he felt her body shaking.

He felt an unaccustomed surge of protectiveness. He wanted to help this girl, shield and protect her from any source of pain. But right now *he* was the cause of her distress. What could he say or do to make that right?

Abby had thought the day couldn't get any worse when she fled the restaurant, but apparently she was wrong. Now he was here watching her toss up her accounts. How embarrassing.

"I'm sorry, Miss Stewart. I wasn't expecting you to be… I had thought… I've made a mess of this."

His hands still supported her elbows and he sounded truly contrite, but what could she say? It was all right? That it was understandable after he had brought her all this way into the middle of nowhere that he was going to abandon her and leave her with nothing?

The nightmare didn't seem to be ready to end. Silence stretched out and neither one knew how to break the uncomfortable tension. At least her stomach had settled to resemble a simple storm instead of a full-blown sea squall.

"Listen, I admit this is a mess." He stated the obvious. If Abby hadn't been so tense, she might have seen a bit of humor in that. Right now she didn't have the energy to be amused.

"Really!" She speared him with a pointed look.

"I'm… Why don't we go back and sit down? Maybe if you eat something…"

"It'll come right back up," she mumbled before he even finished his idea. "All I want is to go home…to have a place to go and lie down, a place that's safe, where I belong."

The last word caught in her throat. A place to belong and to be loved—it was what she had been searching for a long time. Her fight drained out of her as quickly as her ire had ignited. What was she doing, telling this man her heart's desire?

"Um… I was thinking. I've got neighbors a few miles away who might be willing to let you stay with them while you work for us. At least until we can come up with another solution." He paused and then asked abruptly, "Do you know how to ride a horse?"

Abby swallowed hard. He was offering her an option. Granted it wasn't much of an option since it depended on this other family agreeing, but it was a better option than nothing. Clearly he wasn't planning for her to stay permanently since he'd hardly want her imposing on his neighbors for very long, but at least she would have a place to stay for a few days. She nodded, afraid to say anything.

"We've got an extra horse that you could take each day...." He was already planning, but Abby couldn't suppress a shudder. Did he expect her to ride the prairie for a few miles on her own each morning and night? Would it be safe? "We'll work something out, at least until harvest. The winter months we spend closer to the house and I can see to the boys. In the meantime, I'll write to my mother...."

He continued to talk, but she was having a hard time concentrating.

"Well?" he asked, obviously waiting for her to respond.

"Thank you," she whispered. She almost sank to the ground in exhaustion. The entire trip was now taking its toll. From the moment she had received his letter and realized she was finally free of her sister and brother-in-law, she had slept very little, first packing and then traveling by coach and finally by train for the last week. A woman alone, she only dared to catch catnaps and felt so vulnerable. She had assumed that once she had arrived, everything would be calm and she would be shown her room and be able to rest—not sit for almost an hour in a strange town with no one looking for her and then discover that her job itself might fall through.

"I think you need to get in, out of the sun, and rest. Shall we?" Without waiting for her to answer, he slipped an arm around her waist and half walked, half carried her to the front of the building.

"Mr. Hopkins, I can do this on my own," Abby declared as firmly as she could in her shaky voice. She couldn't afford to leave him with the impression that she wouldn't be able to take care of herself, much less do her work. She swiped at the tears on her face and groaned inwardly. Her face must be a sight, all red and puffy.

"All right," he acknowledged, releasing her waist and tucking her arm around his like a perfect gentleman, turning them both toward the front door.

Abby firmly tapped down the hope that things were going to work out. It would be doubly devastating for her to start feeling as if she fit in and then have to pack up and leave. But the way Mr. Hopkins opened the door for her, led her back to the table and pulled out her chair, she felt certain she would be safe with this gentleman farmer.

The boys had both been eating their food, but when they saw their father lead Abby back inside, their eyes lit up and Tommy started his barrage of questions. "Is she okay? Will she come home with us? Are you gonna ask for your food now? Is she still sick? Do you want to try some of mine?"

"Tommy, she's not gonna come to our house 'cuz Pa made her cry," Willy hissed at his brother.

"Well, boys. We've talked and Miss Stewart is going to come with us for a while. I'll see if the Scotts can let her stay with them until we can make some other arrangements."

Abby nodded her head, but even that slight motion sent everything spinning. She just wanted to lie down somewhere quiet and sleep. The waitress came back with a teapot. Before Abby realized what she was doing, the waitress had poured a cup and then sweetened it with a sugar cube that she had plucked from the sugar bowl in the center of the table. The boys' eyes grew large when they saw what treat was concealed in the bowl.

"This might help settle your stomach, miss." The matronly lady spoke softly, placing the cup and saucer in front of Abby. "Why don't you try a few sips at a time? It's chamomile—it always helps me feel better when I've had a rough day." She smiled and patted her shoulder, reminding Abby of Mrs. Gibbons, the reverend's wife from back home. Abby wished that she could let the older woman coddle her a bit more. She managed to keep the tea down and drank yet another cup before the boys became too restless.

She hoped it would be enough to give her strength for the trials that lay ahead.

What had he gotten himself into? Will wondered to himself for the hundredth time as he drove the wagon back toward the homestead. They'd stop tonight at the river. He and the boys could camp out under the stars and Miss Stewart could sleep in the wagon. Getting home and dropping her off at the Scotts' house on the way would be the easy part.

The Miss Stewart he'd imagined had been a sturdy, solid woman who knew her own mind when she said she was unafraid of the challenges of prairie life. This beautiful, delicate girl was another matter altogether. For now she seemed determined to give the job a try, but how long would that last? How long would he have— weeks, maybe a month or two—before she realized that Nebraska was a place where no young woman could ever want to be?

There was no convincing her of that now, of course. She'd have to see it for herself. Until then, perhaps Miss Stewart could help Willy to be more sociable. Maybe she could train Tommy not to say just anything that came to mind—or maybe not. He hoped she could feed them something more substantial than what he normally managed to burn or leave half-raw. Maybe she could get some meat on their bones and make his house feel more like a home… Or maybe he'd just invited trouble to make itself comfortable at his dinner table.

Not that she would be that much trouble. She seemed well educated and her letters bespoke of a nice girl, but to have a beautiful, single, unattached woman out in the middle of the prairie full of single men, all looking to settle down and start families in a place few women would venture… He might just have opened the door to a whole lot more than a housekeeper. Since he employed her, he would be responsible for her safety and reputation, and he'd also have to ensure that she didn't make any decisions she'd later regret. She seemed so set on not returning to Ohio that she might fall into marriage with one of the local men. He'd do everything he could to make sure *that* didn't happen. She needed to be free to leave the prairie whenever she chose—the choice that Caroline had never had.

Out of the corner of his eye, he watched her shift around to look over the landscape. He studied her profile. What must she be thinking? Was she asking herself what she had just gotten herself into, as well? The wind had pulled tendrils of hair out from her pins and he was sure that if she hadn't been so tired from her travels, she would have been trying to control the mass of corn silk better.

Stealing a glance at her sitting at his side on the wagon bench, he pondered how to explain their route. "Listen," he started, trying to broach the subject, then cleared his throat and tried again. "Our homestead is not very close to Twin Oaks. In fact, it's more than another six hours' ride from here, so we'll be stopping at the river to spend the night."

He turned his eyes back to the road, feeling her stiffen next to him. Her words still echoed in his head, the way she had said that she wanted to "Go home... To have a place to go and lie down." He would have let her stay at the hotel tonight and headed out at first light, but that would have meant he wouldn't get her to the Scotts' until late in the night and then it would be too late to get home. Jake would be on his own for five days. It was too much to ask the boy.

"I can sleep with the boys out under the sky and you can have the wagon all to yourself. I know it's not the hotel or anything fancy, but by tomorrow night, you'll be bedding down at the Scotts' house. Mrs. Scotts will take real good care of you and make sure you get the rest you need after this long trip."

The line of saplings and small trees at the edge of the river came into view. "See those trees?" He pointed to the horizon.

"Hmm."

"That's the river. We'll be there in just a few more minutes."

Once they had arrived at the river, he helped her down from the seat and held her upright until her legs stopped shaking and supported her weight. Acting the consummate gentleman, he didn't even look angry. Abby couldn't say if it was the fear of what her future held or the long ride that had her shaking so bad.

"Why don't you walk around here by the wagon for a minute and get your land legs back? The boys and I will go and check that there's nothing around to bother you and then you can freshen up down by the river." His words were soft and she felt protected. Maybe her first impressions had been correct. He made her feel safe.

Within a few minutes, Tommy ran back to her. "We made lots of noise so no critters would come out and scare you, Auntie House." She followed hesitantly, finding Mr. Hopkins and Willy in a small clearing with a sandy bank sloping into the river.

"We'll go and set up camp now, Miss Stewart. You should be perfectly safe here. We'll stay out of sight, but all you have to do is give a yell and we'll come running," the man reassured her as soon as she came into the clearing. As they left, she heard Tommy whine about having to wait for a swim, but she was glad they were gone for a minute. The water looked so cool and refreshing.

When Abby ventured back to camp afterward, she found a small tent erected and a fire started. The boys sat on both sides of Mr. Hopkins and were watching as he cooked some sort of meat.

"Hi, Auntie House," Tommy called out, hopping up and running toward her. "Do you feel better now?"

"Yes, thank you, Tommy. But can I ask you a favor?" she questioned, squatting down to be at eye level with the boy. His chest puffed out a little and he nodded solemnly. "Can you call me Auntie Abby?" Even as she asked, she glanced at Mr. Hopkins and cringed inwardly, wondering if it would be all right with him. "My nieces and nephews call me Auntie Abby and I'd feel better if you called me that instead of Auntie House."

"Sure. You're going to be a much better auntie than our old one. She was mean."

"Well, I'll do the best I can." She tried to cover her surprise as smoothly as she could.

"Now, Tommy, we need to talk nicely about Auntie Shelia. Remember what I told you?" Mr. Hopkins's voice brought her head up quickly.

Tommy stood and thought for a minute and then his eyes lit up. "Always say please and thank you?"

"Well, yes, that, too. But I meant about talking about other people," Mr. Hopkins hinted.

"He means that 'if you can't say nothin' nice, don't say nothin' at all,'" Willy piped up.

"My mother used to say the same thing. I think that's good advice," Abby encouraged. "So, what are you men cooking over there? It sure smells good."

Abby went closer to the fire and watched Mr. Hopkins struggle to flip the meat in the fry pan without getting too close to the fire. "What can I help with?" she offered. If they had been in a kitchen she would have set a table or taken over the cooking. She felt completely out of her element out on the prairie with three strangers.

"Careful of the flames, miss." Mr. Hopkins's voice shook her from her musing. "We don't want your skirt to catch on fire."

"I…" She blushed. She should know better. "Thank you."

"Pa's making venison steaks. He got the lady to give him some bread. Now we can eat like kings."

Tommy's little hand found hers and he tugged her to follow him. "Look over here. The deer and the raccoons and even the foxes and coyotes come to drink at the river at the time the sun goes to bed, so we figure we're gonna bag us a great big one," he boasted, his chest puffed out and his eyes bright with excitement.

"I'm sure you are a fine hunter," she praised. "I'll bet your brother and your daddy both taught you well."

"More like Pa's gonna teach us. I haven't never hunted 'fore. But maybe Pa'll let Willy shoot."

"No, Willy's not going to shoot tonight." Mr. Hopkins's voice was deep and smooth, causing a chill to run up her back. She had almost forgotten the man was there while she had been enjoying her enlightening chat with his son.

"But, Pa," Tommy whined, "you said yesterday that tonight we could bag a big one. Maybe the one with the big horns."

"Those aren't horns, silly. Those are antlers," Willy corrected his little brother. Then he pleaded his case. "But, Pa, you said we could use the venison."

"Well, I've changed my mind." Mr. Hopkins's answer left no room for argument.

"But, why, Pa? Why'd ya change your mind?" Tommy pressed the issue.

"Because I did. We'll go hunting once we're back at the house." Somehow, Abby suspected he had changed his mind because of her presence.

"It's time to eat," Mr. Hopkins announced, ending the conversation.

He slid the last of the meat onto a tin plate. Glancing around, he groaned, handed the plate to Willy with instructions to hold it for a minute and then went around the wagon. He came back a moment later, carrying a barrel for water. He set it far enough back from the fire so that there was ample room and then indicated she could have a seat.

"I'm sorry I didn't think to bring a chair or even a stool."

Once she was seated, he handed her a tin plate, slipped a piece of meat on it and set two dinner rolls on top. The boys were settled with similar plates where they sat on the dirt with their legs crossed in front of them.

"Father God," Mr. Hopkins began to pray, "we thank You for Your provisions and Your traveling mercies on this trip. I ask You to bless the food to our bodies and keep us safe on our journey home. Thank You for keeping Miss Stewart safe and for giving her the willingness to work for this simple farmer and his sons. Please lead us to make wise decisions and trust You every day. Amen."

The word *home* stuck in Abby's head as she ate. How she wished that she was going home. She had until the harvest to convince Mr. Hopkins that she was a hard worker and should be kept on. Only God held the solutions to her problems in His hand, and He hadn't let her know what they were yet.

"Hello, Herbert," Will called to the older of the Scotts brothers as he stepped down from the wagon. Mr. and Mrs. Scotts had attended church alone for so long that Will had forgotten the couple's two grown sons still lived with their parents. Rumor had it, the Scotts brothers thought that riding into Twin Oaks and drinking on Saturday nights was a much better way of spending their free time than worshiping in the Lord's house on Sunday mornings.

"Howdy, Will." Herbert approached from the shadows of the barn where he had been working. His eyes strayed too long on Miss Stewart before he looked at

Will. "And hello, pretty lady. Don't think I've seen the likes of you around here. You—"

"Are your ma and pa around?" Will asked, interrupting Herbert and standing between the man and the wagon. Will was starting to reconsider the idea of leaving a young lady, any young lady, on a farm with the likes of Herbert or Elvin. Why hadn't he thought of them before? A desire to mount back up and head off to his own claim without waiting for an answer almost won over his sense of courtesy, but now that he had come, they needed to at least greet the elder Scotts.

"Naw. Pa's out in the fields, and Ma went off to see to Jankowski's woman. Her time was close and her husband didn't want to see to all their kids and the birthing. Don't see why the woman needs so much help. What with all the little squallers she's already borne, a body'd think she could handle it herself by now."

Will cringed at the coarse way Herbert spoke about such a delicate subject. A glance at Miss Stewart confirmed her surprise. Now he wished he hadn't even attempted to bring her here. She needed a safe, comfortable place to stay—like his mother's home. Miss Stewart had implied that her brother-in-law had been less than respecting to her person, and now Herbert didn't bother to conceal the way he looked too long at Miss Stewart's womanly attributes.

Will had a sudden desire to make her feel safe. Where had that thought come from? Yes, his mother had taught him to be a gentleman, but the powerful need to protect Miss Stewart from Herbert took him by surprise. If the man kept looking at Will's new housekeeper like that, he might just have to teach the younger man a lesson or two about respect.

There was no way he would leave Miss Stewart here. They would have to make some other arrangement. Maybe he could use the barn or fix up the soddy to sleep in so that she could stay in the house. Climbing back into the wagon, he called over his shoulder, "Then I'd best be on my way. You let your ma and pa know we came to visit."

"But, Will, you're not being very neighborly. You didn't even tell me your sister's name," Herbert called after him, coming to stand on Miss Stewart's side of the wagon.

"She's Auntie Abby and she's gonna be our new house…house… What is it again?" Tommy whispered to his brother even as Will clicked his tongue to the horses.

"Housekeeper!" Willy answered his brother. "You don't remember nuttin'."

"Hey, I just can't—"

Will turned the wagon around, knowing he was being less than friendly with his nearest neighbor, but he couldn't stay any longer without losing control of his temper. Miss Stewart was a lovely, respectable woman who deserved to be treated like a lady. Soon enough she'd be headed back East, where she belonged. In the meantime, as her employer, Will knew it was up to him to protect her and make sure she was safe.

"I'm real sorry, Miss Stewart. I didn't know Mrs. Scotts had gone to stay with the Jankowskis." He didn't dare look at the small woman next to him. It was just about two in the afternoon and they still had another hour to go before they made it to the house. What was he going to do for her?

"It's all right. You couldn't have known. I'm sure we

can come up with something. Maybe I can sleep out in the barn if there's no place for me in the house."

"It's not a question of a place for you," Will tried to explain. After all, he had thought ahead and planned for a housekeeper. "You can sleep on the first floor in the parlor. It's been converted into a bedroom." He didn't elaborate that the conversion had been for Auntie Sheila and had never been rearranged once she left.

"It's just that it might not be… It might ruin your reputation to be living on the homestead with two men and two boys and no woman to chaperone." Even as he forced the words out, he felt his face flame. "Not that there would be any reason. We'll… Jake and I will behave as gentlemen at all times and you can sleep in the parlor or up in the upstairs if you want. We'll sleep out in the barn," he offered.

"I don't want to put you out of your own home—but we'll do whatever you say is best." She didn't look at him but kept her face toward the waving grasses stretching out in all directions.

Relieved that he could at least offer some protection from gossips, Will stole a glance at Miss Ab… Miss Stewart, he reminded himself. He supposed it was all right for the boys to refer to her as Auntie Abby, but he would still be reserved and careful around her. He didn't want to be any more familiar with a pretty, young woman than he needed to be. That's what had gotten him into trouble when he was barely able to shave.

Chapter Three

Abby jounced on the wagon seat and took in the view as they drove up to the farmhouse. The house walls were of stout weather-beaten, whitewashed planks settled on a foundation of stones and boulders. Mr. Hopkins hadn't stopped at the front entrance for obvious reasons since the weeds grew knee-high right up to the house. Instead, he pulled around into the barnyard where the dirt was hard and flat, giving testimony to constant traffic. The barn was made of the same planks as the house minus the paint.

Something akin to excitement ran through Abby when she saw a small back porch running the length of the house with a bench swing in one corner. She could imagine swinging out there on cool evenings after her housework was done, just as her mother used to when Abby was small. On closer inspection, Abby's excitement dimmed. She doubted anyone had swung on the swing for a few seasons given the amount of dust and spiderwebs that clung to it. What must the house look like?

One more jerk and the wagon came to a halt. "We're

here, miss. I can't promise that it's very welcoming but…"

Abby looked at Mr. Hopkins and found his expression endearing. He'd mentioned on the trip that he had built the house with his brother and that they had taken the better part of a year to get the main parts done. He said something about having to care for Caroline and the boys, and how that had slowed him down. Now he looked embarrassed as if it wouldn't measure up to what she expected. Mr. Hopkins's humble clapboard home represented an opportunity to prove she was an able housekeeper and educator. While it might never truly become *her* home, she could make it a comfortable one for his family.

"Is everything all right?" His voice called her back to the present. Glancing down from her perch still atop the wagon bench, she found him looking up at her expectantly. His hands were extended to help her climb down from the wagon and she mentally chastised herself for not paying more attention.

"Oh. Yes, Mr. Hopkins. I was just admiring your home." Just a hint of a smile touched the corners of his lips, but the pride that shone in his eyes reminded her of Tommy when she praised him.

Mr. Hopkins's hands were firm and strong as he lifted her at the waist and set her on her feet. "Thank you, miss." He stood a little straighter and surveyed it himself. "She looks a little rough now." He glanced at the house and shook his head. "I guess it must not look like much, but it's dry and warm when it's cold and wet outside. We make do."

"I'm sure it's just fine," Abby reassured him, seeing

a glimpse of an insecure little boy behind the tough exterior of her employer.

"If you want to just go on inside," he said, turning toward the back of the wagon, "I'll get your trunk and other boxes in short order."

"Come on. I wanna show you my room." Tommy took her hand and started to pull her up the stairs.

"Let's go take a look," she agreed, and let herself be led into the kitchen. She blinked as she stood at the threshold and waited for her eyes to adjust to the light. Something smelled as if it had died and was rotting in the middle of the room. It was enough to make her hold her breath. When she finally released the pent-up air, she tried to keep from thinking about what could be making such a stench. As her eyes adjusted, she could take in more of her surroundings. She held back a groan. What could she expect from four men who had been on their own for a number of years?

The floor was the same rough planks as the walls but caked with dirt from the barnyard. The large table stood in the very middle of the large kitchen, its entire surface dirty with lumps of something stuck to its once-smooth surface. Three different-size pots took up part of the wooden counter; each stank of rot and had something decaying inside it. A filthy stove sat in the corner, its pipe connected to a hole just above the grimy window.

It was nice to see that at least there were two glass windows in the kitchen even if they didn't have screens. She would have enough natural light on most days (once she washed the windows) so that she wouldn't even need a lantern or candles. The hand pump connected to the sink looked modern and meant she wouldn't have to lug water from somewhere outside every morning to start the day. But in spite of those conveniences, she clearly had her work cut out for her.

"C'mon." Tommy had run ahead but was now back, tugging on her hand again.

"Ahem." A deep voice from behind startled her, chasing her away from the door.

Mr. Hopkins stood with her hope chest on his shoulder as if it were a bag of feathers. "I'll take this into the room on the first floor and then you can decide where you want to stay. I…" His nose curled as he stepped farther into the room. "Jake!" he exclaimed, frowning as he took in the pots on the counter. "I asked that boy…" he muttered under his breath.

"I'll get the kitchen straightened out in no time, sir."

"It's not right for you to have to start working today. I'm sure you just want to rest after your long trip." His face looked bright red and his eyes didn't meet hers. Abby found his embarrassment charming.

"I'll be fine. I'll just need to freshen up a bit and then I could pull something together for supper."

"Are you going to cook like they do at the hotel?" Tommy piped up, still tugging her hand. Willy hovered at the doorway, trying to act nonchalant.

"Well, I don't know if it'll be just like the restaurant, but it will be enough to fill you up. My nieces and nephews like my chicken and dumplings. We could also make fried venison steaks when you go get a big one with your pa. But today I think I'm just going to have to see what's in the pantry and make something simple. Tomorrow we can make a menu. You can show me how many letters and words you already know," she offered.

"What's a menu?" Tommy turned to his bigger brother, but Willy just shrugged.

"A menu is the list of the foods for you to choose from. At the restaurant, the lady gave one to you to look at so you could decide what you wanted to order. Here at the house we will make a list for the week ahead of what we are going to make each day so you can get really hungry the days that we make your favorites. It helps to know what we want to cook so that we can make sure all the ingredients are available."

"What's 'gredients?"

"*Ingredients* are the things we need to make that food, like flour and butter and eggs.... Now, how about if we go help your pa put my stuff in my room and then we can chat?" Abby offered, following the man who had disappeared into the second doorway on the hallway from the kitchen. Once out of the kitchen, she discovered it wasn't a hallway but a large living room with a comfortable-looking davenport and a rocking chair facing the center of the room. The center wall was a massive fireplace with an ample hearth. The door Mr. Hopkins entered shared the wall with the fireplace. That room would be nice and warm come the winter—if she was still working for the family then.

The bedroom itself was sparsely furnished, with a large bed sagging in the center. The only other piece of furniture was a forlorn nightstand. Everything had a layer of dust, and the spiderwebs in the corner looked like spun cotton.

"Where would you like your chest?" Mr. Hopkins stood in the middle of the room, looking surprised to see the condition of the place. "Um, I hadn't been in here...."

"I think it would be best if you left it out in the living room for a few minutes until I can tidy up just a bit," Abby suggested tactfully.

"Are you gonna sleep on the couch?" Tommy asked.

"No." Abby shook her head and smiled at the small boy, ruffling his hair. "I'll be sleeping in here, but I think it would be better to air out the room and sweep up a little. Don't you agree?"

Tommy nodded energetically. Willy hung back at the door, not venturing into the room but watching everyone else.

"Could you do me a favor?" Abby asked Willy, knowing Tommy would probably follow. "Would you go find me the broom and dustpan?" As soon as Tommy and Willy had raced off, she tried the window, but it wouldn't budge.

"I'll go get your other things, miss. Unless there's something else that you would like me to do first?" Mr. Hopkins offered. His hands resting on opposite sides of the door frame reminded her just how big Mr. Hopkins was. He looked capable of building a house on his own.

"Could you give me a hand with the window?"

Mr. Hopkins crossed the room in five large steps. The room shrank with each step. He towered above her as he stood next to her. He pushed a lock on the top of the lower frame and then grunted as he tried to free the window. It took two tries, but suddenly there was a rush of fresh air sending dust dancing across the room.

"Thank you, sir," she choked out, just before sneezing from the dust.

"No problem. I'll go open the kitchen windows, too. Might as well get it aired out in here. I'll have to put screens on as soon as I can so you'll be comfortable in here in the summer, assuming..." Before he found the words to finish his thoughts, he stalked out of the room.

The boys raced in, fighting about who was going to give her the broom. "Thank you, gentlemen." She acknowledged both of them, causing Tommy to have a fit of giggles. "Now I need you to go out in the living room until I'm ready for you in here. I'm going to get some of this dust out." She tied a handkerchief around her face, covering her nose and mouth, making both boys giggle. Too much in a hurry to change, she told herself that the clothes that she had traveled in needed a good washing anyway, so a little more dust wouldn't hurt.

In a few minutes, she swept up the dirt and dumped it unceremoniously out the open window. She took the bedspread and sheets off the bed, even though there wouldn't be time to get them washed and dried before nightfall. She opted to get as much of the musty smell out as possible. She hung the bedding on the lines extending from the side of the house to a stand twenty paces away. Beating the dusty linens helped to relieve the tensions that had built up over the last few weeks and gave the boys something vigorous to do.

Rinsing off at the outside well, she returned to the kitchen, happy to find that the three pots had vanished. A good breeze flowed through from the two windows and the doorway to the living area. Someone left a fire started in the stove, but she opened the door and checked it anyway. She put water to boil in the only big cauldron she could find in the pantry. She couldn't start dinner until she got some of the grime out of the kitchen. Broom in hand, she made quick work of sweeping the bulk of the dirt off the floor.

Two hours later, she had the table and counter spotless, the supplies Mr. Hopkins brought from town put away in the pantry and dinner finished. There hadn't been time to make bread, but she was glad to see there were all the ingredients she would need tomorrow. For tonight, a simple fare of biscuits and fried meat would be all she could offer. Mr. Hopkins had promised a visit to the smokehouse tomorrow so she could take inventory.

The windows let more than just the breeze in. A bee and a few flies all got a good whack from her wooden spoon for their efforts to visit her kitchen, but the boys' laughter and shouting rode inside on the breeze, too. The latter far outweighed the first. She smiled, listening to them play with their hoops as they ran around the barnyard with sticks in their hands, competing to see who could last the longest before the hoops would wobble and fall.

Finally, the spotless table set with clean dishes, she stretched her arms to the sides and then over her head. She had always worked hard at Emma's house, but today, she did more in a few hours than what she usually would do in a whole day. Traveling left her stiff and out of sorts, and last night's sleep had been fitful. Even with the reassurance that Mr. Hopkins and the boys were sleeping in the tent a few paces from the wagon, Abby had startled awake to every small sound. As tired as she felt now, though, she was sure she wouldn't have any trouble sleeping tonight.

"Gentlemen, it's time for supper," she called, descending the back stairs.

Tommy dropped his stick in the dust and let the hoop roll off as he sprinted to her. "Can we come in now? Pa said we needed to let you sleep, but it sure smells like you were cooking. Can you come see my room now?"

She grimaced at the last question. What would she find upstairs if the downstairs was so dirty? She wasn't sure she could take any more surprises like that tonight. At least the mess gave her hope that if she could do her best job, she would show Mr. Hopkins how much he needed her. It wasn't just a question of taking care of the mess. From the state of the pots and pans, she'd gotten the idea that Mr. Hopkins wasn't a very good cook, either. He was strong and tall but lean. The boys were on the skinny side, too, but with a few weeks of her meals, she was sure that she could have them filling out very nicely.

"Do you want to let your pa and cousin know it's time to eat?"

Without letting go of her hand, Tommy stopped, looked over his shoulder and let out a holler that almost left her deaf. "Auntie House says it's time to eat."

Turning again toward the house, he started to tug again, but she stood her ground. "Is there something else that you need to do before you head on in?" she prompted.

"Nope. I told 'em," Tommy stated matter-of-factly.

"I was thinking about your toys. Do you always leave them in the middle of the yard?"

"Huh?" Tommy glanced around, confused, until he spotted Willy carrying in the other hoop and stick. "Oh. Wait here for me, Abby," he called over his shoulder as he let go of her hand and charged off to collect his forgotten toys.

"Auntie Abby," a deep voice corrected from the open doors of the barn. Mr. Hopkins had been observing

from the shadows. Would he be angry for her famil-
iarity with the boys? Would he approve of her work or
was there something she had done that upset him? If
only she didn't feel like she was on trial.

"Auntie Abby," Tommy repeated.

"Supper's ready," she announced, regretting it immediately since Tommy's voice had probably been heard
into the next county.

"So I heard." His voice held dry humor. Could he
actually be amused by Tommy's antics?

From across the barnyard, Abby thought the corners
of his lips twitched, and she wondered what his smile
would look like. Although Mr. Hopkins seemed very
reserved with her, the boys didn't fear him. In fact, more
than once she watched them climb all over him like
playful little pups. From the wagon she had almost been
sure she heard him laughing with the boys as they had
settled down to sleep by the riverside the night before.

Abby's brother-in-law, Palmer, had never interacted
with his children like that. Trying to remember her own
father, she felt sadness at the faded memories. Closing
her eyes for a brief second, she remembered his scratchy
chin nuzzling her at bedtime, after he had read her a
story and listened to her prayers. Had they wrestled as
well and she just couldn't remember or was it a game
reserved for boys only? Her nephews loved to wrestle
each other and she delighted in tickling them. How
would they be doing now?

Tommy ran back to her and started his now familiar
tugging on her arm. "Let's go!"

"Okay." She smiled again and let him pull her along.

"Tomas Daniel!" It was a command, not a shout, but
it brought Tommy up short and got her attention, as

well. "You should never *pull* a lady. You need to learn to walk at *her* pace," Mr. Hopkins instructed his son, having almost caught up to them with his long strides. He let the others enter first, holding the door open when they reached the porch.

Another young man stood there, too. He was thin and tall, with the same sandy-brown hair and light blue eyes as Mr. Hopkins, and he stood waiting on the porch while she and the boys washed their hands in the sink. Abby wondered where the other man had been as she hurried around to make sure that the table was ready. The boys scampered to their places at the table and climbed up, Tommy kneeling on his chair so he could reach.

"Miss Stewart." Mr. Hopkins turned to the younger man next to him. "I'd like to introduce you to my nephew, Jake Hopkins."

The poor boy's face was beet-red. He looked everywhere but at her. He nodded and mumbled something that she couldn't quite understand.

"It's nice to finally meet you, Master Hopkins. I hope you didn't have too much work to do while your uncle collected me from the train."

"Um, no, ma'am, I mean miss." His voice cracked between words and then he dropped the soap his uncle had just handed him. Although Abby had not thought it possible, his face turned even redder.

"She's Auntie Abby," Tommy corrected, leaving both Abby and Jake with an uncomfortable situation. It was obvious that he was a teen and could not as easily call her auntie, especially since he was living with his uncle.

Mr. Hopkins settled the matter. "Around here we usually use just first names for the boys, so you can address him as Jake. No need for master or mister." He didn't offer for her to call him by his first name, which was just as well. She wasn't sure she wanted to be on a first-name basis with her employer, either.

After a pause, she decided to change the subject. "I hope you're all hungry. I made enough to feed an army."

After everyone was seated, Mr. Hopkins asked for God's blessing on the food and the hands that prepared it. He also asked for wisdom and grace for the adjustments to come. Abby enjoyed the boys' constant chatter as they filled their cousin in on all the things that they saw on their trip into town. It was becoming evident that it was not a common event.

Before she thought it was possible, all the plates were empty once again. "You cook really good. Gooder than Pa. He always burns everything," Tommy announced.

"It was really good," Willy confirmed. He had not yet directed any comments to her. Now that he had, she felt as if she had won a prize.

"The boys are right. You did a fine job with supper, Miss Stewart. Thank you, especially seeing as how you must be completely tuckered out." Mr. Hopkins's gaze confirmed that he was not just being polite but he meant every word. "Is there anything else you'll need tonight?"

"I still have to make up the bed and clean up here, but I think I'm all set, sir. Thank you." She rose to start clearing the table, and everyone scrambled to help. She had left water heating on the stove so she could make washing dishes a quick job once everyone had cleared out. To her surprise, Mr. Hopkins rolled up his sleeves, poured part of the hot water into a basin in the sink and started to shave off a few slices of soap. Soon he had the dishes in the sudsy water.

"Pa, can we show her our room now?" Tommy pleaded.

"That's up to Miss Stewart. She might just want to get some rest," he answered with his strong forearms submerged in the water.

"Not just yet," she answered Mr. Hopkins, then turned to the boys. "Why don't you help me get the blankets off the line outside before it gets too dark and then you can show me your room? I think you said something about blocks your pa made for you. I'd like to see those tonight even if we don't have time to play. Tomorrow we'll have time to explore and see just how much you can teach me about your house."

"I'm not a teacher," Tommy giggled. "That's your job."

"But you know lots about where the clothes are, where the tub is for washing the clothes and what your favorite foods are. You can teach me all those things while I teach you how to read. I even brought some books so I can read you some stories when we get settled."

"Could you read us one tonight? Please?" Tommy cajoled.

After offering to take over the dishes again and being assured everything was under control, she turned to the boys. "How 'bout you help me with my bedding first? Then we'll see what time it is. Maybe your pa wants you to be in bed soon."

She sought a confirming look from her employer but found him silently staring at her. "How 'bout we talk in just a minute, once you're done getting the bedding?" he suggested, and turned back to the dishes before she could answer.

* * *

Her new room smelled fresher now. She stood back and inspected her work… Well, the work she did after the boys "helped" her to make her bed. One more thing she would need to add to her list of lessons for them. Mr. Hopkins had come into the room with a bed key and tightened the ropes under the mattress so it no longer sagged. She closed the window most of the way, leaving only a crack open so the air could continue to circulate without the bugs eating her alive.

"Excuse me, Miss Stewart. Did you want me to put your chest and boxes in your room now or leave them here?" Mr. Hopkins stood right outside her door, awaiting her answer. He took up the majority of the doorway with his broad shoulders and muscled forearms perched on each side of the door frame.

"If you could bring them in here, that would be very nice. Thank you. You could put them right there." She pointed to the corner under the window and moved so he could get past her even as the boys climbed onto the bed.

"Boys, it's time to go get ready for bed." His statement was met with groans, but neither boy argued as they left the room. He looked up to see her watching and grinned as if he knew a secret.

"Now," he whispered, "Tommy will be back in five seconds to ask if you can read—"

"Pa, can Auntie House read to us?" Tommy shuffled back into the room right on time.

Abby fought not to laugh out loud as Mr. Hopkins gave her a knowing glance and a wink above Tommy's head.

"I was about to talk to her about that, but if you don't

get ready for bed, there won't be time for anything other than prayers." His voice was as stern as ever and didn't give away the humor Abby read in his eyes.

"But she could come for prayers, couldn't she?" Tommy persisted.

"Tomas Daniel," Mr. Hopkins said in a deep, low voice.

"Yes, Pa. I'm going but, please." The boy was close to whining.

"Go get ready for bed." The command left no room for argument.

Tommy left the room, walking like a man sentenced to face the firing squad. Abby watched him walk away and then turned to find Mr. Hopkins watching her with a guarded expression, the lighthearted humor forgotten.

"You don't have to go upstairs and help with bedtime, Miss Stewart. You've done more than I expected today. Is there anything you need?"

Disappointment sliced through her. Why should it matter if she helped the boys into bed or not? But it did. She wanted to hear the prayers and kiss their foreheads just as she had done with her nieces and nephews for the last fourteen years.

"I would love to read them a story if it's all right with you." She bit her lower lip, trying to find a nice way to imply that he might not want her involved in such a private family time. "I don't know your routine with the boys. What they do at bedtime or what you will expect me to do in the days to come."

"Well, it will take some time to get used to having a woman around here again," he stated cryptically.

"I imagine. I was wondering… I don't want to ask anything that's none of my business, but just how long has it been since a woman lived here?"

A shadow passed over his face for a minute and she held her breath, afraid she had just offended her employer on her first day there.

"It's been two years since my wife's aunt left." His vague answer left her with more questions instead of answers. Did the boys still miss their great-aunt? How much time would she have to work here before the end of the harvest? Should she hold them at arm's length so that when she left, they wouldn't miss her too much? Would it even be possible to hold them at arm's length? After only two days, Tommy already tugged on her heartstrings and somber, grouchy Willy seemed to dare her to love him.

Minutes later she was sitting between the two boys on the side of Tommy's bed, reading to them. By the time she had finished the story, not only had Tommy climbed up on her lap, but Willy had slid over to look over her shoulder at the pictures. Story done, they took turns petitioning God with their heartfelt prayers for the cows, the horses, family they had never met, for their pa and their cousin, and they included her, as well. She said a few prayers of her own. Her thoughts traveled from her sister's family to the Gibbonses and then all the people she had met on her trip. She asked for God's blessing on this new family that she felt privileged to know.

When she gave a kiss good-night to Tommy, he insisted that his big brother needed kisses, too. She willingly complied and grinned when Willy groaned but turned his face toward her instead of away from her. As she stood, Mr. Hopkins cleared his throat. His eyes had a glassy look to them and she wondered if that was a good sign or not.

Chapter Four

The horses had settled in for the night as if it were the most common thing in the world for Will and Jake to be sleeping up in the hay loft. It was reminiscent of his boyhood visiting his grandparents' farm, when he and his cousins would get to sleep with one of the uncles up in the loft. It reminded him again of all the things his boys were missing out here. Back East, two of his sisters were already married and were starting families of their own. When would his boys meet their cousins?

But his parents understood why he had to stay. Why he had to make this work. It was not just his dream. It had been Mathew's dream first. Up here, in the loft he had built with Mathew, it felt as if his brother were still here on the farm. Will missed him with a deep sadness even after all these years. Sleeping up here with Jake, a replica of Mathew at age sixteen, brought back a flood of memories.

Mathew was five years older than Will. He'd always dreamed of going West to claim a large homestead. When Mathew married MaryAnn, they'd planned to move West just as soon as they saved enough to buy a homestead. Will worked at his father's store hoping to earn enough money to outfit his own wagon and tag along for the adventure of a lifetime. At nineteen, he still couldn't own land, but he could help Mathew settle. Two years later, he could claim the land nearby once he was of age. Everything had worked according to plan—except his marrying Caroline.

At first, Caroline came to Will's father's store to buy little things like penny candy or ribbons for her flaxen hair, but as time passed, Will noticed she often came and spent time there without buying anything. He invited her to a church social in the fall and they got along well. Somehow, without realizing it, he managed to take her to each of the socials and even walked her home from the store a time or two. Most people assumed they were courting and Will didn't do anything to discourage the idea. She was pretty enough and popular. He should have paid more attention when she started bringing sweets she had baked herself. But he hadn't seen the harm. Everyone knew he'd be leaving soon with Mathew and MaryAnn. Yet he couldn't help noticing that every time he mentioned homesteading, Caroline would change the subject or tell of all the perils she had read in the newspapers and dime-store novels.

By February, he and Matt began the process of outfitting their rigs and laying aside the supplies. His head was so full of adventure he didn't pay too much attention to what was going on around him.

Just four weeks before they were to leave, Caroline came crying to the house late one night, making a big scene about his leaving her. He offered to drive her back to her home in his father's buggy, planning to explain to her on the way that they had no future together. Memories of that night still flooded his head. If only he had taken one of his sisters along.

"I'm sorry, Caroline," he tried to console her, holding the reins loosely, guiding the horses to her drive. "I never said anything about us being anything other than friends. I guess you just came to the wrong conclusions. I don't think you would be happy with me. You like your pretty clothes and your nice parties and that's all good and fine, but I'm traveling out to the frontier. There are no shops for pretty clothes out there. There are no parties to go to on Christmas Eve."

"But," she gasped, tears streaming down her cheeks, her nose red and runny, "you took me to all the socials. I told my friends that surely you would ask me to be your wife. I started on my dress and asked Julie to be my bridesmaid. You could wait for a few more months. Let Mathew and MaryAnn go this year and then we could meet them there next year...."

"No, I'm not getting married now! I'm just nineteen. I want to live life without being tethered to a wife and a family. I'm sorry you started to make plans, but I never said..." He stopped the buggy but sat still, wanting to finish their conversation in the semiprivacy of her yard, blanketed in shadows.

"You're leaving me!" Her cry was shrill and carried across the quiet night.

"I'm going with Mathew and MaryAnn. I've been dreaming about it for years now. You knew my plans."

"But I thought you loved me. I thought we'd get married in the spring!"

"Caroline, I'm sorry. I don't mean to hurt you, but I

don't—" Before he could continue, she threw herself in his arms, kissing him soundly on the mouth. The force of her movement almost toppled them off the buggy seat and he reached out, catching her shoulders with his hands to keep them both from falling. Before he could set her away from himself, he heard the creak of the front door opening. Caroline's father stepped out and glared at him.

"Caroline, what is the meaning of this!" Mr. Kellogg roared.

"Oh, Papa!" she exclaimed, spinning around with a smile on her face. "I've got such wonderful news. Will just asked me to marry him and of course I accepted. I suppose we shouldn't have been celebrating quite like this, but I was just so happy to finally hear him admit how much he loves me."

Will remembered feeling numb. Completely numb from head to toe—as if someone had dunked him in ice water. What had he just heard? Had Caroline gone completely mad? Hadn't she heard a word he had said? He was starting out on the adventure of a lifetime in just a few weeks and he had no plans of taking her along.

"Well, boy, now that you've sampled the goods, I expect you to make my daughter an honest woman." Mr. Kellogg clenched his fists at his side and stared Will down as if daring him to refuse Caroline. Swallowing hard, he nodded. Realizing too late Mr. Kellogg would take it as an affirmation of all Caroline had said.

"I expected you to come and talk with me first, like a respectable man would, boy, but I guess there's not much I can do about it now. How do you plan on supporting my daughter?"

"Pa, he's got a job with his father at their store. You

have nothing to worry about," Caroline answered, taking Will's hand in her own and squeezing as if they were the happiest of couples.

"Then I expect you to come here tomorrow night and have dinner with us, young man. I have a few more questions to ask you, but it's late and it won't do to ruin Caroline's reputation by causing a scandal out here. Come along, Caroline, it's time to go inside." Mr. Kellogg assisted his daughter down from the buggy, eyeing Will with a stern look the entire time.

Will finally found his voice. "Yes, sir. I'll see you tomorrow evening." He waited in stunned silence until their door closed behind them and then somehow made his way back to his own home in a fog. What had just happened? How was he going to get out of it? One thing he was certain of. He had planned and dreamed of homesteading in Nebraska, and no one, not even Mr. Kellogg or conniving Caroline, was going to keep him from traveling with his brother. If Caroline insisted on the farce of a marriage with him, it would be on his terms.

The next night, his worst fears were confirmed. Caroline and her mother had already started to make preparations for the wedding. In the days that followed, Will felt trapped in a whirlwind of activities, each one pulling him closer to his doom.

Three days before they were to leave for Nebraska, he and Caroline were married in a small ceremony with his family, her family and a few close friends on hand. At first, he resented Caroline's high-handed way of trapping him into a marriage, but he tried to get along with her. For the first month of travel, she also tried to humor him. Soon all facade fell away as the trip became more demanding. How Mathew and MaryAnn put up with his black moods and Caroline's simpering and sniping sometimes astounded him. Just as he had assumed, Caroline whined about the lack of stores, creature comforts or even basic necessities out on the trail.

Now he looked back and wondered if there had been some other way to avoid hurting each other. She never adapted to the prairie. He never gave in to her demands to move back. At some point, he stopped trying to make her happy. At first, he tried to be a good husband, providing for her needs, helping with the children, but she always found something to complain about.

He didn't regret his boys, however. They were the only good thing that came out of his rushed marriage. They were his inspiration to make the farm a success. Someday they would inherit all that his hands had labored to build. With God's blessings, he wanted to leave them a legacy—something they could in turn pass down to their children. Jake would also be part of the inheritance. His father and mother's dreams had brought them out West to begin with. Will vowed to leave Jake the legacy that Mathew once dreamed of giving his son.

Sighing, he decided to turn the night, his efforts and the coming days over to the Lord. He just wished God would let him know what to do about Miss Stewart.

Just the night before, he'd known that the men in the area would be interested in his housekeeper, and now he was even more certain. She was pretty and soft-spoken, and if dinner had been any indication, she could cook. Both boys were already quite taken with her, and poor Jake hadn't been able to string two coherent words together at the table. Out here, the lack of eligible women meant that even women long in the tooth or dull-witted were courted by many eligible bachelors. Miss Stewart would cause a stampede. Exactly what Will wanted to avoid, for the sake of his own peace of mind, and Miss Stewart's well-being.

He regretted having stopped at the Scotts' homestead earlier in the day, too. Since this coming Sunday was only the second of the month, they still had two more weeks before there'd be another service, and news would spread. Hopefully by then, he would have some idea as to what to do for Miss Stewart. After all, her pastor had written a letter putting her care and well-being in his hands. He would see to her safety and provisions—and it wouldn't be too hard to do if the fringe benefits were meals like the one they had had earlier. But he wouldn't let himself get too attached. Once she realized what life on the prairie really meant, Miss Stewart wouldn't be staying long—he was certain of that.

The first twinges of pink and orange were streaking the sky to the east when Abby groaned, stretched and struggled out of bed. She had slept well for the first night since leaving Emma's house. Seeing the sun pushing up into the sky, she quickly dressed and brushed her hair.

Today she would take inventory of the house. She needed to scrub every single floor, wall and ceiling before she would be satisfied, but she also needed to see about clothing for the boys, do the washing, clean out the pantry... The list went on and on and Mr. Hopkins never did really tell her if he planned for her to stay or if he was set on taking her back into town next week. He had said she could stay until the harvest, but that was when he'd thought she'd be staying with the Scotts. Did the deal still hold true? She shook off her fears. There was no point in wondering about it. Until he told her otherwise, she was still employed as a housekeeper. Her first job was to determine what the most pressing need was and concentrate on it.

Lighting the fire in the stove was actually easier than on Emma's stove. She put water on to boil and then started to look through the pantry. The milk from last night had been kept in a jar and placed in the root cellar under the stairs, so she went down and found it. She wondered if there were fresh eggs.

Heading back upstairs, she heard the kitchen door squeak and paused for a second. Surely it must be Mr. Hopkins, but there was no other noise, as if someone was sneaking in. Fear for the boys' safety sent her rushing back up the stairs, a milk jug clenched in her fist as her weapon.

"Miss Stewart?" The whispering voice was deep and sent her heart into her throat as she reached the kitchen.

"Mr. Hopkins?" she squeaked out, as if anyone else would know she was here, much less come into the kitchen unannounced at this time of the day.

He stood at the doorway into the main house but spun around as she answered. His grin confirmed he realized how silly her question was. It also confirmed her suspicion that he was a handsome man when he smiled. "Good morning, Miss Stewart. Did you rest well?"

"Yes, sir. Did you?" she asked as she set the milk on the counter, commanding her heart to stop beating so loudly. She was afraid the noise would wake the boys.

"I rested very well, thank you." His tone was light and friendly. "Is there something you need?"

"I didn't know if I needed to gather the eggs. Do you need me to go and milk the cows first thing in the morning? Do the boys get up on their own or do you wake them at a particular time?"

He looked at her strangely. "Miss Stewart, do you know how to milk a cow?"

"No, sir. But I learn quickly," she assured him, afraid he would think about taking her back to the train station.

"Well, it's just as well. I'll do the milking if that's all right with you. My cows are my girls and they are very stingy with anyone else. As for the hens, I'll take you out to the henhouse and show you around in a little bit. This morning, however, I brought the eggs and milk." To prove the statement, he backtracked out the door, bent down and reemerged with a pail of milk and a basket of eggs.

"Thank you. Is there something special you would like to eat this morning?" Abby asked, hoping to get off on the right foot.

"Anything other than burnt oatmeal would be ambrosia."

"Ambrosia! I had thought that we'd try for something simple like pancakes and bacon. I'm not sure that I can come up with ambrosia," she teased, knowing that if the pots from the day before were a hint to the breakfasts that were the normal fare at the kitchen table, her mother's light, fluffy pancake recipe would be well received.

The boys and Jake were drawn like flies to the kitchen as soon as she started frying bacon. By the time they washed and dressed, she had a stack of pancakes she figured would hold them for the time being. Instead of eating with the rest, she stood at the stove and continued to flip pancakes, keeping a steady flow coming until everyone had eaten their fill. Jake and the boys made quite a few comments about burnt oatmeal and other cooking failures. Mr. Hopkins took the ribbing in stride and didn't seem at all put out with the boys or his nephew. The easy teasing was refreshing after all the tense meals at her brother-in-law's table.

As soon as the boys and Jake headed out to the barn, the kitchen became silent. The dirty dishes were stacked once again in the sink, but this time Mr. Hopkins remained seated, sipping his coffee as he watched her take the griddle off the stove. "You haven't eaten anything yet," he commented, bringing her attention away from the dishwater.

"Um…" A plate sat on the back of the stove for her as soon as she finished the dishes.

"Have a seat. Eat while they're still warm. Then you can wash everything at once. They were very good, by the way. Ambrosia." He smiled, standing to pull out a chair for her.

"Thank you." She acknowledged his compliment but still felt a little shy as she set her plate on the table, sprinkled sugar over the pile and then returned to the stove for her own cup of coffee. "Would you like some more?" She waved the coffeepot toward him. At his nod, she filled his cup back up before taking her seat again. He returned to his own and sat watching her eat. After a minute he shifted.

"Right after breakfast we usually take the boys with us to the barn and have them sorta help with chores. They're not big enough to handle a shovel and muck out the stalls, so we have them curry the horses while Jake and I do the heavy work. It keeps them occupied and within sight. Now with you here, we can start leaving them in the house, but it means you'll have them underfoot in here. Or would you rather we make them do their chores while you do whatever you need to do in the morning?"

"I'd never presume to tell you what to do, Mr. Hopkins. I am more than willing to care for them the entire day and find ways to get my work done with them 'underfoot' as you say. I also know they need to learn lessons you can teach them in the barn and in the fields. Things I have no knowledge about. I'll leave the decisions to you. Just let me know what you decide."

"Fine," he agreed with a nod of his head. "Then we'll plan on them coming out to help with barn chores right after breakfast. Then they can come back in and you can give them something to work on, whatever works well with your plans. Since you're new to the farm, I'd like to tell you what the boys can and can't do." He paused, waiting for her to acknowledge him, but she had a mouthful of pancake so all she could do was nod. His eyes twinkled and she wondered fleetingly if he had done that on purpose to fluster her.

"They are not allowed to play in the barn or barnyard without an adult with them at *all* times. Little boys tend to move quickly and could spook a cow or horse. An animal's natural reaction would be to kick and that could easily kill a man, let alone a boy. The boys are also not allowed to venture down by the creek or out to the fields on their own. They love to fish and when it gets too hot, we even take them swimming but—" he glanced at her over the coffee cup as he paused to take a sip, his cheeks turning slightly pink "—I don't expect you to have to take them into the water."

The idea of watching the boys fish had a certain appeal as long as they could bait their own hooks. She had never learned to swim, nor did she plan on learning. She would leave the swimming lessons to Mr. Hopkins.

"That sounds reasonable," she said.

"It's not only the animals themselves that pose a threat to the boys. The equipment in the barn is also heavy and some have sharp edges like the saws and the axes. They are not to touch my tools unless *I* am with them. If you need wood chopped or something fixed, please let me know, and I'll get things shipshape."

Again she nodded, the last bite of pancake melting in her mouth. She looked down, chagrined that she had eaten it all. She didn't remember tasting it. Her lukewarm coffee washed the rest of the pancake down and she found Mr. Hopkins's eyes studying her once again.

He had a way of doing that. It made her feel as if he was trying to see into her soul. As if he could really see if she was being truthful or just accommodating. Honestly, she would find it hard to deny him reasonable requests. She was starting to believe again that she had been right to think that God had brought her here. When she'd learned that her Mrs. Hopkins was a *Mr.* Hopkins, she'd started to doubt, to question. But now certainty filled her again. Maybe because the boys pulled on her heartstrings.

It was not that Mr. Hopkins neglected his boys. On the contrary, it was clear that he tried so hard to do everything and he genuinely loved them, but he had no help. Things like table manners, housekeeping and book learning had been forgotten in the attempt to keep the farm running. She wanted to help the boys, teach them what she could and fill them with love and all the mothering they had missed out on these last few years. But what if she were only here for a few weeks or months? Would her presence be missed when she left? Would it be better to keep a distance from the beginning?

No, she couldn't do that. If it was not in God's plan for her to stay, then she'd resign herself to the change later. For now she knew that this was where she belonged, and she'd make the most of it for as long as she could.

"Do you have any questions, Miss Stewart?" he quizzed.

"Well, is there something you want me to work on today? I mean, there are a lot of tasks needing attention." She paused, trying to find a delicate way to say things. "But I was wondering if you have one thing that stands out as more urgent."

"No, ma'am. As you can see, we have been very remiss in our chores around the house, so there is more work to do than I think you'll be able to do in three years." A slight blush colored his ears. "It didn't get this way overnight, and with the boys always underfoot, you may not have as much time as you are used to for tidying up and such. Whatever it is you decide to do, take your time. Just see to it that you don't wear yourself completely out. And if you need anything, you just let us know. It would be nice to have a noon meal right about midday and the dinner ready close to six in the evening. Other than that…you women seem to know better than I do what's what."

"I do have another question. Do the boys know where to find the washtub and the soap? Do they know where to find the dirty clothes? Where do you put the clothes that you need mended?"

This time a full-blown smile filled his face, transforming him into a handsome man, looking years younger than he had looked at the train station two days before. "Miss Stewart, that sure sounded like three questions to me." He chuckled good-naturedly and before she could come up with some sort of response, he continued. "Now, this is a farm where no woman has dared invade in more than two years. If it still stays together on its own, we wear it. Once it falls apart, we discard it. I've never learned to thread one of those itsy-bitsy needles, much less pull one through some shirt that's just gonna get mistreated again."

"I see your point. You may find that I try and change some of those habits in the days to come. Please let me know if I overstep my bounds." Abby kept from smiling, but she was sure the glint in Mr. Hopkins's eyes matched her own. Glancing around the room, still dirty and gritty everywhere but the sink and countertop where she had cleaned yesterday, she wondered if she had bitten off more than she would be able to chew. The only way to find out was one bite at a time, starting with the breakfast dishes.

"I'll be sure to do that, ma'am."

"Huh?" She turned back to him from her perusal of the room, already mentally planning what she would do first.

"I'll be sure to let you know if you overstep your bounds." He smiled at her, and her heart skipped a beat. "And, yes, the boys know where the soap is kept. The washtub is hanging in the pantry and another in the barn if you need it. Are you planning to wash clothes today?" he questioned softly.

"If it's all right with you, sir," she answered just as softly.

"That'd be fine. I'll just go and start the fire in the yard for you, then. I'll also get the water hauled out there."

"Thank you." Thinking their conversation was done, she stood and she noticed he stood as well, whether to get to work or out of respect, she wasn't sure.

"Um."

His hesitance brought her attention back to him from the dishes she had started to place in the dishwater.

"Breakfast was very good. Thank you."

"My pleasure. I love seeing the boys enjoy their food," she confessed, not mentioning that watching the men devour the food had left her just as satisfied.

"Well, it is nice to have someone who knows what they're doing in the kitchen for once." He chuckled as he left the room. Only after the door shut behind him did Abby dare to look back over her shoulder. Through the window she watched his strong, tall form quickly cross the distance and then disappear into the barn.

Chapter Five

"Okay, boys, it's about time to go and check on the laundry," Abby called out to the boys playing in the front room.

She had washed all the clothes yesterday and then worked on washing the kitchen cabinets. Today she had tackled the bedding. The sheets and covers from all four beds upstairs were hanging on the lines in the yard and she had swept the rooms out, including the cobwebs from the corners and the ceilings. Her arms ached, but she was happy with the way things were staring to look—a little more civilized. Given another few weeks, she would have the place clean.

She stepped out of the kitchen and caught Tommy with a hand up under his shirt, scratching again. She had washed that shirt yesterday. Had chiggers or fleas gotten into the wash while it dried yesterday? Her own clothes felt fine. "Come on, boys. Come help me get the sheets for your beds."

They left the city of blocks they were constructing on the floor without complaint but without much enthusiasm, either. As Willy passed her, he scratched his belly, too. Tonight she would insist on a bath for both boys.

Outside, she inspected the bedding and, not finding anything crawling around on it, she carefully took each item down, folded it and placed it in the basket she had found in the pantry. The boys had been subdued the majority of the morning. She wondered if they were already tired of spending their days indoors with her instead of out, playing and working with their father and cousin. It was a depressing thought. She had hoped to become fast friends with them, but chances of that were slim if they were already missing life before her arrival.

With the possibility of little critters on their bodies, Abby opted to leave them playing with their blocks while she wrestled the bedding back on the feather-stuffed mattresses. Making Mr. Hopkins's bed, she let her eyes wander, learning about her employer. Mr. Hopkins had a number of books in his room, stacked on his small nightstand next to the large bed. He had taken his pillow out with him to the barn but had left the rest behind. His clothes had been hung on their pegs on the wall, and his two other pairs of trousers were folded and stacked on the side table under a window. The other piece of furniture in the room was an elaborate dressing table Abby assumed to have been the late Mrs. Hopkins's. Although her things were hidden inside the drawers and a layer of dust sat heavily on everything, it was as if her presence was still in the room.

Did Mr. Hopkins feel the connection to his late wife here, in the room they had shared? Did he miss her terribly? Many men, once they were widowed, didn't wait very long at all to remarry just to have help with the house chores and the children. Society seemed to understand and accept that many second marriages were marriages of need and convenience instead of marriages based on love and friendships, especially on the prairie. Yet Mr. Hopkins hinted he wanted a housekeeper who was older to avoid ideas of marriage. Had his love for his wife been so all-consuming that even a few years after her death, the idea of sharing his life with another woman was unthinkable?

Mr. Hopkins was kind and gentle with just the right sense of humor thrown in. He didn't seem to be a romantic, but what did Abby know about such things? She had never been courted.

A glimpse in the mirror above Mrs. Hopkins's dressing table revealed a disheveled girl who had thin blond hair that never conformed to the knots she fashioned at the nape of her neck and went every which way with the slightest breeze. Her face was slightly flushed with the heat of the late spring sun and the heavy work she had been doing. No wonder no one ever took notice of her.

She hurried to finish straightening out the quilt. It felt as if she were trespassing in a forbidden area. She glanced around once more to make sure everything was in place and then left, closing the door behind her.

Once she was done upstairs, she returned to the living room and found the boys lying on the floor, slowly pushing the blocks around with little interest, both scratching different appendages. For the first time, she noticed that Tommy's cheeks were unnaturally pink and Willy had a glassy look about his eyes.

"Tommy, are you feeling all right?" she asked, anxiously watching his eyes and noting the same glassy look.

"I'm itchy. Som'pin bit me," he complained, and Abby held her breath as she signaled him to come to her.

"Let me see." She sank down on the davenport and reached out for the smaller boy's shirt. He lifted it and she stared, wide-eyed, at the welts all over his torso. "Do you have these anywhere else?"

"Uh-huh, my back is itchy but I can't see it," Tommy whined.

"Let me take a look." She gently turned him. Taking his shirt completely off, she studied the rash marking his back. "You'll be getting this all over in a little while. Willy, do you have these, too?"

"Yeah. They itch!" He was close to tears and Abby groaned, wondering what kinds of medicine and herbs were at her disposal.

When she had been fourteen, she and her nieces and nephews all shared the chicken pox. While it was not any fun, she remembered the doctor telling her it wasn't as dangerous as the smallpox. As long as they kept the fever down and the boys comfortable, they should be all right.

"Well, boys, it looks like you have the chicken pox. We're gonna have to set you in the washtub with some oatmeal so you won't itch so much. I want you to come out to the yard with me and we'll see if we can't help you feel a little better."

"This is silly," Tommy told Abby a little while later as he and his brother sat in the washtub in the shade of the only tree in the barnyard. Willy had been very self-conscious about bathing out in the middle of the yard in broad daylight, but once Abby promised not to look while he stripped down and got in, he quickly complied.

She dragged a stool out from the kitchen and set to mending shirts while the boys splashed each other. She let them play until they looked cool. She helped Tommy out and got him dried off and into his underwear and a large, holey shirt that had obviously once been his father's. Someone had lopped off the sleeves at the elbows so that it would accommodate the boy's shorter arms. Willy insisted on getting himself dressed and demanded she leave him alone. Knowing he was tired, itchy and running a fever, she didn't argue.

Since the front room was cooler than the upstairs, she had them lie down on towels on the floor and she read to them until they were both asleep. While they slept, she checked on dinner and continued to clean the kitchen. She briefly entertained the idea of running out to the far fields to let the men know about the boys, but it wouldn't make any difference in how fast Tommy and Willy got better. In the end she figured it would only worry Mr. Hopkins while he should be concentrating on the fields.

When the boys woke, they were as uncomfortable as they had been earlier and she prayed for patience for the next few days. She settled them to play with the blocks again in the cool of the front room and made frequent trips back to the kitchen. Each time she peeked out to see if the men had returned to the barn. Her heart skipped a beat and then sped up too fast when they finally returned. Would Mr. Hopkins be angry she hadn't told him at once?

"Boys, I'm going to tell your father about the chicken pox. Stay in here and play nicely. I'll be right back." She hurried out to the barn.

"Um, good afternoon, Mr. Hopkins," she called out, making both men spin around from taking the harnesses off the horses. "Jake."

"Good afternoon, Miss Stewart." Mr. Hopkins studied her carefully, his eyes then darting to the house and around the yard. "Is everything all right?" The concern in his voice matched his gaze.

"Um…yes. I was able to do the washing and dinner's on the stove, but…" She bit her lip. How should she tell him? What if he decided to take them to the doctor and leave her at the train station on the way? She hadn't even been in the house for a full three days!

"Is there something you need, Miss Stewart?" Mr. Hopkins's gaze froze her in place. He knew something was afoot.

"I just wanted to tell you that the boys have chicken pox. They started itching just after lunch and now they're covered in the rash. I gave them a bath in oatmeal and lukewarm water and then they took a nap, but I wanted you to know. I can handle this, sir. I took care of my nieces and nephews when we all got the chicken pox a few years ago. It wasn't pleasant, but it's not too dangerous as long as we can control the fevers and keep them from scratching."

"Are you sure it's chicken pox, Miss Stewart?" Mr. Hopkins quizzed her as he all but dragged her by her upper arm toward the house. His grasp was firm but not painful. "Jake, see to the horses. I'll be out in a bit," he called over his shoulder as an afterthought.

"Yes, sir. I remember it well from when I had it myself. And then two years ago, Katie and Peter had it and I took care of them, as well. Since I had already had it, I couldn't get it again and I… Well, Emma was not interested in trying to keep her children comfortable." Abby bit her top lip to stop from rambling.

"Auntie Abby, I want some more water," a small,

cranky voice called out to her as they crossed the kitchen.

"Okay, darling, I'll get you some in just a minute," Abby answered the child, watching Mr. Hopkins to see what his reaction was.

"Pa, Pa!" both boys chorused. They climbed to their feet with less energy than normal, but they still embraced him as he bent down and put himself at their eye level.

"Hey, boys, I heard we have some turkey pox around here," he teased, but the look in his eyes belied his light-hearted banter.

"Auntie Abby said it was chicken pox," Willy corrected. "Right?" he confirmed with a confused glace at Abby.

"Yes, I'm just teasing," Mr. Hopkins reassured the boy. Nodding he turned and studied Abby. "Do they need a doctor? The nearest one is a day's ride past Twin Oaks."

"No, as long as we keep them cool and comfortable, they should be fine." Abby infused her voice with confidence. She had nursed the others through this. Maybe this was the opportunity she needed to prove she was indispensable here. "Have you and Jake had it?"

"Yes, ma'am." He stood and once again towered over her. "I had it when I was a little younger than Tommy is now. Jake had it the fall before…before his parents died. I'll go see about those chores now. Is there anything else you need?" he asked, his attention on his boys.

"Do you have willow bark or something else to keep fevers down?"

"Yes, ma'am, although I don't know how to use the stuff. I bought some just in case when we were in town last fall. There was a bad flu here last year. I wanted to be sure I had some on hand."

"If you would show me where I can find it?"

"Yes, ma'am." Mr. Hopkins gave Tommy's shoulder a squeeze and ruffled Willy's hair. "I'm going with Miss Stewart and then out to the barn to milk old Bess and the other girls. You mind Miss Stewart, now."

Later that night, after the men had bathed the boys once more, Abby stood next to the bed and tucked the boys in their beds. She had listened from the rocking chair near the window as Mr. Hopkins read three stories before their prayer time. Dispensing hugs and kisses to the miserable boys, she had headed downstairs to go to her room when she heard the boys calling out for their father. Since he'd already gone out to the barn, she went up and found herself once again seated on the rocking chair. This time she settled it between their twin beds. She read to them and sang songs she had learned as a small girl from her mother.

When they both were finally asleep, she brought a pillow and the quilt from her own bed and settled on the floor between them so she would be able to hear them whenever they woke. As it turned out, they woke frequently. She didn't sleep more than an hour at a time. By the time the sun was peeking over the horizon, her eyes felt gritty but she forced herself to start breakfast for the men.

The next few days were long and miserable for the boys and Abby. She tried to humor them with stories and singing. More than a few times, she spent hours just holding them on her lap in the rocking chair. Even Willy called for her the minute he woke up. She would bathe them three or four times a day and would always be ready with another glass of water and some bread or cookies. Meals had been simple soups so she could leave them simmering while she spent time with the boys.

"I'm sorry, Mr. Hopkins. I made rabbit stew with potatoes again. I wish I had more time…. I'll have a better meal for us tomorrow," Abby blurted out as soon as Mr. Hopkins had finished saying the blessing on Wednesday night. "I haven't had a chance yet to mop the floors or dust upstairs. I'll get to it as soon as—"

He raised his eyebrows and looked steadily at her as if she were a stranger from another planet. "This is the best rabbit stew that has ever been served at this table and your bread fills in all the rest of the space in our empty bellies. You've been taking care of two sick boys. I don't know how you got to making dinner at all. Don't worry about the housework. It'll still be there in a week from now." He chuckled and returned his gaze to his plate.

That night the boys fell asleep earlier, so she took advantage of the quiet house and scrubbed the kitchen floor until it returned to its original color. Her back protested by the end. If felt as if a hundred splinters still stuck in her hands and knees, but the kitchen was finally clean enough to satisfy her just as Tommy called from upstairs again.

Will wondered what was going on inside the house as he milked the cows. There was no smoke rising from the chimney. In the week since Miss Stewart had arrived, she managed to be up and ready by the time he brought in fresh milk each day. They had all started to get used to the little touches she brought to the house. Although the boys had the chicken pox, they still were eating more than they had before. She had yet to burn anything. Even Jake commented about how nice it was to have two socks without holes and a shirt that had all its buttons.

His wonder changed to worry when he walked into the kitchen, ready to receive the cup of coffee she always had ready by then, only to find the stove still cool and no sign of his housekeeper. Had something happened to her or the boys during the night? Surely if there was something wrong with the boys, she would have alerted him.

Pacing in the kitchen didn't get him any answer, so he quietly headed out to her room, debating if he should knock or just wait in the front room, but the problem was already resolved when he reached her door. It was open. Her bed looked as if it had not been touched and there was no sign of her in any of the other first-floor rooms or in the root cellar.

For a moment, rational thought fled, and he was left with nothing but the deep, aching fear that told him she had left. *She's just like Caroline and Auntie Shelia.* His thoughts ran away, making his stomach churn with anger. *She ran off already.* It was what he had expected, but it still made him furious. At her, for leaving them in the lurch, and at himself for believing—even just for a few days—that he might actually have found a woman he could rely on.

But before the anger had a chance to build, common sense reasserted itself. She couldn't have run off. Where would she have gone in the middle of the prairie? She knew no one out here. The closest neighbors were an hour's ride away by horse, and all the horses were still in the barn.

Rushing up to the boys' room, he held his breath and listened carefully, hoping against his better judgment to hear her soft murmuring with one of his sons, but there was only silence. Similar lumps on each of the twin beds confirmed that both boys were sound asleep and fine. Disappointment knifed him in the gut.

Where could she be? He checked his own room, Jake's and even Matt and MaryAnn's. Neither he nor Jake had ever cleaned out that room. Returning back to check on his boys, he stood at the doorway, wondering where she could have gone off to. Turning to retrace his steps, he halted abruptly and turned around, rubbing his eyes. Two small, shapely bare feet were sticking out past the end of Willy's bed. Drawing closer, he couldn't believe his eyes; she was asleep on a pallet on the floor between the twin beds. Why?

He wanted to shout for joy and yell at her for her foolishness in the same breath. How could she be sleeping on the floor? What was wrong with her bed? She could have used his bed or Jake's if she hadn't wanted to be on the first floor. Was she secretly scared of sleeping in the house without another adult? If she had just said something, he would have tried to find yet another solution.

He knelt down beside her and gently shook her shoulder. "Miss Stewart? What are you doing sleeping on the floor?"

It took her a minute to wake up. "Are the boys okay?" Her voice was gravelly. She rubbed her eyes and blinked at him. Something caught in his throat and he turned away for a moment. Even in her sleepy state she was obviously aware of where she was. Ignoring him, she sat up and checked one sleeping form and then the other.

Will studied the face of the young woman. Why hadn't he noticed yesterday how tired she was? Was she getting sick herself? When she had mentioned something about not getting anything done with the boys sick, he brushed it off as something to be expected with them underfoot all the time. After all, he had plowed and planted his fields in half the time of last year and covered three times more acreage with the boys in the house. If God granted him the sunshine, rain and heat necessary, his wheat crop would be three times as large as last year's.

But as he watched her try and force herself awake with those telling dark circles under her eyes, he realized he hadn't been paying attention to his home. The boys had been sick and all he had done to help was oversee their bath after dinner and then help Abby... Miss Stewart get them into bed. Tommy insisted Auntie Abby be there when they said their prayers. Why hadn't he noticed her fatigue?

"How much sleep did you get last night?" he asked, remembering the clean floor in the kitchen. Had she stayed up and scrubbed the floor on top of everything else?

"I don't know. They slept better last night. I think the worst is probably over." She glanced outside, and color drained from her face. She wrapped her arms around her middle and he remembered the same gesture when she was sick in the alleyway back in Twin Oaks the first day. Her eyes filled with fear.

"Are you all right?"

"I'm sorry I overslept. I need to get downstairs and start breakfast. If you'll just give me a moment—"

"No. You need a few more hours of sleep." He reached out his large hand, placing it on her thin shoulder, and stopped her from standing. "Go sleep in your own bed for a few hours."

Instead of looking pleased, she looked crushed. "I'm sorry. I'll get breakfast going and then there's all the—"

"There's nothing wrong with needing more sleep," he said, more gruffly than he intended to. What drove her? She was almost falling over from weariness and yet she was apologizing for not having breakfast ready.

As he watched, her eyes filled with tears and she turned her face into her hands and sniffed. She stood and fled the room. He watched her leave. "What did I say this time?" he asked himself out loud.

Minutes later, he slunk back down the stairs, careful not to make too much noise so Miss Stewart could sleep. Except he could have made as much noise as he wanted because standing in the kitchen, her feet still bare, was Abby, trying to fill the coffeepot with water from the pump. Tears streaking her face, she wiped them away quickly with the back of her hand as she turned her shoulder to him.

"Why aren't you resting?" he asked, frustration darkening his words.

"I need to make breakfast. You can't go out and plant on an empty stomach."

"I'm not planting today. You need a rest. I didn't realize how much work the boys had been, being sick and all. I'll get breakfast ready. Don't worry about it."

She looked so fragile and small, trying to wake from

her exhausted slumber just a few minutes before, and now barefoot and crying in the kitchen.

He had seen enough tears from Caroline to last a lifetime, but they had never made him as uncomfortable as Miss Stewart's tears. Maybe that was due to his suspicion that Caroline's tears had been a display to manipulate many a situation in her favor. Miss Stewart's were obviously sincere, and the result of exhaustion. In fact, she had worked very hard since the first day she stepped across the threshold and hadn't murmured a single complaint.

To take care of her basic needs would only be the Christian thing to do, especially since she had worked herself to exhaustion caring for his family. It was easy to see why the boys were taken with her. He had seen her when she read to them at night, cuddling Tommy on her lap and wrapping an arm around Willy's shoulders. She had won them over with her kind words and affection. It was only right that they take care of her as if she were part of the family, too—even if it were only for the summer.

That excuse seemed to fit. He clung to it and squared his shoulders, ready to do battle with the feisty, crying lady. She was going to get some sleep, even if he had to force her to.

She hadn't responded to what he had said, just kept going through the motions of putting breakfast together. She set the water on the stove. Picking up the bread from yesterday, she started to slice it.

"Why don't you sit down and I'll cut it up for you?" He stood right beside her and reached out for the knife. She released it with a weariness resembling surrender.

"I'm sorry. I was going to do this. I usually have

more energy than this. I know you need to get out to the fields and I don't want to slow your progress down. I wanted to—"

"I've done more this week than I did in three last year. You've already more than earned your keep." Suddenly it made sense, the way she was wearing herself down, refusing to stop working—she was worried he would send her back East without a referral because she had not been able to keep up with her chores. "You could'a told me they weren't letting you get any rest. I would have come in from the fields earlier so you could have taken a nap, or I could have had them sleep out in the barn with me."

"That's just what I want!" she almost shouted back, clearly frazzled. "I come here to take care of your boys and your home and end up forcing everyone else to sleep out in the barn. I could sleep out in the barn, Mr. Hopkins. Then everyone else could have their own rooms back."

Abby stood looking out the window, her fingers clutching fistfuls of skirt at her thighs. Her tears had stopped but were threatening to spill over the long blond eyelashes framing her expressive eyes.

Standing close, studying her profile, he saw the light glint off the specks of blue and green in her eyes, changing from green to blue and back again with every word she spoke.

"That's not going to happen here, miss. You won't be sleeping out in the barn when there's a perfectly good house here that'd be more comfortable and safer. Now, why don't you just go to bed and get some sleep!" He was too exasperated by the girl to keep his voice down.

She didn't look at him but spun away and fled to

her room. He could hear her muffled sobs a few minutes later when he went as far as the hallway to check on her. He couldn't bring himself to knock on the door. Ma had once said that a woman just needed a good cry every once in a while. He hoped that was all she needed.

When Tommy appeared in the kitchen a while later, Will motioned his son to be quiet. He was amazed Tommy didn't question him until he was seated at the table.

"Pa, where is Auntie Abby? She wasn't in my room when I woke up. I like it when she's there 'cuz she gives me kisses on my head and then helps me get my shirt all buttoned up right."

Inspecting Tommy's shirt, Will realized that Abby's help had been missed. "Here, son, let me help you." He rebuttoned his son quickly as he explained, "Auntie Abby was really tired today because of all the hard work she's been doing around here for us. I told her to go get some sleep so she could play with you boys later. We're gonna be real quiet this morning so she can rest, okay?"

"Yeah, we can be real quiet like we have to be when she's rocking me and Willy is asleep." Tommy's sweet voice added to Will's guilt. His boys had been up in the nights, miserable and grumpy, and he hadn't been there for them. At least Abby had been.

"Pa, we gonna wait for Auntie Abby to make us breakfast?"

"No, I've got it all fixed already," Will answered, ignoring his son's groan.

"But, Pa, I like the way Auntie Abby makes breakfast. She doesn't make it start on fire."

"Hey, that was only once. I was doing better lately. I fried some eggs and put them on bread with butter."

Lifting the platter from the back of the stove, he set it on the table and sat down in his spot.

"I like butter. Why didn't we have it before?"

"Because no one took time to churn the butter. We were always too busy with—"

"Pa, can we make Auntie Abby my new ma?" Tommy's question stopped Will's lungs midbreath. Neither boy had ever mentioned having another mother.

"No. She came to be the housekeeper, and she's not here to stay. She's going to go back," he stated as calmly as he could still gasping for breath. He should have thought about how attached the boys would get to her. After all, she was the first woman who had ever shown them any real affection.

"But I don't want her to go back. I want her to stay here with me, forever and ever. She says 'I love you' and kisses us when she puts us to bed. I want her to do that all the time. I want—"

"There are lots of things that we want in life, Tommy. Most of them we never get," Will retorted sharply.

"But she's really pretty and she sews really good, too. She made a shirt for Willy and is almost done with mine. She said she's gonna have something for us men to wear by the time we go to meetin'."

"Tommy, she's a really nice lady, but she's only here for a short time so that she can take care of you and Willy and teach you some book learning this summer. She deserves to go find some nice place to live in a town somewhere not in the middle of the prairie. Then she can get married and have kids of her own."

"You could marry her, Pa. Jenny said her Ma was telling Mrs. Scotts it was high time you got us boys a new ma. I think Auntie Abby is a good one. She even smells good. Jenny said if you married a new ma, she wouldn't be my ma but my stepmother, and she said that stepmothers beat on their stepchildren. But I don't think Auntie Abby would. Only if I were really bad."

"Well, I have no plan on getting you a new ma," Will stated with enough volume that Tommy sat staring at him for a minute in silence.

Jake chose that moment to come in through the back door, looking around for the new housekeeper. When Will explained that she was resting and that no one was to disturb her, Jake's smile fell and the boy slumped into a chair and waited for his breakfast with a glum expression. Willy finally came down and they all managed to eat the sparse breakfast Will put on the table. Even with the boys still itchy, they all went out to the barn to finish chores.

By dinnertime, Abby made a full meal and had bathed the boys again. She smiled at everyone around the table and thanked them for letting her rest all morning. They all seemed to agree if it meant she was going to go to so much trouble with dinner, including raisin tarts for dessert, they would be willing to let her sleep in more often.

Will had sent the boys up to ready for bed when he turned and noticed Abby's grimace as she stuck her hands in the dishwater. "Did you burn your hands?" he asked, curious more than worried.

"No, I'm fine," she denied through gritted teeth, a fine line of perspiration dotting her forehead and upper lip.

"Let me see." He stepped closer and almost said a few choice words. Each hand looked like a pincushion with ten splinters or more, and her palms had blisters the size of peas. "What happened?" he demanded, clasping her wrists between the thumb and forefinger of each of his hands to keep them in view.

"Nothing. I'll be fine," she denied again, tugging her arms back without success.

"If it were nothing, you wouldn't have blisters and splinters. Did this happen last night?"

She stood still, not even speaking. He was intently looking at her hands when he noticed her trembling. He looked up to find her eyes on the floor, but her fear was almost palpable. He led her to a chair and pulled it out.

"Have a seat. I'm going to pull these splinters out before they get infected. Why didn't you say something earlier?"

Even as he asked, he gently pushed her into the seat. He really didn't expect her to answer. He had benefited from all her hard work and yet he hadn't paid attention to her; just one more reminder why he failed in his marriage. Not that he was looking for another marriage—with Abby or anyone else—but that didn't change his responsibility to her as someone in his care. He was not going to let her get close to him, but he should at least let her know she was safe.

Living on the frontier, he always carried a sharp knife sheathed on his belt. Holding it to the flame in the oven for a moment, he wiped it on a clean cloth and sat down in the chair facing Abby.

"Put your hand out like this." He indicated how he wanted her hand over the clean cloth on the table, and then he started to use the tip of his knife to tease the splinters out. He could tell that she wasn't happy with the arrangement, but she didn't make a noise. Brave woman.

"I remember the first time I tried to help my pa with the boxes in the back of the store." He wasn't sure why he started to ramble, but she relaxed slightly, so he continued. "I must have been about Tommy's age. Pa told me to leave them alone, but I wanted to help. I tried to take them apart with my bare hands and got more splinters than I thought possible, but I broke up each and every box. Too bad my pa planned to use the boxes for produce out front." He shook his head self-deprecatingly and chuckled. "After he pulled the splinters out with his pocketknife, he gave me my first pair of work gloves and then we remade the crates."

Will glanced up from his work and noticed that she looked less frightened. In fact, she was smiling a little. "What?" he asked, a little more gruffly than he had intended. Having shared his childhood memories with her made him feel just slightly vulnerable.

"Nothing." She tensed.

"You were thinking something that made you smile. What was it?" he probed, this time keeping his voice soft and his eyes on her hand.

"I was just wondering if you were more like Willy or Tommy when you were a boy." Her voice was so soft he strained to hear it. When he glanced up again, her gaze turned away.

"I think my parents would say that I was as ornery as Willy and as impulsive as Tommy. I know they were always at wits' end to try and do something with me." He grinned at the thought and went back to prying tiny pieces of wood out of her palm.

"This might hurt a little," he warned before he used the tip to slit her skin open just a bit more and then nab the splinter. Her sharp inhale confirmed the sting, but she didn't flinch.

"That was the last one on this hand," he announced, not yet letting go of her wrist. It was soft and small inside his palm and he was reminded how slender she was. It had been a long time since he'd held a woman's hand in his. Before he could dwell on those thoughts, he let her right hand go and set to work on the left.

"So, you have an older sister and...?" He left the sentence hanging as he forced another sliver out.

"It was just the two of us. She was married by the time our father died of the fever and then, a few weeks later, our mother..." The catch in her breath softened his heart a little.

"How old her were you then?"

"Twelve, turning thirteen. Emma and Palmer took me in. It was their obligation and they never let me forget it. *I* was an obligation." She bit her bottom lip and he wondered what it must have felt like to grow up not being wanted. "So I did as much as I could not to be a bother. I helped with the children. They are really darling."

At the mention of her nieces and nephews, she smiled until he pulled another sliver out and she winced. "At first they had a housekeeper, but after Palmer offended her, she left and they had me do the majority of the work. I didn't mind. It gave me a purpose and I could see to the children, but Emma was never satisfied with what I did."

"I'm sorry your sister didn't appreciate your work. I certainly do. You've made this place much more like a home than it was before. I don't think I've looked forward to breakfast since MaryAnn died. My brother's wife was a good cook. I miss her—and him."

"I'm sorry. How long ago did they die?" Her compassion brought his focus from her hands to her eyes. He hadn't meant to say that out loud. Only Colin, his pastor and close friend, and Jake knew how hard Matt's death had been for him.

"It's been almost seven years. They headed to town in a sled a few weeks before Christmas to buy gifts and something happened to spook the horses, I guess. They ended up flipping into the river. By the time I went to find them, there was nothing we could do." Will cleared his throat, pushing aside the memories of the mangled sleigh and his brother and sister-in-law still trapped under it in the cold, rushing water.

"I'm sorry." Her voice made the memories recede into the past were they belonged. He cleared his throat once more and returned his focus to her hand that still lay limp in his. He knew she was watching his face, but he didn't dare look up and see pity in her eyes. He had seen enough pity in the eyes of the neighbors at the funerals. "It must get lonely out here with all the responsibilities of the farm now on your shoulders."

Her understanding soothed like a balm. A comfortable silence filled the room. Finally every splinter was out.

"You'll need to wash these and then I think I have some salve in the barn that'll help with the sting. I'll go get it."

"Thank you." She stood and he pumped the water so that she could let it run over her hands.

When he returned, she had almost finished the dishes and he forced himself to breathe deeply and take firm command of his temper before he spoke. Why did she insist on doing things that could hurt her?

"You shouldn't be washing those dirty dishes with your hands all cut up like that. I'll finish up." He was proud he'd kept his voice low.

"I…" She looked as if she was about to explain but dropped her shoulders and turned back to the sink.

"Wash them off and we'll get them all bound up for tonight."

Not waiting for her to answer, he started to pump the water again and let her gingerly wash her hands under the cold spray. Holding out a clean towel, he wrapped her hands in the cloth and patted them dry. He used the salve on the cuts and blisters, some of which had opened while she was washing dishes, and then wrapped her hands in strips of clean cloth.

"Thank you," she whispered, without looking up. "I'm sorry to have troubled you. Is there something else I can do for you tonight?"

"No, you were no trouble. I want you to get some rest and take care of those hands. It won't do for one of those cuts to get infected." He wondered if she thought he saw her as an obligation, as well.

Nothing could be further from the truth. She was worth her slight weight in gold. The house was cleaner than it had ever been since he'd built it. The boys were getting better now and he would never have had any idea how to nurse them through the chicken pox. But he wasn't foolish enough to think that she would stay for too much longer. Sooner or later she would be demanding he pay her way back to civilization. He didn't dare dwell on why that thought bothered him tonight. Must be that he'd been missing another adult to talk with.

She shifted on the chair she was sitting on and he realized it was getting late. His cows didn't like him making them wait come morning, so he'd best be getting off to bed, especially since he was starting to feel a friendship stirring between him and his housekeeper. He'd have to be careful not to get too attached.

But maybe a friendship, knowing she was only going to be there for a short time, wasn't such a bad idea. She needed someone to talk with, as well. Maybe he could make a habit of talking with her after dinner in the evenings—just to see how things were going with the boys and their studies—that type of thing.

"I'm gonna head on out now, unless there's something else you need," he offered, reluctantly standing when she shook her head. "Good night."

"Good night," Abby said softly as he strode out into the night. He shut the door behind him and made sure it was secure.

Chapter Six

Sunday dawned bright and breezy. Abby quickly made breakfast and left a chicken baking with lots of onions, carrots and potatoes floating in the water that half filled the pot. Cooking was so easy now that she had the kitchen set up precisely the way she wanted it. It felt as if she had lived there all her life even though the calendar indicated only three weeks had passed. After breakfast, she made the boys put on their new shirts. They looked very handsome in their dark blue matching shirts and she regretted not having found time to make pants for them yet. Mr. Hopkins and Jake had also cleaned up nicely. They both sported white shirts under gray vests she had mended, washed, starched and ironed.

Abby had managed to coax Jake into letting her cut his hair the night before, and he looked dashing. Cutting Jake's hair had reminded her of the times she had done the same for her nephews. She wondered how they were doing and when, if ever, she would get to hear news from them.

The men all sat in the wagon, waiting for her as she stepped out of the kitchen door. Mr. Hopkins drove right up to the steps and disembarked long enough to pick her up by the waist and set her on the wagon seat. They headed to the meeting house before she had time to worry about how she looked herself.

Having chosen to wear her favorite dress of light pink with plum roses printed on the fabric, she hoped the other women at the church would overlook the fact the fabric was slightly worn in places. She prayed her bonnet would hold her curls in place in spite of the teasing prairie breeze. The last thing she wanted to do was to embarrass Mr. Hopkins by arriving at the Sunday meeting with her hair in disarray and her dress less than acceptable.

The boys kept a constant chatter going, telling her about all the children—all five of them—that would likely be there. The children closest to Tommy's age were sisters who lived on the other side of the Scotts' homestead.

"Why couldn't God give us some boy neighbors? All we got around here are a bunch of girls! Uck!"

"Hey, mister, I'm a girl, too," Abby teased.

"Yeah, but you're a nice girl. Not like them. They think that catching frogs and diggin' for worms is gross," he reasoned with her. Abby felt humbled by his admiration even as she shuddered at the idea of actually handling frogs. Mr. Hopkins grinned at her as if he could read her thoughts. In the last week, they had grown comfortable with each other. Abby felt as if she had a good friend in her employer.

Willy told her about the other children who lived farther away. Jake hesitantly filled her in on details when the boys' explanations were confusing. By the time she saw the small chapel in the distance, she was sure she would recognized each of the thirty or so members of the area who frequented the church.

As soon as the wagon stopped, they were surrounded by people. The boys scrambled down the back of the wagon and ran off before Mr. Hopkins could loop the reins around the brake and hop down. He turned and helped her down in a movement as natural as breathing. Mrs. Scotts was the first to introduce herself and expressed her disappointment at arriving at home to the report of having missed her newest neighbor's visit.

Before Mr. Hopkins could introduce her to everyone who gathered, someone started to clang the bell. As one, the group turned and swarmed in through the doors. Before long, they all found seats in the twelve rows of long wooden pews of the quaint church. Abby found herself pulled along with the flow, all the way down to the third pew, and seated between the two boys with Mr. Hopkins on one side and Jake on the other. The tall, young circuit preacher greeted everyone at the door.

"It's a pleasure to finally meet you, Miss Stewart." The preacher gently pressed her hand with both of his as she entered the doorway on Mr. Hopkins's arm. "Will's shared all of your letters and I'm sure he and the boys are enjoying your cooking since anything has to be better than his."

"Except, of course, yours." Mr. Hopkins surprised Abby by being so informal with the young preacher, but the others around them just laughed.

"I confess, Miss Stewart, that my cooking is not much to write home about." Pastor MacKinnon's green eyes danced with merriment and Abby felt at ease. He couldn't be any older than she was, but he made her feel at home.

Abby enjoyed the service. Pastor MacKinnon possessed a gift for making connections to the Bible and everyday life. Surely God had placed her where she was for a purpose. Just like Ruth, the foreigner in an unknown land, God would use her to minister to others. She already saw some of her work paying off just seeing the boys looking so civilized in their dress shirts—until Willy used the back of his sleeve to wipe his nose. She consoled herself with the thought that she had just begun.

When the service finished, Abby was surrounded by the women of the area, and Mrs. Scotts began introducing everyone. Some of the women were openly friendly, while others seemed to hold back a little. All the apprehension she had felt when they had headed out that morning seemed silly now. Her new neighbors seemed to be completely taken with her dress. In fact, her dress was by far the fanciest and newest of all the women's.

Since the area was populated by more single men than families, there were only eleven women over the age of thirteen and all of them were married.

"Now, Miss Stewart, you must try and join us for our monthly quilting bee. We all meet here the last Friday of each month," Mrs. Ryerson suggested. Abby longed to participate and be part of the women's group but what would Mr. Hopkins think about the idea? Would he let her come on her own for a few hours as long as she got all her cooking and cleaning out of the way before she left the farm? Would he let her take the boys? Would he teach her how to drive the wagon?

Just as she was pondering the idea, she noticed that Herbert Scotts had arrived with his brother and was speaking with the preacher toward the front of the church in hushed tones. About to turn back to what the women were saying, she noticed the younger of the brothers gesture toward her, his eyes straying to areas of her body that made her cheeks flame. The women around her seemed to notice the men's presence, and Mrs. Scotts looked surprised to see her sons. Remembering how uncomfortable she had been under the stare of the man on their brief encounter at the Scotts' home the first day Mr. Hopkins had brought her from Twin Oaks, she forced herself to pay attention to what Mrs. Phelps said as she tried to calm her racing heart. The tingling sensation that crept up her neck and left her ice-cold didn't go away. Why was the preacher talking with them about her?

When she glanced back, Pastor MacKinnon had left the Scotts in one corner and retreated with Mr. Hopkins to the other side of the room, where they talked with their heads bent together. Abby couldn't see the look on the pastor's face, but Mr. Hopkins turned shades of red she'd never seen. His anger was almost palpable. What must have been said? He sent the Scotts boys a look that would have cowed lesser men, but they just smirked back at him and then turned their unashamed gazes back on her.

Abby chanced another glance at Mr. Hopkins and Pastor MacKinnon, only to see that they were headed her way. Mr. Hopkins looked like a thundercloud about to burst.

"Excuse me, ladies," Pastor MacKinnon's greeted them all in a congenial voice. He smiled at everyone. "I would like to speak with our newest neighbor for a few minutes alone, if that's all right with you all. Could I ask you to take your visiting outdoors and enjoy the beautiful fresh air and slight breeze God gave us this fine day?" As the woman all gathered their reticules and began to leave, he asked Mrs. Phelps, Mrs. Scotts and Mrs. Ryerson to wait outside because he wanted to discuss something with them, as well.

He extended his right hand out to Abby and once she had placed her own hand in his, he clasped it. "Would you allow me to pray for you and your future?" he asked, waiting for her nod.

"Father God, You know the plans You have for our newest member to this congregation. Plans You promise will build her up and not destroy her. I pray You guide her and be with her as we discuss Your will in her life. Grant us wisdom, understanding and peace. In Your name, I pray, Amen."

The pastor dropped her hand but continued to stand close. Strangely, Abby was more aware of Mr. Hopkins's presence, standing stiffly next to the pastor, only a step away, anger rolling off him in waves like the ripples of water in a river.

"Thank you, Pastor MacKinnon," she murmured. It was reassuring he had asked for wisdom, but she wondered what he was talking about. Surely they had had new people join the community before. Why had his prayer seemed so cryptic and serious? What had happened to the light jesting before the service? Why was Mr. Hopkins still looking like a bull about to charge, his nostrils still flaring?

"It's truly a pleasure to meet you, Miss Stewart. Although it seems that your arrival here has been a series of surprises. I hope we can work some of them out now."

She sent a questioning look at Mr. Hopkins. It was a brief contact, but she saw his look soften slightly and wondered again what was going on. Her mind whirled as she tried to remember anything she could have done that would have provoked his anger, but she came up empty.

"I have known Will since I started preaching in the community about, what, seven years ago, right, Will?" Mr. Hopkins acknowledged him with a nod but didn't comment.

"Will is a man who always looks to God for guidance. One who tries to do the right thing no matter the cost to him." The pastor's words seemed strange and pointed.

"In fact, when he shared the idea of hiring a housekeeper, I encouraged him to follow God's lead. I even carried a few letters back and forth from Twin Oaks. Will tells me there's been some confusion because you are not the grandmotherly woman he expected. He said you expected to find a widow woman, not a young widower at the train stop. Both of those errors may have been completely innocent, but they have caused a bit of a problem. I know God has a purpose in all of this and I suspect I know what that purpose is."

Abby wondered about God's purposes, too. It was such a relief that she had found a safe home with a family who loved God and made her feel useful and appreciated. But the temporary nature of the situation still worried her. She spent a lot of time in prayer about her future.

"However, there is a small complication," Pastor MacKinnon continued with a glance at the young men still smirking in the front of the chapel. "Herbert and Elvin Scotts have come and presented their concerns." He took a breath, as if wondering how to word his thoughts. "They came to inform the congregation that your reputation is at risk because you've been living on a farm with no chaperone and two men. Now—"

"You know I'd do nothing to harm Miss Stewart's reputation," Mr. Hopkins said with a glower.

"I know you fear God and would never intentionally compromise Miss Stewart, but owing to circumstances, I am afraid not everyone in the community will see it that way. The Scotts have come and said that either one of them would be willing to marry Miss Stewart so she can save face and have a secure future."

Abby gasped and felt as if the world were spinning. What had the preacher said? The Scotts had offered to marry her to protect her from Mr. Hopkins? Mr. Hopkins had been a perfect gentleman the entire time, treating her respectfully and sleeping out in the barn. The glances and outright stares the two brothers didn't bother to hide were scandalous. How could they think she would ever agree to marry either one of them? They would be no better than Palmer. The thought made her shudder.

"Miss Stewart, I imagine this must be a shock to you but we need to discuss your options. Are you all right or do you need to sit down a minute?" The pastor's words sounded tinny and far away, but their meaning finally penetrated her foggy mind.

She wet her lips, cleared her voice, testing to see if it was going to fail her, as well. "I would like to sit for a minute," she agreed, unsure if her legs were still under her. She felt numb all over.

Warm, solid arms came to support her right arm and around her waist. Surprised, Abby felt Mr. Hopkins infuse a sense of peace through his gentle grip as he aided her to the nearest pew. Both men hovered near her as she sat, closing her eyes, praying this was just a bad dream. She had finally started to feel safe and at home in Nebraska and now this....

"Miss Stewart. Can you answer a few questions for me?" Pastor MacKinnon asked in a gentle voice, his concern evident in his tone. She couldn't speak past the boulder lodged in her throat, so she nodded.

"Has Will done anything untold or inappropriate to you?"

"No!" The accusation was so ridiculous she lost no time in answering. "He's been a complete gentleman. He and Jake sleep in the barn every night. They have been very kind."

"Good." The young preacher grinned at Will. "I didn't want to have to beat him up. It's been a long time since I've gotten into a fistfight and I'm not completely sure I could take him, but I'd try."

The pastor was trying to make a difficult time a little lighter. She appreciated his efforts, but she doubted Mr. Hopkins did. His expression didn't change.

"The only reason the Scotts knew she was here was that I thought she would be able to stay with Mrs. Scotts," he said, his tone making it clear he blamed himself for this problem. "Now I'm glad I didn't leave her there. I doubt she would have been safe."

Mr. Hopkins glared at the young men. They reminded Abby of vultures waiting for a wounded animal to die before swooping and picking it apart.

"Unfortunately, I suspect you're right. I doubt the Scotts boys would have been as respectful. But they are determined that something be done to 'restore Miss Stewart to her place of respect in our society' and they feel the only way to do that would be to have someone marry her. Since it is widely known you don't want to marry again, Will, they are offering to let her choose between them for the one to take the *responsibility* from you and provide for her."

"Since when have they cared about anyone's respect?" Mr. Hopkins roared.

"Since she came wrapped in such a nice package with nobody to defend her." The pastor looked pointedly at Mr. Hopkins again.

"I was the one who got her all mixed up in this mess—I'll be responsible for my actions. But I did not, in any way, compromise Miss Stewart."

"I know that. But it's not enough just convincing me. If she doesn't marry today, they are threatening to ask the church to vote to excommunicate you both from among us. I don't think they will get enough to vote in their favor, but it will still be humiliating for all of us and leave a shadow of doubt in some people's minds."

"And her having to marry today won't leave the same doubts?" Even with Mr. Hopkins's voice pitched low, his fury was still evident.

"I can't say there won't be those who will see her as having been forced to marry and think the worst, but many will be more open-minded. They'll probably assume that marriage was always your intention, and that this Sunday was your first opportunity. Most of the people around here know you, Will, and they'll take your word that nothing happened between you two."

"So, what are you suggesting?" Will looked pointedly at the pastor, but Abby groaned as she put the pieces together.

"That you marry Miss Stewart today," Pastor MacKinnon answered in a matter-of-fact tone.

"You want *me* to marry *her?* Today!" Mr. Hopkins tried to keep his voice low, but Abby was sure that he could have been heard in the next state.

By the time she had applied to work for the Hopkins, she had already given up on marriage. No man had ever come courting. She never believed she was overly beautiful or graceful, but when she was younger she had harbored dreams that someday she would find a man who would love her for the woman she was… maybe not a priceless jewel but a woman who could care for him and his home and make his life comfortable and fulfilled. After seeing all her friends, even some of the more homely ones, marry and start families, she resigned herself to the fact that she was not marriage material. She repelled eligible men. Certainly Mr. Hopkins had no interest in marrying her. She remembered little things he had said since she had arrived. That he hadn't wanted to have a young housekeeper because it would complicate matters. A man who didn't wish to marry at all would never want to marry *her*.

"Don't worry, Mr. Hopkins. You can just take me to the train and I'll head back somewhere. Maybe there's work I can do in Chicago," she reassured him. "I was hysterical the day I arrived. I didn't think about what I was asking of you or your family."

Both men turned to stare at her as if just remembering that she had been listening to the conversation.

"No, Miss Stewart. The blame lies at my door. I was the one who should have made other arrangements for your housing. Or maybe I could have looked for a companion for you. I sent for you and made the decision to bring you to my home. I will fix this somehow."

Pastor MacKinnon stepped in closer, speaking directly to Will. "I don't think you understand the seriousness of the accusation. If Miss Stewart refuses their option, the Scotts boys are ready to take this to the church elders and demand a vote on whether either of you can be allowed to stay in the church. Even if Miss Stewart were to leave the area, you would still be held responsible, Will."

"But, Colin, you know that's blackmail," Mr. Hopkins rasped.

"I know. And I'd like nothing better than to be able to give you a different answer, but I would hate to see you turned away from the gathering of the brethren and Miss Stewart turned out of a safe home. I know you will be a good provider. I know you love God and would provide a godly lifestyle, bringing her with your family to church on a regular basis and leading the family in Bible study. I can't say the same for either Elvin or Herbert." Having mentioned their names, the pastor glanced at the duo and shook his head.

Turning back to Mr. Hopkins, he hesitated a moment before he started the conversation again. "As for Miss Stewart, you know her better than anyone else here. Is she a believer?"

"Yes, Colin. Her faith is real. I shared the letter she wrote about her conversion with you."

"Then on the basis of that, I would encourage you to consider this as God's opening a door for you. Your boys need a woman's touch in their lives. So do you." Pastor MacKinnon said the last part in a quiet voice, holding Mr. Hopkins's gaze.

"But we both know how that worked out last time," Mr. Hopkins muttered, his hand brushing though his already messy hair, standing the sandy-brown strands straight up in the back.

"You don't have to sacrifice your freedom for me, Mr. Hopkins. I have caused you enough discomfort and irritation as it is. If you could just find a way to get me to Twin Oaks—" she tried to appeal to him once again.

"That is out of the question, Ab… Miss Stewart," Mr. Hopkins interrupted, tripping over her name. For some reason, to hear her given name on his lips, even if unconsciously stated, made her feel a second of peace and belonging. "You don't know anyone in Chicago."

"But I didn't know anyone here before I came. If God brought me here for a purpose, then why is it causing all this trouble? If it weren't for my insistence, you would have sent me back East as soon as I arrived and you wouldn't be having this problem now. If you won't take me, maybe Pastor MacKinnon could see his way to getting me to the train station. Surely he has a wagon, as well."

"Miss Stewart, I think you need to see there are other issues here. Can you tell me if there is a reason you cannot marry Will?"

"He doesn't want to marry me." Humbling as it was, it was the only reason.

She realized the first day she laid eyes on him how handsome a man he was. As each day passed she became more aware of his love for God and for his family and his dry humor. He was a good man, and she was sure he would be a good husband. But he didn't want her. What kind of a marriage would it be to force a man to marry, only to have to live out the rest of her days with him, loving him, but not being loved by him? Surely if she continued to live in close proximity to him, she would quickly grow to love him, while she held no hope that any man would ever love her.

"I think his opposition to my suggestion comes from his issues with marriage itself and what he went through in his first marriage, not with you personally. Is that right, Will?" he clarified, turning to Mr. Hopkins, who just glared at him and then mumbled something resembling a yes.

"Now, are you engaged or do you have an understanding with a beau?" Pastor MacKinnon continued his questioning.

"No, sir," Abby answered, humbled all the more to have to admit it before both men.

"Is there anything we should know about your character that would impede you in being a godly wife and mother?"

"I don't think so...."

"Did your church excommunicate you for unrepented sins?"

"No, sir. Of course not!" She felt her cheeks glow red with embarrassment under their scrutiny.

"I have it on good authority you make a great chicken soup with dumplings and pot roast. You also don't burn the oatmeal for breakfast and you made the boys very comfortable even when they had 'the pox thingys.' Even Jake is coming out of his shell. I have a hunch God put you in their home so you can bring them happiness and complete this family. This day was designed by our Lord because God knew it would be the only way Will would marry again." Pastor McKinnon patted Mr. Hopkins on the shoulder and actually chuckled at the angry look Mr. Hopkins shot him.

"Why don't I let you two talk it over for a few minutes?" he suggested as he headed toward the Scotts, who were looking a little less smug than they had been before.

The pastor guided the men out of the chapel, leaving Abby alone with her employer. Mr. Hopkins began pacing the aisle next to her. The man took one more pass, huffing like the big bad wolf about to blow the little pig's house down. The poor man was in this mess because of her. Would it be better to marry one of the Scotts boys and let Mr. Hopkins off the hook?

She had come to care deeply for Tommy and Willy. The idea of leaving and not seeing them again…it broke her heart. It was different than the pain she had felt when she left her nieces and nephews. They had been staying in a home where all their physical needs were met and where others in the community were on hand to look out for their spiritual and emotional care. But Mr. Hopkins didn't seem to be able to even cook a filling meal, much less see to the care and education of his sons *and* make a go of the farm at the same time. What would he do with the garden she had just planted and the lessons the boys had begun? It was too much for him and Jake to take care of on their own.

"Ahem…" He broke into her thoughts. She hadn't noticed that Mr. Hopkins had stopped pacing and was standing next to her, watching her face. "Could we discuss this for a minute?" he asked, his humility surprising her.

"Of course. Do you have any other suggestions?" She looked up hopefully. His look was a mix of frustration and tenderness. It took her off guard after his anger a few minutes before.

"I'm sorry. I didn't handle any of this very well.

Colin is right." He sighed and ran his hand through his hair once again. "If I were looking to marry anyone, I would be looking for a woman like you. Colin's also right that the boys already see you as part of the family and I don't know what I would do if you had to leave. You have been a blessing to my family and I'm grateful. I just wish keeping you with our family didn't have to involve marriage. For me, the covenant of marriage isn't something to be taken lightly—it's a commitment for a lifetime. And my first go-around wasn't pleasant. In fact, you should know..." He looked away for a minute and then gazed into her eyes, swallowing as if he were swallowing his pride. "You deserve to know that my first marriage..."

He gripped the end of the pew and she instinctively shifted over on the bench so he could take a seat. Whatever he had to say, it was obviously hard for him. Without thinking about what she was doing, she covered his clenched fists with her own small hands.

"My first marriage had a lot of problems." He said it so softly that she wasn't sure she heard him correctly. What should she answer to that? Who was she to judge? She looked down at her hand atop his and bent her fingers around his fist, wishing she could make everything better. He loosened his fingers, turning his palm up to let her hand rest in his. She looked up to find his eyes on their intertwined fingers. Hers were so much smaller and lighter than his, which were so strong and sun-bronzed.

"Caroline didn't like the prairie. She wanted to go back to Philadelphia—but I couldn't leave. Not when I had just started to see my dream and Mathew's become a reality. I worked as hard as I could to give her everything she wanted, but… I don't even know what it was. It was as if she were a plant that just shriveled up in a drought. I tried to be a better husband, father… I did everything I could think of. Everything except go back East. But in the end, she just couldn't survive out here." As he explained, his grip tightened. Abby flexed her fingers and he let her hand go.

"I'm sorry. Did I hurt you?" His concern was sweet, as he rubbed his thumbs over the backs of her hands. She remembered the night he took out all of her splinters. How could hands so strong and callused caress her with such tenderness?

"No, you squeezed a little but I think they're still attached." She smiled and wiggled her fingers in the air to prove her point. The gesture brought a half smile from Mr. Hopkins.

"My mother would have boxed my ears for squeezing a girl's hand that tight." He ducked his head and studied his hands, flexing his fingers out and curling them up.

"Then it's a good thing she wasn't here to see you," Abby quipped.

"That's for sure." They both sat in silence for a moment, both occupied with their own thoughts. Abby's were spinning in her head so fast that she couldn't make sense of anything. Could she really be contemplating marrying a man whom she barely knew? And one who didn't want to marry her or anyone else? Could she pass up this opportunity to marry a Christian man who would do right by her?

All she wanted was a home where she belonged—a family that she could call her own. Was this her chance to finally claim her dream…or would this contrived marriage keep her from ever finding what she sought?

Chapter Seven

How could the day have gotten off to such a beautiful start and end up a disaster? Will sat in the pew next to Abby wondering what must be running through her head. She hadn't dropped his hand when he had confessed his failure as a husband, but maybe she still was too shocked to process it all.

She was bright and pretty. He realized the morning he found her sleeping between the boys' beds just how much he had come to expect a smile and a soft greeting with the cup of coffee when he entered the house each morning. To think that she wouldn't be there anymore…

The boys would be devastated and it would be his fault. His fateful ad had started this whole mess. He had paid her train fare; picked her up—well after they finally realized the mistakes that had brought them together—and brought her out to the homestead. It was his fault she was in this position and there was no way he was going to let either one of the Scotts brothers have her. She deserved better. Even when they were in church, they eyed her like a dog salivating over a T-bone.

If he had never been married before, never seen what it was like to watch a woman fade away in front of his eyes without any way to stop it, he would have jumped at the opportunity to marry a woman so caring and capable. Her cooking was excellent and the house had never been as clean. Even when she was tired, she kept a cheerful disposition and was always willing to do one more task. She was responsible and quick-witted. The boys adored her and she already had Tommy writing his alphabet. Both boys insisted she tuck them into bed each night, craving her kind words and warm affection. He would be a fool if he let her walk away from his family now, but would he be able to give her what she needed?

What would she do once she saw there were no fancy balls to go to on the holidays or stores where she could get the latest fashions? How would she handle the brutal challenges of a prairie winter, or the daily struggles of a farmer's wife living far from civilization? How could he ask her to promise her life to him when she didn't yet know all the shortcomings that life entailed?

Marrying her was the only way to protect her at the moment, but he realized he would have to keep things the same as now—just marry her in name only and continue sleeping in the barn. When the time came that she had her fill of the prairie and the life out on the frontier, then she could ask Colin to annul the marriage. She could go back East and find a place to work. Maybe he could write his mother and ask her to find suitable employment for Abby for the fall.

"Listen, Abby. If we're contemplating marriage, I think we should use our given names. Please call me Will." Wide-eyed, Abby nodded, so he continued. "I know most women dream of their wedding day and being courted and all that, but the situation isn't going to give us a chance. I want to do the right thing, and protect you. In order to do that, I think what we need is a marriage of convenience, in name only. It would protect your reputation and give you a place to stay where you'd be safe—at least until you have a chance to find a different employment back East. Then we could annul the marriage."

Words flowed one over the other, and he wondered if what he had said made any sense. He lifted his gaze to see disappointment for a fraction of a second before she dropped her gaze to the floor, effectively closing him out of her feelings.

Unable to resist contact with her, he lifted her chin with his fingertip. He reasoned to himself it was to get her to respond and let him know if she was even open to the idea or if she was offended by the whole mess. Her eyes shimmered and a tear hung suspended by two eyelashes, slowly losing the battle against gravity. It slipped down her porcelain pink cheek and slid to a stop next to her rosy lip. Will couldn't tear his eyes away from her face, so perfectly combined by God to make an adorable picture. But the picture was contorted in pain and he had the sinking feeling he had caused it. As if it had a life of its own, the finger that had lifted her chin gently traced a path to the tear and swiped it away. If only he could wipe the pain from her heart with the same ease.

"I think what I was trying to say is that I would be honored to marry you, Abby. I'm sorry I made such a mess of all of this." He felt suddenly anxious. He waited, holding his breath without realizing it, for her to answer.

"I'm sorry. I could still go to Chicago...."

Will fought a wave of disappointment. "Is that what

you really want? You want to leave the boys and the farm and all this work you've done and go to a place where you'll be alone?"

"I might be alone here even if I stay," she murmured.

"What do you mean?" he asked, confused. Did she understand he was offering a way for her to stay with him and his family for as long as she wanted?

"Um…" Colin's voice interrupted their silent stare. Will dropped his hand from Abby's cheek as if it had been burned. She straightened her spine as if she had been poked with a cattle prod. "Are you about ready to give us your decision?"

Why couldn't he have just waited for a few more minutes? Will barely kept from growling at him, knowing that Colin was just trying to keep this from getting ugly. Will didn't envy him the task. Abby turned her big blue-green eyes on him as if to ask him to make the decision for her.

"I have just asked this fine young lady for her hand in holy matrimony, but I believe she is still thinking through her options." He called to Colin without taking his eyes off Abby. When this discussion had started, he had not wanted to even consider marriage, but now he was sure that he would be crushed if Abby didn't accept his suit, feeble as it was.

"Are you sure?" she asked, clearly confused.

"Yes. I want you to stay with us. You belong at the farm. We need you to stay." As he said the words he realized how true they really were. They did need her at the homestead and he didn't want her to walk away, especially if she would be walking away as the new Mrs. Scotts. He clutched her hands, and his heart turned in his chest when he felt how cold they were.

"You won't hate me later?" she whispered. He leaned closer to hear her and caught the aroma of her clean hair and the rose-scented soap she used. It made his nose quiver, and his stomach clenched at the idea of having a woman once again at the house for a prolonged time. This time she would be his wife to protect and provide for but not to touch. Could he do it?

He squeezed her hand once more, gently this time, and tried to flash her his most reassuring smile. "I doubt I could ever hate you," he answered honestly. It wasn't her fault they were in this mess. If anyone needed to shoulder the blame, it was him. "Let's go," he encouraged her. "We've got a wedding to get to."

"So, has she given you an answer or is she holding out for someone better looking?" Colin teased, the tension from a while ago still lingering in lines around his eyes.

"She can't get much better than what she's got here in front of her. But she still has me on pins and needles," he volleyed back, hoping to help Abby relax. If only she would smile, even just a little bit, he knew that they would be able to get through the rest of the afternoon. Her wan look did little to reassure him, but he figured that she hadn't run the other way yet and her fingers still clutched his.

As if she could read his thoughts, she looked down at their hands together and then searched his eyes as if she could find some sort of answer there. "Are you sure you want to saddle yourself with me? I could still go."

"I'm not saddling myself with anyone, Abby." Will turned his full attention on her face once again.

If only she knew she would be such a blessing. If only she would be staying forever. She was already becoming a good friend. She took away some of the loneliness he had felt since Matt and MaryAnn died. But he was sure that one day she would grow tired of the hard life in the prairie and choose to go back East.

When that day came, she would leave yet another gaping hole in their lives. He had tried to avoid all this by bringing out someone older. If he wasn't careful he was going to be back to asking the "why" questions again. The questions God chose not to answer last time. Questions he and Colin prayed over and grappled with for the better part of a year after Caroline's death.

"You are a lovely young lady and I would be pleased to have you for my wife. I don't want you to feel pressured, but I don't really see any other way around this. At least God is supplying you with a safe place and a better option than Elvin or Herbert." After he said the words, he realized how arrogant that sounded. "Not that I—"

"No. You don't need to explain. I do thank the Lord that you're offering, but I know you don't want…" She turned her face away and he saw the tears pool against the edge of her eyelids.

"It'll all work out. You'll see."

"Would you do me a favor?" she asked tentatively without looking directly at him.

"What would you like?" He would consider doing just about anything to help fix this for her.

"Would you pray with me about this? Would you pray for God to give us both peace with this decision?"

It humbled him that she had asked for prayer. He should have been the one leading in prayer without being prompted. It was one more reminder why he didn't deserve a godly wife.

"Dear God." It was easy to start, but what was he supposed to say? God knew what was going on in his heart and mind and just how little peace he felt at the moment. Well, he could pray for his future wife. "Guide us and bless this day. Give Abby peace and comfort her."

Colin slid up closer to the pew they were sitting in and rested a hand on Will's shoulder. Will was glad for a good friend to stand with him. When Will ran out of words, Colin took over. "God, we give You honor today, and take solace in the knowledge that You've brought all this together for the best for both Will and Miss Stewart. You have a plan for them and for the family You will form with them today. I pray You will be always the center of their marriage and their home. May Your name be blessed by the way they live and serve You together for the years You give them.

"Be with us as a congregation and teach us to live in a way that is above reproach and a testament to Your faithfulness. We pray for Your peace in our midst today and especially with Miss Stewart. May Your Spirit comfort her and guide her in her new roles as wife and mother. In Jesus's name, Amen."

Colin clapped Will on the shoulder and grinned. "Well, I sure didn't foresee you marrying this morning when I woke and greeted the Lord. I guess you can never tell what the good Lord has in store for a body from one minute to the next. I'll go let the people know there's to be a wedding today. Maybe Mrs. Ryerson and Mrs. Phelps can come and help Abby get herself arranged. We'll have a short ceremony and then let everyone go home since there were no plans for a picnic." He chuckled and Will was torn between punching the man of God in the middle of the church and begging him to stay a moment longer and forestall the inevitable.

Colin must have sensed Will's mood because he moved away but held out his hand in a handshake. "Let me be the first to congratulate the groom. God's seen fit to give you a lovely bride even though you're the ugliest thing He's placed this side of the Mississippi. Congrats."

"Thanks," Will croaked out. He stood and shook Colin's hand, then turned back and offered a hand up for Abby. She stood and he waited for a moment more to see if she had anything else she wanted.

"Are you going to be okay? Do you need anything?" His mother's lessons about how to be a gentleman were rusty, but he determined to put them to use, starting that instant. How he wished his mother were there. She would know how to help. She would have hugged Abby and reassured her that everything was going to work out.

Abby shook her head without looking up at him. What he wouldn't give to know what was going through her head at that moment. But then again, it might be better he not know what she thought of him. There was nothing either of them could do about the situation now.

Before he could say anything else, the door at the back of the chapel opened. Mrs. Ryerson and Mrs. Phelps entered, gushing about how they were going to help Abby fix her hair and get ready for the wedding. They cackled and pecked at him like a couple of hens and he was quick to obey their orders to "get out until his bride had been made ready."

Abby was beautiful just as she was, so he wasn't too concerned about them taking too long with the hair and such…but he did wonder if they knew a way to get both the bride and groom "ready" for a wedding that they had not anticipated or wanted. Getting "made ready" might take a bit longer than they had anticipated. He doubted if they would have been as excited if they knew what had caused all the last-minute plans.

Stepping out into the bright sunlight, he stood still for a minute while his eyes adjusted. Clapping erupted and he looked around to see they were all looking at him. Neighbors, old and new, congratulated him, some men calling out encouragement. Obviously Colin had already announced the ceremony about to take place.

"Pa, Pa!" Tommy's excited voice caught his attention as he started down the stairs. "Is it true? Are you making Auntie Abby my new ma? I told you she'd make a good one. She's nice and smells good and even—"

"Yes, Tommy. I'm marring Auntie Abby, but she's…" He glanced up to see the Scotts brothers standing to the side of the church, not nearly as smug as before. It gave him a sense of satisfaction that he had thwarted their plans. He shuddered at the idea of Abby marrying one of them.

"I just knew it! Yeeppie! I get a new ma!" Tommy went running off to tell Willy. Will searched around the yard and spotted Jake standing next to their wagon, a goofy grin on the teen's face. From the nod he gave Will, he radiated pleasure. Before Will could walk over to talk to him, Mr. Phelps stepped forward to shake his hand.

"It's about time you found yourself a new wife. A young man like you needs a helpmate to keep the farm going and someone to give you a passel of kids. I'll bet you're as pleased as punch."

Will tried to be polite and pay attention, but his

mind drifted off to worries about the boys and how they would react when Abby left in the fall. How would *he* react in the fall? Was there anything he could do to convince her to stay for good? If only their marriage could be for real and not for show. If only he could find some kind of faith that a woman could adapt to the life of the prairie farmer and enjoy it....

If only he could make himself believe that he could ever make a wife of his truly happy.

Abby stood at the foot of the church steps for the second time in one day, listening to the church bells ringing. This time, however, the bells were heralding her wedding. How could it be? She hadn't imagined anything like this would ever happen to her. As a child she had dreamed of marrying some handsome man who would sweep her off her feet with his declaration of love and devotion. Mr. Hopkins fit the handsome part. But where was the rest of her dream—the fairy-tale romance with a man who brought her flowers and proposed on bended knee?

In spite of his promises to not hate her, Abby felt certain that instead of building a marriage or even a friendship, this coerced wedding would create resentment on his part after a time. If only she were more like Emma, it wouldn't be so scary. Emma had married for money and station. It didn't seem to bother her that her husband held her in disdain, as long as he continued to provide their lavish lifestyle. But Abby craved love, affection. Even if Mr. Hopkins—Will—treated her with the same kindness and respect he'd showed thus far, he wouldn't give her what her heart truly desired.

"It's time, child." A soft voice to her right broke

into her thoughts, even as Mrs. Phelps handed her the bouquet of wildflowers hastily collected and wrapped with a hair ribbon from someone's reticule. "He's a fine young man and so handsome," the older woman continued, pulling her by the arm up the stairs. "He's a gentle man, so you have no reason to be frightened. He'll be a good husband—"

Before she could continue, the door opened and Mrs. Reyerson smiled at her. "You look lovely, dear."

Through the open door, Abby could see that most of the congregation had stayed to witness her wedding. Or maybe they were just here to see Mr. Hopkins married against his will. No matter their reason, as she stepped through the portal, they all stood and watched her. On shaky legs, she started forward, unsure where she was even headed until she lifted her eyes and caught sight of her groom standing at the front of the church watching her. He was so handsome. His gaze locked with hers and pulled her toward him. He looked sure of himself. He looked safe.

Unaware as to how she got there, she was suddenly standing in front of him as he extended his hands to cup hers. It felt right—her smaller hand nestled inside his larger, rougher ones. Everyone else in the place disappeared and for a moment, she stepped out of time and felt safe. "It'll be all right, Abby," he whispered just before Pastor McKinnon started to speak.

"We are gathered here today to join the lives and hearts of F. William Hopkins and… Is it Abigail or Abby, Miss Stewart?" he asked, stopping the service midsentence.

"Abigail," she answered, not daring to look away from her groom.

"Yes, and Abigail Stewart in holy matrimony," Pastor MacKinnon continued. Abby felt as if she were an observer on the peripheral, watching a drama play out around her. "Do you, F. William Hopkins, take her to be your..." Pastor McKinnon's voice droned on, but Abby couldn't concentrate. What was she doing?

"I do." Will's voice was steady and sure. He gazed into her eyes and she wondered if he knew how scared she was.

"And, Abigail, do you take William Hopkins to be your lawfully wedded husband, to honor, respect and obey from this day forward?"

Mr. Hopkins squeezed her hands gently and she shook off her fears. It was her turn to speak. "I... I do." Her voice caught, not because she didn't want to be tied to this man, nor because she didn't trust her life in his hands. She did. But in the middle of all of this, she realized it wasn't until death do them part, it was until he could get her off his land and send her back East. It was only until the harvest was in. How could it be that she already wanted to weep for the home she was losing before she ever really had it?

"I now declare you husband and wife." The pastor's voice broke into her confused thoughts once again. "You may kiss your bride."

She had forgotten about this part. No one had ever kissed her before. What if he chose not to kiss her? The marriage was in name only. Will was already standing so close, but he stepped even closer. Letting her hand go, he raised her chin with his finger, forcing her eyes to his. His gaze held her place as his lips descended on hers, or *almost* on hers. His touch was soft and warm, more of a whisper than a touch on the corner of her lips, her cheek. She felt herself tremble as he pulled away. But instead of releasing her as she expected him to, his fingers inched up her cheek and his lips descended once again, this time directly on hers, and the kiss felt like a seal on her heart.

Someone started clapping and Will opened his eyes, lifted his head, squeezed the hand he still held and smiled into her eyes before looking out to the people seated in the pews.

"Ladies and gentlemen, may I introduce Mr. and Mrs. Hopkins," Pastor McKinnon announced to the congregation. Cheers and whistles filled the air.

Chapter Eight

As soon as Will lifted her from the wagon and set her on her feet by the kitchen door, Abby headed inside, her mind on putting dinner on the table for the men. How strange to enter the house she had left only hours before as just the housekeeper and return as Mrs. Hopkins. It felt more like a strange dream. Would she wake at some point and realize none of it was real—not the blackmail threat, or the ceremony…or the way he had kissed her with a gentle passion after they were declared man and wife?

After all, she could still remember the stories her mother had told her about her parents' courting and wedding. Her father had carried his new bride across the threshold of their home after the wedding…. Here Abby was entering with her new stepsons. She didn't even know what Will wanted from her or even how long he had planned to keep her there before he annulled the marriage and sent her packing.

Not that she could blame him, really. He hadn't wanted the trouble of having a wife. Surely he was still in love with his first wife and didn't want anyone to take her place. But in all honesty, Abby knew that she would never take the first Mrs. Hopkins's place. From the color of the boys' eyes and hair, she imagined a beautiful woman who had charmed and enchanted Mr. Hopkins. It was obvious Will blamed himself for not being able to make her happy. He must have loved her very much. Why else would he still keep her things in his room and refuse to consider looking for a second wife to ease his burdens of raising his boys?

She pushed a wisp of hair away from her cheek, and her fingers came away wet. Stunned that she had given into self-pity, she stood just inside the doorway of the kitchen and gave herself a good shaking. If she gave in to her tears right now, she wouldn't get anything done for the rest of the afternoon. She needed to get to work. More than ever she needed to earn her keep while she was here.

Maybe with a little bit of work, she could ingrain herself into the family and workings of the farm to the point she'd earn a permanent position—maybe not as the loved mother and wife, but as the caretaker and homemaker who kept everyone well fed and comfortable. That would be her way to ensure her permanence with the Hopkinses.

Taking her emotions firmly under control, she stepped to the sink and started to get dinner on the table. The boys followed her in and she almost didn't register their chatter as she worried about the chicken that had to be overbaked and burned to a crisp by now. What a way to impress her new husband and the preacher by offering them inedible chicken!

"Something smells good!" Tommy exclaimed. "I'm sooo hungry I could eat a horse."

"Oh. I didn't know that you had a hankering for horse today. I just made plain old chicken!" She forced herself to tease Tommy. Even though her mind was a scramble of different emotions, she didn't want the boys to feel left out. What would today's events change for the boys? For the farm?

"You're silly," giggled Tommy. Even Willy grinned at her joke.

"Why don't you boys go up and change out of your Sunday clothes?" she suggested.

"Yes, ma'am," Willy answered, ushering his little brother up the stairs ahead of him.

Abby knew she should stop to change, too, but the men would only take a few minutes to see to the after-noon chores, and then they'd be ready to eat. She just hoped she had something to offer them. She tugged an apron over her favorite dress, glad that she had worn it today.

Who would have thought that today would be her wedding day? And yet she didn't feel any more mar-ried now than she had felt before the ceremony. Shocked and disappointed better described her state of mind. She figured with the expectation of annulment in the near future, she might never feel married. She wasn't the kind of woman a man would want to be married to forever. The sooner she accepted the truth, the sooner she would be able to resume her chores and life would go back to normal.

Pushing her unruly thoughts aside again, she pulled the large pot out of the oven. She said a silent prayer and held her breath to see what was left of the chicken she had set in the oven hours ago. The impromptu wed-ding meant that they had been away much longer than she had planned, and almost all the water had dried out, leaving a mush of potatoes, onion and carrots. Still, maybe it would be edible after all. It did smell good. She scraped out the vegetables and put them all in a big serving bowl. Minutes later, she stared at her concoction. Instead of white mashed potatoes, they were orange, but she added butter, milk and salt and tried a taste. It was actually pretty good.

The boys appeared back at the door as she finished doctoring the "mush" as she dubbed it in her mind. They stood just a pace away from the table and watched with fascination every move she made. The chicken fell apart when she lifted it onto the serving platter. What little juice remained she drained off to make gravy.

"Auntie Abby, can we eat now?" Tommy looked longingly at the platter as if he wanted to eat the whole chicken by himself.

"Not yet. Your pa, Jake and the pastor haven't come in from the barn yet. As soon as they come in, then we'll eat." She made a face at him. Giggling, he made one in return.

Turning back to the stove, she could hear Willy and Tommy whispering. They often discussed things like they were little old men. Tommy came up with all sorts of ideas and Willy, always claiming to know it all, explaining the whys and hows of life.

"But she is, too," Tommy argued, louder this time. "Aren't you, Auntie Abby?" he asked, his voice belying how much he wanted to be right.

"What are you talking about, Tommy?" she asked pleasantly, remembering the times she intervened between her nephews. She just hoped it was something that she knew the answer to. Her nephew Peter would come up with questions about why the sky was blue or why the geese flew away from the pond in the town square every winter and where they went to.

"I told Willy that you're our new ma. Pa said he was marring you at church and Jill said if you married our pa, that made you our ma. Can we call you Ma? I'd like you to be our ma since our old one is dead." Tommy's matter-of-fact statement caught Abby completely off guard. How could she answer the boy when she didn't know the answers herself? She had so many questions and she was afraid that even if she and Will were to sit and discuss things, they still wouldn't be completely settled for a time.

Abby searched for words, ideas, anything to be able to reassure the boys, but came up with nothing.

"I told you she didn't want to be our ma. Our real ma didn't even want to be our ma, so why would a stranger?" Willy's words only tore at Abby's heart and confused her. What had Mrs. Hopkins been like? Why did Willy say that she hadn't wanted to be his mother? Had she been sickly or more uninterested in children, like Emma? Either way, it helped her to understand his belligerence and why he held himself away from others.

Abby slid the pan off the stove and set it aside. The gravy could wait. The boys were more important. Kneeling before them, a hand on each boy's shoulder, she gazed into Willy's eyes and then Tommy's.

"It would be the biggest honor in the world for me to be your ma. But that's a question you need to ask your pa. I know that things are hard to understand…." She paused to organize her thoughts and beg God silently for the right words. "I will always love both of you and I will be here as long as God gives me the opportunity.

Everything that happened today was a surprise and I'm still trying to figure out what to do. I don't know what your pa would think if you called me 'Ma.'"

She swallowed hard. She would love to be "Ma" to these precious boys. After all, her heart's desire had always been to be a mother. In many ways, she had been a second mother to her nieces and nephews, but she'd had to leave them behind. Even if she would never have children of her own, she had already come to care for these boys deeply. But was it fair to let them get attached if Will was planning to end their marriage and send her away in a few months? Would he think she was trying to usurp his first wife's place in the house and with the boys?

In spite of all her questions and doubts, she couldn't resist pulling the boys closer to her and hugging them tight.

Willy was less receptive, but having nursed them through the chicken pox, she had gotten used to the facade he showed at her attempts of affection. The first day the boys had been sick, she had tried to give him more space and not baby him as much, but then she saw the look of longing on his face when she held Tommy. She slowly began to touch his shoulder, forehead or finger his hair out of his eyes since then.

"I want you to be our ma," Tommy said with a pout, but before she was able to correct his attitude, they heard the men clomping up the back steps.

"How about we talk about this later?" she offered, not wanting to have this discussion with everyone else in the room. Maybe later in the afternoon, she would be able to approach Will about the changes that were happening on the farm and what he wanted from her. In the meantime, she had dinner to put on the table.

"Something sure smells good in here!" exclaimed Colin as soon as the door opened. "I can tell that you've been hard at work, Mrs. Hopkins."

Will glared at his friend. He wasn't sure what to do in this new situation he found himself thrust into, but he knew that it didn't make him look good to have his friend beat him to the punch on complimenting the new bride. Colin was right about the food smelling good. It made his belly growl and he realized it had been hours since breakfast.

He waited while Colin and then Jake washed their hands and faces. When he had walked in, Abby had been kneeling in front of his boys, hugging them close. He noticed that she and the boys looked upset, but he wasn't sure what to do about it. Maybe once they had eaten, he could think a little more clearly.

After Colin had asked the blessing on the food and "the newly formed family," everyone dug in. Abby was hard put to get more than a few bites before someone needed something. As soon as the boys finished their food, they begged to leave the table. Without giving it a second thought, Will waved them away and Jake followed them out into the barnyard. The door slapped shut behind them before he glanced at Abby and the strained look on her face.

"Pastor MacKinnon, would you like more?"

Her voice was as pleasant as always, but Will suspected that he had done something wrong and hadn't an idea what it was.

"There's plenty of mush. I'm sorry for the appearance…" She was repeating the same excuse for the third time.

"Don't worry about a thing, Mrs. Hopkins. I happen to be a confirmed bachelor, so it's a real treat to have such a good, home-cooked meal."

Colin was his usual congenial self, but this fact bothered Will today. His friend was more at home with Will's new wife than he was. It grated on his nerves that Colin insisted on calling Abby "Mrs. Hopkins," as well. The formality was just another reminder to everyone of the big changes that had happened that afternoon.

"Mr. Hopkins, did you want more?" Abby asked, starting to rise even though her own plate was still half-full.

"Not until you finish what's on your plate," Will answered gruffly. "And remember, we agreed that you'd call me Will from now on."

Humbly, she sat back down and began to eat without lifting her eyes from her plate. Guilt assaulted Will as he realized that she was acting afraid of him. Colin caught his eye—his look condemning.

"Listen, I'm sorry if I spoke harshly, but you didn't even sit down to eat!" His voice rose as he struggled to keep his temper. He hadn't wanted to be married ever again. Now that he was, he hadn't even gone for a full three hours without having to apologize to her. In the last three weeks, they had become friends and now he felt as if he didn't know what to say to her.

"I guess I'm not really that hungry," she mumbled, pushing back from the table and standing once again. She had reached out to collect his dishes when he stopped her by clasping her wrist. A jolt ran down his hand to his arm, stunning him, and he released her.

"Wait." His conscience got the best of him. It wasn't her fault he was in a bad mood. It wasn't even her fault that they had this problem to begin with, and now he had ruined her meal. "Listen, Abby." Will didn't know what to ask, but he didn't want her to leave the table, either. "How about if I help with the cleanup while you rest for a bit?" he offered.

"No, I can do it." She took his plate.

Standing, Colin started to stack the boys' plates in a pile and headed over to the sink. Abby followed with her dishes and Will's. She took a pot off the back of the stove and poured the warm water into the basin, added soap and set the dishes in to soak. Will placed the platter of chicken bones and the empty serving bowl next to the sink on the counter.

"Thank you, Mrs. Hopkins. Dinner was excellent."

"Thank you, Pastor MacKinnon. I'm glad you enjoyed it." She turned from the sink and took a platter and the sugar bowl out of the cabinet. "I have cookies. Would you like to sit and have a cup of coffee with dessert?"

"That's a tempting offer, ma'am, but I don't know how wise it would be. I think I'm about as stuffed as I can get before I burst one of my seams. I might be able to handle a little more coffee, though."

Will fought the jealousy rearing its ugly head. She hadn't offered any to him. But then again, he hadn't commented on her cooking. Instead, he almost bit her head off for trying to get him something more. If he told her now that he had enjoyed her cooking, it would look as if he was just trying not to lose face.

"W-Will, would you like some more coffee or some cookies?"

"Sounds good," he managed to mumble, feeling more miserable by the minute.

Abby held the kettle up and poured coffee into a big earthen mug instead of the fine china that she had used at the dinner table. Obviously, she had learned a few things about men's habits during her stay. She filled the second mug, set them both at the table. The sugar bowl and a small pitcher of cream came next, followed by the plate of sugar cookies. Once everything was on the table, she glanced hesitantly at Will and then the back door.

"I hid these from the boys so that they wouldn't ask for any until after they had finished their meal, but I hadn't expected them to be done so soon. Should I call them back in?"

"No, that's fine. We'll enjoy a little peace and quiet and then they can have some," Will answered, selfish enough to exclude his own sons from dessert in an effort to find some more solid footing with his housekeeper turned wife.

Nodding, Abby turned back to the sink and started her washing again.

"Aren't you going to join us?" Colin asked, obviously uncomfortable.

"No, thank you. I need to finish this. Is there something else you need?" She lifted her hands from the sudsy water and started to wipe them on her apron.

"No. Everything is fine," Colin reassured her.

Will sipped his coffee, scalding his mouth in the process. Looking at Colin, he could see his friend was having a hard time trying to piece everything together. Within a few minutes, Abby left the kitchen spotless and excused herself to go outdoors. Will wondered if she was going to see the boys or just wanted away from him.

Colin asked about some of the families in the area and the farm in general and they sat talking and sipping the now-cooling coffee for a time. Even as Will answered questions about the neighbors, Abby's face came to mind. With her face came a list of questions that he had no answers for. For years, he had concentrated on getting through each day and then each season, providing for his family and caring for his boys. Now he was going to have to learn how to live comfortably with Abby and yet not let her tear his heart out the day she chose to leave.

"Hey, Will, you'd think I was boring you!" Colin's voice yanked him back to the present. "I think you've got a pretty little blonde on your mind and I imagine I don't quite compare." Colin's teasing grated on Will's raged nerves.

"Knock it off, Colin. It's not something to tease about," Will barked.

"Hey, easy there, my friend—she's young and pretty. No one would blame you for thinking about her instead of listening to an old, ugly preacher. I know this marriage wasn't what you expected, but God's hand of providence brought her out here to be your helpmate. You said yourself that God would have to all but put a gun to your head before you'd marry again. I'd say He did just that today." Colin's words were lighthearted, but his eyes were somber.

He had listened through the years while Will fought God about the turns his life had taken. Colin had arrived in Nebraska Territory just a month before Matt and MaryAnn's accident. He'd officiated at the funeral.

And afterward, he'd done what he could to try to counsel Caroline and Will through those last, hard years of their marriage. Will trusted him more than anyone else in the world, but the events of the day had left him out of sorts. It was probably a good thing Abby had gone out and given him some distance.

"Why don't you go out and look for your little lady?" Colin asked, a smirk in his eyes.

"Because she's *not* my little lady!" Will lashed out. He regretted the words as soon as they came out.

"What do you mean?" Colin's head snapped up, all teasing gone from his eyes.

"She's not going to last out here. No young, pretty woman wants to make her life out on the prairie," Will explained. "It's not settled enough for someone so delicate. She might make it through a summer, but she would never endure a winter. I won't watch another woman shrivel up and…and die like Caroline. I won't do that to her. She has her whole life in front of her." *Not to mention the fact that she's good, wholesome and beautiful,* his heart reminded him. There was no way he would be part of her destruction.

Silence answered his outburst and Colin sat staring at him as if he had grown another head. "So, why did you marry her today?" Colin finally asked.

"So she could be safe. So she wouldn't have to marry one of the Scotts boys. So she can stay the rest of the season until the harvest and find a good position before she goes back East."

"But she's your wife now. You can't just let her walk away." Colin looked incredulous.

"Wife in name only. I'll still be sleeping out in the barn with Jake."

"Does she understand this arrangement?" Colin's voice was deeper than normal. Sparks flew from his emerald-green eyes, reminding Will of the stories he'd heard about the Irish temper.

"Yes. We spoke of it before the ceremony," Will answered tersely. He had invited Colin out to the farm so he could be a character witness when the time came to annul the marriage. He hadn't expected Colin's opposition to his plan.

"So, then why did you kiss her like you did?" Colin's eyes were burning holes into his, and Will tore his gaze away and fiddled with his empty mug. He'd been asking himself the same question since the minute he pulled his head back, wishing he could keep kissing her forever and realizing that he had taken the intended gentle peck on the lips to a whole other level.

In all the confusion of the hurried wedding, he hadn't gotten a chance to ask Colin not to have the groom kiss his bride, so when the moment came, he had to make it look real. The Scotts brothers were standing by, waiting for proof that he wasn't going to send her packing on the next train. He'd intended to only touch his lips lightly on the corner of her mouth, but then she'd shivered with the small contact.

She had kept her eyes open, staring at him as if frightened, so he put a hand on her cheek and held her closer. He wondered if his had been her first kiss. The reality of her innocence had sent a current through him and he hadn't been able to pull away from her. Instead, he'd deepened the kiss and felt her relax at his touch as his hand caressed her cheek and his lips met hers. They were both strangely short of breath and blushing when they glanced around and found everyone's attention focused on them. It had been believable, all right. Even Will had believed that it was something more than a simple kiss.

"I don't know. I had…" The admission made him angry with himself, but he lashed out at Colin. "I was still in shock. You know I didn't want to marry ever again. I wouldn't have done it if it hadn't been for you and those troublemaking Scotts," he accused.

"Hey. I know this was sudden, but you'd be a fool to let that woman walk out of your life now. She has done wonders with this house. It's clean! And her cooking beats your burnt oatmeal any day. She's wonderful with the boys, and I saw the way you watched her today, at the table and even in the wagon. Don't let what happened to you and Caroline ruin your future."

Everything Colin said was true. Will knew it in his head, but that didn't mean he wanted to hear it. It wouldn't keep Abby from walking away from him and the boys someday. He'd see to it that she was provided for—that she had a good job waiting for her out East when she left, and that she had a comfortable home until then. But he wasn't about to let himself get caught up in caring about another woman. It was just a matter of time. He had already sent a letter for his mother to look for work for Abby.

"My future is fine. I've got a good homestead, the crops are in and the house is built. I was thinking about next year. I could put in twenty acres more to the east of the fields than I've got planted now."

"Your future is lonely. The boys will grow up someday and start families of their own. God didn't mean for a man to live out his days alone. He created a helpmate for Adam. I'm thinking the good Lord sent you one, as well."

"If you like her so much, you should have married her yourself!"

As soon as the words were out of his mouth, Will felt sick. He didn't want anyone else to marry Abby. She was *his* wife, and the boys had become attached. If he had to give her up, it would be only to keep her from becoming another victim of the prairie. He would send her back East, but he didn't want her marrying anyone else, not even his best friend.

"Nah, I couldn't do that," Colin replied.

"Why not?"

"'Cuz I value my life," Colin snapped, but his eyes held mischief in them. "I saw the way you stiffened as soon as people started to crowd around the wagon today. You flanked her with your boys during and after church. You might say you haven't got attached yet, but I have eyes in my head. And if I had doubted before, that kiss that you gave her at the end of the ceremony confirmed everything." Colin chuckled and Will once again fought the urge to hit his friend.

"She came at my request, to my farm, and I am responsible for her well-being," Will argued, more to himself than even to Colin.

"Well, then all the more reason to treat her right. She is your wife now and you need to see to all of her needs and comfort." Colin's look reminded Will of his mother's when she was laying down an order. "And if you're still so intent on being the biggest fool this side of the Mississippi, then you'd better not trifle with her, either."

"I know what I've got to do! I'd appreciate if you'd

keep your nose out of my business. You sound like her father," Will growled.

"It became my business when I performed the ceremony. I'm not sure I would have done it if I had known that you don't plan on trying for a real marriage. As of today, Abby happens to be one of my parishioners and therefore my business. Since she doesn't have family in the area, I have to assume the role of older brother in Christ. You need to watch the way you treat that woman. She's a godsend and if you can't see it, well, then, my friend, you've got about as much sense as a fence post." Colin shook his head in disgust and scraped back his chair.

Will didn't take being called a fool easily. He regretted having invited Colin to stay with them for a few days. When Colin set his mug in the sink and then left the room without a word, Will sat back and breathed deeply. His hands were shaking and his breath came fast.

Of course he would see to Abby's needs. Colin's implication that he would do anything else offended him. Colin knew Will well enough to know that he was a responsible man. Abby would be fed, clothed, protected and provided for while she was here. He would make sure her reputation was still intact and that she found a good home to work in when she was ready to leave.

His needs were what worried him. How was he going to face his kitchen alone, morning after morning, once she was gone? Colin was right; his boys would grow up and start lives of their own. In just the three weeks she had been on the farm, he had gotten used to her coffee first thing in the morning and a cup of tea on the back porch after the boys were in bed. A lifetime of loneliness was close to forever, but he wouldn't ask her to give up her happiness to keep him from a little loneliness. What kind of man would ask a woman to give up her life for his dreams? He had done it once and because of it his first wife now lay in a grave at the top of a knoll overlooking the farm. He wasn't going to ask that kind of sacrifice from another woman.

He stood from the table, picked up his mug and left it in the sink. He was almost out the door before he realized what he had done—expecting Abby to clean up after him. He retraced his steps and made quick work of washing the two mugs.

Wanting to be alone with his thoughts, he went out to the barn, saddled his horse and headed out to the fields. Abby was nowhere to be seen. Maybe she needed some time to herself, as well. Now, if only the memory of her face would stop filling his mind, maybe he could find a little peace.

"Thank you, God, for my pa and for my new ma. Thank you for giving me a family like Jill's. Bless Bess and Buttercup and help them to give us more milk and help my new ma to have lots of babies so that I can have little brothers an' maybe even a sister. Bless Jake and Willy and help him not to win again at horseshoes next time. Amen."

Abby sat at the side of Tommy's bed and listened to his prayers. Many times Tommy's ideas made her want to giggle in the midst of prayer time, but tonight's prayer had the opposite effect. He staunchly refused to call her anything other than "Ma" and since Pastor MacKinnon was here, there was no time to talk with Will and make sure that that was all right. She hadn't wanted to talk to him anyway. She needed some space and time to adjust. But even with space and time, she wasn't sure she would ever adjust. If things went the way Will planned, she would be out of the house before the first snowfall.

She turned her thoughts back on Willy's prayers even as her own heart cried out to God about her loneliness and need to find a place where she was loved and wanted. As soon as the boys were tucked in and she had placed a kiss on their smooth, cool foreheads, she turned and fled down the stairs, leaving Will behind.

She rushed to her room, shut the door and leaned her back against it. She felt foolish, acting like a small child who had been chased by the fear of a monster down the hallway. Her breathing was heavy and she tried to concentrate on slowing it down so that no one would hear her. She didn't even light the lamp on her nightstand or have her routine cup of tea. She wasn't about to risk coming face-to-face with Will in the kitchen now that everyone else was bedded down. They would have to talk things out but not tonight. Not with his words bouncing around in her head—"If you like her so much, you should have married her yourself!"

She hadn't meant to eavesdrop and she hadn't stayed to hear much more. What she had heard was enough. Still puzzled about what made her unlovable, she poured out her heart to God.

Her most secret dream lay within reach and yet had never seemed further away. A wonderful man had shared his name with her and promised to protect her, held her hand during the challenges of the day and kissed her lips as sweetly.... The dream she pushed into a closed corner of her heart, too extravagant to contemplate for a girl who had never once been courted, felt in some moments as if it had come true. Will personified the man she dreamed of—but he admitted to his friend he regretted having married her even before the ink had dried on the parchment. When she heard Mr. Hopkins suggesting Pastor MacKinnon should have offered to marry her so he wouldn't have had to, she'd known he would never come to love her. They were bound by a vow and all the witnesses from the ceremony, but she was more alone than ever.

As if her thoughts could conjure him up, his steps sounded on the stairs above her and then drew closer. Her heart pounded against her ribs faster with each footfall.

Tonight was her wedding night! Most new brides would be looking forward to being alone with their new husbands. Instead she was cowering in her room. They had already agreed that nothing would happen tonight or any other night. What did she have to fear—other than the loneliness that had been her constant companion for so many years?

"Why, God? Why is it that no man can love me?" she cried quietly, wishing that Will would just go away even as she tensed, aware he stood silently outside her door. Was he angry that he was stuck in this situation? He and Pastor MacKinnon appeared to be good friends and yet he had yelled at him.

The floorboards creaked under his feet as he shifted, standing just on the other side of her door. Would he knock? Would he send her away? Maybe it would be better for everyone if she just left once and for all. Her hand was on the handle, gripping it so hard her fingers had turned white, and she couldn't feel the tips anymore but she couldn't find the strength to turn the knob.

The flooring creaked once more, making her jump and hold her breath as she heard him move away from the door. His footsteps echoed back to her as he left the house, the back door closing almost soundlessly behind him. Relief and grief mixed together and suddenly the weight of everything was more than her knees could bear. As if her bones had turned into wet sand, she collapsed on the floor, a puddle of grief, hot tears streaking down her face. She hugged her legs to her middle and cried out her longings for a home, a family, for someone to love her.

Morning came too early. Or maybe it was the lack of sleep. Abby had sat on the floor crying for what seemed like an eternity the night before. When she finally did get up, she changed clothes and hid under blankets that she pulled over her head even though the night was too warm for them. She tossed and tuned but didn't sleep until very late. When she awoke, she was aware of dreaming about looking for something lost and never finding it.

The rooster crowed once again and Abby realized the sky was already tinged with pink. She was late getting up and starting the fire in the stove. This was not a good start if she wanted to prove what an asset she was to Will. Rushing, she pulled her hair out of the braids she hadn't even undone the night before and brushed out the kinks as best she could. She rebraided her hair but didn't even bother coiling it into a bun again. She would deal with it later.

Donning her tattered housedress, she splashed her face with tepid water and rinsed out her mouth. Without looking at the mirror she rushed out to the kitchen. Her face felt stiff and her nose was stuffy, but she couldn't worry about that when there were hungry men to feed. As she fed the embers of the fire she was starting, she gave a wry laugh. She had never thought herself vain, but what else could you call it when she was concerned about how she looked even when the two men that were coming to the table for breakfast had both clearly indicated their lack of romantic interest in her?

The coffee had barely started to heat when the door opened and Will stepped into the kitchen. His face was pale and his hair still stood on end on one side. His eyes had fine lines around them and he looked as if he hadn't slept all night. Before she could say anything, Pastor MacKinnon followed through the door.

Abby felt relieved and disappointed at the same time. This morning would have been almost like all the others if it hadn't been for the pastor's presence and the *minor change* of marriage. If the pastor hadn't been there, would Will have acted more like his usual self or would there still be the stilted formality between them?

"Good morning, Mrs. Hopkins!" Pastor MacKinnon greeted her jovially. He looked well rested with a glint of mischief in his eyes. Was there a reason that he insisted on calling her by her new title? Did he do it to goad Will? She had assumed the pastor was just being formal with his parishioners earlier, but now she wondered.

"Good morning, Pastor MacKinnon, Will. I'll have your coffee in just a minute." She turned back to the stove and wished that she could make the coffee boil faster.

"She's Abby. We don't go by titles here, Colin." Will's voice was deep and husky.

"That's fine by me, as long as it's fine by her." Both men had come to wash hands in the sink and Abby stepped away, pretending not to hear the conversation as she reached for the mugs. Pulling ingredients for pancakes out of the pantry, she returned to find both men studying her face.

"Are you feeling all right?" Will asked, concern etched in deep lines on his brow.

"I'm fine. I'll get you the coffee in just a minute." She offered what she hoped looked like a smile even though her face felt tight and dry.

"No need. We just brought in the eggs and milk." He indicated to the items that sat in their usual places on the counter.

"Thank you. I'll—"

"Don't worry about us." Will stood blocking her path to the stove where the coffee now boiled. "But are you sure you're all right? Your face is…well…it's all blotchy. And your nose is red. Are you getting sick?"

Heat burned her face as she realized why her face was blotchy. She'd cried herself to sleep. Her eyes must be all puffy and red rimmed. She should have soaked her face with cool water last night before bed or at least looked at a mirror this morning.

"I'm fine." Even as she spoke, she realized that her voice sounded deeper and a little raspy.

"Then why—"

"I think she's had a long night pondering her current state, isn't that right, Abby?" Colin jumped in and saved Abby from having to explain herself but at the same time, proved that her worst fear was true. Everyone would know that she had been crying last night.

"Abby, is that true? Were you up all night crying about what the Scotts said about you?"

She didn't raise her eyes to meet Will's but focused on his hands clenched into fists at his sides.

"I wasn't up all night," she denied, unsure what else to say. There was no way she was going to admit that she had been crying about what *he* had said, not the Scotts' behavior. "If you'll excuse me." Stepping past him, she lifted the kettle from the stove and poured coffee into the mugs. Scooping a spoonful and a half of sugar into the first one, she stuck the spoon in and gave it a good stir before handing it to Will. She poured milk into the other and handed it to the pastor.

"I didn't notice you take any sugar yesterday, Pastor McKinnon."

"No, this is just how I like it, thank you."

"Breakfast will take a few more minutes, so if you would like to take a seat…" She motioned to the kitchen table, but both men shook their heads.

"There are stalls to muck out and horses to check on," Will answered, glaring at the pastor.

Silence reigned over the kitchen as Abby turned back to the stove. Soon the smell of ham frying and pancakes browning in a pat of butter filled the kitchen. The only sounds were the occasional sip of coffee from one of the men and the sizzle from the stove.

Pastor Colin finally set his cup down next to the sink. "Thank you, Abby. That hit the spot. You make mighty good coffee. I think just the smell of breakfast is gonna make us work twice as fast today." He smiled good-naturedly and headed out toward the barn.

"He's right. Your coffee's always good," Will said begrudgingly.

"I'm glad you're pleased, Mr. Hopkins." She didn't turn around but kept her eyes on the stove, embarrassed that she'd used his formal title after he'd asked her to call him Will. It was easy enough to think of him by his first name in the privacy of her own thoughts, but when she was nervous while speaking to him, she'd accidentally slipped up. Would he scold her for forgetting his request?

"I'd be more pleased if you'd just call me Will," he said, his voice soft and gentle—almost wistful. Then he headed out without looking back. If he had looked he would have seen surprise and confusion written on her face.

Why did that woman have him all tied up in knots? Will knew he wasn't handling things well, but why did she have to look as if she was about to burst into tears? It broke his heart and made him sick to think he had brought all this about. If only he had been more careful. She was far from home and in a marriage that was nothing more than a sham. The least he could have done was to be a friend for her. But all he had managed to do was trip all over his own tongue.

Judging from the look on Colin's face, he was going to hear all about how much he had to change to be worthy of that lovely young lady cooking his breakfast back in his kitchen. Hoping not to have to listen to any more accusations than what were already flying around his own head, he gave wide berth to Colin mucking out the first stall.

Will couldn't ask for a better friend. In fact, Colin had been his closest friend since he had lost his brother. But even Colin had skated on thin ice yesterday, telling him to hold on to Abby and not let her go. Didn't Colin realize Will was trying to do the right thing?

Seeming to sense the tension, Jake worked silently instead of jabbering on about a lot of nothing as he normally did. Not that Will minded most of the time. He'd become more of a son than a nephew to Will. They had worked side by side since the day Matt and MaryAnn had died. It worried Will that in private, Jake wouldn't stop talking, but he wouldn't utter a word around most people. Abby was changing that, slowly earning his trust and then openly chatting with him about topics she was sure he would be knowledgeable in. Will had noticed that yesterday at church, Jake had seemed much more comfortable chatting with others, bringing up things Will had overheard him discussing with Abby.

The silence from both his best friend and his nephew pricked his conscience. If only his own thoughts would leave him alone. They were making up for the silence of the other men. Finally the chores were done and the smell of breakfast was pulling them all like a lasso looped around their middles.

"Why don't you go on in, Jake?" Colin suggested. "I have something I need to say to your uncle." Will looked up and found a solemn gaze pinning his.

"Don't waste your breath. I know I didn't handle that well back there," he admitted with a long sigh.

"Last night I thought you had the sense of a fence post. You proved me right this morning. Of course she was going to have a rough night! She's a newlywed who spent her first night as a married woman all alone. Not only that, her new husband is snorting like a bull that got into loco weed. If I were a betting man, I'd wager she didn't cry over what the Scotts said. Did it cross your mind that maybe she feels you've rejected her?"

Will stared at his friend. Abby knew the marriage was just to save her from either marrying one of the Scotts or putting up with their disgusting accusations. It provided a way for her to stay at the farm until other arrangements were made. It would take some time, but she would be leaving.

And how do you know that she won't want to stay come wintertime? The question crossed his mind for the first time. He bit his lip to avoid answering out loud. The answer *Because it's happened before* bounced around in his head.

She was a better person than Caroline—braver, kinder, more honest and honorable—but in the end, she wasn't that different from his first wife or her aunt. Caroline and Shelia had both made it clear to him that they deserved better than the rough prairie life he had to offer. If it was true of them, then it was definitely true of Abby. She deserved to be coddled, to have parties and nice, fancy dresses with lace trim and the ease of living in a town. He wouldn't make Abby give up a life she would enjoy to be stuck on a farm with only hard work and worries as her daily companions.

"What do you think I should do? Make her my wife and let her shrivel up and die like Caroline? There's no way I'll let that happen to Abby. I have already sent a letter to my mother to see if she can arrange some sort of work for Abby where she'll be safe and happy. Somewhere she can go to dances and get all dressed up. Ma knows many people in Philadelphia."

Colin's hand gripped Will's shoulder. Will expected

anger or even contempt in Colin's eyes, but the sympathy he saw caught him in the gut like a sucker punch.

"She's not Caroline. Don't sell her short. She's got *grit*. I only met Abby yesterday, but I see a lovely woman who would be a good mother to your boys. And since they're already calling her 'Ma' you're gonna have the fight of your life to convince them she doesn't belong to your family."

"She's not Caroline but she still deserves better than this life, just like Caroline always said."

"Don't let the past ruin the future, Will," Colin stated seriously. "You'd have to be blind not to notice how lovely your wife is. Don't let her get away or you'll regret *that* for the rest of your life."

Colin released his hold of Will's shoulder and headed toward the house. Will stood still contemplating his friend's words.

"I don't know about you," Colin called back without breaking stride, "but your wife's cooking has my mouth watering. If you don't hurry, I'm gonna eat my share and yours, too."

Chapter Nine

Almost a full month had passed since the fateful day that Abby went to the chapel and came home married. More than three weeks of slow adjustments to a strange loneliness even as Abby found things to occupy her hands and her mind. Life on the farm had started to fall into a routine. The cooler mornings were for chores and then she and the boys would stay inside in the shade and focus on schoolwork until suppertime. She faithfully watered and weeded the garden. Any day now she would have lettuce, celery, cucumbers and tomatoes to add to her meals. The potatoes and pumpkins would take a while longer.

Each day was an adventure with the boys, who were now baked brown by the sun. On Mondays she washed the laundry and then they made a game of hanging all the clothes on the line. Tuesdays and Thursdays she took the boys down to the creek to fish for dinner while she read to them.

One morning they got so involved in the adventures of their hero that Willy lost his fishing pole to a large catfish. He jumped in the water after his pole and barely caught it. Abby hesitated for an instant, but as soon as Willy's head went under a second time, she splashed in herself. She might not know how to swim, but she wasn't going to let Willy struggle alone.

She found the water was only up to her waist and the current wasn't strong enough to knock her off her feet. Relief made her giggle. Even with her sodden skirts, she had no trouble catching hold of Willy, who was still battling with the catfish. She held him tight around the waist as he reeled in the fish. Tommy extended the net as they brought in the fish together. Having scored victory over the catfish, Abby and Willy climbed the bank of the creek and lay out in the dappled sunlight filtering through the tree branches overhead, letting the warm breeze dry them.

"Thanks, Ma. I was scared till you caught me! I can't wait to show Pa and Jake I got the big one."

Abby lay there in the warm afternoon and breathed deeply to keep the tears scratching her throat from cursing down her face. It was the first time Willy called her Ma. If only she could be assured she would always be here to catch the boys....

She and Jake became friends, too. After dinner and the boys' bedtime stories, Jake would find Abby on the porch out back. They took advantage of the twilight hours for her to teach him math and science. His mother had taught him to read when he was small, but he only read when forced to, until Abby lent him some of her books. As Abby encouraged him, he started to tell her more and more about his life and his memories of his parents. They realized that they had been about the same age when they had each lost their parents.

The common ground helped them both to understand each other.

Her husband was the only person on the farm who held her at arm's length. While she had grown accustomed to calling him by his given name, an uncomfortable civility could be felt in their everyday encounters that hadn't been there before. Often, she would barely lay eyes on him from sunup to sundown.

Foolishly, she waited for the minute she saw him walking toward the house and felt something akin to relief at the sight of him each night. Just to see his face made her heart beat a little faster. She never gave in to the desire to fling the kitchen door open and embrace him, but she would silently cherish his arrival.

Often he would spare her only a few words although he listened to the boys chatter happily about what they had done during the day. He looked over the slates they showed him with a critical eye. Was he happy with the progress she had made with them or was he just resigned with her presence here until she left? He would often sit on the stairs of the porch and listen to Jake read or Abby explain something from the text but rarely added to the conversations. Unsure if he stayed for the company or the mug of tea Abby always had ready for him, she cherished even the encumbered moments, stealing glances at her husband when she believed he wasn't looking at her.

She tried to do all she could to ease his life and make him comfortable. She learned which foods were his favorites and how he liked his clothes cleaned and pressed. She made more clothes for the boys and two men. This Sunday, when the Hopkins family walked into the chapel, each of the men would be wearing a new shirt and matching pants.

While he didn't outwardly show much interest in Abby, she began to note little things he did for her to make her life easier. At least she hoped they were to make her life easier. He always made sure there was a huge supply of buffalo chips for burning stacked against the wall on the porch. The smell took some getting used to, but with wood so scarce, it was an easier fuel to come by.

Most nights, he would stay and dry the dishes while she washed. He'd send the boys up to get ready for bed, but he'd have Jake sweep the kitchen floor, as if not wanting to be alone with her. Every evening, before he went out to the barn, he checked that the door was latched and that she had everything she needed.

As the days passed, she wondered how long before they would get a letter back from his family with job prospects for her after the harvest. She prayed that none came. If she were honest with herself, she'd have to admit she didn't want to leave…ever. She wanted to somehow win the affection of her husband even if it seemed impossible.

The third Sunday of the month approached and Abby once again felt apprehensive. Colin had arrived on Thursday afternoon, entering the kitchen with Will at dinnertime.

"Hello, Abby. How are you doing?" His eyes searched hers, as if he would be able to tell if she was being truthful or not.

"Just fine, Pastor Colin. How have you been?" she asked, taking another plate out of the cabinet and setting a place for him at the dinner table. *So this is what is feels to have an older brother,* she thought to herself. She hoped that this visit would be better than the last. Will looked pleased to have his friend back.

"I've been just fine. But I must be getting old. I wrote back to the seminary where I studied and asked if they would send more preachers out this way. I'd like to buy up some of this good-for-nothing sod and try my hand at settling down." He shot a quick glance at Will and then washed his hands. "I was even thinking that this area is as good a place as any to settle. You have any suggestions about where I might want to stake a claim, Will?"

Will mentioned some land to the west of theirs. He shot a strange look at Colin and then Abby but kept talking about streams and land formations as the men took their places at the table. After dinner, the boys played in the front room with their blocks while Abby cleaned up the kitchen. The men sat around nursing their second cup of coffee. Their talk ranged from land and farming matters to families in the area to the last chapter that they had been studying in the Bible.

It was nice to see Will relax around the table again. Sadly she learned more about her husband's thoughts and current concerns from watching him interact with his friend than from their own stilted conversations in all the time they had been married. The realization made her long to know him better. Maybe if she could learn more about him, she could make him more comfortable with her staying for good. Maybe someday she would fit here as part of the family, not just some hired hand.

Saturday nights were the nights that everyone got a bath, whether they needed one or not. Abby let Will take care of bathing the boys and then she had the kitchen all to herself for her own bath. Back in her room, she brushed out her hair. It was still too damp to braid, so she took a walk. Feeling restless, she headed down toward the creek where the boys loved to fish. The sun was about to set and she didn't plan on being away too long. Tomorrow was church Sunday and she would see all the people who had witnessed her marriage just a month before.

Colin planned a picnic with some of the women of the congregation for after the service tomorrow. It would serve as both a welcoming celebration for Abby and a belated wedding reception. During the week she had made cookies and other sweets as well as baked bread and prepared a large hunk of ham from the smokehouse. Will tried to reassure her that the other women would see to everything, but Abby wanted to do her part.

As Abby stood next to the creek meandering slowly through the flat prairie, she watched the sun sinking to the west with a beautiful display of God's creativity in burnt reds, auburns, oranges and plums. If God could do that for the sunset that had no real significance except to mark the end of another day, couldn't He make her lovely enough to inspire something in the heart of a man who needed a helpmate? "Sorry, Lord," she whispered, struggling again to be content with His unknown plan.

The rippling water and the gentle breeze soothed her spirit even as the mosquitoes started to buzz around her. Noise from behind her caught her attention, and for an instant, she panicked, realizing just how vulnerable she was alone out on the prairie without a gun. Grabbing the closest stone that fit into the palm of her hand, she spun around. Laughter spilled out from sheer relief when she saw the form lumbering toward her was only Colin.

"Good evening," he called out in greeting, eyeing her strangely as she released her rock and tried to control her giggles.

"Good evening," she answered, her laughter bubbling out in spite of herself.

"Something out here amuses you?" Colin stood a few paces from her, staring out at the sunset as well.

"I wasn't sure you weren't a coyote or something else interested in carrying me off for its dinner. I was glad to see it was just you."

"It's reassuring you consider me better than a coyote," chuckled Colin, his green eyes glancing her way and then holding her stare.

For a preacher, he looked very human out by the creek at sundown with his strawberry-blond hair and freckles. His eyes registered concern. "Are you all right, Abby?"

"It's just been so long since…"

"Since you were able to laugh with an adult?" He finished the thought that she didn't dare express. She didn't want to be unfair to Will. It almost felt as if she was betraying him for laughing with someone else, even if it was his best friend and their pastor.

Colin sighed deeply and turned his gaze back to the sunset. "How have you two been getting along?" he asked quietly, and she sensed he was asking as much as her friend as her pastor.

"I don't know. I…" She bit her lip and waited. She had longed to confide in someone since the day she had become Mrs. Hopkins. She wished her mother were still alive so she could ask her how a woman went about making a man fall in love with her. But to confide in Colin just didn't feel right. It wasn't the kind of subject she would have been able to speak with Pastor Gibbons about, either, and he was old enough to be her father. She also felt as if she was somehow betraying Will's privacy.

"Just give it time. He'll come around. He's not going to admit he needs a woman in his life just yet, but I know God sent you here to be his helpmate. I've been praying for you to come for a long time. He needs to see that not all women are like his first wife. I don't know if he explained anything about her, and I won't say anything more, but you should know that she left him very disheartened and convinced he never wanted to love, much less marry again."

"She must have been very beautiful. He doesn't seem to notice me at all," Abby said wistfully. She was lost in her own thoughts and didn't realize that she had said the last part out loud.

"On the outside, yes, she was lovely. But bitterness cripples both the heart and the spirit. God's word says He sees the heart and judges man by what He views on the inside. I know God finds you very lovely and I suspect Will does, too, whether he'll own up to it or not. Just don't give up. I know this wasn't what you expected when you answered his ad, but the boys need you and so does Will. He is just too stubborn to admit it yet."

"He still is waiting to hear back from his mother about another job for me," Abby blurted out.

"God has a way of working things out. Just keep trusting." There was a moment of silence and then Colin broke it with a question. "You've come to care for him, haven't you?" He had lowered his voice, watching her again.

She had not admitted to herself how much Will and the boys had come to mean to her, but now, with Colin's green eyes drilling into hers and seeing past her facade, she knew she needed to be honest with him and herself. She nodded, closed her eyes and prayed that God would protect them all.

"Good. God put that love in your heart. You're a very special woman. You're a wonderful mother to the boys, and I know you'll make Will very happy, once he lets you. If he starts to get too grumpy you just let me know. I'll knock him upside that big, hard head with a two-by-four."

Before she could respond, she heard a rustling sound from the direction of the house. Abby and Colin spun around at the same time, Colin stepping closer to her as if to shield her from whatever was coming at them. They both relaxed when they saw Will. At first, the relief that no wild animal or Indian was heading straight for them caused Abby to smile, but her smile faded just as quickly as it had spread when she saw the fury in Will's eyes.

"What are *you* doing *here?*" His glare pinned her to the spot.

"I…" She swallowed, trying to figure out what had happened. He never told her she couldn't take a walk. "Is everything all right? Did the boys wake?" She suddenly realized how far from the house she was. She wouldn't have heard them if they had called for her.

"The boys are asleep. They have nothing to do with this. Why are you here with *him?*" His voice was pitched low and shook with anger. He glared at her as if she had just committed some grievous crime.

He had never reacted like this before and for the life of her, she couldn't understand what had happened. If the boys were fine, then why was he so agitated? Colin bristled at her side. She'd forgotten he was even there.

"I saw her come to the creek and decided that it would be smart to keep an eye on her," Colin answered before she could form a coherent reply. "She and I were just discussing how the last few weeks have been. As her pastor, and *your friend,* I wanted to make sure she was adjusting and all was well." Colin moved closer yet, as if still wanting to protect her. "As for her being here with *me,* I think she needs a friend from time to time."

As Abby watched, Will stood rigid, his face darkened like the powerful storm clouds she had seen unleash torrents of water on the open prairie. She skirted around Colin, unwilling to hear any more of their argument. Words from their last visit still replayed in her mind. *"If you like her so much…"* She forced herself to stop the thought and headed toward the path back to the house. They could work out whatever they needed to without her. With her growing feelings for Will, she didn't think she could stand hearing him declare his apathy toward her or their marriage.

As she tried to pass Will, his hand snaked out and caught her upper arm. His grasp was firm but not painful. His sudden movement stunned her and an energy zinged up her arm and left her short of breath.

"I'll walk you up. You shouldn't be out here alone at this time of night." His voice was gruff but his hand gentle as he released her and then tucked her arm around his elbow as if they were out for a walk in the city. It made Abby feel protected. She would have been almost pleased if he hadn't glanced over his shoulder and glowered at Colin.

"I'll see you in the barn." His voice promised that they still had unfinished business.

"I'll be there," Colin promised without heat in his voice or his eyes. "Good night, Abby. Get a good night's sleep so that you can stay awake tomorrow. I hear the preacher can sometimes get a little long-winded." His lips twitched and she tried not to smile at his teasing. Surely Will would take her laughing with Colin all wrong.

Once they were out of hearing distance, Will glanced at her, his scowl telling her all she needed to know. He was still upset.

"What were you thinking?" he questioned as if he were sure that she had gone completely crazy.

"I only wanted to take a walk. I wanted some air," Abby argued, hurt that he would treat her like a small child. Tears threatened to spill over, frustrating her. In the last few months she had cried more than she had in years back in Ohio.

"You've been here long enough to know better. There are animals that hunt at night, coyotes and wolves, and there is still the possibility of Indian unrest. I don't want you out at night. I don't want…" The anger in his voice diminished as he talked.

"You never said I couldn't take a stroll after dinner." She dropped her voice and slowed her pace, forcing Will to slow with her. Suddenly she felt forlorn. Whom was she trying to fool? She had only managed to bother Will again. Sighing deeply, she trudged on.

"It gets dark fast. You should be in the house, safe

and sound." His voice carried on the still air of the evening and she wondered if Jake could hear them from the barn as they came into view of the barnyard. She had left the boys' window open and didn't want them waking at the sound of grown-ups arguing, either.

"Are you feeling all right?" His voice dropped and he slowed to a stop, turning her to face him in the shadows near the front of the house.

"I'm fine." It wasn't really a lie. She was healthy and uninjured—well enough to do all of her duties. If her heart was troubled… Well, he didn't need to know that, did he?

"No, you just shivered. Did you get a chill down by the creek?" His voice spoke of his concern and it warmed her somewhere close to her heart.

"No. I'm fine," she asserted more convincingly.

She wanted to tell him that she was shivering because he was upset with her and the fact broke her heart. That she cared about him, and hated the distance that had sprung up between them. But he didn't want to hear any of that, so she mumbled an excuse and fled into the house. Once again, she curled up into a ball in her bed, hidden under her sheets, and cried her heart out to God.

Why did loving Will hurt so much? And now she knew that she did love Will. She longed to see him smile, wished he would hold her close and kiss her again, as he had done the day of their wedding. She missed him when he was out in the fields, away from her and the boys, and she missed him when he sat across the porch from her, within a stone's throw and a million miles away. If only he could love her in return.

Chapter Ten

"So, my brothers, God is telling us here in Psalm 90 verse 12 that the true measure of wisdom is to 'number our days' so we can live in a way that serves God and his children. Now, you may say to me, 'But, Colin, how am I supposed to count my days if only God knows how many days or years I have left?'

"And I would answer you that you are correct. It's the very point Moses is trying to get us to understand. Just a few verses before, Moses writes that the days of man are fleeting and a thousand years for the Lord is like a day. He depicts our life like the grass that spouts in the morning and withers by the afternoon. We may have the next fifty years at our disposal or we may be standing in God's presence later on this very day. Since we don't know what the number is, then prudence would dictate we live every day as if it were to be our last— as if what we do with the next ten minutes may be the only legacy we leave behind."

Colin looked out and caught Will's eye. The church was crowded and Will wished there were more windows to open. It was stuffy inside and he felt grumpy and fidgety—though those feelings probably had less to do with the airless room and more to do with the way he had mishandled everything last night. Like a snorting bull, he had seen red when he finally found Abby contentedly conversing with Colin by the creek.

Colin's words about treating each day as your last gave him a guilty shiver. Thank goodness the previous day hadn't been his last one, because he sure would like to have done better. After dinner, he'd had the urge to stay and talk with his wife, but she had needed to bathe and get ready for the Lord's Day. Finally settling on the pretext of checking to see if she was ready for the picnic the following morning, he'd gone back to the house. When he didn't find her in the kitchen or in the boys' room, he dared go toward her room only to find the door was still standing open. Assuming that she was in the outhouse he headed out the back door. His heart plummeted to his toes and his hands felt like ice when his search gave no clue as to where his wife had gone.

Searching the barn and the yard around the house, he started to suspect she had gone somewhere with Colin. For a minute that reassured him, until he began to wonder if they were even then whispering sweet nothings. Colin had already admitted he admired her cooking and her mothering skills. Now he was talking about settling down. Didn't he understand that Will wanted to save Abby from the hardships of being a farmer's wife? If she was going to stay in Nebraska, then it should be by *Will's* side—he was the one whose sons needed her. He was the one who knew and appreciated all her wonderful abilities. He was the one who cared for her…more deeply every day, for all that he tried to avoid her.

But because he cared for her, Will was the one who

was going to do the right thing. He was going to find a job for Abby in some comfortable city far from the prairie. She'd be happy there, which was what mattered most. And he wasn't going to let Colin convince her otherwise.

As the trail to the creek twisted around and he could see the two of them standing a few paces apart, relief made his heart leap because she was safe! Then his anger returned because she was out for an evening stroll with his best friend.

When Colin came back to the barn, he had not so much as said a word about their exchange by the creek except to chuckle about how quickly Abby had gotten under Will's skin. It was the final straw as far as Will was concerned. He'd told Colin to keep his nose out of other people's business and not follow Abby around in the evening without staying within view of the house. Colin had just laughed and offered to pray before they hit the hay. Now he stood calmly preaching to his congregation and Will wondered, with a sinking sense of dread, if Colin's sermon was personally motivated. Had Colin decided that the best way for him, personally, to live life to the fullest would be to settle down on a claim in Nebraska…with Abby as his wife? He'd have to talk Colin out of it and make his friend see that Abby didn't belong in Nebraska—and certainly not as any farmer's wife. Not even Will's.

"Here in this very community, we have had our share of heartbreaks and funerals." Colin continued his sermon, his eyes roaming the congregation and once again settling on Will. "None of the brothers and sisters who have gone before us woke on the morning they were to meet their Savior knowing it was their last day. They went about, living their lives as they always did and then, without God asking them leave, He collected them to Himself.

"While we may have mourned them for a time, and still miss them, I doubt any of us who truly understands where our departed loved ones are today would ask to have them returned from Paradise to the suffering in this fallen world. I have to confess there are days when I grow weary of the drudgery and suffering here and plead with God to take me to my eternal rest, but most mornings I rise with the desire to see another sunset and another sunrise. I hope to someday settle down and find some nearsighted girl who will take pity on my sorry hide and decide to make a family man out of me. There are mornings when I beg God to hurry that day and others I resign myself to the life God has chosen for me to serve Him, even if it means living the rest of my life like a Gypsy, not having a home to call my own or a family waiting for me around the hearth at the end of the day. But while I can't know what God has planned for me, I *can* make the choice to embrace His blessings to the fullest of my ability, enjoying every day I'm given and never holding back from all the happiness life offers. No matter how many days the Lord grants every one of us, we need to spend each day full of joy for the wonders of His gifts, and praise for His name."

Soon Colin brought the service to a close with a prayer of blessing and protection for the families of their church. "Don't forget, we have a picnic planned for after service. I have been informed by a very reliable source that there's enough food out there to feed an army. Since we're all part of the army of the Lord, I hope that's true. Once the ladies have the food set out, we'll ask the good Lord to bless the food and our fellowship. This is a special day when we get to welcome Mrs. Hopkins to our community. As you all know she and Mr. Hopkins were married just last month in a ceremony after the service. Today we'll have the reception."

In a matter of minutes, the women assembled all manner of tempting dishes on the two long tables made out of sawhorses with flat boards laid across that the men had set up earlier. Once Colin said grace for the food, the serving began. Mothers collected their children and filled their plates before withdrawing to the blankets that had been laid out in the shadow of the church. Then the men surged around the tables like a swarm of bees. Will saw to Willy and Tommy and then stood to the side and watched as Abby graciously greeted everyone and helped serve.

He was just about to get into line when Abby's eyes found his and she smiled shyly. His pulse tripled and he could hear his heart pounding in his ears. A hurt look crossed her face and her smile slipped away as she busied herself with the plates of two more farmers while he edged closer. Had she expected him to smile back? Of course, he reasoned with himself. She was the stranger here and she deserved to know that he was so proud of how well she was getting along with everyone. What a dunce he was to squash what little joy she was getting from the potluck.

Stepping up in line, he stopped in front of her and found that she had already served a heaping plate of all his favorites. "You look like you're enjoying yourself," he stated, hoping to make up for his coolness just seconds before.

"Everyone is so nice and welcoming," she answered

without looking up at him. It bothered him that he had hurt her again.

"Thank you for the food, Abby."

"You're welcome." She started to prepare another plate of food—presumably hers since everyone else had their plates—so he waited until she finished. "Did you need something else?" she asked, clearly surprised to find him still waiting on the other side of the table when she reached for a slice of bread.

"I thought it only proper I escort my lovely wife to our blanket with the boys," he explained, proud that he had managed to compliment her. Her eyes found his for a second and then she nodded.

"Oh, we need to appear to be together for the Scotts," she whispered as he led her across the thick grass he and Colin had cut down the day before in preparation for the picnic.

"In part, but I also wanted to say you look lovely and did a wonderful job with the meal. Everything looks delicious." Her surprise looked turned to pleasure and a slight blush graced her cheeks, but before he could say any more, they arrived at the blanket the boys occupied and the opportunity to talk privately was gone.

He held her plate for her while she twisted and settled all her skirts so she could sit on the blanket and then she held both plates as he flopped down next to her. The boys, their food half gone, crowed around and kept a constant chatter as he and Abby started to eat. Will watched Abby as she patiently answered all of Tommy's questions and told funny stories to him and Willy. To everyone around them at the picnic they must have appeared to be a real family—especially with both boys calling her Ma.

"Pa!" Tommy plopped down next to Will, his hazel eyes bright and happy. "Did you hear me, Pa?" Tommy's little hand nudged his arm, pulling his focus back on his little boy.

"Sorry, what did you say, son?"

"I said Ma taught me to count all the way to thirty. Wanna hear? She showed me a cal…can…calendar—it has boxes and numbers. Just like Pastor Colin said today. Ma taught me to be wise 'cuz she taught me to number the days."

Will cast a questioning look at Abby. The knowing grin she sent him told him that not only had she followed Tommy's strange logic but she also knew Will didn't have a clue. She had come to understand his boys better in a few months than he had done in all the years he raised them. If only she could stay.

"Tommy, Pastor Colin was talking about something a little different today, sweetheart. I taught you how to number a calendar to tell us what day of the week it is or what month of the year. But what Pastor Colin was talking about was that if we really want to be wise, we will learn to live every day for God as if there might not be any more days here for us. I hope you grow up to be very old and have children and grandchildren…."

"Yeah, and you'll get all wrinkly and your hair'll fall out like ol' Mr. Patterson," Willy added.

Abby took control back of the conversation. Grinning at Willy, she fingered his hair out of his face as she continued. "Sometimes God wants us in heaven before we get to be all old and wrinkly. The Bible says no man knows when he will be called to stand before God and give an account for his life. We can't wait till we're old like Mr. Patterson to start living the life God wants us to live."

"What's that mean?" Tommy asked.

Will took a deep breath, praying for wisdom and answers, but Abby already started to explain. Nodding his encouragement, he started praying that God would give her the right words to share the message of salvation with Tommy.

"God's got plans for all of us," she began.

"Like when you make plans for our lessons?" Tommy asked.

Abby laughed. "Well, a little like that, I guess. God's plans tell us where we're supposed to go, and what we're supposed to do to be good people, and find happiness."

"Did God tell you to come out here to us?" Willy questioned, leaning against Abby's side. She wrapped an arm around him in a hug.

"He certainly did." The words hit Will like a pleasant shock. She still believed that—that God had brought her out here, that their humble home in Nebraska was where she was supposed to be? He pushed down the sense of hope that that gave him, reminding himself that she still didn't understand just how grim prairie life would be. She'd come to hate it, just as Caroline had. And she'd come to resent him if he tried to keep her there. He needed to remember that.

Will listened as Abby explained God's ultimate plan—to save mankind with the gift of His son. As she talked about sins and the forgiveness God offered through Jesus's sacrifice, Will was reminded of his own shortcomings. If he'd been more careful, if he'd paid more attention, then he wouldn't have led Caroline on, leading to their disastrous marriage. If he'd been more considerate, more aware of her needs, maybe she wouldn't have wasted away. If he'd been more diligent getting information from Abby before hiring her as his housekeeper, maybe they could have avoided the misunderstandings and complications that led to—

That led to this: sitting on a picnic blanket, surrounded by a happy, healthy, well-fed and well-dressed family while a kind, beautiful woman gently spoke of God's message to his youngest son. How could he regret this? How could he repent his actions when they led to the gifts Abby had brought to his family?

Was there any chance that his marriage to Abby was truly part of God's plan? Was this really the life that God wanted him to lead?

"Someday," Abby concluded, "each one of us will reach the end of God's plan for us, and it'll be time to go home to Him in Heaven. If you want to be able to go to Heaven, you have to tell Jesus that you know you are a sinner and you accept the gift of His forgiveness. He promises in the Bible that He will forgive anyone who asks Him to. Would you like to ask Jesus to forgive your sins today?"

Tommy nodded his little head and Abby took him into her arms, snuggling him close. She told him to close his eyes and she led him in a prayer to open his heart to the forgiveness Jesus promises to all who ask.

"I bet Pastor Colin would very much like to hear that you just asked Jesus to be your Savior, Tommy," Abby suggested. "Would you like me to go with you so you can tell him or do you want to take your pa?"

"I want you both to go with me," Tommy answered.

"Sure thing, son," Will managed to choke out. "I'm so glad you let Jesus be your Savior."

"Did you ask Him to forgive you, too?" Tommy asked innocently.

"I did. I wasn't much bigger than you are now. I remember my grandpa took me to go fishing and while we were waiting for the first fish to bite, he started to talk to me about how life is too short to wait until we get big to make the most important decision in our lives. He said that I needed to get my life right with God before I could be a good man."

Tommy stood and threw himself into Will's arms. The force almost knocked him onto his back, but he managed to keep upright. "I love you, Pa. I'm glad you could be a good man 'cuz then you could be my pa."

"I love you too," Will whispered as he hugged Tommy tight. He hooked his other arm around Willy and pulled him into the hug, as well. Seeing Abby watching them, he smiled and mouthed, "Thank you" to her. She smiled back and he felt the force of it all the way to his toes. She had a lovely—powerful—smile.

Both boys pulled away and cuddled with Abby for just a moment before they were ready to run off and tell Colin. Will stood and extended his hand to Abby to help her stand. Her fingers slid into his palm, and their eyes caught for just a second before she looked away. The same burning question from before filled his head. Was she the one God wanted for him—part of a life that followed God's plan? He wanted to believe it, but he couldn't be sure. He'd been selfish with his first marriage, forcing his choices onto Caroline, believing he knew what was best for them both. Was he letting his own selfish wishes get in the way again? Until he was certain, he couldn't open his heart to Abby with all of his feelings for her. But there was still one thing he had to say.

"Thank you. I… I'll always be beholden to you for taking the time to get to know my boys and being sensitive to the Holy Spirit working in my son's heart. Today his eternity was determined and I have you to thank for that."

"No. You have the Lord to thank for that. The time was right and God just chose to use me to explain to him. I'm sure you would have said the same things, or maybe Jake or Colin. But I am glad I was here for it. No matter what happens, I'll always remember this day." Her voice cracked at the end and she turned away, following the boys.

Chapter Eleven

"Good morning, Jake. How are you today?" Abby greeted the young man she'd truly come to see as her nephew. In the last five months since she had arrived to Nebraska, they had become as close as she had been with Emma's boys.

"Great, Abby. Uncle Will is thinking we'll be done harvesting in a few more days. He thinks maybe I could go into the town with him when he goes to sell the wheat and extra vegetables."

The news shouldn't have been surprising, but it still shook her. Will hadn't said anything to her about it. Despite the rocky beginning, they had managed to return to friendship during their four months of "marriage." Friendship—but nothing more. Will and Jake continued to sleep out in the barn and even though Jake didn't ask questions, Abby felt his curiosity at times. Will treated her no differently than he had when she was just his housekeeper. It was a relief to have the odd distance between them from their first month of marriage gone, but she still wished their relationship could be something more. Sometimes she wondered if Will felt the same way. There were times…times when she felt him watching her moving around the kitchen or when she was on the porch and he would sit in the quiet and just wait. It felt as if he were being pulled toward her but was holding himself back.

"That sounds exciting. How long has it been since you've gone to town?" Abby asked, forcing herself to sound interested instead of panicked. Would Will expect to take her to the train station then or would he leave her back at the farm with the boys? She would rather stay on the farm for the next ten years and never see the town again if it meant staying with her family.

"We went every fall with my parents. It's been a few years. Not since they passed," Jake answered with a shrug, but by now Abby knew the young man too well to be fooled by his pretended nonchalance.

"That was almost seven years ago! Why haven't you gone back?"

"Well…someone had to stay with the livestock." Jake explained it away but Abby saw something else in his eyes.

"Didn't you want to go this last time, when the others came to meet me at the train? I'm sure Will could have gotten someone from another farm to come out and check on the livestock or even take them over to someone else's spread until you got back," Abby argued.

"I was fine staying here. See, I'm not…" His face turned a bright red and he ducked his head as he tended to when she had first arrived.

"You're what?" Abby prompted in a quiet voice, waiting for him to raise his eyes and answer.

"I'm not very cultured or educated. I'm just a country bumpkin and I, well, I'm not really fit to go to town."

"Since when? You are a very well-mannered young man. If you weren't, I would have let you know by now. You were terribly shy when I first came, but you do really well now, talking with everyone at church."

"But I don't have any schooling," Jake disputed.

"You've been taught the basics of reading and writing and I've helped you with some of the more advanced math. You're very smart."

"No, she said…" Jake turned away and seemed about ready to head back out the kitchen door without breakfast.

"Wait, Jake. Who said what?" Abby pressed, grabbing his hand to keep him from leaving.

"It doesn't matter. She was right. I'm just a simpleton. I don't know how to treat a lady or how to act in public."

"Who said that to you, Jake? Was it someone from church?"

He shook his head and Abby tightened her grip.

"I want to know who lied to you, Jake. You're a wonderful person. It's been a pleasure to get to know you. Your own parents and then your uncle raised you very well. I'd be proud to introduce you to my nieces if they were here. You have nothing to be ashamed of. You might find some things in town confusing because you didn't grow up there, but that doesn't mean that you're worth any less than any city boy. You just need to learn." He stopped fidgeting and listened but he didn't look her in the eye.

"Jake, I want you to believe that God made you special. You're young yet, but you're so handsome we're going to have to beat the girls back with a broom one of these days." Abby grinned, but he didn't even smile.

"Who said those horrible things to you, Jake?" Abby entreated.

"My aunt," Jake stated flatly, in a voice just above a whisper.

"Do you mean your aunt Caroline?" Jake didn't answer, but Abby didn't really need the confirmation. Caroline was the only aunt Jake had known, growing up in Nebraska.

"She lied. I'm so sorry that she said those horrible things to you, but they were lies. You can't possibly believe her." Abby moved to stand directly in front of Jake. "You have to understand—I never met her and don't want to speak ill of the dead, but she lied to you. Don't let the words she said dictate who you are or who you become. When I see you, I see a wonderful young man who is very smart and capable. Someday you can have your own farm just like this, or breed hoses or cattle or anything else you want."

"No. I'll always just be a stupid farmhand. Uncle Will needs me and he has given me everything I've ever needed. It's an okay life. I don't mind."

"Have you ever thought about what you'll do for yourself?"

"No. I can't run my own farm. I'm too stupid. I can't read enough and someone would just swindle me out of everything."

"Is that what you know or what your aunt told you?" Abby pressed; her gaze was steady as she waited for Jake's answer.

"That's a good question, Jake. I'd like to hear the answer to that myself," Will said, startling both Jake and Abby.

"I heard what Abby was saying through the window," Will informed Jake.

After a pause, Will took a seat and motioned Jake to take the one next to him. "I'm sorry I didn't realize what Caroline had said to you, or how it's hurt you all these years."

Jake flopped down in the chair at the foot of the table. Abby turned back to the stove, caught between the urge to leave to give the men some privacy for their conversation and to stay so that she could be of help. Will looked like a fish out of water, trying to deal with the fragile ego of his nephew. Emotions didn't seem to be his area of expertise.

"You were always so busy trying to keep everything together. She was always saying stuff about you being…" Jake stopped and looked down at his lap.

"I don't care what she said about me," Will answered, his voice soft. "I know she was angry with me. That's nothing new. But I didn't know she'd hurt you, as well."

Will reached out across the empty chair between the two and briefly squeezed Jake's shoulder. "Listen, Jake, you're your father's son and I knew Mathew better than anyone. So I know, for certain, that he'd have been very proud of you. You are very smart. You have a special way with horses, and I wouldn't be able to get nearly as much done without your help. I can't believe you didn't tell me about these doubts you've got about yourself. All this time I just thought you didn't want to go to town because it brought memories of when your parents went and didn't return."

Silence filled the kitchen. Both men sat staring at their hands, resting on the table in much the same loose fold. If Abby hadn't known that Will was Jake's uncle and not his father, she wouldn't have been able to tell by looking at them. She knew that Will loved Jake as much as he loved Tommy and Willy.

"Jake, I need to ask you to forgive me. I was struggling so much with all that was going on that I didn't pay enough attention to you and how you must've been feeling." Will looked Jake in his eyes and Abby held her breath, waiting for Jake to acknowledge his uncle.

"It's no big deal. You had your hands full with everything else. I was just glad that you didn't send me back East to live with Grandma or in some orphanage." Jake ducked his head and didn't make eye contact.

"Jake…" Will stood and cleared his throat. Squatting down next to his nephew, his hand on the teen's shoulder, he looked him straight in the eye. "Your pa and I had a covenant, kind of like David did with Jonathan in the book of Samuel. I promised to see to you, your ma and any other of his kids if anything ever happened to him. He promised to do the same thing if the tables were turned. Half of this homestead is yours when you come of age. You've worked by my side like a man and deserve it. This was his dream before it was mine. If, when the time comes, you want to concentrate on breeding horses or raising cattle or anything else God puts in your heart, you have my blessing and my help if I can."

Will stood and Jake unfolded from his chair, as well. Both men stood face-to-face, Will only a few inches taller than the boy. Soon Jake would be as tall as his uncle. Neither one seemed to know what to do or what to say.

"Come on, now, give each other a hug. If you don't, I'm not gonna feed you for a week." It slipped out so easily she was turning back to the stove to give the men some privacy when she realized what she had said and felt her face turn the shades of sunset. While she was Will's wife in name, she was just his housekeeper in truth, and wanted to keep that position as long as possible. Threatening to not comply with her work was not exactly the way to ensure her stay.

Jake was the first one to laugh. "Well, now, Auntie Abby, you sure know how to threaten a man. You've got us so spoiled we'd probably starve to death the first day."

"So don't make me do it," Abby threatened playfully, pleased that Jake was teasing her.

"You heard the woman," Will mock-growled at his nephew. "I guess we've been given our orders."

A moment later, they both shook hands and then Will pulled Jake into his arms. The hug resembled a wrestling match between bear cubs as Abby watched it in her peripheral vision. She swallowed back the lump in her throat and sniffed to keep from crying, forcing a smile instead.

Ever since Pastor Colin had preached about "numbering one's days," she had tried to do just that—live each day as if it would be her last day to interact with Will and the boys. She looked for ways to encourage them or to teach them so that when she left, they would have a host of memories that would keep her alive in their hearts.

She also prayed for them and their daily growth. Even as she sewed seam after seam into their new winter clothes, she prayed God would sew His Word in their hearts so they would carry it with them always. Abby thanked God with tears streaming down her face the night of the picnic when she had the privilege to help Tommy accept Jesus as his Savior. Now she added to her precious memories the privilege of seeing Jake and

Will draw closer and Jake overcome hurtful lies his aunt had told him years ago. Lies that had kept him from enjoying social activities with his peers and other adults.

She placed a cup of coffee before each man and returned to her work. Listening to Will and Jake take their seats again in the kitchen and just sit in silence, a peaceful silence that no one wanted to spoil with words, she felt as though this had been part of the reason God had brought her all the way out to Nebraska. He had a divine plan to use her in the boys' lives and in Jake's. Even as she resigned herself to the truth that she might not have many more days with the Hopkins, her heart cried out to God. If she had been able to bless them in little ways, it would only stand to reason that staying for a lifetime would bring a lifetime of blessings.

But the words *Teach me to number my days* rang in her mind. Hers were but a few days on earth. She would have to find a way to survive when the allotted number had been spent here and then she'd have to accept when it was time to move on.

Later that night, the boys already tucked in bed and the kitchen set to rights, Abby slipped out onto the porch with a cup of tea and a light shawl draped around her shoulders. Now the evenings cooled quickly once the sun began to set. The nice part was the bugs didn't bother nearly so much as they had done in the heat of the summer. She settled into the swing with her knitting on her lap. There was a lantern on in the barn and she could hear the frogs still singing in chorus down by the creek.

She had often been tempted to take a stroll down by the creek at this time of night, just to get away from the house and enjoy God's peace and quiet. No wonder He had chosen this time of day to meet with Adam and Eve in the Garden. But she had never ventured away from the house again. She had sensed Will's deep concern for her the night he had found her and Colin talking by the creek, and she hadn't wanted to worry him again.

As if just thinking about him conjured him up, he emerged from the barn and headed toward the house. "Good evening," she called out from the shadows of the porch. "Everything all right?"

"Good evening," he called back. His eyes searched her out in the shadows and then, when he spotted her, a smile lit his eyes and his lips curled at the edges. It was a warm, friendly smile. She reminded herself not to read anything more into it than that. "Everything's fine."

"Want a cup of coffee or tea?" Abby offered, setting her knitting to the side and starting to stand. In a blink, Will was up the stairs and held out a hand to steady her on her feet.

"A cup of tea sounds good tonight. But stay put. I can get my own," he reassured her, motioning her back toward her chair.

"No, sir. I just washed up in there and I'd rather make a little mess than have to deal with the bigger mess you'll make," she teased, rewarded by his boyish grin in return.

He held the door for her, then waited as she prepared the tea. By mutual accord, they returned to the porch with their mugs. She settled on the swing and he sat next to her, leaving as much space between them as possible.

"I wanted to say thank you for your help talking to Jake earlier today. You've done wonders pulling him out of his shell. You've done wonders for all of us, really. I don't know what I would have done without your help this summer," he started, his gaze holding hers.

Abby bit her lip and tried to calm her racing heart. What was he saying? Was this the opening of a discussion about how she'd done enough for them, and now it was time for her to leave? Until now, he hadn't heard back from the East. At least he hadn't told her about anything from his family in the post. In fact, just a few days before he'd commented how strange it was that his mother hadn't sent her regular letters.

In the same span of time, her nieces, Megan and Hanna, had both written letters to her, telling her how much they missed her. Her breath caught in her throat when she dreamed about having her family around her. If only her marriage had been a real marriage, maybe her husband would have let her bring out the girls for a visit.

The second letter had arrived just before meal time last month. Colin had brought it for her. She waited to read it until right after they had finished the meal. She had sat at the table and drunk in the information from her nieces. Their words had her missing them so much that they sent her rushing to her room for a good cry, leaving behind three confused and uncomfortable men. A few minutes later, the boys knocked on her door and then came in and curled up on the bed on each side of her and offered her a handkerchief until she had calmed down. Tommy asked if he could kiss her "owie" and make it better, but she had explained that it was an "owie" inside her heart that was sad without her nieces and nephews.

She cringed at the thought of how sad her heart would be missing Willy, Tommy, Jake and Will if the time had finally come for her to leave.

Sitting out on the porch, Abby felt at home. It felt so natural to enjoy the calm of twilight by Will's side. For a moment, she let herself indulge in the dream that this would be her life. Working hard and laughing at life, hand in hand with a godly man, was all she could ask from God.

"I…" He shifted, then stood and paced to the railing, leaning on it with his forearms, his gaze taking in the barnyard, his back to her so she couldn't read his expressions.

"We're almost done with the threshing and I'll need to be taking the wheat to Twin Oaks so I can get it to the miller and then get our winter supplies. I had expected to have heard from my mother by now."

Abby held her breath and waited as Will kept his back to her. "I don't have any place to send you to. I'm sorry. I bet you're champing at the bit to get out of here. Do you have a family or somewhere…"

"No. I don't have anywhere to go. But I don't mind it here. In fact, I've become quite attached to the boys." Abby swallowed hard, not willing to expose all of her feelings. For all their warm, friendly conversations over the past few months, this was something they had never discussed. The topic of what would happen when she left had been studiously ignored. Now that they were finally talking about it, she had no idea what to say. What words would convince him to let her stay? "I feel safe here."

She watched Will's shoulders relax and it almost seemed as if he had let out a sigh. Did he truly think that she wanted to leave? "I don't know how you can say that. There's always the threat of bad weather, insufferable heat in the summer and harsh cold that penetrates the bones in the winter. Then again, the Indians could pillage the farm or we could get a swarm of locusts like there was three years ago. Or a draught could kill off the plants.…"

"If life is so hard here, why do you stay?" Abby blurted out, shocked at Will's pessimistic outburst.

"Now, don't you start! I've put too much work into making this dream happen. I've lost Matt and Mary-Ann and even Caroline to this place. I'm not leaving."

"If you're staying, then shouldn't I stay, too? You need someone to take care of the boys. And someone to see after your needs, as well. You can't even cook. What'll happen to the boys once I go?" Abby's question was more a whisper but carried on the still night.

"They'll be brokenhearted. It was what I wanted to avoid. I didn't want them hurt."

Abby stared through the gathering darkness and tried to understand this man. "Would it have been better for them to not have had someone to feed them and take care of them all summer than to have heartbreak and know someone out there loves them even across the miles? My life will forever be richer for having known your family, for having loved your boys." She bit her tongue before she could add "for loving you."

Will shifted his weight against the banister and breathed deeply but didn't reply. The silence stretched out. Finally, Will turned toward her but didn't make eye contact. "I don't know. I…" He swallowed and shook his head. "Good night, Abby. Thank you for the tea."

He strode away to the barn as if someone were chasing after him. Abby didn't move until he was inside the barn and the door had shut. Collecting her mug, her knitting and the mug Will left behind, she went into the house, still pondering the abrupt end to their conversation. Could Will possibly consider it better to never experience love than to love and have to say goodbye?

Chapter Twelve

$\mathcal{C}\!\!\!\sim$

Will watched the horses plodding along and smiled to himself. He and Jake had left early and were making good time with their heavy load. His wheat had gotten a good price and now he had barrels of flour to get him and the boys through the winter. He'd purchased sugar, spices, limes, apples and raisins, too. All the ingredients Abby had on her list and a few extras.

The vegetable garden Abby had painstakingly cared for all summer had yielded an overabundance of tomatoes, onions, carrots, beans, lettuce and a number of herbs. She'd spent the better part of the last three weeks canning the produce and had sent some with him to sell, as well. The pumpkins vines slowly twining around the border of the garden all summer promised some large pumpkins for pies in the next month. This growing season had been a success and he admitted it was in large part due to the woman who would be waiting back at the house with dinner ready for them. He fought the urge to hurry the horses.

"So, you miss her?" Jake asked from the wagon

bench next to him, bringing Will's focus back to the road and the here and now.

"The farm?" he responded, ignoring the jab in his conscience. He knew exactly whom Jake was referring to.

"Uncle Will—you taught me never to lie," Jake tsked.

"I think I liked you better when you weren't quite so mouthy," Will quipped, but even as he said it, he knew that the changes in Jake were due to Abby's attempt to bring out his shy nephew. She'd coaxed Jake into trusting her and then taught him a few social graces. If Will didn't keep a close eye on the young man, he was going to start thinking about things like courting and noticing the girls.... Not that there were many to notice in the area.

Abby was the youngest over the age of thirteen in the whole area.

"Come on, Uncle Will. You've got to admit you miss her just a little bit," Jake insisted.

"Yeah, she cooks a lot better than either of us. I can't wait to get back and see how she fared with the boys and the farm while we were gone."

"She had Colin there," Jake reminded him innocently.

"I know. I'm sure that everything is fine." Will said it as much to himself as to his nephew. It had been the best solution to have Colin stay in the barn so he could see to the livestock and chores while Will and Jake were away. His friend's presence should have served to reassure Will, but he also felt jealous. He was worried that Colin had been a better companion for Abby than he had been.

The men continued traveling in silence, Jake still

smirking and Will fighting a battle with his emotions. Truthfully, he missed Abby something fierce. He even contemplated asking her to stay…to make their marriage a true marriage, not just a business arrangement. But he knew it wasn't fair to her to ask her to make her life with him in the middle of the harsh, wonderful prairie.

"Uncle Will, are we gonna keep sleeping out in the barn?" Jake interrupted his thoughts again.

"I… I don't know." It was another topic he had been debating.

The weather wasn't going to let him put off the decision much longer. The last three mornings he'd woken to frost on the ground. Soon the snow would come and then he and Jake would need to be sleeping indoors. Maybe he should rebuild the soddy where they had first lived. But was he being foolish to ignore the warm, sturdy house he'd built just because he'd have to share it with Abby? They were married, her reputation was secure—and of course, they'd continue to sleep not just in separate rooms but on separate floors. There'd be no harm in that, surely…except for the way it would make it feel as though they were all one, united family that would be staying together all winter. And that was something he knew couldn't be true.

Abby had been listening for the sound of a wagon since the day before, or more honestly, since the minute Will and Jake pulled out of the barnyard a few days before, but when it finally came, she almost missed it. She was canning some of the late tomatoes from her garden, her face matching their color from the heat of the stove. Will had promised to bring more canning jars for the squash and pumpkin, as well.

"They're here! They're here!" Tommy came bursting into the kitchen and swept past Abby, out the door and into the yard before Abby could even react. Willy was only two steps behind his brother, leaving the door wide open in his haste to see his father and cousin.

"Willy!" she called after him. He rushed back long enough to slam the door behind him. She had to fight the urge to hike up her skirts, dash out after the boys and throw herself into Will's arms just as his boys were doing now. Instead, she turned back to the stove before she gave in to the impulse. She tried to rein in her thoughts; she had never before wanted anyone to hold her, save her father when she was small. She gave herself a sharp rebuke about wayward daydreams and forced her attention on the tomatoes.

But even her eyes wouldn't obey and they kept straying to the window where she could see the men hugging and laughing with the boys. The sound of the boys' happy chatter mixed with the deeper notes of praise and questions from Will and Jake. All the voices floated on the wind and comforted her in the lonely kitchen. Colin met the group at the door of the barn.

By the time they had all trooped back to the house, Abby managed to set the table and have the roast, mashed potatoes and salad served and ready. Glasses of chilled milk were poured and standing at attention as the door opened. She had wanted everything to be perfect, not that the men would ever really notice little details.

The minute Will entered the room, Abby felt her breath catch in her throat and her heart speed up. The noise of the boys and men talking seemed to fade into silence, and for an instant, her eyes connected with Will's. His face lit with happiness and he stepped closer. She thought maybe he would pull her close and hug her as a normal husband would, but then the light in his expression dimmed to something more controlled and polite. Friendly, but nothing more.

"Looks like a meal fit for a king, Abby," Will commented, taking his place at the head of the table, not having come close enough to shake hands, much less hug her. Her disappointment choked her and she just nodded.

"How were things here while we were gone?" he asked as she settled in the chair next to his.

"Fine, everything went just fine. And how did your trip go? It's good to have you back," she blurted out.

"It's good to be back!" Jake answered from down the table. "Uncle Will's cooking hasn't gotten any better since you've been here, that's for sure. I'd like to have starved if it weren't for the thought we'd be coming home to your fine meals. Ain't that right, Uncle Will?" Jake tossed his uncle a knowing grin and ruffled Tommy's hair.

Colin said grace and thanked God for His protection on the men who had traveled and the family left behind. Once "Amen" was uttered the silence was broken only by the scrape of a fork on the plates and the boys chewing with their mouths open. The boys seemed to be in a race to see who could finish first and then they waited impatiently while the others finished, peppering their father and cousin with questions and squealing with delight when Will promised if they helped unloading supplies, he just might be able to find the stash of peppermint sticks he'd bought.

Soon, Abby was alone again with the dirty dishes. As she worked in the kitchen, she smiled to herself and hummed a hymn. At least for the night, her family was all home, safe and sound. Tomorrow would bring enough worry. As the men started filling her pantry with the sacks of flour and sugar, spices and dried fruits, Abby thanked God for the provisions for the winter months. It looked to her as if Will had purchased enough to hibernate for two winters.

She put some water on the back of the stove to heat for tea for the men as Will went up to tuck the boys into bed. They had missed their father the last few nights he was away and she wanted to give them time together.

"Ma," Tommy called down the stairs almost as soon as he had dressed in his nightshirt. "You need to come up and hear me say my prayers."

"Why don't you let your pa listen to them tonight?" Abby called back up, standing at the foot of the stairs.

Not only did she want to give Will some time alone with his boys, but she was also afraid of what would show on her face if she were in the room with just him and the boys when her heart was so full of happiness to have them all together again. If only Will shared her joy at their togetherness! But it was his right to want her out of his house and life, as much as it hurt to think that after almost six months, he hadn't grown to care for her the way her heart had become attached to him.

"No, Ma, we want you to tuck us in. You need to give us hugs and kisses and all that," Tommy argued.

"I'll be up in a moment." Abby sighed, looked around the room for something else to straighten up. Wouldn't you know that everything was in its place? She ducked into her room to search for her knitting but couldn't find it.

"Ma?" Willy stood at her door, his eyes following her search.

"Yes, Willy?" Abby answered absentmindedly.

"Are you coming up now?"

"I was going to, but I can't find my knitting."

"It's up on the chair next to our beds. Don't you remember? You started to knit there last night when Tommy was scared."

"You're right. Thank you, Willy. Let's go on up."

Willy took her hand and they ascended the stairs together. He let her go only to climb between the sheets and then patted the bed so she would sit down next to him. Once prayers were said and the boys had been given their good-night hugs and kisses, Will escorted her back downstairs. It was the first time they had been alone in more than a week and she found herself suddenly shy. Her nerves weren't helped by the worry that a letter had come from his mother that he'd collected while in town. Would this be the conversation where they made the plans for her to leave?

"So." Will sounded as uncomfortable as she felt. "Did the boys behave for you?"

"Yes. You should be proud," she answered, glad he had chosen a safe topic.

"Most of their good behavior comes from what they've learned from you these last few months."

"It's been my pleasure to be here with them, but you laid the foundation." Her mother had always encouraged her to say something nice and true at the same time. If ever a statement were true, it was that. Abby had so enjoyed getting to know and love the boys. How could she possibly walk away from them now? She bit her lower lip and tried not to give in to the urge to cry at the thought.

"I really appreciate all you've done out here. I know the conditions aren't what most women would expect and we're certainly a little rough around the edges…." By now they had entered the kitchen and Abby started to prepare two mugs for tea without even asking.

"I don't mind. I've come to value all your hard work and sacrifices to make this place work. And look what a harvest God's blessed you with. Out here, it's easy to be mindful of our Creator. After all, if He doesn't send the rain, you don't have a harvest. If He sends too much rain, you won't get a harvest, either. I can see why Jesus asks God for our daily bread. In the city, we can forget our food and livelihoods don't come from the market but from God. The silence and the richness of this land, the flowers, the plants, the sky…."

"It sounds like you have gotten used to this place. But you haven't seen a winter here. That might change your mind a bit."

"Hmm… I don't think so." She bit her lip and wondered if he would give her the chance to make up her mind for herself or if he was even now holding the tickets for her to return to the East.

He swiped his hand through his hair, standing it on end. Abby recognized his tic, hinting at his frustration. Maybe it was a good sign. Maybe he was at least a little bothered to have to send her off.

She handed him his mug of tea and instead of leading her to the table, he motioned to the door. "It's still light out. How about sitting out on the porch awhile?" he offered.

"Sure, let me go get my shawl." She was gone and back in a few seconds.

Seated on the rocking chair, she waited for whatever news Will wanted to share with her. He seemed suddenly nervous as he settled on the swing. He sipped his tea, looked over his land, put the swing in motion and then tried to sip more of his tea, succeeding only in spilling some down his shirtfront. Abby had to bite the inner part of her lip to keep from chuckling. He set the mug down on the windowsill behind him and continued swinging.

"Listen, Abby, I don't know what to tell you. I was hoping that by the time I got to Twin Oaks I would find a letter from Ma. Not that I want to get rid of you. Just the opposite. I see how much the boys have come to depend on you. They love you. Jake wasn't joking about my cooking. It hasn't gotten any better over these last months. If anything, it's gotten worse or maybe it's just that we've gotten spoiled by your expertise. And you have to know how good you've been for Jake, how you've helped him believe in himself. While I… I can't tell you how grateful I am for all that you've done.

"But it's not fair of us to think only about us and not about you. You need a family of your own. You need to be in the city where you'll have everything you want and someone who can give you more than just a load of dirty laundry and backbreaking work from sunup to sundown."

He stopped the swing and stared straight into her eyes. "I have to admit that I don't want to see you go. You lighten our day and make me smile. You should've seen Jake in town. I was afraid I wouldn't be able to get him to come back home. He had so much fun talking with all the young ladies. And I happen to notice the shirts and pants you made for us were as nice as the ones that Mayor Hoffman was wearing. Somebody, I think it was the waitress at the restaurant, made a comment about how nice Jake's hair looked."

"So, why are you so set on sending me back?" Abby whispered, her heart breaking with each word.

"Caroline always said, 'No woman on the face of the earth would want to be stuck out here, in the middle of nowhere.' She said she 'didn't want to spend her dying days out here,' but that's just what happened. This land is inhospitable for most, especially women.'"

Caroline had really said all of that? Abby knew Will's first wife hadn't liked the prairie—he'd told her as much on their wedding day—but she hadn't known the woman's opinion of the place had been that low. It went a long way toward explaining why Will was so convinced she'd be better off somewhere else.

But why wouldn't he believe her when she tried to tell him otherwise? Maybe Caroline hadn't wanted to spend her dying days out on the prairie, but Abby did. She wanted to spend every day she had left cooking and cleaning in this house, laughing and playing with the boys, being part of the family that Will had made. Maybe it would have to be enough for her to see his family was well cared for. Maybe they would never truly be her family, but it would be the closest she would ever come to having one of her own. After this summer, she would never be the same. She was sure because she would be leaving the biggest part of her heart behind with Will and the boys. Maybe there was still time to convince him. She could be happy as long as they were happy.

"Ma didn't write back," Will said, breaking the silence. "At least, I haven't gotten a letter from her yet. I'm of half a mind to send you on back to stay with her until she can get you established with someone from town. I don't know what's taking her so long, but if you stay too long, you're liable to get snowed in and then you won't be able to get out for a few more months."

"Please don't send me away yet," Abby urged. "I'm not ready to leave. There's still so much to do...." She thought franticly of all the chores she still had before she felt ready for winter. "I haven't gotten the entire garden in yet. And the pumpkins are just about to ripen. You can't possibly tell me you know what to do with pumpkins or how to make pumpkin pie if you can't even make oatmeal! There's still the sweaters I'm knitting for the boys. That's why I asked you to bring me more yarn. I need to still take a look at all of your winter wear and patch anything that's gotten threadbare. I—"

"Abby, there's nowhere I can send you just now, so don't get yourself all worked up. I don't want a repeat of the first day." His eyes, full of compassion and something else, held hers for a moment before she remembered what he was referring to.

"There's something else we need to talk about," Will stated, and once again Abby held her breath. "It's gonna get too cold at night to have Jake and me sleeping out in the barn. I was wondering if it would be okay with you if we started sleeping upstairs, in our old rooms." He hesitated a moment and then continued, "You could still keep the parlor and of course we'd respect your privacy like always. If there were some other way I'd do it, but the snow is going to come soon and I don't want Jake getting sick."

"Of course!" Abby exclaimed, laughing out loud. The silliness of the owner of the house, asking her to let him sleep under his roof, tickled her funny bone. Or maybe it was the relief that Will wasn't set on sending her away quite yet. "I'll make up the beds right away."

"No, not tonight, Abby. Tomorrow will be soon enough," Will reassured her. "In fact, it will be some-time next week since Colin will be staying for a few more days."

Abby watched as Will looked out toward the barn. He looked distracted, probably thinking of all the things that needed to be done around the farm now that the harvest was in. The chill of the night stole into her bones, making her tremble with the reminder that sum-mer was truly over, and her remaining days in Nebraska would soon be coming to an end. "I think I should be going in now," she said in a quiet voice.

She stood and picked up her mug. Will stood just as she tried to pass him and she tripped while trying to avoid a collision. His hands caught her upper arms and kept her from falling. Instead of letting her go once she was steady, though, he waited, seeming to force her eyes to meet his. When she did, she wondered at the emo-tions there. She saw fear, kindness, endearment and something more. Something that made her confused and excited all at once.

With a start, she realized that this was the first time in months that Will had touched her for more than the bare moment necessary as he handed her up and down on the wagon when they went to church. Maybe it was his warmth that pulled her like a magnet or maybe he really did pull gently on her arms, but suddenly she was taking a step closer and found herself engulfed in his arms, buried in the strength of his chest. She closed her eyes and pretended she would never have to leave the shelter of his arms.

"Oh, Abby. I…" He swallowed but didn't continue.

This was what he had kept himself from doing earlier in the afternoon. This was what she had seen in his eyes—the need to hold her close. His hand slid in a circular motion on the center of her back and she felt safe, protected and cared for. She let her arms wrap around his waist and felt as if she had finally come home. Was this what it felt like to be loved by a man? There was no doubt now, *she* loved *him*.

Almost as if he could hear her thoughts, he pulled away from her, holding her at arm's length. "I'm sorry, Abby. I guess I'm just tired tonight. I'm not thinking straight. You'd better get inside and stay warm."

The trembling started again, as the cold rushed in to embrace her much as Will had. Only this time, the cold started from inside. It had been too good to be real; Will hadn't held her close because he had feelings for her but because he was tired and lonely.

Without saying anything more, Abby rushed into the house and straight to her room. She heard Will enter a few minutes later, put the dishes in the sink, walk halfway to her door, then retrace his steps and leave out the back. Once again, she found herself weeping on her bed, wondering if she wouldn't be better off leaving. Living here, near a man she loved, and yet never having him return her feelings, would be harder than living miles away from him with just the memories to keep her company. Memories of being held and a fleeting kiss on her wedding day. Those two precious memories might be all she'd ever keep from her marriage to Will, but she cherished them and would remember them always.

"God, only You know the plans You have for me.... But I'm not happy about them right now. It hurts to not belong to Will while he holds my heart in his hands."

"I know the thoughts that I think toward you..." The verse from Jeremiah echoed in her heart. *"Thoughts of peace and not of evil, to give you an expected end."*

"But, God, if they're supposed to give me peace, why do they hurt so much? Why did You bring me here to fall in love with a man who can never love me? Why did You bring me here to be part of a family that will never be mine?"

Chapter Thirteen

Will kicked a rock as he made his way out to the barn. He probably looked like Tommy having a temper tantrum, but he didn't much care. How could he have lost his head so easily? He had almost kissed her! He had taken her in his arms and held her close and she had fit perfectly in his embrace.

Not only had she fit, but she had melted against him so innocently, without knowing what that was doing to him. He would never forget the feel of her in his arms. Until the day he died, he would remember how he held her and she'd come willingly. But he couldn't let himself forget that he had her interests to consider. Whether she realized it yet or not, the prairie wasn't where she belonged. He was going to stay away from her as much as he could until she left, and then…then he'd have the rest of his life to miss her smile and laughter. He'd have the rest of his life to know that he had done the right thing by her. At least he could be proud that she would be able to go on and find a true love who would give her everything she needed.

"You don't have to come and sleep out here on my

account," a voice called out to him from the doorway of the barn. "I'm sure it's much nicer in the house."

"Night, Colin." Will acknowledged his friend, even though all he wanted to do was turn and stomp away. He didn't want another lecture from his friend about how he was making the wrong decision. Right or wrong, it was his decision to make—and he was going to do what he knew was best for Abby.

"Why don't you just go back in there and tell that woman of yours that you love her?" Colin pried.

"'Cuz you know if I do, she wouldn't go back East when my ma sends for her." A second too late Will knew his answer confirmed Colin's suspicions.

"Well, I'm glad you're not denying that you love her. And we want her to go back because…?" Colin left the sentence hanging as if to prompt Will to admit to his own folly. Sometimes Colin was like a dog with a bone; he just wouldn't let it go.

"Just leave me alone, Colin," Will answered grumpily.

"No, not until you explain this to me. I saw how she wore a hole in the floor by the window, watching for you to come home. She took pains with that meal tonight and you know it's because you were back. Don't you see the gift God has given you? A beautiful woman who loves your boys and has fit into your life as if she had always belonged? How many other men in this territory would give their right arm to find a jewel like her? And here God just dumps her in your lap and you want to send His precious gift back East as soon as possible. Can't you see she wants to stay here with you?"

"She's young and doesn't know any better."

"She's older than you were when you first came out

here. Have you ever asked her what she wants? You and the boys aren't going to know what to do if she goes. Most men would have made sure she didn't have a reason to leave here long ago."

"I'm not most men. I wouldn't leave for Caroline and look what happened. I don't want to be responsible for another woman shriveling up and dying out here."

"When she first arrived, I admit, there were a number of people who doubted she'd last more than a month or two. But no one doubts her anymore. She's shown herself to be a true farmer's wife."

The decisions Will made were for Abby's sake. He might be sacrificing the greatest gift short of salvation to let her go, but it was for her own good. His heart wanted him to go back to the house and let Abby know how he really felt. As much as he wanted to deny it, Colin was right about one thing. He loved Abby. If he didn't love her this much, he might be more tempted to try and convince her to stay.

Poor thing, she was probably all confused and upset. Just the thought that he might have caused her distress was tearing him up inside, but it was better this way. It would be better for her and for him in the long run if she believed that he didn't harbor any feelings for her. Not that he believed it was all that likely he could convince her he had *no* feelings for her. If she hadn't figured it out from the kiss on their wedding day, tonight must have proven his folly. But as long as she didn't realize how deep his love ran, she wouldn't feel obligated to stay out with him on the prairie where he was sure she could never be truly happy.

Will shouldered his way past Colin and climbed up

the ladder to the loft. Jake was already bedded down. He shot a pitying look at his uncle.

"Colin, you might as well come on up and get some sleep. Trying to talk to my uncle now is like talking to a brick wall," Jake called out, then turned on his side and pretended to doze off.

Before the rooster even could crow his "good-morning" to everyone, Will headed down below, mucking stalls and milking the cows. By the time most of the chores were done, Jake and Colin still hadn't bothered to come down. It was probably better they leave him to work in peace, but now he had to face Abby. He'd planned to send the milk in with Jake, hoping to avoid her unless others were around, but Abby had had the fire started for a while and she would need the milk soon. She'd already been out to the outhouse and then the henhouse. Feeling every bit the coward, he watched her from the shadows of the barn as she had stood on the back porch for a minute, studying the barn as if pondering what to do about life or maybe just what to do about him.

Well, there was nothing more to do than go bring her the milk. He gritted his teeth as if he were about to face the firing squad. He trudged across the yard and up the stairs, tempted to just leave the pail inside the door, but the smell of coffee called to his grumbling stomach. As soon as he opened the door, he saw her square her shoulders and take a deep breath. Not a good sign.

"Good morning, Abby." He hadn't wanted to sound so pleased to see her, but his voice betrayed him. What he really wanted was to cross the room and take her back into his arms as he had done the night before.

"Morning," she answered, not turning to look at him. That was definitely a very bad sign. It was the same thing his mother would do when she was upset with his father.

"Here's the milk." He stated the obvious, wanting to find some neutral ground.

"Thank you." She half turned and he could see her profile. Her eyes were puffy and her cheeks and nose were red. Stray wisps of her hair were pulling free from her bun, making her seem more vulnerable. He fisted his hands and stuffed them in his pockets before he gave in to the urge to hold her close again.

Before he could think of some excuse to leave, she was handing him his mug of coffee, their fingers brushing accidently. The contact burned a trail of fire all the way to his soul. "Thanks," he murmured. He'd planned to leave it at that, but the look of pain in her eyes undid all his best intentions, breaking his heart.

"You're welcome," she whispered, and spun away, back to the stove to care for what looked like the beginnings of French toast. He involuntarily took two steps closer.

"Listen, Abby. I don't want you all upset and all." His hand reached out on its own accord, ignoring his common sense. He pushed a wisp of hair away from her face, hooking it behind her delicate ear. His index finger tracing a path from her ear to her jaw, but warning alarms in his head finally broke through his fog and shook him. He dropped his hands to his sides.

"You know that this is better this way. You need to be in a place that's safe. This is the prairie. There's always the threat of an Indian uprising, of bad weather, of the harvest not giving us enough to get through the winter…. I can name a hundred other ways that a body can become just one more victim of this barren place. It's the place that I love and I won't leave, but it's not right for you."

"What gives you the right to decide that for me?" Abby turned and glared at him. He had never seen her look angry, not even when the boys were fighting. "I don't think I've said anything about the prairie being wrong for me. In fact, if you had been listening to anything I have been saying in the last few weeks, you would have heard how much I've come to love this farm, this family, the land. This place isn't just the land you dream about. It's become my dream, as well. But you're too busy playing God to listen to anyone else."

"I'm not playing God!" Will gritted out. He was a God-fearing man. He would never—

"Of course you are. 'I'll not be responsible for another woman dying out here….'" she parroted him. "As if you appointed the time for Caroline to die! As if there are not any dangers in the city. What if I go where you send me and I die of influenza? Would that also be your fault? What if someone attacks me in the city or I get trampled by a runaway carriage? Or is danger only here in the horrible wilderness?" Her sarcasm surprised him. She had never once been sarcastic before.

"All Caroline wanted was to go back to the city and I wouldn't go. She…"

"She what?" Abby exclaimed, but then she dropped her voice and a look of compassion filled her eyes. "I know you still love her. You must miss her something fierce, but you've got to realize God appoints each of us a time. He called her home, just like He called my parents home before I felt ready to let them go. But no one can tell God how or when to work His will. He does as He sees fit and He loves us. It's for our good."

"But I didn't love her!" Will exploded, but stopped in shock as his words echoed in the now-silent kitchen. He dropped his eyes to the floor, wanting to leave and never return to see condemnation that must be in Abby's eyes at that moment.

"I don't understand. You married her.... Had children with her. You still have her things in your room." Abby swung away from him and scraped the now-burnt French toast from the skillet. She pushed the fry pan onto the back of the stove.

"I married Caroline because *she tricked me.* I didn't want a wife since I was already planning to come out here with Matt and MaryAnn that spring. I think Caroline believed she could talk me out of my plans once she forced the engagement, but I held firm. She got the husband she wanted and I got the journey I wanted, but neither one of us was happy. Once we were married— especially once the boys came along—I tried to be a good husband, tried to tell myself that I loved her, but, well..."

Had he really not loved Caroline? Even now it hurt to admit it. It made him feel like even more of a failure as a husband.

"I made a lot of mistakes," he admitted. "Did a lot of things that I now regret. I'm not sorry I came out to Nebraska, or that I helped build this farm along with Mathew, but I am sorry that I made Caroline so unhappy."

"I think there's a part of you that felt you should have left and seen to her comforts and yet another part that feels you were justified in staying since she was the one who forced the marriage," Abby said. "You need to forgive her. You need to let God be God and control life. You aren't going to be able to protect all those you love. You aren't going to be able to change God's will. If He calls me to Him today, you won't be able to keep me here no matter what you do. But if He sees fit to let me spend the next fifty years here on this earth, I'd rather spend them with you and the boys than going to the city, no matter the conditions." Abby swung around and faced him, squaring her shoulders once again. She bit her lower lip and it was all Will could to not to reach out and wipe away a stray tear.

"I guess what I'm trying to tell you is I'm not Caroline. She and I might both have forced you into marriages you didn't want, but we had very different reasons. I don't expect you to love me or find me appealing like you must have found her, but I want a chance to prove I can be a good mother to your children. Maybe even a good wife to you."

"But you'll be missing out on your own life," Will countered. It was all he could come up with. He was not going to give in now. Not when he had kept his emotions in check for so long. He would not be responsible for another woman dying on the prairie.

Even as the thought crossed his mind, he recognized it as the very thing Abby said was sin. But it was what had kept him from getting too close. And if he got close, when she did finally get tried of the prairie life, he would be truly heartbroken because unlike with Caroline, he really did love Abby. She was right; she would be a great mother for his children and a very good wife. If only he could claim her as his without endangering her life or her happiness.

Knowing he was too close to giving in and letting her win the argument, he did what any self-respecting man would do. He turned on his heel and left. Stalked out the door and let it slam behind him. Even as the smell of coffee and French toast enticed him to return, he kept on walking. He'd survive on water and whatever bread Jake could smuggle out to him later. At least that's what he told his rumbling stomach. He had lots of work to do—work that wouldn't get done unless he saw to it himself.

Work that would distract him from the woman he loved, and wanted to beg to stay by his side forever.

Chapter Fourteen

The Monday after their return from town, Will, Jake and Colin left as soon as morning chores were done and spent the day building the foundation for Colin's cabin. He'd filed on a homestead a half hour's ride from theirs. It was close enough to church that anyone could find him if they needed the preacher in a hurry.

The next morning, the three men did their morning chores and then left for Colin's cabin, returning at afternoon chore time and eating the evening meal with Abby and the boys. The pattern continued until Friday morning.

"Well, Abby, I am forever indebted to you for feeding me so well." Colin thanked her after breakfast on Friday morning. "I reluctantly have to bid you and the boys goodbye until Sunday. My cabin's finished enough for me to sleep in it and not have to worry about unwelcomed visitors or water dripping on my head. I imagine that being such close neighbors, you and Will can invite this poor preacher over from time to time to enjoy your good cooking."

He stood and hugged her close as a big brother

would. Stepping back just a space, he whispered, "I'll be praying for you both. Don't give up. Even though he denies it, he loves you. It'll just take time. Trust the Lord. You're the best blessing the Lord has ever lavished on that old hardhead."

Colin winked and it made Abby giggle. It felt good to smile. As the three men saddled up, Abby stood on the porch and waited for them to wave goodbye. Will circled back and kept his horse prancing at the foot of the steps. It put him eye level with Abby. She liked not having to look up to him while they spoke.

"Listen, if you get a chance, could you make up my room, and Jake's? I guess there's no need for us to be sleeping in the barn when there are two perfectly good beds inside to use."

Abby nodded.

"Well, I'll see you tonight." And before she was able to come up with a fitting reply, he reined his horse around and trotted off after the others.

That night, Abby noticed that she felt safer somehow, knowing Will slept just upstairs instead of out in the barn. It made the house seem smaller, cozy. She liked having everyone under one roof. If only Will would admit that this was the way things should be. But he remained stubbornly insistent that she would never be happy out on the prairie. At times she wondered if it wouldn't just be better to move back East somewhere and bury herself in mundane work, far from the reminders that she was married to a man who didn't want her. A man who refused to even entertain the idea of making her his.

But no matter where she went, she knew she would always be able to close her eyes and picture his face, his blue eyes sparkling as he laughed with Tommy or his forehead wrinkled in thought as he tried to answer the boy's questions. And when she closed her eyes, she could still almost feel the gentleness of his lips on hers on their wedding day or smell his scent as he hugged her close the day he returned from his trip to town. She'd cherish the time she had with Tommy, Willy and Jake, too. But her heart had become attached to Will more than any other.

Abby hesitated at the door of the church. She felt tired and discouraged. Will barely took the time to spare her a word much less take a cup of tea with her on Friday or Saturday nights. She had hoped that now that Colin was in his own home and Will and Jake were staying indoors, they'd have more opportunities to talk, but it hadn't worked out that way at all.

Mrs. Scotts and Mrs. Becker both greeted her as she entered the church building, but what she longed for was a true friend. Someone like Mrs. Gibbons, the pastor's wife back in Ohio, or even her own nieces. A woman whom she could confide in and who would understand her. Instead, Colin greeted her as she followed Will and the boys to their pew. He was kind and a good friend, but he didn't make up for a woman who could understand her heart.

"Before you leave, I need to speak to you," Colin whispered. Abby nodded just before sitting down next to Tommy.

During the service, Abby had the strangest sensation that Colin's message was somehow directed toward her and she tried to drink in every word. He spoke about how God's plans and timing are not always ours. He pointed out that God made promises He fulfilled years later, sometimes even centuries later. Colin read from Genesis and from Hebrews about how God used faithful men and women to do His work, many of whom never saw a reward for their labor this side of heaven. As Colin spoke, Abby felt torn. She knew that Colin was using these passages to encourage everyone to keep serving the Lord, letting God use their lives for His purpose. But she also understood that Colin's message meant that sometimes God answered prayers only after the faithful souls reached heaven. Was that His plan for her prayer for a home and family of her own?

By the end of the service, Abby dreaded speaking with Colin because she suspected he held news from the East.

"Good morning, Abby, Will," Colin greeted them as they exited, Will right behind her. "Before you go…" He reached out, stopping her, and didn't let go of her hand. "I just wanted to tell you I will continue to pray for…for what we talked about last time. I'm sure God has a plan and it's just His timing, but…keep in touch." He finally looked up into her eyes and she knew he was saying goodbye.

She didn't trust her voice. She swung away and fled down the steps to the wagon. The boys were playing with their friends and ignored her. She was almost to the sanctuary of the wagon when Mrs. Scotts called out to her.

"Hello, Mrs. Hopkins. How are you doing, my dear?"

The older woman had always been pleasant with Abby even though Abby had chosen to marry Will instead of one of her sons. Abby swallowed the lump in her throat and tried to force a smile, as if her life weren't falling apart once again.

"Hello, Mrs. Scotts."

"How have you been?" The older woman's eyes were sharp and she looked Abby over from head to toes. "Do you need me to help you into the shade?"

"No, thank you. I'm fine. I've been busy. This is the first year I've been on a farm. It's a little different than what I'm used to." Abby found herself blurting out anything that came to mind.

"Have you been feeling all right? You look a little pale." Mrs. Scotts eyes looked more merry than concerned. "You aren't nauseated in the mornings or lightheaded? Do you get extra tired?"

For a moment, Abby wondered what Mrs. Scotts meant. Then realization hit. She felt her face turn crimson and swallowed back the taste of tears. If only she could be concerned about being in the family way.

"There you are, Abby." Will's deep voice called out from behind her, making her heart speed up and her stomach flip. He came to stand beside her, resting a hand on her shoulder. It was odd that he should do that now, after weeks of avoiding her, especially when he must now hold in his hands the letter that would send her away.

"Good afternoon, Mrs. Scotts," he greeted the other woman. "You'll have to excuse us. We need to get home to the chores. We'll see you next week." He didn't even wait for a reply before he was leading Abby toward their wagon, calling out to Jake and the boys to say goodbye to their friends and come along.

He lifted her up by the waist. Though he released her as soon as she was seated, she could still feel the heat of his hands halfway home. Why did the letter have to come now? Her heart and mind raged at God even as she sat silently on the wagon bench, mindlessly gazing out at the prairie. She couldn't help noticing its changes since she had arrived all those months before.

Now everything was dry and brittle. The plants that were light green spouts when Will brought her home from Twin Oaks in May had already grown, flowered, given their fruits and seeds and were now dying. The breeze that would have brought cool relief from the scorching sun just a few months ago now tore through her like a sheet of ice, numbing her face and fingers. She pulled her woolen shawl tighter around her shoulders.

Strange how her life mirrored the plants. She had been here just for a while, growing to love Tommy, Willy, Jake and especially Will, but that love seemed only to have planted seeds to what would never be. The plants, though, were fortunate enough to be staying in Nebraska. Next spring they would once again burst out of the seemingly dead ground, but Abby would be miles away. It would be only a memory, the prairie and her instant family…. The one her heart claimed as its own even though Will never wanted her.

It had finally come. Will hadn't realized what Colin was handing him until he glanced down and saw his mother's flowing script on the envelope. Now it all made sense. All those looks that Colin sent Abby during the service this morning were because Colin knew that Ma had finally written back. It was a good thing the letter had come today. He wasn't sure if he could have made it through another week. Each day had been harder than the last to get through without seeking her out and confessing that his life was never going to be the same once she left.

Abby hadn't said a word since they'd left church. At first, Will thought she was just in a quiet mood, but when she didn't even answer the boys' constant chatter, it dawned on him that she must have realized he'd be receiving the letter, too. His glace at her confirmed his thoughts. She was looking out at the landscape, turning her face away from him, her shoulders slumped and her chin down. An urge to fix it, make things better almost loosened his tongue. Almost. But maybe it would be better this way.

He was going to get home and read the letter and then tell her that she could leave during the week…assuming his mother had found a place for her to work. It had better be a good place, where they would treat her right and pay her well. Abby worked hard and deserved much more than what he could offer.

His barn came into view, then the rest of the property, and without too much thought he pulled up by the house, tethered the brake and jumped down, ready to help Abby from the wagon. It was a habit formed from good training on his mother's part and had never meant much to him before. But as he stood next to the wagon, waiting for Abby to stand up, he found himself looking up into her eyes. They were red rimmed and her nose was also red as if she were getting sick.

"Do you feel okay, Abby?" Concern colored his voice and his words.

Instead of answering right away, she looked away, cleared her throat and nodded.

"Were you cold on the ride?" he tried again. "You should have said."

"No, I'm…" Her voice sounded husky and cracked before she could finish her sentence.

He reached up and caught her around the waist, stepping forward to examine her more closely. He studied her eyes carefully, sure something was wrong.

Her face was drawn, as if she was tired and hadn't been sleeping enough lately. Under her eyes were dark, purple smudges, reminding him of the time she had nursed the boys through the chicken pox and in the process, worn herself completely out. Seeing them made him want to send her to her room to rest, as he had done back then. Who would pay attention to her when she needed rest if she went back to Philly?

"I, um, need to get down." Her voice brought his wandering thoughts back to the present.

He lifted her down, yet even when she was planted on solid ground, he couldn't take his hands away. He held his wife, the one he had come to love, knowing that she would be going within the week. Something caught in his throat. His arms ached with the longing to pull her closer and hide her in his chest, letting her find comfort in his tenderness. He tried to remind himself that he was sending her away for her own good, but the reminder was no comfort now.

She pulled away and fled up the stairs, leaving him to wonder if she was fleeing from his touch. Just before the door shut, he heard her sniffle and then she was gone. What had just happened? She had looked so forlorn. Turning away, he found three pairs of eyes watching him with accusing looks.

He pulled the wagon around and put it away in the barn. Jake and the boys played horseshoes out in the yard, but Will puttered around the barn, looking for something to do with his hands. A part of him was tempted to read the letter from Ma once and for all. He had impatiently waited for it for so long, but now that it was finally in his hands, doubts filled his head.

What if the employment his mother arranged for Abby didn't meet his approval? Should he take her back to Philadelphia himself to make sure that she arrived safely? It would be almost impossible to leave the farm for that long unless Colin was willing to stay with Jake. In his mind he started to plan what needed to be done. Until that moment, he hadn't really considered that he was planning on sending a beautiful young woman on a train without anyone to see to her welfare. It was amazing that nothing had happened to her on her trip out.

"You're too busy playing God." Her words echoed in his ears again. He was forgetting that God would be with her. God would take care of her. But what if God had wanted Will to be the man to protect her and he let both God and Abby down? He had given his word. To honor, protect, provide…until death do them part. What if…

What if she wanted to stay, just as she had claimed a week ago? The thought snuck in and blindsided him, stealing his breath. What if she actually learned to live out on the prairie? Mrs. Scotts and Mrs. Phelps had. Would it be too much to hope for?

Sooner or later there would be other settlers closer to their farm. Now that Colin was going to be just a quick ride away, others would surely start to settle near the church and a town would spring up in no time. His heart quickened with the thought. Before, he had dreaded the idea of more neighbors, busybodies nosing around in his business, but more neighbors might mean a school for his boys someday, other women friends for Abby to chat with, to trade recipes with, to visit and hold sewing bees with. A town would mean a sheriff. Maybe she would be willing to…

He had to stop this silliness. He was daydreaming like some young schoolgirl with her first crush. He called himself every kind of fool for not thinking about this until now. What he should really do was read the letter, but he didn't want to now. He wanted to see Abby. He wanted to sit across the table from her and be able to let her know that he didn't want her to leave. That he wanted her to stay with him, on his farm, until they were both old and gray. A sudden image of Abby carrying his child came to mind and stole his breath away. Could it be possible?

Abby called from the back step for everyone to come in for dinner. He set his letter in the tack room and went into the house. For at least one more meal he would act and think as if there were no changes coming.

Dearest Son,

It is so good to finally hear from you. I waited expectantly for word all summer. I pray and trust that you are all fine and healthy. I pray for you all each night.

I believe God has a hand in everything that has happened to you this year. I'm glad the woman who responded to the advertisement is truly a Christian, even if you do not find her acceptable for your wife or family. (I admit I hope God impeded your first letter from coming to me so you could come to care for your unexpected wife.)

I have found a family who is looking for additional help, but I would rather meet your Miss Stewart first. I want to make sure she is able to do the work you claim she can do and at the same time, determine if she will be comfortable with the Standish family. Please send her whenever it is convenient.

Ma's letter rambled on, asking about her grandsons and then telling all the latest news about his sisters and their families.

He had waited until he was alone in his room in the quiet of the evening before he had dared open it. Now that he had done that, he was surprised his mother wanted him to rethink sending Abby back. Could this be a sign that God was showing him? He already had a head full of doubts about pushing Abby away. But in the end, he kept coming back to the idea that he needed to protect and provide for her. What was the best for her? God couldn't possibly want her to waste away in the prairie when she had so much to give others. Joy, laughter, love, attention…. What a blessing she would be to any family and yet Will knew he selfishly didn't want to bless anyone else. He wanted her to stay with them, and if he were truly honest with himself, he was selfish enough to want her to stay for *him*.

Daybreak came with little light peeking through dark, thick clouds the color of dirty wool. Will climbed out of bed, shivering with the cold, and quickly dressed, heading out to the barn and the cows before he could find himself face-to-face with Abby. He stirred the embers to flame and then tossed two logs on the fire in the kitchen on his way out. The air smelled of winter. The grasses were covered in frost. Would they get an early snowfall? That might force him into making a decision about Abby. One way or the other.

His stomach soured with dread at the thought of sharing his mother's letter with her. Would she be happy or disappointed with the news? He hadn't done anything to make her feel welcome for a long time. Maybe she had all her things packed already.

Will sent the milk in with Jake. By the time he actually returned to the house for breakfast, the boys were seated around the table and there wasn't another opportunity to talk with Abby alone throughout the day. It was only at night, when the boys were in bed, that Will worked up the courage to speak with her.

"Um, Abby?" he asked quietly as she poured her nightly cup of tea. "Could I talk with you for a bit?"

Instead of responding, she bit her lower lip and reached for another mug. As she turned to face him, Will saw tears already filling her eyes. The sight broke his heart and his resolve. She nodded and he debated a moment before leading her out to the front room. Taking a seat on the rocking chair, he motioned for her to sit on the davenport.

"Well, Abby. On Sunday…" He hesitated, unsure how he wanted to explain his mixed feelings.

"You received a letter from your mother." She finished his sentence in a quiet, sad voice when he didn't continue.

"Um… Yes." She'd known and yet she hadn't said a word. He studied her face, wondering what was going on behind those beautiful blue-green eyes. She didn't smile, nod or even flinch. She just sat there, staring at the floor. His heart lightened a little bit when she didn't jump for joy at the prospect of leaving.

"How is she?" Abby finally asked when the silence drew out too long.

"She's fine."

"And your father?" she asked after another pause.

"Pa's fine. She said she hadn't gotten any mail from me since last spring. I guess the first letter I sent got lost somewhere."

She straightened her shoulders and glanced at him but quickly let her gaze fall back to the floorboards. "So, when do I leave?" Her question sank heavily into the air and extinguished the small flicker of hope he had felt a minute before. If she had indicated even the slightest interest in staying, he would have been overjoyed, but she didn't even mention it. She must have changed her mind about wanting to stay. He swallowed hard.

"The outbound train comes every Monday, early, roughly eight in the morning. You'd have to spend the night in the hotel the night before."

"Then we'll leave on Sunday?" she asked, still not meeting his eyes.

He clenched his hands in tight fists until they shook from the effort. His heart cried out to lift her chin, push her hair away from her forehead and ask her if she still wanted to stay or if she wanted to go…but he refrained. If she said she wanted to go, he'd be crushed. And if she said she wanted to stay… He didn't know if he'd be able to resist letting her, in spite of the regrets he was certain would follow.

"Um, well, no. I think we should leave on Saturday. That way we won't be traveling much on the Lord's Day. We could stay at the hotel where we met." He stopped talking as memories of that day flooded his head— her tears, how small and vulnerable she'd seemed to him then. He hadn't recognized her that day. But now her face, etched in his heart as if carved into stone, was more familiar to him than the backs of his hands. When he became old and gray, he might forget his own name but he wouldn't forget the shape of her eyes or the curve of her smile, the sound of her voice or the smell of her hair....

"Then I'll be sure to pack. Is there anything else you wished to discuss with me?" she asked in a voice so soft and forlorn he inched closer to hear her. The smell of cinnamon wafted to him.

"Um…" He searched for anything that would keep her here with him in the quiet of the night a few minutes longer but came up empty. "No, that was it." His mouth obeyed his head even as his heart threatened mutiny.

She stood and left the room. For a very long time, Will sat in the living room, wondering if he had done the right thing.

"God, You know best. If You want her to stay, You're gonna have to do something between now and Friday. Not that I have any right to put any limitation on You or tell You what to do, but I can't do this…. I don't know if I can let her walk out of here. Give me strength to do the right thing."

For the first time since Abby's parents' death, she didn't feel like dragging herself out of bed the next morning. She wanted to hide under the covers and pretend Will hadn't said she needed to leave on Saturday. How could she possibly tear herself away from the boys? They had been calling her Ma for the better part of the summer. It would be like cutting off her arms. She couldn't believe she had come to love them so quickly, nor so completely.

Why couldn't Will just let her stay? She didn't have to be part of the family. He didn't have to claim his husbandly rights—she understood there was something lacking in her that kept him from loving her. But if he never planned to marry again, then would it be so bad to live with a wife whom he didn't find attractive as long as she fed his family and taught his boys?

The rooster crowed for the second time and Abby forced herself up. If not for herself, she would make these last days special for the boys. Hopefully they would always remember her just as she would keep them in her heart. They were the closest she would ever come to having a family of her own. From now on, she would guard her heart. She would work whatever job God provided for her, but she wouldn't let herself love anyone again.

"Ma! Ma! Look outside! It's snowing! It's snowing!" Tommy shouted right before lunchtime, running into the kitchen at full steam. "I wanna go out and play. We can go sledding! Come on, Willy!" Tommy jumped and wiggled like a happy puppy in his excitement.

"No, not yet. It's almost lunchtime. When your pa and Jake come in, then you can ask them." Abby didn't want to make promises. She knew what to expect for a November snowstorm in Ohio but not out here in Nebraska.

"But, Ma! We just gotta—"

"Did your ma just tell you no to something?" Will's voice caught them both up short. He stood just inside the kitchen door with an armload of wood for the wood box.

"Yes, sir," Tommy answered, his head down. This was not the first time they had had this discussion.

"Then I expect you not to argue. Understood?" Will's eyes glued his small son to the spot until Tommy nodded.

"I'm sorry, Ma," he mumbled, glancing up at her and then away.

"It's okay to be excited about the snow, Tommy. You just need to get your father's permission before I can let you go out," she reassured him, pulling the boy into her arms and squeezing him close.

"Your ma's right," Will said, surprising Abby with his use of the title. He usually referred to her as "Auntie Abby" even though the boys had long since adopted "Ma." "I'm going to go get the cattle in from the south pasture right after lunch. I don't want you boys out there until I get back. The wind feels right for a whiteout."

"Aww, Pa. But I want to go sledding," Tommy whined.

"I think we'll have more than enough snow and winter to get you out sledding at least once or twice before spring comes," Will reassured Tommy, finally glancing at Abby and sending her a wink.

She almost dropped the dishes she was carrying to the table. He hadn't winked at her since the first month she was there—before they had been forced to marry. Could his returning jovial attitude be attributed to her leaving come Saturday? The thought brought unexpected tears to her eyes and she turned back to the stove in order to disguise her distress. How could he look forward to her departure while she dreaded it worse than the hangman's noose?

Somehow, Abby managed to keep from rushing out

of the room during lunch. She even pretended to pay attention to Tommy's detailed stories of sledding in years past. Willy interrupted more than once to correct his little brother. Will kept sending her puzzled looks, but as soon as they finished lunch he headed out with Jake to bring in the straggling herd.

With dinner already made, she cleaned and dusted all the rooms upstairs, including Will's. She normally didn't go in there since it made her feel as if she was trespassing on his private sanctuary, but today she had wanted to make sure that the house was perfect when she left. His clothes and room had his lingering scent and it calmed her nerves about the snow. She could barely see across the barnyard to the outline of the barn. Abby returned to the kitchen and began to pace. They had been out for more than three hours. Where were they? Wasn't it past time for them to have returned?

She had been watching the snow come down harder and the wind howling at the windows and the chimney. What little dim light there had been during the day was now fading to darkness, and her worry grew exponentially. Were Will and Jake still out in one of the fields or had they both gone into the barn? She wanted to believe they were snug and warm with the cows in the sturdy building, but her fears whispered that they were trapped out in the snow.

"I'm sorry, Lord. I just don't want anything to happen to him… I mean them," she amended for the hundredth time. "What would I do without Will? What would happen to the boys? God, You know what they've already suffered. Don't take their father, as well. Or their cousin."

"Why are you out here again, Ma?" Tommy stood watching her from the doorway.

"I'm…um… I was just checking on dinner."

"It smells just fine. I want you to read another story to me. The one about the little boys."

With one more look over her shoulder toward the back door, Abby forced her trembling legs to carry her back to the living room with the boys. She sat and read for the better part of an hour but couldn't remember any of it. Even as she read, her ears were cocked, listening for any sound that would alert her to Will or Jake coming into the kitchen. She set the book down and had read three pages of the next one when the back door opened.

She was off the couch, almost upending Tommy in the process, and was halfway into the kitchen, before either boy could react. "Hello?"

Jake stood just inside the kitchen door, his coat covered in a layer of snow and ice. He took his hat off and even his hair underneath was wet from the thick snow. "It's miserable out there. That wind could freeze a man solid!" he exclaimed as he pulled his boots off.

"Where is your uncle?" Abby rushed to the stove, pulling the hot water forward to boil once more.

"He went out to find the last cow. Foolish heifer. Gerty never comes when we call her. She'll freeze out there, but will she follow the others to the shelter of the barn? No, she needs a special invitation. Uncle Will said to get the others in and bedded down for the night while he went out looking for her." Jake stepped out of his snowy boots and handed her the bucket of fresh milk.

"Could he be lost? How long has he been out there? What if—"

"Abby, Uncle Will knows this land better than anyone. He saw Gerty up on the north side of the pasture but wanted to get the rest in so if he had to coax her, he wouldn't have to do the same for all the others. Cattle can be some of the dumbest animals, but when they want treats, it's amazing how they learn to beg." Jake hung his coat and hat in the cellar stairway, letting the water drip onto the earthen floor beneath instead of Abby's clean kitchen floor.

"Are you sure your uncle's all right out there? Maybe we should go out and look for him." She handed Jake his mug of spiced tea and crossed over to the window, peering out into the fading day.

"He'll be in pretty soon. It's milking time for Gerty and she'll come along easily if he offers those sugar cubes he has. The rest of the chores are done. Don't worry, Abby. He'll be fine. I'm going up to change."

Abby stood in the kitchen waiting for what felt like an eternity, but Will still didn't come in. Too frantic to stay inside any longer, she pulled on her boots and long winter coat, hat and gloves. She trudged out, fighting the wind that whipped through her clothes as if she were dressed in her summer dress. How cold must Will be by now? He'd been out for hours. What if he had gotten hurt?

She would only check the barn, hoping he was there. She knew better than to stray too far from the house in this weather. Everything seemed to look the same with the snow and wind in her face. At the barn door, she had to shove with all her might to get the big wooden beam out of its place to open the door. Stepping inside, she realized that if the door was closed from the outside Will couldn't have possibly been inside. Logic told her she should turn around and go back to the house, but the peace and relative warmth of the barn drew her in. Pulling the big door closed behind her, she ventured in, never having been inside in all the time she had been on the farm. While Will and Jake slept out here, Abby felt as if it was their private domain and she had chosen not to trespass. Now that she was out there, she wondered what she might find, even in the muted light.

Honestly, large animals spooked her. She liked the horses Will owned, but even those she preferred to see from afar, up atop the wagon on the way to church. In the dusky light of the barn something moved toward her. As her eyes adjusted to the scarce light, she saw that the cows weren't in stalls but were all around her and one was behind her, about to bite her. It nibbled at her hat and its tongue, moist and rough like sandpaper, scratched her neck. Shrieking, she fled to the ladder in the middle of the aisle. Tripping over her skirt, she battled her way up the ladder as if she were being pursued by a band of warrior braves. Only once she was up in the hay loft did she turn to see the cow happily munching on her hat, the scamp.

Afraid to come down for fear of the large animals, she sat on the edge of the loft and wondered how she could get out of this mess she had made. She should have at least told the boys where she was going. What if Will came in before she was able to get back down? He'd have all the right in the world to say that she was not suited to be a farmer's wife, and send her back on the next train just as he wanted to.

Pushing back from the edge of the loft, she looked around. It was full of hay for the winter, but there was a pallet still set out in the far corner with a pillow and a blanket. She sat down and plumped up the pillow. The now familiar smells of livestock, hay and Will wafted up to tease her nose as well as a crinkling sound that puzzled her. She lifted the pillow up completely. There were letters under the pillow. Her letters, all addressed to F. W. Hopkins. They were creased and worn at the edges as if someone had read and reread them. Why would Will have them here? Had he been trying to find a reason in the letters to send her packing earlier?

Thud! Something hit the door of the barn, causing her to jump and scatter the letters. She collected them again and hid them back under the pillows. Determined not to let the bovines get the best of her, she prayed for courage and breathed deeply. If the boys could come and play in the barn with all the animals and show no fear, then so could she. Armed with a false sense of valor, she pulled her skirts up above her knees, glad no one was around to see her folly, and then she struggled down the ladder.

Thankfully, the cattle were happy to ignore her. They all seemed to be more interested in a trough of oats. Strange, it hadn't seemed to be that full before.

Abby sighed with relief as she made contact with the door, sure she would escape safely now, except the door wouldn't budge. It was as if she were pushing on a solid wall. Had the snow drifted against it so quickly? Panicking, she shoved harder, again and again, until her foot slipped on something slippery and smelly. Crying, she pushed off the floor and once again made her way to the ladder.

For the first time since entering into the barn, she heard the wind howling outside and shivered. It was much warmer in the barn than out in the weather, but it was still cold. The heat from the animals helped, but she couldn't start a fire or the whole barn might burn down. What if she had to stay the night out there? She crawled back to Will's pallet and wrapped his blanket around her shoulders. It would keep her a little warmer while she thought of another way to get out.

Will pushed the kitchen door closed with his boot and dropped the last load of wood into the wood box. He'd brought in enough to hopefully last for days if need be. If it were up to him, he wouldn't be going out into the wind again until chore time tomorrow. What he really wanted was a nice cup of Abby's hot tea and her sweet smile to warm him all the way to his frozen toes. He'd asked God to intervene and keep him from sending Abby away and it had snowed. Maybe God had a message here.

Strange, the kitchen remained quiet and Abby hadn't appeared as she normally did every time the door opened. Dinner was on the stove and the water was boiling, but there was no sign of his wife.... His wife. Could he really ask her to stay? Would she be willing? After the snowfall today, maybe she would see the dangers of the prairie and change her mind. But he had to at least try.

Footsteps sounded on the stairs and he peeled his gloves off quickly, shedding his coat and hanging it in the stairwell to the cellar as he crossed the kitchen to greet Abby, except it was Jake who descended the stairs.

"So you finally came out of the cold." Jake chuckled. "I bet Abby's glad to see you're safe."

"I haven't seen Abby yet. Is she upstairs?" From the doorway he could see the boys were playing blocks on the front-room floor, but Abby wasn't with them.

"No, she's not upstairs. She was in the kitchen when I came in. And she was powerful worried about you." Jake grinned, like the Cheshire cat.

"Well, maybe she's down in the cellar. I'll go look." Will had turned around and was headed back to the cellar when he remembered what he had wanted to talk to Jake about. "Jake, next time you go out to the barn, especially in this cold, remember to shut it up well."

"I did. I made sure the doors were secure before I came in."

"Then why did I find Gerty back in the yard while I was bringing in more firewood?"

"I don't know. I haven't gone back out since I came in an hour—" But Will didn't wait for Jake to finish.

"Boys, have either of you seen your mother?" His voice must have conveyed urgency because both boys popped up from the floor and looked at him strangely.

"She put on her coat and hat after Jake went upstairs. Then we heard the door open and close a whole bunch of times. I think she was bringing in firewood," Willy reported.

"Maybe she went to go sledding," Tommy volunteered, blissfully unaware of the dangers of being out too long in a storm.

"I brought in the firewood," Will said, "and I didn't see her at all. Jake, go check back upstairs. Boys, I want you to stay here. I'm going to go back out to the barn. Jake, did she say anything to you? Did you tell her where I was?"

"I told her you were looking for Gerty but not to worry because you'd be in in a little while. Do you want me to go out to the pasture?"

"No. I'll check the barn first. Then, if she's not there,

we'll go looking. But look for her inside first. And pray, boys. Pray that she's safe and out of the storm."

His heart pounding as if it were going to explode at any time, he retraced his steps through the kitchen, not even bothering to button his coat correctly and pulling his new knitted cap, compliments of his missing wife, haphazardly over his head. His fingers were still numb from being out so long, but he shoved his wet gloves back on his hands as he rushed across the slippery barnyard.

Just as he had left it, the barn door was shut from the outside. He hefted the beam and set it on the ground. Pulling the door open, he peered into the darkness of the warm barn. Only the moos of the cows greeted him. He lit a lantern and hung it from its peg. "Abby! Abby, are you here?" he yelled out, knowing the panic in his voice betrayed his feelings more than anything else. Rustling above him over by his pallet drew his attention to the loft.

"Will!" Her voice floated down to him above the din of the animals. "Are you all right?"

He pulled the barn door closed behind him, latching it from the inside this time, and raced over to the ladder as if the barn were on fire. He wanted to shake her silly for scaring him so bad but then he wanted to kiss her silly in relief. He was halfway up the ladder when her face peered out over the edge.

"Are you all right?" they both asked at the same time. She giggled and then sat back as he reached the top rung, putting him eye level with her.

"What are you doing out here?" he demanded, out of breath from his climb.

"I... I was worried about you and wanted to make

sure you were okay. I couldn't stay inside any longer and came out, hoping you were in here. Then one of the cows tried to eat my hat and I got scared and climbed up here. When I came back down, the door was stuck and I couldn't go back to the house. I'm sorry. You're probably cold and hungry and here I am—like such a fool—making you come back out in the cold and worrying you...." He could see her shaking and wanted to hold her tight, to promise her she would never be frightened again.

"Shush, don't worry, Abby. I'm so glad you're all right. You are all right, aren't you?" He pulled off his glove and caressed her cheek. Even with numb fingers, he felt her warm, silky skin and the moisture of fresh tears. She nodded, looking down below them instead of into his eyes. He'd do anything for this woman. If she couldn't be happy on the prairie, he'd leave. They could find somewhere else to live, he didn't care where, as long as they could be together.

"Don't worry about anything. We'll move South, where there aren't any snowstorms to scare you. I can sell the land or maybe leave Colin to sell it and take what we have. Texas is always warm, they say. We can start over. It won't be as nice right away and we'll have to work hard, but—"

"What are you talking about?" Abby stared at him as if he were out of his mind. He grinned. How foolish it must have sounded.

"When you weren't inside the house and I knew you could be out in the storm, I was so scared. I had promised to take care of you, protect you. You could have been hurt or worse...." He couldn't force himself to even finish the thought. "I realized no piece of land is worth losing you, Abby. I want a real marriage, and I'll do whatever it takes to prove to you that we can make it work. If you want me to move back to Philly, I'll do it. I'm just sorry I held you at arm's length for so long." He drew a ragged breath, wondering if it was already too late for them.

"But I don't want to leave here! I don't know why you think I do. I love the prairie that goes on and on forever. I know it's a dangerous place, but God is just as able to keep me safe here as He is in Philly or in Texas."

"You don't want to leave here?" Will asked, afraid to hope.

"No, I don't want to leave you, or the boys or the farm. I have come to love you all. This is my home, my family. I—"

"You still want to stay with us? Even now that you've seen how the winter storms can be? And this is just the start. There will be more storms."

"Yes. I want to stay." Abby nodded but turned away.

Joy exploded in Will's chest, squeezing the breath from his lungs. She wanted to stay. She wanted to stay! Had she really said she loved him? Or just his family? It didn't matter. He could be patient. He'd learn to court her. He'd bring her flowers and tell her how lovely she was to him. Why had he waited so long?

"I know that you didn't want a wife either time you married and I…" She swallowed and he saw her struggle with some hidden emotion. "I don't understand the way it is between a husband and his wife. I guess I was too young when I lost my own parents and my sister never took the time, not that her marriage was a good model. Anyway, I guess I never will be a woman to attract a man's attention in that way, but—"

"Abby, sweet, beautiful, darling Abby," he whispered, his finger having silenced her ramblings, relishing the feel of her sweet breath across his fingertips. "There is nothing lacking in you. You had my attention from the day you fell into my arms at the train station."

"I—I did? But I—"

"Shush. Yes, you did. I did everything I could to keep from showing you how I felt because I thought you needed to move back East. I thought… I was a fool. Jake and Colin both told me, but I didn't listen to them. I didn't believe you could come to love us enough to want to stay. I do love you, Abby. I've loved you for a long time. That's why I wanted you to go, so you would be safe, not because I didn't care for you or want to be married to you. It was tearing my heart out to even think about letting you go."

Her bright eyes turned up to meet his, glinting in the semidarkness of the barn, the lantern he had hung down below sparkling off the green-blue specks in her eyes. Eyes filled with wonder and tears. "You—" she swallowed hard, staring at him "—you said you love me?"

"Yes, ma'am, Mrs. Hopkins. I love you." His fingers smoothed over her cheek, tucking her hair back behind her ear. She shuddered, whether it was from his touch or the cold he wasn't sure. "I'm a fool for not telling you or showing you before. I'll try and make up for that."

He grinned, wondering at how the cold and wind seemed to be in another time and place. Even his throbbing fingers as they thawed out didn't bother him nearly as much as they normally did. He needed to get her back to the house, back into the warmth of the kitchen and to the rest of their family so they could stop worrying, but he didn't want to spoil the moment.

"I love you, too," she whispered softly, her eyes closed, her face turned away. "I want to be your wife." Her voice almost inaudible.

"Do you, Abby?" Will asked, hoping she knew what she was saying. His fingers pulled her face back toward him. "Do you really want to be my wife? To live your life here, with me? To let me love you like a man loves his wife?" He held his breath for her response.

Instead of words, she nodded. Unable to keep her at arm's length anymore, he surged up over the lip of the loft and unceremoniously sat on the floor next to her. Without warning, he slid his hands once again over the softness of her cheeks and into her silky hair. Then he guided her lips to his own. Gently at first; he didn't want to scare her. She was precious to him. So precious he wanted to treat her like fine china. He let his kiss confirm his declaration of love for her. She might not understand how much she moved him or how much he had come to love her yet, but he was bound and determined to show her. It might take years, but someday she would know.

Finally, his lungs burned for lack of air and he knew he needed to give her a chance to catch up, to tell him to back off if she wanted to. He pulled his head back slightly, his arms around her shoulders, holding her to his heart, right where she belonged. He breathed in the scent of her hair and felt her shudder as he buried his face in the curve of her neck.

"Abby, we need to get back to the house. You're gonna catch cold out here and the boys have got to be worried by now." He sat up slowly. "Now, how did you get up this ladder in those skirts?" he wondered out loud as he started back down.

Instead of answering, she blushed. He grinned at her sweet innocence. "Here, let me help you." He showed her how to sit on the edge and find her footing as she turned. He let his body serve to protect her as they backed down the ladder, her back to his chest, his arms around her. A foreshadowing of how he would protect her in any way he could from now on. Once on the floor, he stepped back and waited for her to turn away from the ladder, right into his arms.

"Oh, I'm sorry—"

He stopped her apology midsentence with a kiss. Good thing Gerty started nibbling at his hat or he might have kept Abby there for a long time. Placing a final kiss on her nose, he sighed as he turned her around. "Let's go see what your boys are up to, Mrs. Hopkins."

Tucking her under his arm, he led her out of the barn, stopping only to put out the lantern and to bar the door. As they entered the kitchen, both boys raced up and tugged on her, pulling off her gloves and peppering her with questions.

"Did you get lost?"

"Did you go sledding?"

"Are you all right?"

"When are we going to eat dinner? I'm hungry."

Laughing, she smiled down at them. "One thing at a time, boys. I went out to the barn and couldn't get back right away. We'll eat as soon as I can get the table set and the food out of the oven. Go wash up while I get out of my coat."

Jake stood by the table, grinning from ear to ear. When Will looked at his nephew, the boy had the audacity to wink and nod as if in approval. "Auntie Abby, is there anything I can do to help?"

"You never call her 'auntie,' just Abby," Tommy corrected.

"Well, she's my uncle's wife now, so she's my auntie, as well, I figure." Jake smiled at her surprise and stared to set the table.

Abby's eyes shone with happiness as she rushed around getting dinner on the table. Will watched her from a corner of the kitchen, a cup of tea warming his hands, and felt his heart expand with love for this beautiful housekeeper who came to keep his house and ended up capturing his heart.

Epilogue

Six months later

As soon as Will walked into the kitchen, Abby snatched the telegram from his hand and tore into it. He inhaled the fresh scent of his wife as he circled her small waist with his big arms. Pillowing his chin on her head, he gazed out to the barnyard from the kitchen window. He had gone over to Colin's homestead early in the morning to help Colin clear a field, and Colin had given him the telegram that had come to the church the day before. It was almost dusk and there were chores to do, but for just a moment, he held his wife close. Spring was forcing its way into their beloved prairie. Snow was melting, leaving puddles of mud and slush everywhere. But there was a promise of new things as green shoots started to push out of the frozen ground.

Ma and Pa had sent word that they planned to come out for a visit later in the summer. His poor, sweet wife had been in a flutter for days after the letter arrived. Abby foolishly worried they wouldn't like her. If only she knew how much they already loved her.

"Um, Will?"

"Yes, sweetheart?" he answered absentmindedly, his thoughts still on her meeting his parents.

"Remember about how I talked with you about an addition?" she asked, her voice sounding pinched.

They had lain in bed one night last week, talking about how they could expand the house if they added to their family. It was Abby's desire to have more children and Will couldn't have been more pleased. He wondered if there would be time to put a full addition on before his folks arrived with all the work that it took to get the fields planted. But they hadn't come to any decisions, except one. He and Jake had finally opened the door to Mathew and MaryAnn's room after so many years. Abby had cleaned it and Will suspected she was sewing a quilt to put on the bed for when his parents arrived. If they already had a room for his parents, why would she be talking again of expansion so soon unless…?

"Yesterday you said that you weren't…" he started, spinning her in his arms, his hand going to her flat belly, expecting to see her eyes alight with joy. Instead she looked worried.

"It's not that. The telegram is from my niece, Megan. She said she'll be arriving April fifth with her sisters and brothers for a visit."

Will studied Abby and then pulled her closer to the table, sitting on the closest chair and tugging her on to his lap. "So why the worried look?" he whispered against her ear. She shivered and he sensed she needed his reassurance.

"It's just that your parents are coming in a couple of months and I wanted to have everything ready for them.

Now, what are they going to think about your wife who comes and brings all her family along, as well?"

"They'll love her all the more when they see how good she has been to their son and grandsons. Don't worry about the space. We'll figure something out. How many kids are there anyway?"

"There's Megan, Hanna, Peter, Harold and Katie." She leaned back into his arms and he smoothed his thumb over her elbow.

"We can have the boys sleep together and the girls can share Jake's room. He can take the parlor. My folks can still have Mathew and MaryAnn's room. See, honey, it'll all work out." He brushed a kiss on her forehead.

"Will." She sat up a little straighter. "Today is the third."

"That means they'll arrive the day after tomorrow. I'll go get them," he promised, wishing he could do more to reassure Abby.

"Thank you, Will." She ran her fingers over his rough cheek, sending a shiver down his back. "I think God's blessed me so much more than He's blessed you. He gave me an instant prairie family." She punctuated her statement with a kiss, but before he could return the favor, small footsteps thundered into the room.

"Ma, I'm hungry. You ever gonna stop smooching with Pa and make dinner?" Tommy demanded, pulling at her arm.

"I think you're just jealous," she teased with a glint in her eyes. "Come here and I'll kiss you, too!" To which Tommy ran shrieking, only to collapse in a puddle of giggles when Abby caught him in the living room and peppered his face with butterfly kisses.

"Young man, you'd better be nice to my wife. You

hear?" Will pretended to be stern, masking his smile behind his hand.

"You can have her. I don't like yuckie slobbery kisses. Uck!" Tommy yelled just before he broke out in a gale of giggles again.

"I'm gonna go see about my chores, Abby," Will announced from the doorway to the front room, smiling at his wife and son playing so contentedly.

"Hurry back, dinner's almost ready." Abby came into the room and stole another kiss from him, one he forfeited gladly. "I love you, Mr. Hopkins."

How could he have possibly thought he could let her walk away? "I love you too, Mrs. Hopkins."

* * * * *

Florida author **Louise M. Gouge** writes historical fiction for Harlequin's Love Inspired Historical line. She received the prestigious Inspirational Reader's Choice Award in 2005 and placed in 2011 and 2015; she also placed in the Laurel Wreath contest in 2012. When she isn't writing, she and her husband, David, enjoy visiting historical sites and museums. Please visit her website at louisemgougeauthor.blogspot.com.

Books by Louise M. Gouge

Love Inspired Historical

Four Stones Ranch

Cowboy to the Rescue
Cowboy Seeks a Bride
Cowgirl for Keeps
Cowgirl Under the Mistletoe
Cowboy Homecoming
Cowboy Lawman's Christmas Reunion

Lone Star Cowboy League: The Founding Years

A Family for the Rancher

Ladies in Waiting

A Proper Companion
A Suitable Wife
A Lady of Quality

Visit the Author Profile page
at Harlequin.com for more titles.

COWBOY
TO THE RESCUE

Louise M. Gouge

Except the Lord build the house
they labor in vain that build it.
—*Psalms* 127:1

This book is dedicated to the intrepid pioneers
who settled the San Luis Valley of Colorado
in the mid- to late 1800s. They could not have found
a more beautiful place to make their homes than in
this vast 7500 ft. high valley situated between the
majestic Sangre de Cristo and San Juan Mountain
ranges. It has been many years since I lived in the
San Luis Valley, so my thanks go to Pam Williams of
Hooper, Colorado, for her extensive on-site research
on my behalf. With their permission, I named two
of my characters after her and her husband, Charlie.
These dear old friends are every bit as kind and wise
as their namesakes. I also must thank my
dear husband of forty-nine years, David Gouge
(a U.S. Army veteran), for his help in character
development, especially for my military characters.

Chapter One

June 1878

Daddy wouldn't make it through another bitter-cold night. Susanna wasn't even sure how she'd managed not to freeze to death on this Colorado mountainside over the past ten or so hours. Maybe her anger had kept her alive, a real rage like some folks back home in Georgia still felt toward the North and all Yankees. For the first time in all her nineteen years, she understood firsthand how they felt.

The only trouble was that she had no idea whom to hate. Still, if God brought them out of this predicament, she would see to it that justice was meted out on whoever robbed Daddy, beat him almost to death and left him to die amid their scattered belongings. If Susanna hadn't been over the hill fetching water for their supper, she had no doubt those men would have done their worst to her, as well. Always the protector, Daddy had managed to tell her that when the villains had demanded to know who owned the female fripperies in the wagon, he'd told them his wife had been buried on the trail. Such a lie must have cost her truthful father dearly, but it had saved her from unknown horrors.

She placed a small log on the fire and used a poker to stir the flames she had somehow kept alive throughout the night. The sun had just begun to shed some light on La Veta Pass, so the day should soon warm up enough for her to make plans about how to get out of this mess. Daddy's fever didn't seem too high. Or maybe the cold just made his clammy skin seem cooler. No matter. She had to find a way to get them down into the San Luis Valley to a ranch house or town. One thing was sure. His silver prospecting would have to wait until he recovered.

A familiar ache smote Susanna's heart, but she quickly dismissed it. No use reminding herself or Daddy that if they hadn't left Georgia, they wouldn't be in this fix now. Oh, how she longed for her safe, comfortable home back in Marietta. All she had ever wanted was to marry a good Christian gentleman and raise a family in the hometown she loved so much, just as her parents had. Many of her friends had already married. Some had children. She couldn't think of a more satisfying life. But before Mama died last autumn, she'd made Susanna promise to take care of Daddy. She didn't regret her promise, but she was fairly certain Mama never dreamed he'd want to go prospecting out West. She'd had no choice but to pack up and go with him, deferring her own dreams for his and leaving her future to the Lord. After last night's attack, surely she would have no trouble convincing Daddy to return to their safe, happy life in Marietta.

"Belle." His raspy voice cut into Susanna's thoughts.

"No, dearest." She swallowed the lump in her throat.

Several times in the night, he'd cried out for Mama. "It's me, Susanna."

"Ah, yes. Of course." Daddy's eyes cleared and seemed to focus on her. Then he grimaced in pain and clenched his teeth. After a few moments of clutching his ribs and writhing, during which Susanna dabbed his fevered forehead with a cloth, he shuddered as if to shove away his pain. "Young lady, have you made my morning coffee yet?"

His gruff, teasing tone would have encouraged her if she didn't know the terrible extent of his injuries. The thieving monsters who had attacked him seemed not to have left an inch of his body unbeaten. She knew he had some broken bones, yet he was being brave for her, as he always was. Now she must somehow be brave for him.

"Coffee, is it? I guess I could manage that." She tucked the woolen blankets around him, then gathered her rifle and bucket. "I'll get some water and be back before you can whistle a chorus of 'Dixie.'" She waited a moment for one of his quipped responses, but his eyes were closed and his breathing labored. *Please, Lord, watch over him.*

Trudging up the small, tree-covered rise, Susanna paused to stretch and shake off the stiffness that had crept into her limbs while she'd slept on the cold ground beside Daddy with only a few blankets for cover. She hadn't been able to lift him into the prairie schooner, and she couldn't leave him alone outside.

The thieves hadn't simply stolen their horses, her favorite cast-iron pot and her silver hairbrush; they'd slashed the bedding and dumped out their flour and cornmeal in search of hidden money. Still, they'd found only the paper bills Daddy had kept in his wallet for just such encounters. Even though they'd destroyed just about everything in the wagon, the secret compartment below its floorboards remained secure, as did the gold coins sewn into her skirt. But she'd trade all that gold to be sure Daddy would survive his injuries.

Once over the small hill, she made her way down the shadowed slope to the snowy banks of the rushing creek. Imagine that, snow in June. Back home in Marietta, she reckoned folks were already feeling the summer heat.

Resting her rifle against an aspen, she anchored herself by gripping a budding green branch with one leather-gloved hand, then dipped the metal pail into the surging waters with the other. It filled in seconds, and she hoisted it back to the bank with little effort, snatched up her rifle and began her trek back to the campsite.

What would Mama think of her newfound strength, her growing muscles? Mama had always said that a lady should never be too strong or too capable when it came to physical labors. Such work was for men and servants. But these past months of crossing mountains, rivers and plains had put Susanna through trials harder than any Mama had ever faced.

The moment she thought it, she changed her mind. After all, when those wicked Yankees had gone and burned down the plantation house, Mama had risked her own life to save Susanna and her brother, Edward, Jr. After the war, she'd helped Daddy and Edward build a dry-goods business in Marietta. She'd become a respected society maven, greatly beloved because of her charitable works. Surely, all of that had been harder than walking across America as a pioneer, even considering the rattlesnakes and coyotes Susanna had encountered.

She sniffed back tears. Oh, how she missed Mama. But Mama always said dwelling on the past wouldn't help. That was how she'd managed to go on after the war. Susanna would honor her memory by having that same cheerful attitude. Surely, after Daddy got his fill of searching for silver, he would take her back home to Marietta. But he would have to recover from his beating first. She forced down the fear and doubts that assailed her. Daddy *would* recover. She would take care of him, as she'd promised Mama.

She came over the hill, and her heart seemed to stop at the sight of a man kneeling over Daddy. Had the thieves come back to make sure he was dead? She set down her pail and lifted her rifle.

"Put your hands up and move away from him." Her voice wavered, and fear hammered in her chest, so she leaned against the trunk of a giant evergreen to steady herself. "Do it now, mister, so I don't have to shoot you." She'd shot a coyote on the trail, but faced with killing a person, she wasn't sure she could do it. But this villain didn't have to know about her doubts.

Hands lifted, he stiffened and rose to his feet, turning slowly to face her. Lord, have mercy, how could a murdering thief be so well put together? Maybe twenty-three years old, he was tall and muscular and wore a broad-brimmed hat tilted back to reveal a tanned, clean-shaven complexion and pleasing features—the kind of face that always attracted the ladies and weakened their good sense. But Mama hadn't raised a fool for a daughter. Even as Susanna's knees threatened to buckle, she gritted her teeth and considered what to do next, sparing a glance at Daddy before glaring again at the stranger. If he went for that gun at his side, would she be able to shoot him first?

"Put your gun down, daughter." Daddy croaked out a laugh and paid for it with a painful grimace. "This gentleman has come to help."

Nathaniel Northam wanted to laugh, but with that Winchester cocked and pointed at him, he didn't dare make the lady mad. My, she was a cute little thing, all bundled up in a man's bulky winter coat over her brown wool dress with blond curls peeking out from her straw bonnet. That turned-up nose just about couldn't get any higher, or those puckered lips look any more prim and prissy in her brave attempt to appear menacing. The gal had spunk, that was certain. Fortunately, the old man on the ground spoke out before she took that spunk too far and shot Nate.

Should he lift his hat in greeting or stay frozen with hands uplifted until her father's words got through to her? *Lord, help me now. The Colonel will kill me if I get myself shot before I bring Mother's anniversary present home, not to mention my death would ruin that big anniversary shindig she's planning.*

"To help?" The girl blinked those big blue eyes—at least they looked blue. He couldn't quite tell with her standing up there on that shady rise. To his relief, she lowered the gun, and those puckered lips spread into a pretty smile. "Oh, thank the Lord." Before he could offer to help, she hefted her bucket and hurried down the slope. "You can't imagine how I prayed all night long that the Lord would send help." She swept past him. "And here he is." She set down her bucket with a small splash and knelt beside the old man. "Oh, Daddy, it's going to be all right now. Help has come." She didn't seem to notice the absurdity of her own words.

Daddy? Once again, Nate withheld a grin. That genteel drawl in both of their voices and her way of addressing her father marked them as Southerners, as sure as the sun did shine. Oddly, a funny little tickle in his chest gave evidence that he found everything about the young lady entirely appealing, at least at first glance. Time would tell if there was more to her than beauty and spunk. That was, if they had more time together. Seeing the state her father was in, Nate was pretty certain they would. He'd never go off and leave a wounded man in the wilderness, not when he had the means to help.

"Ma'am?" He put his hands down but didn't doff his hat because she was facing her father and the gesture would be meaningless. "Maybe we ought to get your father up off the ground."

She looked up at him as if he were a two-headed heifer. Then her eyes widened with understanding. "Oh, mercy, yes. Of course."

"Zack." Nate called to his companion. "Get over here and help me."

The short, wiry cowhand jumped down from their low, canvas-covered wagon, secured their lead horses and hurried to Nate's side. "Yeah, boss?" Zack's gray hair stuck out in spikes from beneath his hat, and Nate wished he'd made the scruffy hand clean up a bit more before they started out this morning. But then he hadn't known they'd meet a lady on the trail.

"Let's get this man into his wagon." He wouldn't ask the young miss why she hadn't moved her father there, for it was obvious a little gal like her wouldn't be able to lift him, and the man was in no condition to move himself. But at least he was resting close enough to the brown prairie schooner for it to shield him from the wind, and he had plenty of blankets around him. "Hang on a minute. Let me check inside."

Moving aside the once-white canvas covering, he struggled to calm a belly roiling with anger over what he saw. Just about everything had been destroyed, from the smashed food crocks to the shattered water barrels to the broken trunks. Only a few tools and hardware remained hanging on the outside of the wagon box. Obviously, the thieves had been searching for money and no doubt had left this little family of homesteaders penniless. A strong sense of protectiveness swept through Nate. God had sent him here and, like the Good Samaritan of Scripture, he would not refuse the assignment. If the Colonel got mad, Nate would just have to deal with him later.

He squatted beside the girl, his shoulder brushing hers, and a tiny tremor shot through him. He clamped down on such brutish sensations, which dishonored his mother and sister and all ladies. "Sir, if you'll let me, I'll divide my team, and we'll pull your wagon down to the hotel in Alamosa. They can help you there. Would that be all right?"

He'd offer to take them to Fort Garland just down the road, but a Southerner probably wouldn't like to recuperate among the Buffalo Soldiers stationed there, those soldiers being black and some of them former slaves. Nate ignored the pinch in his conscience suggesting his real motivation was to get better acquainted with this young lady.

"Obliged," the man muttered, giving him a curt nod,

but Nate took no offense. Clearly, the old fellow was in pain, and all of his responses would be brief.

"I'm Nate Northam, and this is Zack Wilson." He tilted his head toward his cowhand.

The old man's eyes widened, and his bruised jaw dropped. "Northam, you say?"

"Yessir." Nate stood up. "You know the name?" His father, referred to as the Colonel even by his friends and some of his family, had a powerful reputation from the War Between the States. Maybe this man had met him on some battlefield.

He shook his head and grimaced, almost folding into himself. "No. No. Nothing." He tried to extend his right hand, but it fell to his side. "Anders. Edward Anders."

"Well, Mr. Anders—" Nate reached down and patted the limp hand "—you just give Zack and me a few minutes, and we'll get things all fixed up." Nate didn't know how he managed to say all that without choking on the emotions welling up inside, especially with Miss Anders staring up at him as if he was some kind of hero. My, a man could get caught up in those blue eyes and that sweet smile. Those golden curls only added to her appeal. Nate cleared his throat and turned back to deal with the wagon.

Lord, what have You got me into this time?

Susanna forced her eyes away from Mr. Northam to focus on Daddy, her stomach twisting over his lie. This was so unlike Daddy. She understood why it wouldn't be wise to let these strangers know they had money, but his insistence that they make this trip across the country under an assumed name continued to disturb her. And although Daddy had denied it, she could tell the man's last name meant something to him. She wouldn't press him to tell her, at least not until they were alone and maybe when he felt better.

"Daughter, where's my coffee?" The artificial gruffness in his tone further encouraged Susanna. The earlier hopelessness he hadn't quite been able to hide seemed to have disappeared with the arrival of these good men, that and the bright sun now warming the campsite.

While she poured water into the battered tin pot and checked the fire, her own mood remained wary. Not about the men, but about Daddy's health. He always tried to put on a good front, so she would have to watch him carefully to keep him from overdoing.

"Miss?" Mr. Northam gave her an apologetic frown. "If it's coffee you're wanting, I have some in my wagon."

She eyed him as his words sank in. Of course. Their coffee had been dumped on the ground along with their other supplies. Why hadn't she realized it before? "That would be very kind of you, Mr. Northam."

"Call me Nate, please. Out here, we younger folks mostly use first names." He shrugged in an attractive way and gave her an appealing grin. "Of course, I won't assume—"

"You may call me Susanna." She could just hear Mama's disapproving gasp at her agreement to such informality, especially when it was obvious from their speech that these men were Yankees. But this was not the South, where a strict code of manners ruled the day, accompanied by a strong dose of hatred for all things Northern. She didn't doubt the people out west had a similar code, but maybe not quite as strict, as she'd noticed among the folks in the wagon train from St. Louis. Not once had she heard the war mentioned. Not once had any Southern traveler scowled at or refused to obey their Yankee wagon master, not even Daddy.

In any event, Mama had also taught her that a lady never treated other people as if she were better than they were, even if she was, for kindness never went out of fashion. Susanna hadn't yet figured out this cowboy's social status, but his older friend called him *boss,* and he had a commanding air about him, suggesting he was a landowner. Otherwise, she might have thought twice about granting him that first-name privilege. If he turned out not to be a gentleman, she could always withdraw her permission.

Nate returned from his wagon carrying a cast-iron kettle and coffeepot.

"Thank you." Susanna reached for the items, but he held them back.

"You look after your father." He gave her a brotherly wink. "I'll fix you some breakfast."

Her heart lilted into a playful mood. "Well, as I live and breathe." She shook her head in mock disbelief. "A man who cooks when there's a woman around."

"Yes, ma'am." He chuckled. "Out here, men have to learn to do a lot of things some folks call women's work." He placed the covered kettle over the fire and stirred up the flames. "Otherwise we'd starve and wear the same clothes for a month of Sundays."

In spite of herself, Susanna laughed, and it felt good clear down to her toes. For the first time since she'd returned from the creek the night before, she thought everything might indeed be all right.

"Of course," Nate continued, "you understand that the ladies sometimes have to take on men's work, too." He sent her another teasing wink. "Milking cows, plowing fields, breaking horses, that sort of thing. If you're out here to homestead, you have that to look forward to."

"Well, I never," she huffed, turning away to hide a grin. "The very idea." This was getting entirely too silly. She'd just met this man. But how could she stop when their teasing back and forth encouraged her so much? Should she tell Nate that Daddy was a prospector, not a homesteader?

Nate saved her from the dilemma. "Go look after your father." His soft tone and gentle touch on her arm made her pulse skip in an entirely different way. "I'll bring you something to eat before you know it."

Not trusting herself to answer, she went to tend Daddy, only to discover him watching the whole thing. He said nothing, and his mild expression, marred only by an occasional wince, held no censure. With his strong sense of discernment, he would warn her if her behavior was improper or if Nate did not appear to be a gentleman.

In a short while, Nate brought them each a tin cup of steaming coffee and then a tin plate of beans and bacon, with a wedge of corn bread on the side. Susanna had been eating beans all across the prairies and mountains of this wide land, but never had they tasted so good. Even Daddy grunted his approval. Susanna struggled not to eat too large a portion, but the desire to make up for missing last night's supper almost overwhelmed her. Fortunately, Mr. Northam—Nate—had busied himself dividing his team between the two wagons and had no idea how much she devoured.

In just over an hour, the horses were hitched up and ready to roll. Even the campsite had been cleaned up and the fire doused. Nate and Zack lifted Daddy into the cleaned-up schooner, and Susanna tucked him in. They made him as comfortable as possible on his canvas cot, supplementing the torn ticking and reclaimed straw with evergreen branches and providing pillows from their own bedrolls. Susanna climbed in beside him and settled back to endure the ride. In spite of the bumpy trail and an occasional groan from Daddy, she managed to drift off into a light slumber.

Once Nate's two-horse team got over the initial surprise of pulling the extra weight, they settled into a slow, steady pace. He wouldn't have tried this arrangement if they were on the east side of the mountain pass, because it took all four horses to make it up the many inclines. But the worst of the trip was over, and the valley floor was just another two hundred yards or so downhill. If all went well, they could make half of the journey today and arrive home tomorrow.

Following behind the prairie schooner, he waved away the dust it stirred up, at last resorting to tying on a kerchief over his nose and mouth. Had he made the right decision to tell Zack to drive the schooner? If he were up there right now, maybe he could learn more about Susanna and her father. But the Colonel would be angry enough over this arrangement, so Nate had chosen to drive this specially rigged wagon with its irreplaceable cargo. If anything happened to Mother's anniversary gift, he would need to take the blame, not Zack. What was he thinking? If anything went wrong, the Colonel would blame him regardless of whose fault it was.

As the morning wore on, the sun beat down on Nate's back, so he shed his light woolen jacket. A quarter mile north of the trail, the Denver and Rio Grande train sped along on its daily run, sending up a stream of black smoke that draped behind the engine like mourning crepe.

Up ahead, Susanna poked her head out the back of the schooner and honored him with a wave and a smile. He didn't fault her for her response to his teasing at the campsite, even though they'd just met and hadn't really been properly introduced. Once again, if there was a fault, it was his. From the state her father was in, he figured they both needed all the encouragement they could get. He'd always found that humor lightened a person's load. Fortunately, just like his sister, Susanna cheered up when she was teased and gave back a bit of it herself. Besides, teasing her kept his thoughts in the right place.

He wouldn't put too much into her friendly waves and smiles. After all, she was likely motivated by gratitude. Of course, that didn't keep Nate from hoping to further their acquaintance. They would arrive in Alamosa by midmorning tomorrow and there part company. Somehow he had to figure out a way to have a nice long chat with the young lady to find out whether they had any interests in common. Once he got home, the Colonel would keep him busy for the rest of the summer, and he wouldn't risk his father's anger by coming back for a visit unless he had a good enough reason.

He blew out a sigh of frustration, and his kerchief fluttered in front of his face. Thoughts of his father's controlling ways never failed to ruin his day, and humor rarely worked to cheer him up. The Colonel had it in his mind that Nate would be marrying Maisie Eberly from the ranch next to theirs as soon as she turned eighteen.

While Maisie was a nice girl, he'd never felt a desire to court her, nor had she shown any interest in him. The Colonel didn't seem to think that mattered, nor did any of Nate's other opinions.

A familiar anger stirred in his chest. One of these days he would find the courage to take a stand against his father's control, even if it meant he had to leave home and give up his share of the ranch. He didn't like the idea of leaving the land he'd worked so hard to cultivate, the community he'd helped to build, but a man could only take so much and still call himself a man. He would make his decision by mid-July, when the whole community would gather for his parents' anniversary party.

As if a boulder had come to rest inside him, setting that deadline sat heavy on his soul. But what other choice did he have?

Chapter Two

"What do you put into these beans to make them taste so good?" Taking a ladylike bite, Susanna leaned back against the wagon wheel to savor it. Nate had provided a stool for her so she didn't have to sit on the ground, making this meal all the more pleasant. With Daddy fed and taken care of, she could finally eat her own supper—beans again, but wonderfully mouthwatering.

"Now, don't go asking about my cooking, young lady." Seated on the ground, his back against a bed-roll, his long legs stretched out in front of him, Nate spoke in that teasing tone so much like her brother's. "Angela—she's our cook and housekeeper—would tan my hide if I gave away any of her secrets."

"Humph." Susanna sniffed with a bit of artificial pique. "As if I didn't have a few secret recipes of my own." Not many, but enough to impress folks back home, especially at church dinners. Like Nate's family, hers had employed a housekeeper who'd taught her some basic cooking skills, which had come in handy on this journey. But she wouldn't mention that they'd had servants, for that would reveal their financial status.

"I'm sure you have some very fine recipes." He chuckled and shoveled in another bite.

On the other side of the campfire, Zack whittled on a stick, his empty plate beside him. He stretched and yawned, then took himself off toward the horses grazing nearby.

Susanna busied herself with finishing her meal before sitting back to relax. After a long, hot afternoon of riding into the sun, they sat facing the trail they had just traversed, taking refuge on the shady side of the prairie schooner. Now as the sun went down behind them, it cast a deep purple hue over the eastern range bordering the San Luis Valley.

"What a wondrous sight," she murmured. "We have our beautiful Appalachian Mountains back home, but these are so much higher. They're truly awe-inspiring."

"They are indeed." Nate pointed his fork toward the tallest peak, which still wore a snowy white crown from last winter's snow. "That's Mount Blanca, and the whole eastern range is called Sangre de Cristo."

"Sangre de Cristo. That's Spanish, isn't it?"

"Yep. Just about every place around here has a Spanish name because Spaniards were the first Europeans to settle here." Nate's soft gaze toward the east bespoke a love of the scene. "*Sangre de Cristo* means *blood of Christ,* an allusion to that deep, rich color."

"Ah." Agreeable warmth filled her. She'd never dreamed she could enjoy the companionship of a Yankee man this way. But Nate hadn't said or done anything that was even slightly improper. "Those Spaniards were people of faith."

"At least the old *padre* who named these mountains was." He shot a curious glance her way. "And you?"

His question confused her for only a moment. "Oh, yes. My mama always said that after all the South suffered in the war, she didn't know how anyone could go on without the Lord." She instantly regretted bringing up the devastating conflict that had shaped her entire life. But Nate didn't bat an eye, so she hurried on. "I made my decision to follow Christ when I was nine years old, and He's never let me down." His understanding smile invited her to echo his question. "And you?"

"Yep, around that same age. Ten, actually." He stared off as if remembering. "When the Colonel came home safely from the war in answer to our prayers." A frown briefly creased his brow, though Susanna could not guess why. "Of course, lots of fathers came home badly wounded or didn't come home at all. But at ten, I was only concerned about my own. As time went on, praying and trusting God became as natural as breathing." He grunted out a laugh. "Now, don't get the idea I see myself as somebody special. Just the opposite, because I need the Lord's help all the time to do the right thing."

Susanna's heart warmed at his guileless confession. "I believe we all do, Nate." She'd watched Daddy's faith dip after Mama's death, but as they headed west, he seemed to grow more encouraged. Although she would never understand his urge to go digging for silver, anything that gave him a reason to live had her approval, even if she had to be dragged along on his quest. Even if she had to wait to see her own dreams come true. She supposed parents were always a mystery to their children. "Do you always call your father the Colonel?"

"Yep, just like everybody else." Nate grimaced. "If you ever meet him, you'll understand why."

"He's that intimidating?" Susanna knew many former military officers, Daddy included, but they were Southern gentlemen and never made a lady feel uncomfortable. Maybe Northern officers didn't have the same good manners. They'd certainly treated the South badly.

"You could say that." Nate stood and took her empty plate, setting both of them in a metal pail.

"I'll wash the dishes." She rose and brushed dust and twigs from her skirt.

"Nope." Nate held up a hand. "You go see to your father. Maybe you can light a lamp and read to him. I'm sure he'd like to have his mind on something other than…" He shrugged, a charming gesture that conveyed sympathy and understanding.

"Thank you. I'll do that." Tears stung Susanna's eyes, but she managed to keep her voice steady. "We've been reading Charles Dickens's *Bleak House* on our journey. Fortunately, those thieves weren't interested in stealing books. I'm sure hearing another chapter will take his mind off his pain." How kind and thoughtful this man was. Not at all like the Yankee carpetbaggers she'd learned to distrust and avoid. But she quickly shut the door on the warm feelings trying to invade her heart. Mama would turn over in her grave if Susanna even considered finding a Yankee attractive.

"*Bleak House*. That's a good book. My folks sent me back east for a year at Harvard, and that's where I first read Dickens's works."

So Nate had an education and liked to read good books. Now she had something to discuss with him, something that would keep her thoughts off how handsome he was.

She climbed into the back of the wagon to find Daddy staring at her with a slight grin on his dear bruised face.

Heat flooded her cheeks. Had he been listening through the canvas to her conversation with Nate? She searched her memory for anything that might have sounded improper but came up with a clear conscience. Why had she worried? Probably because Nate was a Yankee, and Daddy had always said nothing good ever came out of any Yankee. But here he lay with more mischief than censure in his eyes.

"What are you up to?" She would get the upper hand before he could say anything.

He chuckled, then coughed, then grimaced and groaned.

"Oh, dearest, don't laugh." She knelt beside him. "Zack said you probably have some broken ribs and should try not to laugh or cough." She eased him up and gave him a drink of water from a canteen. "Would you like for me to read to you?"

He gave a brief nod. "First take this." He handed her a wrinkled, sealed envelope from the broken remnants of their traveling desk.

"What on earth?" She accepted it only to discover its unusual weight. "Is this one of our gold pieces in here?"

"Shh." He gently clasped her free hand and whispered, "Tomorrow when we reach that hotel, slip this to the manager—before Northam speaks to him, if you can. And don't say anything about it to these cowboys."

"What?" Her mind could conceive of no sensible reason for Daddy's request.

"Shh!" He glanced toward the back opening of the wagon. "Just do as I ask, daughter." He patted her hand. "Will you?"

Susanna swallowed hard. In all her born days, she'd never seen Daddy do anything dishonest. Back home in the dry-goods store, he'd always taken a loss rather than offend a customer. Surely, she could obey this simple order. "Yes, sir, I will."

But an odd foreboding crept into her heart and kept her awake far into the night.

After breakfast the next morning, Nate and Zack hitched up the teams and prepared to head out. As he had several times a day since leaving Pueblo, Nate checked the cargo in his wagon, lifting a silent prayer that they could get it home without any difficulty. So far they'd managed, but they still had the river to cross.

He'd just replaced the canvas cover when Susanna approached and stared up at him with those pretty blue eyes. Without her coat, she appeared much thinner, the mark of most people who had crossed the prairies. This little gal could use a regular diet of steak and potatoes so she could put some meat on those bones.

"Would it be rude of me to ask what's in your wagon?"

He couldn't imagine thinking she was rude. Nor could he imagine denying her any request. He loosened the ropes but paused before lifting the canvas covering. "Can you keep a secret?"

"Pretty much."

Her impish grin tickled his insides and made him chuckle. *Whoa.* He really needed to get a handle on these wayward feelings. "Well…" He drawled out the word. "I guess I'll trust you, anyway." He pulled the canvas back a few feet to reveal one of the four crates. "It's a gift for my mother. My folks will be celebrating their twenty-fifth wedding anniversary, and the whole community plans to take part in the festivities." Tucked around and between the crates were supplies that he'd bought to divert Mother's attention from the real purpose of his trip. "If the Colonel has any say about it, it'll be the biggest party ever given in the San Luis Valley."

Instead of being impressed, Susanna pursed her plump lips into a silly pout. "You're giving her wooden boxes?" She slid him a sideways glance. "Now, you know I'm going to ask what's inside them."

He laughed out loud. "All right, then, Miss Curious." For the first time in his life, he understood how Samson must have felt when Delilah kept wheedling him to learn the secret of his strength. "It's china. The Colonel had it imported from England." Imagining the joy Mother would feel when she received it come July, Nate felt a kick of anticipation. "Wedgwood," he added for effect, though why he was trying to impress Susanna, he didn't know. "Of course, Mother thinks her present is the new addition to the house."

The wonderment brightening her pretty face gave him the answer, for he had a hard time tamping down the strong urge to give her whatever she wanted. What was wrong with him? They'd just met yesterday. He didn't really know all that much about her. All he knew was that no other lady had ever affected him this way. Certainly not Maisie, who was more like a sister than someone he wanted to court. Not that he wanted to court Susanna, either. Until he settled some serious matters within himself, he couldn't in good conscience court anyone.

"Wedgwood china all the way from England." She breathed out the words in an awe-filled tone, and her blue eyes rounded with unabashed curiosity. "How on earth did you get it here?"

"Let me see, now. Across an ocean." He held up his hands and ticked off on his fingers the legs of the journey this valuable cargo had taken. "Around through the Gulf, up the Mississippi, then the Missouri River to Westport, Kansas. A freight company hauled it over the Santa Fe Trail to Pueblo. They were accompanied by replacement soldiers headed to New Mexico, courtesy of the Colonel's old army friends, so they arrived without incident." He paused to take a breath and to consider whether or not to tell her everything. She probably didn't need to know that the freight drivers had unloaded the cargo at the fort and had taken off for the gold fields outside Denver. Their desertion had meant the Colonel had to send Nate to bring the china home. It also heightened his father's already deep hatred of prospectors.

"And you met them in Pueblo." Susanna grasped the important parts of the story, meaning he didn't have to include the unpleasant side. "Well, Mr. Nate Northam, it remains to be seen whether your Colonel has that intimidating presence we spoke of last night, but I already like him for going to so much trouble to get his wife such a fine gift as this." Her approving smile further melted Nate's insides. "Tell me, how do you keep it from breaking?" She raised herself up on tiptoes and peered down into the wagon bed. "I see. The boxes are suspended on rope webbing." She reached in and pressed down on the ropes, testing their flexibility. "That must keep them from bouncing around as the wagon goes over bumps." She gave him another admiring glance. "Why, Mr. Northam, how extremely clever of you."

Nate lifted his chin and returned a playful smirk. "Clever indeed, if I do say so myself." Even the Colonel had been impressed by his invention. In truth, he'd given a nod and a grunt, the nearest thing to praise he ever dished out to Nate.

"No more compliments for you." She waggled a finger at him and clucked like a scolding schoolmarm. "Pride *goeth* before destruction, and a haughty spirit before a fall."

"Ouch. Guess I'd better repent of my pride." He shuddered comically. "We aren't safely home yet, and I sure don't want any destruction to fall on Mother's china."

Sobering, she touched his hand, sending a pleasant spark up his arm. "I believe God cares about these things, Nate, so I'll be praying all goes well for the rest of your journey."

That promise refocused his emotions, and he placed a hand over hers. "I'll pray the same for you, Susanna. Seems to me you've already had enough things go wrong."

Her eyes brightened with moisture, and his heart warmed. He was doing the right thing to help her and her father, of that he felt certain.

Within two hours, they met their first test of those prayers when they reached the banks of the Rio Grande. Alamosa lay just across the shallow but rapidly flowing river, causing a mixture of emotions in Nate's chest. Soon he would have to say goodbye to Susanna and her father, but first they all had to get across the wide waters. Both would be challenges.

"I don't know, boss." Zack gripped the reins to keep the restless horses from bolting into the water or shying away from it. "Looks like we might need help."

"Maybe." Standing beside the prairie schooner, Nate surveyed the scene. "Let's use all four horses to get this wagon across. Then we can bring them back across for mine." He didn't like the idea of leaving the china unguarded, even though the other wagon would be in view at all times. But they had no choice.

"Can I help with anything?" Susanna poked her head through the front opening of the schooner and peered over Zack's shoulder at Nate. Her gaze dropped to the river, and her eyes widened. "Oh, my. That must be the Rio Grande River. Not quite the Mississippi, but no easy crossing, I'd guess."

"No, ma'am. It's a good forty feet across these days because of runoff from the mountains." Nate hated to think of the punishing ride her father would have if they took the usual mode of getting to the other side. "How is Mr. Anders doing?"

She disappeared behind the canvas for a moment, then reappeared. "He says not to mind him, just do whatever you have to do." Her usually smooth forehead was creased with concern.

"What do you think?" He could at least give her a chance to decide.

"Do whatever you must." A steely look narrowed her eyes and tightened her jaw. "That's what our wagon master said more than once on the trip out here."

Her courage continued to impress him. Leaving her behind would be all the more difficult in a couple of hours. Maybe he could make it easier with more teasing. "By the way, it's just Rio Grande."

"I beg your pardon?" Her cute little grin appeared.

"You said Rio Grande *River.* That's like saying Big River River."

She laughed in her musical, ladylike way. "Spanish, of course."

"Yep." He could see her mood growing lighter. "And if you really want to get it right, it's Rio Grande del Norte." He used his best Spanish inflections, as Angela had taught him. "Great River of the North."

Susanna put the back of one hand against her forehead in a dramatic pose. "Mercy, mercy. How can little ol' me evah learn all of that?" Her sweet drawl oozed over him like warm honey.

"Poor little thing." He clicked his tongue and shook his head. "I have no idea."

Zack coughed softly, shaking Nate loose from his foolish teasing.

"All right. Let's get this done."

He drove his wagon into the shade of some cottonwoods, then unhitched the two horses and joined them to the team in front of the schooner. Like old friends glad to be together again, the horses nickered and tossed their heads as much as their harnesses permitted.

Nate considered carrying Mr. Anders across the water on foot, but it wouldn't do for the old man to get wet, even in this hot weather. Instead, he instructed Susanna to cushion her father as best she could, then brace him for the crossing.

Taking the reins himself, with Zack beside him to help as needed, he circled the schooner around and away from the water to give the horses a running start. Then he slapped the reins and cried, "Hyah!"

His team didn't let him down. They gamely leaped into their harnesses, built up speed and plunged into the water, their momentum more than matching the current as they angled downriver to conquer the forty-foot expanse. The water covered the wagon's axles but did not breach the box. With a final lunge, the lead horses emerged from the river, then the second pair, at last pulling the wagon onto dry, solid ground. All four animals shook their manes and whinnied almost as if they'd enjoyed the bath.

But Nate had felt every rock and tree branch submerged under the water's surface; he'd heard every clatter of the contents of the prairie schooner, along with a yip or two from Susanna and her father. Now to go back and get his wagon. The prospect made his chest tighten with trepidation.

He'd conveyed Mother's china this far without mishap, but the Great River of the North might just put an end to that. He found it impossible to please the Colonel with his good, hard work, so there was no telling what his father would do if Nate let the china get damaged.

Chapter Three

Susanna's pulse finally slowed enough for her to step down from the prairie schooner. Before climbing out, she checked on Daddy, only to find he'd fared better on the crossing than she had because of the thick padding Nate had put in his bed. Shaking out her wobbly legs, she approached Nate and Zack, who were unhitching the horses so they could go back across for Nate's wagon.

A sudden protectiveness for Mrs. Northam's anniversary gift stirred within her. No matter that she'd never met the lady. If she'd reared this kind gentleman, Susanna already liked her.

"Surely, you don't plan to bring the china across the river that same way." She posted her fists at her waist for emphasis. "Every plate and cup and bowl will be broken." Maybe there was even some crystal glassware in the crates, and that most certainly would not survive no matter how well it was nestled into the straw packing.

Nate shoved his hat back, revealing the tan line on his forehead and giving him a charmingly boyish appearance. He looked down his straight, narrow nose at her. "I suppose you think I haven't thought of that." His tone held a hint of annoyance, but his green eyes held their usual teasing glint. "You have a better idea, Miss Smarty?"

"Humph." She crossed her arms and tapped one foot on the ground. "As a matter of fact, I do." Sliding her gaze northward along the river, she pointed toward the raised railroad trestle. "Have you ever heard of a little thing called a train?" She shook her head. "I can't imagine why you didn't just have the crates shipped that way over the mountains."

Now serious, Nate frowned. "The Colonel didn't trust them to show due care, especially over La Veta Pass. Sometimes trains jump track or run into fallen trees." His tone suggested he didn't quite agree with his father. "He didn't want to risk it."

At the mention of railroad tragedies, Susanna could think only of the stories she'd heard all her life. Sherman's army destroyed the Confederacy's entire rail line, digging up the tracks and wrapping them around trees, burning train stations and cutting telegraph wires. Maybe Colonel Northam participated in that same kind of destruction somewhere in the South. She shook off the memory and forced her thoughts to Mrs. Northam's certain appreciation of her husband's extraordinary gift. After all, Northern ladies hadn't participated in the war, and surely nice things meant as much to them as they did to Southern ladies.

"Maybe he wouldn't mind just for the crossing?" She lifted her eyebrows with the question and smiled at Nate.

He glanced between the bridge and her, and his Adam's apple bobbed. This man liked her, she could tell.

But she wouldn't play with him, as she had some of the boys back home. Southern boys understood and even expected flirtation. Yankee boys might get the wrong idea if she behaved as she had back home, and so far their teasing had fallen short of real flirting.

"I wouldn't have you disobey your daddy, Nate, but isn't the most important thing getting the china safely to your mother? That would honor both of them most of all, wouldn't it?"

He grinned in his boyish way. "Yes." He eyed Zack. "Let's unhitch Henry." He nodded toward one of the lead horses. "I'll ride up the tracks a ways and flag down the train to see if they'll carry it over for us."

"It'll cost you, boss."

Nate shrugged. "Broken china will cost me a lot more."

The moment Nate rode away, Susanna heard her father's faint call. Zack gave her a worried look as he helped her climb into the rear of the prairie schooner.

"I'm sure he's all right," she whispered as she gave the cowboy a nod of appreciation. Then she ducked inside. "Yes, Daddy?" She knelt beside him and brushed the back of her hand over his cheek. "You're hot. How do you feel?"

"Don't worry about me, sweet pea." A glint in his eye contradicted the set of his jaw. "While Northam's gone, you walk on up to that hotel and give that note to the desk clerk."

"What? Now?" She retrieved the envelope from beneath her tattered bedding. "Daddy, please tell me what this is all about."

"Now, daughter, you've never been one to question

me." He fumed briefly. "Oh, very well. I'm not partial to being laid up in some hotel in a tent city where no one knows or cares about us. I want that proprietor to turn us away. Then Northam won't have any choice but to take us on to his place." He coughed, then held his ribs and groaned with pain. When he recovered, he gave her an apologetic grimace. "Out here in this wild country, it's hard for a man to be so helpless he can't even take care of his own daughter. I trust Northam. He'll do the right thing by us, he and his family."

Susanna studied him for several moments. He'd slept fitfully last night, and no doubt the river crossing had been hard on him. Maybe he wasn't in his right mind. But that didn't give her an excuse for disobeying him. Still, he had never asked her to do anything this close to lying in all her born days. Unless she counted his changing their last name and pretending to be poor. She still hadn't reconciled herself to those ideas.

"Will you go?" He tried to sit up. "If you won't, I will."

"Shh." She gently pushed him back down. "You rest, dearest. I'll do as you asked." Her stomach tightening, she climbed out of the wagon and tied on her bonnet. "Zack, please tell Mr. Northam I'll be on up the road arranging tea and sandwiches for all of us." At least that part wouldn't be a lie.

Nate emerged from the hotel scratching his head over the manager's refusal to take in Mr. Anders. He thought everybody out here in the West knew that when decent folks suffered terrible losses, other good men needed to help them out. But Nate's offer of up-front payment and his promise to return in a day or two to check on them were rebuffed. Even mentioning his father had no effect because the man was new to the area and didn't know the Colonel's position in their burgeoning community to the west.

Granted, the one-story wooden hotel wasn't much to look at, but it was serviceable. New in late May when Nate and Zack had come through the tent city of Alamosa on their way to Pueblo, it already had a well-worn appearance. Like the other premade wooden structures lining the main street, the six-or seven-room establishment had been transported by train one room at a time and set up in haste. No doubt something more substantial would soon be needed to house the many travelers riding the newly laid Denver and Rio Grande railroad line, which would soon extend both south and west.

Nate glanced across the dusty, rutted street and snorted in disgust. Of course, they'd brought in a building for a saloon to keep the railroad workers happy. There would be none of that over in his as-yet-unnamed community. The Colonel always made it clear up front to everyone who came to his settlement that no liquor would ever be allowed there. Apparently, the founders of Alamosa didn't feel the same way. Even now in midmorning, several disreputable-looking men loitered outside the swinging doors, their posture indicating they'd already had a few drinks. Nate couldn't help but think Mr. Anders and Susanna would have been better off in Fort Garland, Buffalo Soldiers notwithstanding. But he couldn't take them back there now.

Nor could he put off delivering the bad news about the hotel to Mr. Anders. Peering into the back of the prairie schooner, he waited until his eyes adjusted to the dimness before speaking.

"Everything all right, Nate?" the old man croaked.

"Yes, sir. No, sir. I mean—" He couldn't manage to say the words. "Is Susanna back from getting her tea?" Foolish question. Obviously, she wasn't in the wagon. "Maybe I'd better go check on her."

"You do that, son." Mr. Anders lay back with a groan.

His belly twisting, Nate turned back to the hotel just as Susanna came up the street carrying a tray laden with a teapot and sandwiches.

"I finally found some refreshments at a cute little tent café down the road." She tilted her head prettily in that direction. "I brought enough for everybody." She held the tray out to Zack, who was eyeing the food like a hungry bear. "Help yourself."

"Much obliged, miss." He tore off one leather glove and snatched up a sandwich with his grimy paw. "A mighty welcome change from all them beans."

At the sight of his dirty hand, Nate cringed, but Susanna didn't seem to notice. Or chose to ignore it, as any lady would.

"Did they give us a room?" Her expression revealed a hint of conflict, almost as if she hoped they hadn't.

Once again, that feeling of protectiveness welled up inside Nate, and his concerns vanished. He knew what he had to do. "No, ma'am, but don't you worry your pretty head about it. It's just a few more hours to my ranch. We'll put you up until your father recuperates."

With some effort, he willed away his anxieties about the Colonel. Mother was hospitality itself, and she would more than make up for his father's reaction. If worse came to worst, Nate could always take the Colonel aside and point out that Susanna was the one who insisted he take the china over the river by train. Otherwise, Nate would tell him, he wouldn't have dared come home, because all the dishes would doubtless have been broken coming across the river's rough bottom in the fast-flowing current. That should convince the Colonel she and her father deserved some help.

For Nate's part, he was grateful for the Denver and Rio Grande engineer and conductor, who had been more than obliging. Once they'd learned the shipment was for the Colonel, they'd ordered their own men to give a hand. And once they'd learned it was imported china, the other men couldn't have been more careful. Seemed every one of them understood a man wanting to do something nice for his mother. When all was said and done, Nate couldn't have been more pleased, and it had only cost him ten dollars for the lot of them.

Nor could he say he was disappointed when the hotel manager turned Mr. Anders away. After all, Nate had wanted more time with Susanna. Now he had it. The Colonel might have ideas about him marrying Maisie Eberly, but he could never feel the attraction for his longtime friend that he already felt after only two days with Susanna.

As they resumed their journey, Susanna noticed how pleased Nate seemed. In spite of the brisk wind whipping up all kinds of dust, he'd left off his kerchief and kept smiling her way. It was plain as the nose on his handsome face that he didn't mind his Good Samaritan role, and she kept thanking the Lord for his kindness.

She really shouldn't be hanging out the back of the wagon, but she couldn't help herself, even with all that dust threatening to choke her. Many weeks ago, she'd resigned herself to landscapes far different from the verdant fields and forests of Georgia. When they had viewed a large area of the San Luis Valley from the mountain pass, she had observed vast expanses of green and several broad lakes glistening in the sunlight. But the valley floor had some stretches of desertlike land, as well, and she wondered how anyone could expect to farm it successfully.

Thank the Lord that Daddy had chosen to be a prospector instead of a homesteader. He was far too old to till unbroken sod, and even his prospecting was more of a hobby than an occupation, at least in her mind. After all, they had enough money to live on. If they hit hard times, Edward would send more. Once Daddy was back on his feet, she'd let him have his fun searching for silver and gold for a little while. Let him find a silver nugget or two, and then she would persuade him to take her back home to Marietta.

Being in the company of a kind, compassionate, educated man like Nate reminded her of her yearning to find a good *Southern* gentleman to marry, someone with whom she could build a home and family in the hometown she loved so much, among the friends she'd known all her life. For now, however, she must set aside those longings and take care of Daddy. She whispered a prayer that the Lord would tell Mama she was keeping her promise.

At last the dust won out, and she pulled her head back inside the schooner and closed the flap. Daddy was bearing up quite well, although he still had moments of incoherence and slept fitfully when he did manage to sleep. She prayed there would be a doctor near Nate's ranch who could help him.

By midafternoon, they had reached a small settlement of several houses, some buildings and a white clapboard church with a high steeple. Nate had said they would take time to stretch their legs and water the horses before going on, and now he hurried to help Susanna out of the wagon.

"Shall we get a bite to eat?" He waved a hand toward another white clapboard building, this one with a sign over the door that read Williams's Café. "Those sandwiches didn't last me very long, and it's a few hours until supper at the ranch."

A sudden nervous flutter in Susanna's stomach extinguished her appetite. Supper at the ranch meant at last meeting that intimidating Union colonel. Would he still be fighting the war, as most Southerners were, if only with words? Habitual animosity filled her chest, but she wouldn't let on to Nate.

"Maybe a piece of pie, if they have some." She nodded her head toward the wagon. "I think it would be good for Daddy, too." As Nate tipped his hat and started toward the building, she touched his arm.

His eyes widened with apparent surprise as he turned back. "Yes, ma'am?"

"Do you suppose there's someplace where I could, um, well…?" She shook her brown skirt, and dust flew in every direction. "I would like to be a bit more presentable before I meet your mother." *And especially your father.* Maybe he would take more kindly to them if they didn't look so bedraggled.

"Now, don't worry about that." Nate grinned. "I'm sure she'll understand that you've been on the road." He glanced toward the building. "But I'll see what I can do."

Mrs. Williams, the café owner, could not have been

more accommodating. It seemed that the Northam name held much more power in this unnamed settlement than it did in Alamosa. Miss Pam, as she asked to be called, had a permanent smile etched in the lines of her slender face. She appeared to be around fifty years old, and her warm brown eyes exuded maternal kindness as she invited Susanna into her own quarters at the back of the café.

"Charlie—he's my husband—he'll see what your pa needs." Miss Pam set a pitcher of warm water on her mahogany washstand. "You go ahead and clean up. Is that your fresh dress?"

"Yes, ma'am." Susanna held up the one dress the thieves had managed to overlook in their destruction. They'd stolen her favorite pink calico, so this green print would have to do.

"It's a pretty one." Miss Pam gave Susanna a critical look up and down, her gaze stopping at her hair. "Do you have a brush?"

"No, ma'am." She tried hard not to sigh, but a little huff escaped her. Almost everything she depended upon to make herself look presentable was gone or ruined.

Miss Pam gave her a sympathetic smile. She reached into her bureau drawer and retrieved a boar-hair brush with a tortoiseshell back, holding it out to Susanna. "You take my spare one."

"Oh, my." Her heart warmed at this woman's generosity. While Susanna could afford to buy her own if she found a mercantile nearby, it seemed best to accept the brush and pay Miss Pam back later. "Thank you."

While she helped Susanna brush her hair and fasten the back buttons on her dress, Miss Pam chatted about the big anniversary party coming up in July. "Out here, we're always looking for something to celebrate, but this one is going to be special. Colonel and Mrs. Northam have done so much for this community, bringing in a preacher and building a church, just generally taking care of everybody. The Colonel says he has a doctor arriving next month. Too bad he's not already here for your pa, but Charlie's pretty good at tending injuries, being a former mountain man. You know how they have to be self-sufficient living out in the mountains by themselves the way they do."

Not giving Susanna a chance to comment, she went on to list various ways Nate's parents had helped folks. Every word and tone suggested only respect and affection for the Northams, especially lauding the Colonel's leadership, but that still did not diminish Susanna's apprehensions about meeting the man.

In less than an hour, Susanna felt sufficiently refreshed, and Miss Pam's husband had taken care of Daddy. Charlie offered his expert opinion that Daddy's left leg was indeed broken, as were several of his ribs. He made a splint for the leg, wrapped torn sheets around Daddy's ribs and gave him a dose of medicine to ease the pain. Nate told Susanna that while the community awaited the doctor's arrival, Charlie was often called upon to help folks out.

After they had enjoyed some of Miss Pam's delicious gooseberry pie with a splash of thick fresh cream over the top, they headed south. Unable to bear riding inside the schooner another minute, Susanna sat beside Zack on the driver's bench watching the beautiful green landscape dotted with occasional farmhouses nestled among the trees.

In less than an hour, the two wagons passed under

a majestic stone archway emblazoned with an intricate cattle brand and the name Four Stones Ranch. A long drive between two fenced pastures took them toward the two-story white ranch house built on a stone foundation. To one side were a giant red barn and numerous outbuildings. Susanna noticed the addition Nate had mentioned, also two-storied, on the north end of the main structure. A wide brook ran some fifty yards from the house, and young elm and cottonwood trees grew in clusters around the property.

Nostalgia swept through Susanna at the sight of the beautiful ranch. Back home, magnolias would be in bloom, and maybe a few spring gardenias would still be filling the air with their lovely perfume. Catching a whiff of roses, she searched without success for the source of the fragrance.

As if someone had blown a trumpet to announce their coming, several people poured forth from the barn, while a solitary man emerged from the house.

Nate jumped down from the wagon and gave instructions to his cowhands, who took charge of his wagon and drove it toward the barn. Then he turned toward the other man.

An older version of Nate, and just as tall as his son, the dark-haired Colonel exuded authority before he even spoke a word. Susanna could hardly breathe as she listened to Nate's brief explanation for the presence of the prairie schooner and its inhabitants. All the while, the older man glared at her through narrowed eyes. No one had ever looked at her with such disdain, perhaps even hostility. Yet she didn't dare reveal her own bitter feelings against this Union officer. Maybe it was just those feelings speaking to her mind, but he looked like someone who would chase women and children from their plantation house and burn it to the ground.

"So I thought they would make a fine addition to our community, Colonel." Nate sounded a little breathless, and from the way his right hand twitched, Susanna thought he might salute his formidable father. "Being homesteaders, that is."

The Colonel walked to the back of the schooner and threw open the flap, then returned to face Nate, eyeing his son with obvious disgust. "What's the matter with you, boy? These are no homesteaders. Where's their furniture? Where are their clothes? All I see is a pickax and two gold pans. Can't you tell a money-grubbing prospector when you see one?"

Chapter Four

Nate saw the hurt in Susanna's eyes and the way she cringed almost as if she'd been slapped. He ground his teeth as protectiveness once again roared into his chest. He had long ago learned that arguing with the Colonel was a useless exercise, but he'd never tried to beat some sense into the man. His hands ceased their nervous twitching and bunched into involuntary fists as if they wanted to do that very thing. Only by hooking his thumbs over his gun belt did Nate manage to control the impulse. How would he ever learn to control his temper when his father continued to rile him this way?

"Nathaniel!" Mother bustled out of the house and down the front steps, her fuzzy brown hair streaked with flour and her white cotton apron stained with jam. "You're home at last."

At the sight of her, Nate's anger softened, replaced by the joy her presence always brought him. Spreading his arms, he welcomed her eager embrace. "Mother." He held her tight and savored the aroma of fresh-baked bread that clung to her like perfume. Her nicely rounded form reminded him of Susanna's need to put on a few healthy pounds. But if the Colonel had his way, the Anders family wouldn't be enjoying any steaks at the Four Stones Ranch.

Mother leaned back and brushed a flour-covered hand over his cheek. "Angela and I have been baking all day, but I didn't know when to have her cook your favorite— Oh! What's this?" She broke away and moved toward the prairie schooner. "Why, Nate, you've brought us a guest." She glanced at the Colonel. "Frank, help this young lady down so we can be properly introduced."

Nate gulped back a laugh. His father never tolerated so much as a grin when Mother took charge this way.

"Of course, my dear." His face a mask, the Colonel stepped over to the wagon and held out his hand. "Miss?" Even his offer sounded like an order.

Susanna eyed him with confusion, then gave Nate a questioning look. He returned a short nod, hoping she would accept the Colonel's curt invitation. With a graceful elegance Nate hadn't known she possessed, she lifted her chin like a duchess, then rose and stepped to the edge of the driver's box to place her hand in his father's.

"Thank you, sir." Her posture stiff, her voice coldly polite, she permitted him to assist her to the ground beside Mother.

Nate usually waited to be addressed by his father. This time, however, he approached the little group and said, "Mother, Colonel, may I present Miss Susanna Anders? Miss Anders, Colonel and Mrs. Northam."

Her expression filled with warmth and hospitality, Mother gripped Susanna's hands. "Welcome, Miss Anders. Do come in the house. Supper will be ready shortly, and I'm sure you would welcome a chance to—"

She started to usher Susanna toward the house, but the young lady gently resisted and turned back toward the wagon.

"Thank you, ma'am, but my daddy requires my attention."

"Oh." Mother didn't bat an eyelid. "Another guest. Is he ill?" She shot a look at the Colonel. "Frank, my dear, don't just stand there. We must help these people."

The Colonel also didn't bat an eyelid. "Of course, my dear." His expression unchanged, he once again walked to the back of the wagon. "Nate, get over here and help me."

Nate had to turn away and regain his composure before obeying. Mother and the Colonel rarely did battle, but when they did, Mother never lost.

Susanna threw dignity aside and pulled down the tailgate so she could scramble into the back of the schooner. Finding Daddy sound asleep, she lifted a prayer of thanks he hadn't heard that awful Colonel's rude words. Daddy wasn't the slightest bit money-grubbing. He didn't need to be because he already had plenty of money. And what on earth was wrong with being a prospector? Suddenly, camping beside the road they had just traveled seemed a better idea than accepting the hospitality of this Yankee family.

"Dearest." She gently touched Daddy's cheek. "We're here at Nate's house." Only by thinking of it as Nate's could she consider going inside.

"Hmm?" Daddy raised a bruised hand and swept it over his eyes. That medicine Mr. Williams had given him had probably muddled his thinking. He inhaled deeply, then winced. "What?"

Susanna glanced at the three Northams, who were peering into the wagon with varied expressions. She decided to ignore the pity in Nate's eyes and the hostility in his father's, and concentrate on the warm concern beaming from Mrs. Northam's sweet, round face.

As if the older woman realized how the situation appeared from Susanna's viewpoint, she gave Nate a little shove. "Go on inside, son. Tell Angela to get your bed ready. We'll put Mr. Anders in your room. Then come back and help your father."

"Yes, ma'am." He disappeared, and the thumps of his hurried footsteps resounded through the canvas walls of the wagon.

Daddy caught sight of their hosts and tried to rise. "Help me up, daughter. I should greet our company."

A faint growl sounded in the Colonel's throat, and Susanna gulped back sharp words, while Mrs. Northam shushed her husband. As she helped Daddy to a sitting position, Susanna gave a little laugh that sounded a bit too high and a bit too nervous in her own ears. "Actually, dearest, we are the company."

As if he finally grasped the situation, Daddy's eyes cleared. "Ah, yes, of course." He nodded toward the Yankee couple.

Susanna briefly considered presenting Daddy to them, as would be proper, since they were the hosts, but something inside her refused to comply. After all, the prairie schooner *was* her and Daddy's home. "Daddy, may I present Mrs. Northam and Colonel Northam?"

If he noticed her breach of etiquette, he didn't indicate it. "How do, ma'am, sir?" He leaned into Susanna's shoulder. "Edward Anders."

"We're pleased to meet you, Mr. Anders," Mrs. Northam said. "You just rest a minute, and Nate will be back to help you inside." She looked up at her husband and raised one eyebrow.

The Colonel cleared his throat and pursed his lips. His wife elbowed him in the ribs. "So you met up with horse thieves, did you, Anders?"

Daddy coughed out a wry laugh and grimaced. "Indeed we did. Took most of our belongings and supplies and did their best not to leave a witness." He patted Susanna's hand. "The good Lord protected my daughter, as she was off fetching water when they came."

"Oh, my." Mrs. Northam's eyes reddened. "Praise the Lord."

"That I do, ma'am. That I do."

Slightly out of breath, Nate appeared once again beside his parents. "Angela was waiting by the door. She'll have my room ready by the time we get there."

"I don't want to put you out, Nate," Daddy said.

"Not at all, sir. I—" Mrs. Northam began.

"They won't be here long," the Colonel said. "I'm sure Anders is anxious to get on his way to the silver fields." He waved Nate toward the wagon. "Get on in there and help him out."

Instead of the instant obedience Susanna expected to see, Nate fisted his hands at his waist. "He'll need to recuperate for quite a while before he goes anyplace. And they'll need another team of horses." His father started to respond, but Nate hurried on. "We need Mr. Anders to give us a good description of those horse thieves so we can put the word out to everybody. They're a threat to the whole valley. If they get away with what they did, all sorts of criminals will think—"

"You think I don't know that?" The Colonel silenced

Nate with a dismissive wave of his hand. "Now, let's get this done."

Despite her outrage over the Colonel's behavior, Susanna could not fail to be impressed by his and Nate's strength as they lifted Daddy's cot from the prairie schooner and carried it toward the house. Daddy was not a small man, so they set him down and summoned two men—she guessed they were called cowboys—to help carry the invalid up to the second floor of the house. Susanna didn't have time to notice much as they entered and climbed the stairs, but what she did see impressed her with its beauty and grandeur, much like the mountains surrounding this high valley. While she wouldn't call it a mansion, it certainly was an imposing domicile.

Within ten minutes, Daddy was resting in a charmingly masculine room, where guns and antlers decorated the walls, and pine furniture and woven rag rugs contributed to the rustic atmosphere. Above Nate's handsome pine secretary, a glassed-in bookcase held several leather-bound books. Susanna didn't take time to read the titles, but she longed to know what he read besides Dickens.

"And now for you, Miss Anders." Mrs. Northam took Susanna's arm and led her down the hallway to another bedroom very different from Nate's. Frilly white curtains fluttered in the breeze wafting through the two windows. A pink-and-blue patchwork quilt covered the four-poster bed, and a blue velvet overstuffed chair sat nearby on a patch of carpet. The scent of roses filled the air, although none were in the cut-glass vase on the bedside table. "This is our daughter Rosamond's room. When she returns from her friend's house, she'll be pleased to learn she has a roommate. Maisie's coming with her to spend the night, but we can bring in an extra mattress."

"You're so very kind, ma'am." Susanna's eyes stung. Would these other girls truly welcome her? Would Rosamond be like her mother or more like her inhospitable father?

Sudden weariness filled her, and she eyed the feather bed with longing. As if reading Susanna's mind, Mrs. Northam gave her a brief hug.

"Why don't you lie down? I'll send our girl Rita up to wake you when it's time to eat."

"How can we ever thank you?" And how could she think any evil of this sweet Yankee lady?

"I will speak to you in my office, Nate. Now." The Colonel didn't grant Mr. Anders so much as the courtesy of a parting word, but strode from the room toward the front staircase. The two cowhands followed after him.

Nate gritted his teeth as he watched his father leave. Pasting on a more pleasant expression, he turned to the bed where Mr. Anders lay, his gaze on Nate.

"You get some rest, sir." Nate bent forward to adjust the quilt. "If you need anything—"

"You've done a lot, young man." The look of approval in his eyes caused a stirring in Nate's chest. How would it feel if his father looked at him that way? "You're a true Good Samaritan, just like the Good Book says."

Nate cleared his throat. He wanted to say *aw, shucks,* like his youngest brother might. Instead, he offered, "Don't mention it, sir. I'm glad to help. We all are."

Mr. Anders coughed out a laugh, then grimaced and

clutched his ribs. "I wouldn't say *all,* son, but I'll let it go at that."

Nate took his leave, shutting the door behind him and offering a prayer for the old man's recovery. At the top of the stairs, he hesitated. The Colonel had ordered him down to his office, but Nate couldn't just go off and leave Susanna. He walked to Rosamond's room and tapped on the door just as Mother swung it open.

"Nate." She reached up to give him another welcoming hug. "Oh, it's so good to have you back home. I miss you so much when you make these long trips for supplies. I don't know why your father can't just send some of the hired men." She cast a quick look at Susanna, and her eyebrows arched briefly. She opened and shut her mouth as though she had started to ask him something, then changed her mind. Instead, she patted his cheek. "I'm going downstairs to finish helping Angela and Rita with the baking. Then we'll prepare supper. You may stand right here in the doorway and speak to Miss Anders for two minutes. Then I expect to hear your boots on the downstairs floor fifteen seconds after that."

Nate pursed his lips to suppress a grin. "Mother, Susanna and I have been out on the trail together for two days, with her father looking on the whole time. You don't have to worry about any improper behavior."

"Susanna, is it?" Mother looked at her. "And I suppose you call him Nate?"

"Yes, ma'am." Susanna returned a sweet smile. "That is, if you don't mind."

"Hmm." Mother got a speculative gleam in her eyes. "No, dear, not at all." She swept past Nate, wearing a soft grin and watching him the whole time as she headed for the back stairs that led to her kitchen.

All of a sudden, the kerchief around Nate's neck seemed awfully tight. Mother often teased him about girls. It seemed to him that was what most mothers did to their sons. But she'd never said anything so bold in front of a young lady.

"I hope you don't mind her." He leaned against the doorjamb, crossed his arms and offered Susanna an apologetic grimace.

"Not at all." She untied her bonnet and hung it on the back of Rosamond's desk chair. "She's very kind and hospitable." Now serious, she leveled a steady gaze on him. "I'm afraid your father is not quite so pleased to have us as guests." Biting her lower lip, she stared out the window. "Maybe we should go back to the café. It seems Mr. and Mrs. Williams would be—"

"No." Nate spoke more sharply than he intended, and she blinked. "I mean, they're the salt of the earth, but they run their place without help, so it might be a burden for them. We have servants and cowhands and a big family." He rolled his hat in his hands. "Besides, I feel it's my responsibility to see that your father gets back on his feet." That thought had just come to him. Yet hadn't the biblical Good Samaritan taken responsibility for the beaten merchant even after taking him to the inn? Nate knew he could do no less.

Susanna's blue eyes were rimmed with tears. "I don't know what to say."

He barked out a laugh that didn't sound quite as cheerful as he intended. "I do. We're having steak for supper, and I can't wait to bite into a big juicy one."

Smiling again, she laughed, too. "You mean no beans?"

"Nathaniel Northam!" The Colonel's voice thundered up the staircase.

Nate gave an artificial shudder. She didn't need to know how much he was truly quaking inside over his father's angry summons.

"That's right. No beans."

Her soft feminine laughter followed him all the way down the stairs, and he barely had time to wipe the grin off his face before stepping into the Colonel's office for his scolding—undeserved but nonetheless expected.

Chapter Five

Susanna's laughter died away, and with it her good feelings. Unless she'd missed something, Nate didn't deserve to be yelled at or scolded like a mischievous boy. In her opinion, it was that Yankee colonel who needed a scolding, and she would be glad to give it to him. He had a noble, good-hearted son, and yet he was beating him down for no good reason.

She'd noticed the difference in Nate the minute they arrived at the ranch. For two days, she'd watched a capable, authoritative, helpful man take care of business. But the moment his father stepped out the front door, Nate became an awkward servant trying without success to please an implacable master.

An uncomfortable sensation stirred in her stomach. Back home in Georgia, it wasn't just the carpetbaggers who mistreated people. She'd seen for herself how some Southerners treated their former slaves as if no war had happened, as if no Emancipation Proclamation had freed them. She was thankful Daddy and Mama got rid of the plantation and moved to town. There they didn't have to deal with such things as getting enough

people to work in the cotton fields, work they'd always
done as slaves but now had to be paid for. The house
servants Susanna's parents had employed received a sal-
ary and were well treated. She'd never heard Daddy or
Mama speak to a servant like the Colonel spoke to his
own son. The Southern man she married would need
to understand she expected no less for their servants.

Weariness once again overtook her. She untied and
slipped off her walking boots and lay on the bed, but
could not sleep. Despite Nate's being a Yankee, she must
somehow find a way to pay him back for his kindness.
Even knowing the trouble he would get into with his
father, he had saved Daddy and her from untold grief,
perhaps even death. That was worthy of a reward of
some kind. But what could she do? The Northams were
obviously wealthy ranchers, so he didn't need any material repayment. All she could do was pray and let the
Lord work things out.

Her eyelids grew heavy, but she managed to whisper
a prayer for Nate to make it through his current scolding
without too much difficulty. Even if he was a Yankee…

"Did you check the entire shipment before you
loaded it up?" The Colonel stood behind his large oak
desk, bracing himself on his fists as he leaned forward
in a threatening pose. With him standing, Nate didn't
dare sit down, no matter how weary he was from his
travels. "Every plate? Every cup?"

An unfamiliar thread of assurance wove briefly
through Nate's chest, just before the more familiar anger
roared up and closed his throat. Of course he'd checked
the shipment before loading it onto the wagon. How
stupid did the Colonel think he was that he would have

the horses haul home a broken cargo? But a bitter re-tort never got him anyplace, so he said, "Yessir. Every-thing was in perfect condition." He made sure he spoke loudly, clearly and respectfully so his father wouldn't have further cause to yell.

Yet he couldn't leave it at that. "It was a good thing Miss Anders was with us."

Snorting, the Colonel straightened and stared at him as if surprised he would offer additional information without being asked.

Nate hurried on. "When we got to the river, she sug-gested that we take it over on the train. I mean, the water was fast, and when we took their wagon through first, we drove over a lot of rocks and branches. So I flagged down the train and—"

"And you needed someone else to suggest that ob-vious solution?"

Nate stepped back, and the heel of his boot hit a chair. Somehow he managed not to lose his balance. "W-well, you had it brought by wagon all the way from Westport because you didn't trust the trains, so, no, sir, I didn't think of it."

Again, the Colonel snorted out his disgust, although Nate had no idea what had him so riled. His father ran a hand across his jaw and sat in his leather-covered desk chair. "Now, about those people—"

"Yessir." Nate still wouldn't sit until invited to do so, but the ache in his legs didn't help his temper. "Those people. I know for a fact that you couldn't have driven on past them any more than I could." Where had he got-ten the courage to say that? "And you would have been ashamed of me for not stopping to help."

The Colonel's eyes narrowed. "That didn't mean you

had to bring them home to burden your mother. You should have left them in Alamosa."

Nate explained the situation at the hotel. "Even your name didn't affect the proprietor." He offered a sheepish grin.

The Colonel didn't react. "Just make sure your mother doesn't have extra work. And make sure they leave as soon as possible. That Anders fellow seems like the kind of lazy Southerner who will sit around expecting people to wait on him like his slaves used to do."

Nate wouldn't ask how he knew whether Anders had kept slaves. Not everyone in the South had. But his father often spoke disdainfully of Southerners, as if they were all the same, all except Reverend Thomas, the preacher he'd brought from Virginia.

The Colonel snatched up the packing list for the china and thrust it toward Nate. "The first time your mother goes out visiting, you check the shipment again to make sure nothing broke on the way from Pueblo. If it did, I may be able to get a replacement from San Francisco by the time our party rolls around." He waved a dismissive hand. "I expect you back to work on the new addition before dawn tomorrow. Anders and his daughter may get to sit around, but you're back on the job."

Nate started to say he'd been *on the job* during this whole trip to Pueblo, but his father slapped the paper back on the desk, causing him to jump.

"And don't be getting any ideas about that Anders girl. Maisie Eberly will turn eighteen in a few weeks, and George and I expect an announcement from the two of you right after her birthday." The Colonel pulled out a ledger and opened it, scanning the pages as if prospecting for gold, effectively dismissing Nate.

He stared at the top of his father's head. No, he would not be getting any ideas about the lovely Miss Susanna Anders, not her or anybody. He had too many things to work out in his life before taking on a wife or even a sweetheart, not the least of which was whether or not he would keep working like a slave for his father. And he certainly wouldn't be proposing to Maisie. It wasn't fair to either one of them. But George Eberly was as domineering as the Colonel, so avoiding marriage could turn out to be the hardest thing Nate—*and* Maisie— had ever done.

"I'm so grateful to you for sharing your room with me." Rested after her nap, Susanna sat in the blue velvet bedroom chair while Rosamond Northam and her friend Maisie Eberly sat side by side on the bed. Dark-haired and green-eyed like her brother, Rosamond had her father's lean face and her mother's sweet smile. "I'll try real hard not to put you out." She'd never had to share a room and had no idea how this girl would react to such an intrusion.

"Oh, don't worry about that. We'll have a good time." Rosamond nudged her friend. "Won't we, Maisie?"

"You bet we will." Maisie giggled, and her curly red hair bounced as she nodded her agreement. "Just like the Three Musketeers." She leaned toward Susanna. "Have you read Dumas's book?"

Caught up in the younger girl's merriment, Susanna offered a more ladylike laugh. "Yes, but I'm a little rusty with my swordplay." She searched her mind for specific scenes from the exciting tale. "And I doubt we'll find any queens to rescue."

"Maybe just a cowboy or two." The girls giggled and

bounced and put their heads together in a familiar way. Despite their differing coloring and features, they were like two peas in a pod.

Susanna's heart warmed. What nice young ladies, although at sixteen and seventeen, they still had some growing up to do. She had no doubt Mrs. Northam was responsible for any measure of decorum her daughter displayed, but the way they had noisily run up the front staircase a while ago revealed that both of them also possessed a bit of Colorado wildness. Someone should establish a finishing school out here. They would probably find many students among ranchers' daughters. Of course, Susanna would never correct them, for that in itself would be a dreadful breach of etiquette. All she could do was set an example of refined behavior.

A soft knock on the door interrupted their merriment, and a dark-eyed girl of perhaps fourteen poked her head in the door. "Miss Rosamond, Mrs. Northam requests your presence in the kitchen."

"Thank you, Rita. Tell her we'll be down soon. And bring us some hot water and towels so we can wash up."

"Yes, miss."

Rita disappeared, and the other two girls continued their discussion of musketeers and scheming cardinals, comparing them to the cowboys they knew. Although they mentioned several names, giggling all the while, not once did they say anything about Nate. Susanna couldn't imagine why she had even thought about that. Clearly, Maisie was too young to be interested in him, at least romantically.

Those few moments revealed much to Susanna. While the Colonel was stern to the point of rudeness, his family was more lighthearted. Further, she was glad to see they treated their servants with courtesy. But she guessed that Rosamond, being the only daughter, was a little bit spoiled. Susanna had never failed to go immediately when her parents called. Indeed, she would gladly answer Mama's summons once again.

She thrust away the grief that tried to engulf her. She couldn't go back to those days, and until she could get Daddy back to Marietta, she must learn to live as a pioneer woman, whatever that meant. Although she was about two or three years older than these girls, she would open her heart and let them teach her. And maybe she could teach them something in return.

With Maisie on one side of him and Rosamond on the other, Nate could hardly enjoy his steak for all of their chatter and giggling. In contrast, Susanna sat across from him eating her supper with the grace of a duchess. Funny, that was the second time he'd thought of her in that way, yet he'd never even met a duchess. He must have read about one in a book. The thought made him grin. He'd enjoyed their brief chat about books while they were on the trail. Maybe they'd have a chance to do it again.

Guilt wove through him. The Colonel would probably do all he could to keep Nate away from Susanna. He glanced toward the end of the table. His father, watching him with an inscrutable look, bent his head toward Maisie. Nate groaned inwardly. She was a sweet little gal, but still just a child, despite being almost eighteen. How could the Colonel think she was ready for marriage? In Nate's opinion, the way she and Rosamond acted was just plain silly, something that had never bothered him before, but now got on his nerves.

Rebellion kicked up inside him. He looked at Susanna again, determined to talk to her rather than Maisie, and his rebellion turned to—jealousy? Chatting with his middle brother, Rand, on one side and his youngest brother, Tolley, on the other, she hadn't even glanced across the table at him except to give him a smile and a nod before the Colonel said grace and they all sat down.

Rand was yammering on about something, bragging, really. Until this moment, Nate hadn't given a second thought to a match between the two of them. Even at twenty, his younger brother was about as grown-up as his sister and her friend. Yet here was Rand obviously trying to impress Susanna with some tale about how cattle brands were designed, of all things. As if a refined young lady wanted to hear about that. Yet she focused on him and responded with interest, even including Tolley in the conversation.

Tolley's beaming response earned Susanna another surge of Nate's admiration. Hardly anybody paid attention to fifteen-year-old Tolley, and the boy had begun to show signs of rebellion. Nate was worried but had no idea how to help him.

"But Nate wouldn't want to do that, would you, Nate?" Maisie elbowed him in the ribs and laughed in her schoolgirl way.

"Uh, what?" He glanced at Rosamond, silently quizzing her with a raised eyebrow. Fortunately, she sat adjacent to Mother's place at the end of the table nearest the kitchen door, so the Colonel couldn't see his confusion.

"Of course he would." Rosamond gave him a furtive wink, then leaned around him to address Maisie. "Who else would escort us up into the hills to get flowers for our flower beds?" She lifted her coffee cup and saluted her friend. "Mother agrees with our idea. Columbines will make a beautiful addition to our garden. Being native to Colorado, they sure won't take as much work as Mother's roses. We can fetch home enough to fill that new garden patch, and they'll be all rooted and growing by the anniversary party."

Her foolish chatter gave him all the information he needed, and he offered his sister a grateful nudge. "Girls, I hate to disappoint you, but I'm afraid the Colonel needs me here at the ranch. I can't run off for a picnic when this house has a two-story addition I need to finish." He shot a glance at his father, expecting his agreement, but the Colonel's expression was surprisingly agreeable.

"I believe a day trip to acquire some columbines for your mother would be a fine idea." He served himself another helping of mashed potatoes and ladled on a large portion of beef gravy. "You three youngsters can go tomorrow. Ride horseback instead of taking a wagon, and you'll be back in time for milking." He dug into his supper as if that settled the matter.

The girls chirped like baby birds as they made plans for the upcoming day trip, but Nate could only stare across the table at Susanna in dismay. No wonder the Colonel gave his permission for such a trivial excursion, for it would force him into Maisie's company. Nate should invite Susanna along, not only for good manners but also so he would have some intelligent conversation along the way. But if she didn't know how to ride like his sister and Maisie, he'd be stuck with two chattering magpies for a whole day.

* * *

Susanna had learned in finishing school that a lady didn't talk across the table but rather engaged in conversation with those seated beside her. In this case, it wasn't too difficult. Rand was almost as funny as Nate, and he could spin a yarn nearly as well as her own brother back home. But the quieter Tolley touched her heart. His sad brown eyes made her think of a puppy pleading for approval, and when she turned her attention to him, he all but jumped around in happy little circles. A glance across the table from time to time gave her a new perspective on Nate. Those girls were making him dizzy with their back-and-forth chatter, but he took it in good spirits, another admirable quality.

She was surprised that Colonel Northam said very little beyond blessing the food and telling poor Nate that he had to take the girls out to pick flowers. If she wasn't so worried about Daddy, she would hint that she'd like to go with them, as she hadn't ridden a horse since they left Marietta four months ago. The girls had been quick to welcome her into their friendship, and she could almost see herself feeling at home here for as long as she had to stay in Colorado.

A glance at the Colonel canceled those thoughts. He was glowering at her as if she were some sort of bug that needed to be squashed. Her own uncharitable thoughts back toward him crowded out all of her good feelings. She and Daddy would never be welcomed even as temporary guests in this community. This Yankee colonel had not ceased to make that very clear to her.

Oh, she couldn't wait for Daddy to get back on his feet so she could take him home where they belonged.

Chapter Six

"You go on, daughter." Daddy's short, shallow breaths seemed an attempt to mask his pain. As always, he was putting on a brave face for her. "After our long journey, you need to have a little fun with other young people."

Seated on the edge of his bed, Susanna raked her fingers through his brown hair to comb it back from his face. In the shadow of the lamplight, she could see he was long overdue for both a haircut and beard trimming. If she left him looking this scruffy and the Colonel saw him, their unwilling host would have all the more reason to despise him, as if his condition was his own fault. Even on the trail, he'd always kept himself well-groomed, quite a feat for a man who all his life had a body servant to tend him.

"Tell you what. I'll clean you up a bit, and if they haven't left, I'll see if they still want me to go with them." Last night after supper as they were preparing for bed, Rosamond and Maisie had insisted that she accompany them to the foothills. They planned to leave at dawn, and soon the sun would rise over the distant Sangre de Cristos. The Colonel's hostility notwithstanding, she longed to accompany them. Yet she was worried sick that something would happen to Daddy in her absence.

A soft knock on the door interrupted his response. "Señor Anders?" A feminine voice with a Mexican accent identified the speaker as Angela, the Northams' cook and housekeeper, whom Susanna had met the night before.

Susanna stared at Daddy. "Isn't it a bit early for breakfast?"

An odd little grin flitted across his lips, and he shrugged. "Get the door, daughter."

Susanna hurried to obey, admitting the servant to the room. Angela brought in a tray holding a pitcher of steaming water and some masculine grooming supplies. Over her arms, she carried several towels and what appeared to be brown trousers and a white shirt. The sturdy, dark-eyed woman, perhaps forty years old, glanced briefly at Susanna, doubt filling her expression.

"Is this time good?" Her question was directed at both of them.

"Well, I—"

"Of course." Daddy coughed and grabbed his ribs. When he recovered, he spoke with effort. "You go on, Susanna. Angela came up last night and offered to help me. She said Mrs. Northam sent her."

"But—" An odd sensation swept over her. Not quite censure, but not quite approval, either.

"Miss Susanna, I am a Christian and a servant." Angela's warm gaze exuded understanding of her confusion. "Nothing improper will happen. On this, you have my word."

"Mine, too." Daddy chuckled and paid for it with another spasm of pain. Again he clutched his ribs, then gave her an artificial glower. "Are you going to obey me, daughter?"

"Oh, very well." She returned to his bedside and kissed his forehead. "Thank you, Angela." She wagged a finger in Daddy's face. "Now, you behave and get your rest."

Her heart light, she hurried back to her room to don her brown woolen skirt. Rosamond had promised a side-saddle was available for her, as though that was unusual. Then Susanna noticed the other two girls wore skirts that were split to accommodate riding astride. With some difficulty, she hid her shock. On the other hand, their boots appeared to be much more appropriate for riding than her walking shoes. If she rode often, she'd have to get a pair of those boots.

The three of them had talked late into the night until travel weariness had overcome Susanna. Strangely, she woke feeling refreshed, and the younger girls seemed just as energetic. While she'd checked on Daddy, they'd gone downstairs to fix an early breakfast, so she mustn't keep them waiting. Happiness kicked up inside her. Nate would be waiting, too. It took a few moments for her to remind herself that this was a Yankee household. As kind as the children might be, their father's behavior more than negated their generous actions.

Nate drank his second cup of coffee while the girls cleaned up after their breakfast and packed a picnic. Mother had a rule that they had to leave Angela's kitchen the way they found it, so they were taking special care. Still full from last night's steak and potatoes, he'd managed to eat a plate of griddle cakes and eggs so he wouldn't get hungry on the trail. After waking up early to prepare the horses, he couldn't wait to head out.

As restless as he felt, he kept an eye on the kitchen door hoping, even praying, that Susanna would join them. The Colonel had sent him out on chores after supper last night, so he hadn't had a chance to invite her on today's outing. He knew he could count on his little sister to think of their guest, even if it turned out she had to refuse the invitation because of her father's condition.

The door opened, and Susanna peered in almost as if she doubted her welcome. Nate jumped to his feet as relief flooded him. This lady's presence would make today a lot more tolerable. No, make it downright enjoyable.

Before he could speak, both Rosamond and Maisie rushed over and hugged Susanna.

"I'm so glad you decided to come." Rosamond spoke in a hushed tone as befit the early hour.

Maisie retrieved a plate of griddle cakes they'd set back. "You hurry and eat while we finish the cleanup."

She then ushered Susanna to the kitchen table, and Nate held out a chair for her.

"Oh, thank you." Susanna, always the lady, laid her napkin across her lap, bowed her head briefly, poured a dainty amount of chokecherry syrup on her griddle cakes and began to eat.

Nate sat across the table from her and propped his chin on his fists. "How's your father?"

"He had a hard time sleeping last night." Worry skittered across her face, but then she smiled. "Your mother very kindly asked Angela to see to him, and he insisted that I come with you."

"Well, you can see we're all pleased you can go." Nate glanced at the other two girls, who were watching them with identical smiles. He shot them a frown. The last thing he needed was to have them tease about Susanna and him. "I haven't had a chance to ask if you ride, but I put Mother's sidesaddle on a sweet little mare for you, so you'll be all right even if you don't."

"Humph." That playful glint, which he hadn't seen since yesterday at the river, returned to her eyes, sending an odd little thrill through his chest. "La-di-da, Mr. Northam, what must you think of me? We Southern ladies know very well how to ride. But mercy me, where are my manners? I do so appreciate your accommodating me with that sidesaddle."

Her mention of being a Southerner reminded Nate of the Colonel's assumption that she and her father were lazy, which Nate found nothing short of unfounded prejudice. On the other hand, he noticed she didn't seem to hold the bitterness he'd seen in some Southerners. That alone showed real character. He couldn't ask her, of course, for he'd learned long ago not to open discussions about the war with those on the losing side. He could only hope she would overlook the few times he'd slipped.

While he ruminated on that, the other two girls giggled softly, as if they were enjoying this exchange. He needed to take Rosamond aside and tell her to quit it or else. For now he'd stick with teasing Susanna.

"Well, then, if you're an expert rider, maybe I should go put that sidesaddle on our stallion, Malicia." He puckered away a grin. "In case you're wondering, *Malicia* is Spanish for *maliciousness*."

"Don't you dare, Nate Northam." Maisie came over

and punched Nate's shoulder. "I wouldn't even ride Malicia, and I've been breaking horses since before I could walk."

"Shh." Rosamond held a finger to her lips. "Don't wake the whole house. Let's get going." She nodded toward the broad window, where sunlight had begun to brighten the eastern hay field. "The sun's crested Mount Blanca, and we have a long way to go."

The group left the kitchen and made their way through the narrow hallway to exit the house through the enclosed back porch. Bringing up the rear, Nate noticed Susanna eyeing the boots lined up by the back door.

"Rosamond, hold on." He touched Susanna's shoulder to stop her, too. "Let's see if a pair of Mother's riding boots will fit."

A quick try-on proved successful, and the group was soon out the door and on their way to the stable.

With no mounting block available, Susanna relied on Nate to help her onto the horse. He gripped her waist to lift her, and a thrill streaked up her spine. One would think she'd never had a gentleman's help to get on a horse before. As he adjusted her left foot in the stirrup and made sure her right knee was comfortably positioned over the pommel, she shushed her irrational feelings and settled into the saddle. As if equally pleased with their arrangement, the pretty little brown mare nodded her head agreeably.

"Her name is Sadie." Nate handed the reins to Susanna. "Her mouth is soft, so a little direction is all you need to give her. Just use the reins, and she'll know what you want her to do."

His frown revealed more than a little apprehension for Susanna, a notion she found altogether appealing. After her long, arduous trek across the country, during which she'd stifled every complaint and worked as hard as any of the other ladies, it felt good to have a gentleman worry about her. If only the gentleman in question weren't a Yankee. Summoning the willpower to dismiss her foolish inclinations, she leaned down to pat Sadie's neck.

"Never you mind, Mr. Nate Northam. Miss Sadie and I will get along just fine."

If his sudden grin was any indication, he rather enjoyed her flippancy. "All right, then." He ambled over to his own horse and swung into the saddle. "I'll put my worries to rest."

"If you two are finished jawing, I'd say it's about time we hit the trail." Maisie reined her horse away from the stable, dug in her spurs and led out with a whoop.

Rosamond followed, urging her gelding into a slow gallop. Mindful of her own need to reclaim her riding skills, Susanna stayed back with Nate. He set a slower pace as he led the packhorse carrying their picnic baskets and gardening supplies as they rode across verdant fields toward the low-lying hills ahead.

The early-morning air smelled of fresh grass, with the pungent odor of cattle occasionally wafting by on the breeze. Quiet lay over the scene like a cozy blanket as the sun inched above the horizon to wake up the land. Sudden birdsong erupted from somewhere nearby in a marshy ditch, their *chit-chit-chit-terree* stirring Susanna's soul like a welcoming wake-up call. She glanced at Nate to see if he noticed the sound.

"Redwing blackbirds." He gave her that charming

grin of his, with one side of his upper lip a little higher than the other, as if he knew something she didn't.

Indeed, how had he known what she was thinking? She answered his intense gaze with a tilt of her head and a slight smile. As much as she tried to resist it, a warm peace settled over and within her. Maybe just for today she could give herself permission to enjoy the companionship of the handsome young cowboy beside her. The handsome young *Yankee* cowboy beside her. Somehow she must rein in this foolishness, but she found her emotions far more difficult to control than the horse she rode.

She glanced westward toward the distant San Juan Mountains, Daddy's ultimate destination. What dreams had drawn him to those silver fields? He possessed all the money he'd ever need. Unlike some former plantation owners, he'd made a successful new life for himself after the war, and the family had never wanted for anything. Maybe prospecting had been a boyhood dream, and only after Mama died was he free to pursue it. The thought stung so much that Susanna quickly dismissed it. Mama's death had made a gaping hole in Daddy's heart, so he'd had to fill it with something. If prospecting made him happy, Susanna wouldn't fault him for it.

Unlike the Colonel.

The thought brought her up short, and she unconsciously pulled on Sadie's reins, bringing the little mare to a halt.

"What is it?" Nate stopped and turned back to face her. "You all right?"

There he went again, showing that gracious concern. This time his worried frown didn't sway her emotions in the slightest. Yesterday when the Colonel had spoken of prospectors as if they were just the same as horse thieves, Nate hadn't disagreed, hadn't defended Daddy *or* her. But what had she expected? After all, an apple didn't fall too far from its tree. In fact, if she'd told him right away that she and Daddy were headed to the silver fields, he probably wouldn't have helped them.

That wasn't fair, and she knew it. He'd never asked any nosy questions about them, just helped. But she couldn't let that sway her feelings.

"I'm fine." She nudged Sadie with her left heel and loosened the reins.

The mare resumed her pace, even prancing a little bit as if eager to catch up with the other horses. Susanna held her back, and after a while, Sadie settled back into a steady pace beside Nate's mount.

They rode in silence for some time, following an irregular trail toward the rolling green hills where Rosamond had promised they would find a field of columbines. Susanna could see in the corner of her eye that Nate kept glancing at her, but she refused to acknowledge him. It just wouldn't do any good to let her heart go. In fact, she should make herself as unappealing to him as she could so he would stop being so nice.

"Just what does your father have against prospectors?" She watched with satisfaction as dismay swept over his fine features.

For a short time, he just looked away from her across the open field. At last he turned back, his eyes full of regret. "I'm sorry you had to hear him say those things yesterday. It wasn't much of a welcome, was it?"

She doubted she was supposed to answer, so she kept her gaze on the trail. Some hundred yards ahead, Rosamond and Maisie had slowed to a walk and appeared to be chattering in their usual sisterly style. Once in a while, they'd glance back and wave. Susanna couldn't resist returning the gesture. After all, she'd found no fault in the girls other than their lack of social graces. Manners could always be learned, but prejudices were rooted deep in the soul. She'd seen plenty of that back home when some of the men had taken to wearing white sheets to scare former slaves out of trying to make something of their lives. Mama had forbidden Daddy to take part, and it spoke well of him that he'd honored his wife's wishes. Any man Susanna married would have to respect her opinions that same way. She had to admit even the Colonel had acquiesced to Mrs. Northam's will yesterday.

"The Colonel is pretty free with his opinions, isn't he?" Nate's question broke into Susanna's thoughts, but again she doubted she was supposed to answer. "But sometimes his anger is justified."

Susanna offered him a questioning look, both eyebrows raised, but no smile.

"That shipment of china? It was supposed to be delivered all the way to the ranch. The freight drivers left it at the trading post in Pueblo and headed out to the gold fields near Denver." He huffed out a sigh edged with frustration. "That's why Zack and I had to go get it."

Susanna stifled a gasp. If Nate hadn't gone to the fort, he wouldn't have been on La Veta Pass, wouldn't have been there to save Daddy's life. Why, he'd been an answer to prayer, and the Lord set it all in motion long before those thieves stole their horses. She started to mention that important fact, but Nate kept talking.

"'Course, the Colonel never did think much of prospectors, even before that." Nate grimaced as if he knew it was rude to say so. "You see, he's trying to build a decent community out here, a Christian community where everybody works hard and helps his neighbor."

"Unless that neighbor is a prospector?" Susanna couldn't keep the crossness from her voice.

Nate shrugged. "Most prospectors are out for one thing, finding a fortune, sometimes at a terrible cost to themselves or others."

Susanna held her peace. What good would it do to tell him Daddy already had a small fortune? That prospecting was only a pastime, an enjoyment in his old age?

"'Course, you and Mr. Anders aren't typical prospectors." Nate offered one of his charming smiles, and Susanna had to look away to keep from smiling back. "It'll take some time for your father to heal up so you can continue your journey. I'm sure by the time you head out, the Colonel will see you're decent Christian folks."

His statement, so simply spoken, sent another one of those pleasant but traitorous feelings through Susanna's chest. At his core, Nate Northam was an upstanding man, one who gave people a chance to prove themselves beyond appearances. Her heart reached out to attach itself to him, and she could think of only one way to stop it. *Yankee! Yankee! Yankee!* she shouted in her mind. Yet somehow that epithet failed to engender the usual sense of anger and dismissal.

How could she hate a man who had saved Daddy's life and showed her only kindness?

Chapter Seven

The Colonel would change his opinion of Mr. Anders? Nate had no right to advance such a notion. His father was as unpredictable as a San Luis Valley winter and often just as cold and bitter. But Nate couldn't let Susanna go on feeling bad about the Colonel's remarks. Maybe with Rosamond's and Maisie's help, he could cheer her up, at least for today. This brave little lady had a lot weighing on those slender shoulders, and he longed to lighten her load.

"How was your father this morning?" The moment the words came out of his mouth, he wanted to kick himself. He'd asked the same question back in the kitchen and learned the old man hadn't slept well.

He could see she caught his mistake, because she grinned and looked the other way, ducking behind the brim of her bonnet. When she turned back at him, the smile was gone and her eyes had a misty look. "Brave, as always. Trying to hide his pain from me."

Brave would fit Susanna, too. "Don't let it worry you. Charlie told me yesterday that broken ribs are just about the most painful injury a man can have, sometimes even worse than a broken leg. But he'll heal." At her doubtful expression, he added, "Angela has a real gift for taking care of people. She'll make him comfortable."

Susanna favored him with a slight nod.

He'd let her be for a while. She needed healing, too—heart healing. After almost losing her father to murderous thieves, she could do with a little bit of happiness and security. Rosamond and Maisie, for all of their immaturity, had welcomed her like a long-lost sister. And of course, Mother had relished the rare chance to show hospitality. He'd leave it to the ladies to take care of the happiness. As for the security, Nate would have to keep her away from the Colonel as much as possible. Susanna didn't need to wonder whether he would throw her and Mr. Anders out before the old man was well enough to stand on his own two feet and provide for the two of them. Not that Mother would allow such a thing to happen. The dear woman loved everybody and never let anyone leave her house hungry or in need.

As often before, Nate pondered his father's disposition and the way it differed so completely from Mother's. The Colonel made quick judgments about people and seldom changed his mind. Yet he had an uncommon ability to inspire loyalty and to gather good people to himself, a trait that no doubt came in handy during the war and never left him. To a person, everyone in the community thought the sun rose and set in the Colonel and looked to him for leadership. No wonder everyone was eager to make the upcoming anniversary celebration an event that no one would ever forget.

Nate knew his father rose early every day and went to his study to pray and read the large, leather-bound family Bible. He had observed the Colonel's faith many times in the ten years since they had come to the San Luis Valley. But he often seemed to Nate like an angry Old Testament prophet rather than a man saved by the grace of Jesus Christ. His favorite target to preach at? Nate himself. And it wearied him into the very depths of his soul.

He could leave. The thought was never far from his mind. But then he would remember these past ten years. The long journey from Boston, mostly by wagon. Helping the Colonel with the hard jobs. Helping his brothers and sister when things got tough. Coming over the mountains. Finding the right acreage. Building the house. Nate could remember every board, every nail, every stone cleared from the fields and laid for the foundation. He had more skin in the house, the barn, the stable and the church up the road than a man of his age had a right to claim. That alone gave him a reason to stay in the community. He must not let his father drive him away.

"How much farther?" Susanna's question was a welcome relief from Nate's dismal musings.

"You getting tired?" He challenged her with a smirk, hoping to lighten her mood and his own.

"La-di-da, Mr. Northam, not in the slightest."

When she spoke in that sassy way of hers, how could he not cheer up?

"Well, I was just checking. Wouldn't want you to wilt away in the summer heat."

"Now, there you go again." She stuck her pert little nose in the air. "We Southern ladies may look delicate, but we're made of steel. You'll see." She sniffed with artificial haughtiness, adding a little lift of one shoulder. "Besides, I can't seem to locate this summer heat you're so busy talking about. Have you evah been to Georgia in August? That's a heat you'll never forget.

Why, it gets so hot, the chickens lay hard-boiled eggs. It gets so hot, our candles melt into little puddles before they're even lit."

Nate threw back his head and guffawed. He hadn't laughed this hard in he didn't know how long. "That's pretty hot."

They rode in silence while their horses waded through the fast-flowing Cat Creek. Once they reached the opposite side, Susanna gave Nate a saucy look. "Go on, now. Try to outdo me."

It took him about four seconds to understand what she meant, another ten to come up with a retort. "I don't suppose I can beat you for hot weather, but I'll give you a warning about the cold."

"I'm waiting." Susanna looked so pretty sitting up straight and proper on Sadie, just like a duchess. Oh, mercy, there he went again.

Remembering how Zack told tall tales in the bunkhouse on a winter's night, Nate got a faraway look in his eyes. "Well," he drawled, "it was nigh on five years ago I learned a mighty hard lesson about Colorado winters." This was harder than he'd thought. His quip wasn't that complicated. A glance at Susanna revealed her interest… and amusement. He had to come up with something fast.

The thunder of hooves broke into his panicked thoughts. Rosamond and Maisie were racing back to join them, each one bent low on her mount's neck, determined to win the spur-of-the-moment contest. Rosamond won, pulling her horse to a stop as if she was set to rope a calf for branding. Nate wouldn't be surprised if she jumped off and lassoed something, maybe that jackrabbit that just took off running from the thicket a few yards away. Despite being a little embarrassed by his sister's rowdy ways, he couldn't complain about the reprieve he'd just been handed. Maybe Susanna would forget the subject of their banter. Or maybe he could use the interruption to come up with some clever yarn about the cold.

"Hurry up." Maisie pulled up beside Rosamond. "We found the columbines just over that hill." She tipped her head in that direction, knocking her wide-brimmed hat askew. She didn't seem to notice.

"What's the hurry?" Nate looked mighty relieved over being interrupted.

Doubting he actually had a cold-weather story, Susanna laughed to herself. But guilt quickly swept away her amusement. What was the matter with her? Against everything she'd ever been taught, she'd been flirting with this Yankee boy. Mama had taught her never, ever to flirt with a man she didn't think she could marry. *Forgive me, Mama.*

"Let's go." Nate urged his horse to a brisk trot, with the packhorse trailing behind.

Instead of pulling up beside him, Susanna held Sadie to a slower pace. Nate sent her a questioning look over his shoulder.

"I want to enjoy the scenery." She used that excuse to avoid resuming their teasing conversation, but it was also the truth.

The past four months had been constant motion, yet as slowly as she and Daddy had traveled west, they always seemed to be in a hurry. Hurry to catch one train then another on their way to St. Louis. Hurry to purchase a wagon and supplies so they could make it across the plains in good weather. She wanted, no, *needed* to relax and enjoy this beautiful country.

She drew in a deep breath and let it out. The air smelled clean and fresh, with a hint of alfalfa. Above her, the sky was a deeper, richer blue than she'd ever seen. A pleasant breeze brushed over her with a featherlike caress. An occasional deer appeared in the distance, then danced away into the cottonwoods, while numerous long-eared rabbits scurried around in the tall grass. Every sight, every smell, seemed to call out to her to surrender to the happiness trying to invade her soul. Oh, how she longed for the freedom to enjoy this place, this day. These people.

Nate slowed his pace but remained ahead of her, checking back often and waving or touching his hat brim in a salute. No one could say he wasn't a considerate man. But she'd known that from the moment she met him.

She must remember who she was and where she came from. Georgia had its fields and flowers and beautiful skies. That was where her friends and relatives lived. That was where she belonged. Somehow she must guard her tongue, her heart, her mind and not let these Yankees invade her soul as their soldiers had invaded her beloved homeland. She must not lose hold of all she'd ever been taught.

As depression threatened to overshadow her, she reached the top of the hill where Nate awaited her. The instant she pulled up beside him, all sadness vanished at the breathtaking sight. Below in the shallow valley lay a carpet of blue columbines, their rich, sweet perfume rising on the breeze to fill her senses.

"Ohhh," she breathed out on a sigh. "How beautiful." In all her life, the only flower fragrance to rival this came from the gardenias in Mama's garden. She glanced at Nate to find him studying her, and her foolish heart skipped. "Yes? You have something to say?"

He grinned in his charming way, with one side of his upper lip higher than the other. Did he give that same smile to all the girls?

"No, ma'am. I'm just enjoying the look in your eyes." He gazed down into the valley. "It truly is something, isn't it?"

Rosamond and Maisie had already dismounted and were studying the flowers. Rosamond beckoned to them. "Come on down."

Instead of answering Nate, Susanna moved the reins on Sadie's neck, and the mare began to pick her way down the slope, zigzagging until she reached her friends. The other two horses nickered and tossed their heads as if to say *What took you so long?* If only Susanna could enjoy the similar welcome Rosamond and Maisie offered her.

"Come take a look." Rosamond held Sadie's reins so Susanna could dismount.

Not waiting for Nate's help, Susanna freed her right knee from the pommel and her left foot from the stirrup, then jumped to the ground. Her landing on the hard ground sent a sharp pain through each of her feet and up her ankles and calves, causing her to yelp in a most unladylike way. She never should have worn Mrs. Northam's boots, for they weren't really a good fit.

Nate jumped down from his horse and hurried to her side. "Why didn't you wait for me? I'd have helped you down."

"I'm fine." Pride forced a smile to her lips, even as the other two girls voiced their sympathy. Even as the balls of her feet continued to sting. "What have you found?"

The girls appeared to accept her quick recovery, but Nate didn't dismiss it so lightly.

"Are you sure you're all right?" He gently gripped her elbow, and a pleasant sensation swept up her arm, clear to her neck.

She shook it off as best she could without jerking away from him. "Yes. Don't give it another thought."

He released her but held her gaze, his green eyes boring into hers with a commanding intensity. "Next time, you wait for me. Your father doesn't need for you to be injured." How could a man's tone of voice be so stern and gentle at the same time?

Susanna felt the wind go out of her attempt at aloofness. She could not dislike this man, for he showed nothing but concern for Daddy and her. "You're right, of course. Thank you."

With considerable difficulty, she broke away and limped over to the girls. "Tell me about your plans to transplant these." Mama had taught her how to move flowers about the garden, but she wouldn't show off her knowledge unless asked.

"I dunno." Maisie at last straightened her wide-brimmed hat, a boyish creation that resembled Nate's and Rosamond's. "Just dig 'em up, I suppose, and put 'em in a sack." She indicated the burlap bags on the packhorse.

"Do you have any ideas?" Rosamond asked.

Susanna took a minute to kneel and study the plants and dig a gloved finger around the base of one cluster. "Well, I don't know about columbines, but I would suppose they're not too much different from jonquils or Johnny-jump-ups." She brushed the dirt from her leather gloves and stood. "Do you have a small spade?"

The girls retrieved their equipment from the packhorse, and Susanna set about teaching them how to dig up the flowers. She wasn't sure this was the best time of year for transplanting, being that the columbines were in full bloom. But here they were, so she would make the best of it.

Kneeling back down, she dug into the ground with the spade Rosamond had given her. "If you come across runners, don't worry about cutting them. I can tell these are hardy flowers, surviving out here in this climate, so they'll be fine. Just be sure you keep enough soil around each cluster of roots. We'll wait to separate the roots until we're ready to plant them in Mrs. Northam's garden."

Maisie dug into the ground with enthusiasm, while Rosamond proceeded with more care. Susanna reasoned it was because the flowers were for her mother. Nate situated himself on a rough woolen blanket on a patch of grass, propped himself back on his elbows and chewed on a green blade. When Susanna glanced over at him, he grinned in that dangerous way of his and touched the brim of his hat. She wanted to say *Stop that!* But that would only reveal the effect his smiles had on her and encourage him to keep it up.

After an hour or more of digging up the plants, wrapping the roots in burlap squares and dousing them with water from their canteens, the girls joined Nate on the blanket. They removed their gloves and splashed more water over their hands, then unpacked sandwiches, cold chicken and potato salad, a jar of pickled vegetables and another jar filled with cold coffee.

Once they'd finished their picnic, the other girls wandered off, chatting in their usual way. Susanna knew she should go with them, but her feet still ached, the pain made worse by the narrow boots she never should have borrowed.

"My, just look at those puffy little clouds." Nate tipped his hat back and stared upward. "Looks like a flock of sheep."

"Humph." Susanna eyed the same clouds. "I'd say they look more like a field of cotton bolls ready for picking." Oh, would she never learn to stop teasing? Why hadn't she simply agreed with him?

He chuckled, a deep sound that rumbled in his broad chest. "Well, seeing as how I've never seen a cotton field, I wouldn't know." He held out the coffee jar, silently offering to pour more into her tin cup, but she shook her head. "Did your father grow cotton in Georgia?" A strange little frown flitted across his brow, almost as if he wished he hadn't asked the question.

For a moment, she considered her answer. Maybe if she mentioned how General Sherman's troops had destroyed their cotton plantation, how they'd very nearly destroyed her family, it would expose the unbridgeable gulf between them. To gather her thoughts, she looked off to the southern hills, and a gasp escaped her.

Several Indians on horseback were staring down at them, and if their threatening demeanor was any indication, they were not at all pleased to see Nate and Susanna.

Fear shot through her. *Dear Lord, please help us!* Had she made it all the way across the country without a serious encounter with Indians only to die by their hands in this remote mountain valley?

Chapter Eight

Nate stood and pulled Susanna to her feet. "Get behind me." He tried to keep the tension from his voice. "I'm sure they don't want trouble. They'll ride away shortly." He doubted that, but no need to alarm her.

He glanced in the direction Rosamond and Maisie had gone. They were running back through the columbines, determination on both of their faces. If he didn't stop Maisie, she might shoot first and ask questions later. At least Susanna had the good sense to obey his order to move behind him. But as the Indians rode down the hill toward them, his chest tightened.

The girls reached him just as the Indians—Utes, more accurately—rode into the edges of the columbine field.

"Keep you gun in your holster, Maisie," he said. "Let me handle this." He understood why her father insisted she carry it, but along with teaching her how to shoot, he should have taught her to control her temper. "You girls help Susanna mount Sadie, then mount up."

To his relief, all three girls obeyed without argument or comment. He would stay on the ground so as not to appear combative to the approaching men. Lifting his empty gun hand to wave—and to show good faith—he called out, "Greetings. It's a fine day." *Lord, please let one of them speak English or Spanish.*

As they drew closer, he noticed they were leading extra horses, and cautious hope sprang up in his chest. This was a trading party, not a war party. In fact, the Utes had peacefully settled in the southwest corner of the San Luis Valley a few years back. But a man could never be sure younger men like these might not go on a tear over something or other, just as the Plains Indians did.

"Greetings." One man returned Nate's wave, but all of them were focused on the girls.

The hair on Nate's neck stood up. Could he defend them against four men? Maisie would be some help, and Rosamond had a rifle on her saddle.

"We're just headed home, so help yourself." He gestured toward the columbines. Angela had told him that Indians used these flowers to spice up their food, but she wouldn't have them in her kitchen because parts of the plant were poisonous.

"Wait." The man who seemed to be the leader rode closer to Nate. "We had a fever last winter. Lost our wives." He nodded toward the girls and held up the reins of the two horses he was leading. "You trade?"

Nate could feel the heat rising up his neck, but anger would only create problems. Besides, this was an honorable custom for these men. They meant no insult. Behind him, however, he'd heard Susanna gasp and Maisie snort. He could imagine Rosamond clapping a hand on her rifle, but he dared not look around to be sure.

"Now, friend, you know we don't do that." He decided to end the matter as quickly as possible. "Colonel Northam won't appreciate your coming our way looking for wives. Why don't you head down toward Santa Fe or the pueblos?"

The instant he'd mentioned the Colonel, all four men stiffened. Conferring among themselves, they turned their horses southward and rode away without a word. Nate heaved out a sigh, then turned to check on the girls.

Rosamond and Maisie continued to glare at the men, but Susanna's face was as white as those clouds they'd talked about a few minutes ago.

"We'd best head back to the ranch." Nate mounted up and gave Susanna what he hoped was a reassuring smile. "Gotta get those flowers in the ground before supper. Go on, now." He would stay at the rear, just in case.

The other girls led out, with Rosamond taking charge of the packhorse, but Susanna stuck close to Nate. He didn't mind that at all, especially since his pride had suffered a pinch over having to use the Colonel's name to close the matter with the Utes. But on second thought, he was grateful to be the son of a man whose name meant something to folks, at least in these parts. In times like this, he doubted he could ever leave the community, no matter how harshly the Colonel treated him.

He looked over at Susanna, whose face was hidden by her bonnet brim. "You doing all right?"

She cast a sassy little glance his way. "Now, Mr. Nate Northam, you were saying something about how cold it can get in Colorado? Did you ever come up with something clever, seeing you've had all this time?"

He laughed so hard, he almost choked, but part of that was probably pent-up feelings of relief over the safe ending to their encounter. As for Susanna, well, she was an amazing lady to recover so quickly from her fright and return to their earlier teasing. Fortunately, he had figured out a response. "I sure did. That winter, it was so cold that when I went to milk the cow, she gave me ice cream instead."

Susanna rewarded him with a soft laugh and a tight smile. "I guess that'll do, since you can't come up with anything better." She turned away from him to hide behind her bonnet again. If she said anything more or tried to control her quivering lips, she might burst into tears. She'd had enough trouble saying those few sentences, hoping to divert Nate's attention from her terrified reaction to the Indians.

Never in all her life had anyone looked at her as those men had. But she'd seen that expression before. Back home, men studied horses or dogs or items in Daddy's mercantile with that same speculative look as they considered whether or not to make a purchase. Sometimes she'd even seen men, not gentlemen, of course, but others, studying women that way. But she had never been the object of such bold stares. Even Colonel Northam's rude looks had acknowledged her as a person, no matter how unwanted a guest she was in his home. And now she could not even begin to describe the feelings churning about inside her. She was not a piece of merchandise, not something to be bought and sold at the whim of other people.

Something nagged at the back of her mind, but she couldn't pull it forward into her conscious thoughts. Something that happened a long time ago when she was very small, before the Yankees came and destroyed the South and her family's way of life. A slave auction, that was what it was. She wasn't supposed to see it, but she'd wandered away from Mama on a shopping trip to Atlanta and come face-to-face with another little girl, a dark-skinned one, on sale just like a horse. For the first time in her life, she understood the terror in that child's eyes. And not for the first time, she was grateful slavery had been abolished, especially for the sake of that little girl.

"Say, Susanna." Nate's overly cheerful voice cut into her thoughts. "I think Angela's cooking up some of her excellent chili for supper tonight. Have you ever eaten chili?"

Using a trick Mama had taught her, she took several quiet, deep breaths to steady her nerves before she answered him. "My, my, is food all you think about? First ice cream, then chili?"

He laughed, again sounding a bit too cheerful. Her brother had used that same tone when she'd confided her fears about the trip west and he'd done his best to calm her worries. Bless Nate for showing such brotherly concern for her. "After eating Angela's chili, I think we'll all agree that ice cream is just the thing to cool us off."

Susanna surrendered to a real laugh, and it felt good deep inside. They were all safe, and just as some of the dangerous incidents that happened during the trip west, this one needed to be put behind her. If it could.

After tending to the horses, Nate wandered over to the flower bed to see how the transplanting had progressed. Both Rosamond and Maisie appeared to be covered with dirt from head to toe, but Susanna didn't have so much as a smudge on her cheeks. Once again, her characteristic elegance brought the word *duchess* to his mind. One of these days, he was going to slip and call her that. Such a blunder would reveal how tender his heart was growing toward her, which would be a big mistake. He just couldn't afford to fall in love, not until he had matters settled in his own life, especially his anger toward the Colonel. Maybe the only way to avoid trouble was to tease Susanna some more.

"You girls about got this job done?" He plopped himself down on a nearby cottonwood stump and pulled out his folding knife to whittle on a stick. "I just unsaddled and brushed down five horses all by myself, got 'em fed and watered and sent out to pasture. Seems like the three of you could manage to stick a few flowers in the ground in all that time."

Rosamond and Maisie traded a look, and he knew he was in trouble. He didn't know which one lobbed the first handful of mud at him, but before he could put away his knife and take off running, he found himself being bombarded with wet dirt from both sides by giggling girls. No matter which way he tried to escape, they cut him off like cow ponies corralling a calf and rubbed soil into his hair and down his shirt.

"Help me, Susanna." He managed a glance in her direction, only to find her backing away from the scene, her expression going from dismay to amusement and back to dismay again. She'd probably never in her life been in a mud fight. Before he could stop himself, he snagged up a handful of wet dirt and slung it at her.

She nimbly sidestepped. "Ha. Missed. Now, Nate Northam, don't you dare—"

Splat! A wad of mud struck her cheek. She stared in disbelief at a blissfully guilty-looking Maisie. The shock on Susanna's pretty, *dirty* face was a sight to behold. Nate almost fell over laughing, but he thought it best to stay upright to defend himself.

"Well, I never!" Susanna's indignant tone matched her regal bearing. "The very idea!"

Everyone else froze, while disappointment pinched at Nate. Surely, a little mud couldn't offend her that badly.

"Oh, dear." Maisie looked stricken. "I'm so sorry."

Rosamond hurried to Susanna's side. "Here, let me help you." She pulled a handkerchief from her pocket and started to dab away the offending dirt.

"Never you mind." Susanna politely took the white cloth and scrubbed it across her cheek, leaving a streak of gray. "Now, if you'll excuse me, I have flowers to finish planting."

She walked slowly to the flower bed, where about half of the columbines had been planted and the rest of the separated clumps lay awaiting their new home. Something in her ambling gait dispelled Nate's disappointment, but he held his peace and watched. Sure enough, Susanna knelt down and made a mud ball, and before he could blink, she sent it hurling through the air to land smack on Maisie's chin.

Maisie shrieked louder than Nate had ever heard her, and then all three girls fell into a fit of laughter. He allowed himself to sit back down on the stump as they all looked around at each other and enjoyed the moment.

"You know, I thought for a bit that Nate was going to take those horses." Rosamond wiped her sleeve across her face, causing more damage than repair. "But I couldn't figure out which one of us he was going to trade for 'em."

Both she and Maisie guffawed like cowpokes, and neither seemed to notice the horror on Susanna's face.

"Now, girls, you know I wouldn't—"

"Oh, my, what a mess." Mother emerged from the side door and studied the scene, her hands fisted at her waist.

"Yes, ma'am." Nate gave his sister a wicked grin. "These girls have been impossible to control all day long, and now look what they've done."

Mother gave him one of her no-nonsense glares. "And of course, you're entirely innocent. Well, I won't have any of you leave the cleanup to Angela or Rita or any of the hands. You'll clean up this yard, and you'll do your own laundry." The lilt in her voice belied her stern words. She started back toward the door, then stopped to study the flowers. "These columbines look lovely, girls. I'm sure they'll recover from the shock of moving by the time we have our party." Her voice softened, as it always did when she spoke about the big anniversary event. Nate couldn't wait to see her face when the Colonel gave her the china. "Now, don't forget tomorrow is Sunday, and we're all going to church, so everyone will need a bath. Nate, you'd better get busy pumping and heating water and bringing it to the back porch." She went back inside, shaking her head, but Nate had no doubt she was laughing to herself.

As for Susanna, he hoped this bit of tomfoolery had lifted her spirits after this afternoon's fright. Once they cleaned up and sat down to supper, he could count on the Colonel to ruin any feelings of inclusion he and the girls had conveyed to Susanna.

Chapter Nine

Wrapped in a borrowed robe, Susanna hurried up the back stairs to Rosamond's room. As the least dirty of the girls, she had taken the first bath and now had time to visit with Daddy while the other girls bathed. She couldn't imagine what had gotten into her, participating in such a brawl.

Well, no, she really did know. Her first instinct had been to flee the scene when the girls started throwing mud at Nate. But when Maisie had impulsively included her in the fight, then looked so stricken by her own behavior, Susanna could not bring herself to add to the girl's chagrin. In finishing school, Mrs. Sweetwater had taught that all good manners should be motivated by a desire to make the other person feel comfortable and to save him or her from embarrassment, no matter how awkward the situation.

The only way to save Maisie from humiliation had been to serve her a dose of her own medicine. Susanna was fairly certain Mrs. Sweetwater would have been shocked by the entire affair, but it certainly worked out well. Even Mrs. Northam found the whole scene amusing. And all of that foolishness showed Susanna that the other girls were as unnerved by the incident with the Indians as she was. They'd all had a good laugh, the best antidote to any fright, the best first step to any recovery.

As she entered Rosamond's room, another memory of finishing school surfaced. In spite of all the manners taught there, the girls always had to initiate newcomers. Susanna's initiation had included sugar in her reticule, which of course drew hordes of ants. By laughing it off, she'd won many friends. The same had happened today, and it felt good deep inside her. Even though the girls were Yankees.

Rita had laid out several of Rosamond's outgrown dresses for Susanna to choose from. Her hostess was a few inches taller and a bit broader, but by no means too large. If anything, Mama would say Susanna was entirely too thin. She'd lost the last of her childhood chubbiness on the trail, and while she wouldn't wish it back, she could afford to gain another pound or two in order to feel at her best.

She selected a blue print dress, then thoroughly brushed her windblown hair. Fortunately, no mud had lodged there, so she hadn't had to wash it. Soon she was dressed, groomed and ready to visit Daddy. She found him propped up in the bed reading *Bleak House*.

"You were asleep when I peeked in a while ago." She pulled a chair up beside him. "Did you have a good day?" His clean-shaven cheeks had lost their gray cast, and his newly trimmed hair had restored his handsome appearance. Susanna could only be encouraged.

"Fair to middling." He offered a weak smile, but his eyes exuded peace and a hint of amusement. "How was your day?"

Susanna hesitated. He appeared recovered enough to hear the truth, so she told him about the entire trip to the columbine field and back. No, not the entire trip. She could talk about the lovely flower field and the nice little mare she rode. She could minimize the dangers of the encounter with the Indians and her fright, though she could see the situation troubled him. She could even describe the mud fight, which gave him a good laugh that resulted in some pain in his ribs.

But she dared not tell him what a fine man Nate Northam was turning out to be. Not that he needed any further proof after Nate's Good Samaritan actions in bringing them here. But she must not speak of her struggle to keep from caring too much for him. Daddy had been teasing her about beaux since she was born, but never about any of the young Yankee men who'd come around their prairie schooner in the wagon train. A few cold words had been sufficient to drive away their interest in her, so she could not, *would* not, dishonor him by forming an attachment to Nate.

"And what about your day?" Best to deflect any possible questions he might have. "What did you do?"

"As you can see, I'm in a bit better shape than when we arrived. It's remarkable how much better a bath can make a man feel."

Susanna gasped. "Angela gave you a bath?"

"Of course not." He lowered his chin and gave her a chiding look. "You know my stance on such matters. Have you ever seen me do anything improper with a female servant?"

"No, sir." Susanna held back a laugh. My, he looked indignant—a good sign his old self was returning. "But don't tell me you did all this yourself." She waved a hand over his clean presence.

"When Miss Angela saw the task was bigger than she'd thought, that cowboy Zack brought up the tub and water, then helped me." He went on to explain how the process had wearied him, and he'd slept most of the day.

Susanna barely heard the rest of his remarks. *Miss* Angela? Since when did a servant merit that courtesy title used in the South?

Voices and footsteps down the hall indicated Rosamond and Maisie had come upstairs, and Susanna glanced toward the door. Maybe she should offer to help with supper.

Daddy patted her hand. "You go on, daughter. I know you want to be with your new friends. I'll be fine."

"All right, dearest. You rest now." She bent down to kiss him and caught a whiff of a woody cologne. Seemed Zack and *Miss* Angela had made an extra effort in their care of Daddy. That wouldn't entirely make up for the Colonel's attitude, but it surely would make things easier as long as they had to stay here.

The girls were busy combing out tangles from their freshly washed hair, but rather than stay and chat, Susanna felt compelled to go downstairs and see if she could help with supper. Perhaps if she made herself useful, the Colonel wouldn't object so much to Daddy's recuperating in his home.

Two steps before she reached the landing where the back staircase made a right turn, she stopped at the sound of the Colonel's voice just below.

"Monday morning, when Mrs. Northam is away visiting, you slip away just like we planned. I've made all

the arrangements for you to ride one of the horses."
His soft tone held an unmistakable note of affection.

"*Sí,* Señor Colonel." Rita's voice!

A sick feeling churned in Susanna's stomach. What
kind of wickedness was this? Obviously, this man did
not hold the same moral convictions as Daddy regarding female servants. And to think this girl was younger
than his own children. What would poor Angela think
if she knew her employer had designs on her daughter?

Hearing Rita's light footfalls ascending the steps,
Susanna backed up as quietly as she could and hurried
through the hallway to descend the front staircase. To
her chagrin, on her way down the center hall to the
kitchen, she encountered the Colonel. Fighting the urge
to back up against the wall to let him pass, fighting the
urge to tell him what she thought of his character, she
forced a smile Mama and Mrs. Sweetwater would have
been proud of.

"Good evening, Colonel Northam. Did you have a
chance to see the columbines we planted?"

Instead of bowing politely as any Southern gentleman would, he stopped short and stared at her as if
trying to remember who she was. A scowl quickly replaced his confusion. "I trust your father will be back
on his feet soon." It sounded more like an order than a
friendly inquiry.

"Never you mind, Colonel." Susanna put on her
sweetest voice. He might not be a gentleman, but she
was still a lady. "Once he can walk, we'll be out of your
house faster than a jackrabbit running from a coyote.
You can count on that." She punctuated her words with
a perky smile, picturing him as that coyote she'd shot

out in Kansas. "Now, if you'll excuse me, I should go peel some potatoes or something."

She brushed past him and made her way to the kitchen. While the welcome Mrs. Northam and Angela gave her didn't entirely make up for his inhospitable behavior, it went a long way to soothing her disquieted soul.

"Did you get their names?" The Colonel sat behind his desk grilling Nate about the Indian encounter. At least this time, he didn't stand in his usual intimidating way.

"No, sir. The only name mentioned was yours, and they took off as soon as I said it." Flattery had never worked with the Colonel, and it didn't this time, either.

"Humph." He brushed away the idea as one would a bothersome fly. "I doubt they meant any harm. But just to be sure they don't come up here again, I'll send a message to the commandant over at Fort Garland." He waved a hand toward a chair, wordlessly ordering Nate to sit. "Now, about that china. On Monday morning, your mother and Rosamond are driving up to Swede Lane to deliver some food to those folks during their convalescence. That's when I want you to check for any broken pieces. You think you can get it done in a few hours?"

"Yessir." Nate started to say Susanna could help him, but it probably would be best just to have her do it and tell him later.

"You be careful with it."

"Yessir." In spite of his resolve not to get angry at his father, Nate felt heat rising up his neck. "Of course I'm careful with Mother's gift."

The Colonel sent him a scowl. "After that, you can work on the addition." He grunted in his usual dissatisfied way. "That carpenter from Denver had better show up to complete the woodwork." He seemed to be speaking to himself, as if making a mental list of all the things that needed to be finished before the anniversary party. "All right, you can go." Again he waved his hand, this time in a dismissive gesture toward the door. "And check on that Anders fellow. Make sure he's not faking his injuries so he can loaf around here at my expense."

"Yessir." Nate stood and stretched. It had been a long, tiring day, especially coming right after his trip to Pueblo. These were the times when it was hardest not to respond to his father in anger. "He could be faking the broken ribs, but it's kind of hard to fake a broken leg." He hurried from the room before his father could holler at him for talking back.

One thing was sure. His stomach was hollering at him right now. Drawn by the mouthwatering aroma of Angela's chili, he ambled down the hall to the kitchen to see if he could find something to hold him until supper. When he opened the door, Susanna's lovely face was the first thing he saw, and his heart skipped. What was the matter with him? It hadn't been two hours since they parted company to go clean up, yet he felt as if he'd been away from her for two days. And that was just short of how long he'd known her. The smile she gave him seemed a little strained. If the Colonel did something to hurt her feelings, he'd go right back to the office and give him what for.

"Nathaniel." Mother looked up from her work over a large crockery bowl. "Just the man I wanted to see.

Come over here and stir this cookie dough. It's so stiff I can't manage to blend all the ingredients together."

"Yes, ma'am." He grabbed the wooden spoon and took a turn at mixing the heavy dough, which contained candied fruit, nuts, spices and molasses. "You know I'll do anything to have some of my favorite cookies." Once he'd blended everything to Mother's satisfaction, he pinched off a piece of the dark brown substance and popped it into his mouth. "Mmm. Just right."

"You'd better leave some for baking." Mother sprinkled a little flour on the kitchen table, then spooned out a chunk of dough and began to flatten it with her rolling pin. "This recipe has to go a long way if all the hands are going to get some."

"Yes, ma'am." Turning a chair around and straddling it, he propped his chin on his hands to watch Susanna cut carrots and other vegetables. This was where they'd started the day some twelve hours ago, yet she still had enough energy and the good manners to help in the kitchen. That spoke well of her. So much for the Colonel's talk of lazy Southerners.

"May I help you do that?" He hoped she'd give him one of those *la-di-da* answers he found so appealing.

Instead, she shook her head and gave him a tight smile. "No, thank you. I believe I can manage." She scooped up the vegetables and set them in a bowl, then carried it to Angela, who was stirring the chili in a large cast-iron pot on the stove. "Is there anything else I can do? I could start washing those dishes." She nodded toward a collection of items by the dishpan.

"No, *gracias, señorita.* That is Rita's responsibility. She will do it soon." She put the vegetables in a pot, then moved to the side table and began to assemble the ingredients for tortillas.

Watching the ladies cook had always been one of Nate's favorite pastimes, but usually he was busy with his own chores at this time of day. He noticed the disappointment on Susanna's face when Angela refused her offer, and tried to think of some way to divert her.

As if reading his mind, she glanced in his direction, and he felt the little jolt in his chest that was getting all too familiar.

"If it's not too much bother," she said to Angela, "could you teach me how to make tortillas?"

"*Sí, señorita.*" Always accommodating, Angela made room on the table for Susanna to work beside her and began her instructions.

Susanna's persistence in wanting to help deepened Nate's admiration for her. He glanced toward Mother, hoping she would appreciate their guest's good manners, too, and found her watching him. The sly smile on her face cut short his enjoyment of the moment. He frowned and shook his head, but her smile merely broadened. He wanted her to like Susanna to make up for the Colonel's rudeness, but he didn't need her to play matchmaker.

He stood and headed for the back hallway. "Guess I'll go check on those columbines."

Mother chuckled. "You do that, son."

Susanna said nothing. Didn't even look his way. Nate was surprised at how disappointed that made him.

Susanna tried to concentrate on Angela's instructions, but Nate's presence made it impossible. She was glad when he left. No, not glad at all. Just plain sad. In any other time or place, regarding any Southern gentleman with the same depth of character, she could let her heart lead her. But here and now, these feelings just would not do. Even if she and Nate did fall in love, they had no future together. But she mustn't even entertain the word *if.* She would not love this man. Would not! To distract herself, she pictured the house in Marietta she loved so much and her dreams of having her own children growing up and playing on that same grassy lawn, as she and Edward Jr. used to do. She must never lose sight of those dreams.

"No, no, Miss Susanna, too much water." Angela laughed as she reached over to add more finely ground cornmeal to the bowl she'd given Susanna. "Make the dough like this." She held up a round lump that appeared pliable enough to flatten without falling apart.

"Oh, dear." That was what she got for not paying attention. "Have I ruined it?"

"Do not worry, Miss Susanna." Rita had entered the room moments ago and begun washing the dishes. "I still cannot make tortillas like *madre mia.*" She reached to place a glass jar in the rinse pan, but it slipped from her fingers and crashed to the floor. "Oh, no."

"Be careful," Angela and Mrs. Northam chorused.

Rita grabbed for the shattered jar too quickly, then gasped and pulled back her hand. Trying not to cry, she gripped her injured palm with the other hand, but blood seeped through her fingers. "Mama," she whimpered.

With a worried gaze on her daughter, Angela rinsed her hands, while Mrs. Northam left her cookie-making to come help. Susanna waited until they moved to the center table to tend the wound before finding a broom to sweep up the shards. She could not help but wonder how this would affect the poor girl's assignation with Colonel Northam.

She soon found out. Once the hand was bandaged, they all went to work again and within a half hour had supper ready. As Susanna and Rita set plates and silverware around the table, the Colonel entered the room, spied the wounded hand and demanded to know what happened. After hearing Rita's explanation, he summoned Angela and Mrs. Northam.

"This child is not to wash dishes again. Is that clear?" Both women appeared surprised by the vehemence of his order, but both agreed to obey him.

But Susanna wasn't the least bit surprised. The Colonel would likely do anything to protect the girl who was the object of his favor.

Chapter Ten

The moment Reverend Thomas opened his mouth to speak, Susanna felt as if she'd come home. His Southern pronunciations varied slightly from hers and Daddy's, but it was clear the man was no Yankee. She couldn't imagine why the Colonel had let this Southerner take such a prominent place in his community, but she expected to enjoy his sermon. Maybe the minister would visit Daddy, who'd insisted that Susanna must attend church with the Northams.

After a few words of welcome to Susanna and two other visitors, Reverend Thomas announced the Scripture verses he would address in his sermon. Seated beside Susanna, Nate held his Bible up so she could look on, just as he had the hymnbook at the beginning of the service. When they'd begun singing, she could barely hold back a giggle. Nate was no singer, but what he lacked in pitch, he made up for in enthusiasm. From the light in his eyes as he sang "When I Survey the Wondrous Cross," she could see that he held deeply the faith he'd spoken about on the trail. She might as well admit, if only to herself, that a Yankee could be a true and decent Christian, despite what his people did to the South during the war. Despite what his father said in the back hall of their house.

Before they'd left the ranch, Nate had gone out of his way to make sure she was comfortable in the family carriage with Mrs. Northam, Rosamond and Maisie. Everything he did prompted warm sentiments in Susanna's heart. Somehow she must find a way to cool that warmth before it blazed up and burned her.

She quieted her thoughts and settled back to enjoy the sermon. The verses they'd just read in Hebrews 11 might be the very thing to help her. All those Bible folks had acted in faith in the midst of serious difficulties, and most had suffered terribly for it. While staying in the home of a Yankee colonel wasn't exactly perilous, spending time with the man's son could well be dangerous to her heart.

As it turned out, the minister focused his message on the faith these congregants had in building this new community in such a harsh land. In faith, they had all left their comfortable homes back east at the invitation of Colonel Northam. His purpose? To build a Christian community where all would be welcomed with the love of Christ.

The moment the pastor mentioned the Colonel and the Lord in the same sentence, Susanna stopped listening as Rita's sweet, innocent face came to mind. Oh, the deeds done in secret! Wasn't there a passage of Scripture about how those deeds would be brought to light? If it wouldn't cause a scene, she'd grab Nate's Bible and hunt that verse right here and now.

* * *

Figuring he should dodge Mother's matchmaking efforts outside of church, Nate didn't mind when she put him next to Susanna in the pew. Susanna was wearing Rosamond's Sunday dress from last summer, so he would just think of her as a sister.

Who was he fooling? No man in his right mind could lightly dismiss the effects this beautiful lady had on him. When she'd worn that blue dress yesterday afternoon, her eyes had sparkled like the rare gems in Mother's sapphire necklace. And now in this frilly pink gown, her ivory complexion glowed like one of Mother's alabaster vases, the ones painted with roses like the soft blush on Susanna's fair cheeks. How had she managed to cross the entire continent without turning brown? Or freckled like Maisie. Maisie, whom the Colonel had seated on Nate's other side.

He forced his thoughts away from his woman troubles and tried to concentrate on Reverend Thomas's sermon. Faith. That was what he needed. Faith that the Lord would continue to build this community. Faith that in spite of the Colonel's domineering ways, Nate could stay and make a contribution worthy of the Northam name. Faith that one day he would earn his father's approval.

With that thought, his spirits sank. The only way for him to get the Colonel's approval would be to become Rand. And there at the other end of the pew sat his middle brother, dozing after his late-night doing who knew what with Seamus and Wes, two of the Northam cowhands. They'd probably been gambling, something the Colonel had made clear he wouldn't permit in his community. Yet he refused to come down hard on Rand when he did it.

The familiar resentment against his brother crowded out Nate's attempts at worship. Yes, those Bible heroes had great faith, but right now, he just wasn't up to joining their ranks.

After the sermon, Nate listened halfheartedly to the announcements. The fever that had spread through the Swedish community was now under control, thanks to Charlie Williams and his herbal remedies learned from the Indians. With the plan Mother already had in place, meals would be delivered to those folks until they could stand on their own feet again. Finally, Reverend Thomas commended the congregation for their donations to the charity fund, for several needy families had been helped.

As usual, the congregants lingered in the churchyard, chatting and catching up on news and innocent gossip. Then hunger sent them scattering to their respective homes. The Northams parted company with Maisie with a promise to send Rosamond for a return visit in a few weeks.

Nate couldn't help but notice that Susanna had been very quiet. Other than brief chats with Pam Williams and Reverend Thomas, she had stood by the carriage waiting to go home.

Except she didn't have a home. And Nate didn't have one of his own to offer her.

Susanna spent part of Sunday afternoon reading to Daddy and the remainder of the day alone in Rosamond's room. The Northams took the Sabbath seriously, resting after church just as her family had back home in

Marietta, so no one came looking for her. She'd wanted to take Daddy out into the sunshine, but he wouldn't be able to go down the long staircase for some time. An upstairs veranda opened out from Colonel and Mrs. Northam's suite, but she wouldn't go anywhere near that end of the upstairs hallway.

Rosamond had told her that even Sunday supper was quiet and simple, with Angela and Rita away visiting family in a small Spanish settlement to the southeast. Susanna wondered if Rita would find a confidante, maybe a grandmother to whom she could expose the Colonel's reprehensible behavior. Obviously, she had not been able to tell her mother, probably because she feared they would lose their employment.

Not wanting to encounter either Nate or his father, Susanna waited to fetch supper until she observed through the bedroom window that the two men had walked toward the stables, no doubt to tend to chores. In the kitchen, she found a tray laden with food and a note for her to take all that she and Daddy needed.

As they ate in the bedroom, Daddy seemed to grow more cheerful, while Susanna's heart grew heavier. How long must they stay in this place? After only two days of bed rest, Daddy's leg hadn't healed enough for him to find new horses, much less hitch them up and drive the wagon. She certainly didn't have the strength to manage all the work required for traveling.

After church, she'd thought about asking Miss Pam if they could stay with her and Charlie, maybe camp out behind the café. Before she could say a word, however, Miss Pam had told her how fortunate she and Daddy were to be in the care of such good people as the Northams. When Susanna thought to make her plea for other accommodations to Reverend Thomas, the young minister had gone on and on about what a good man the Colonel was.

In this small, developing community, no hotel had been built, and none of the homes had been made into boardinghouses. Susanna found it more than frustrating to have plenty of money to move out of the Northams' house, yet to have no place to go and no means to get there. All she could do was remember Mama's everlasting optimism and try to make it her own.

The next morning as she sat again beside Daddy's bed as he ate breakfast, Nate came to the half-open door and gave them both a big smile. That cute smile of his, with one side of his upper lip higher than the other. Despite her determination to shield herself from his charms, her traitorous heart skipped.

"Susanna, would you be able to help me with something?" The twinkle in his green eyes did nothing to fortify her resolve.

"Well…" Having left Daddy alone too much these past two days, she'd turned down the invitation to go with Rosamond and her mother to deliver food to the needy. "I planned to read to Daddy—"

"Nonsense, daughter." Daddy gave her arm a little nudge. "You go on. I'll be fine."

Her heart tried to pull her out of the chair, while her mind refused to budge. "Exactly what do you need help with?" In spite of herself, she couldn't keep the sassiness out of her voice.

He glanced back down the hallway, then ducked into the room and closed the door. "The Colonel wants me to make sure none of the china is broken. Mother and Rosamond are going out calling all morning, so this is the perfect chance to go through the boxes. I figure it'll take two of us."

His eager expression added to his charm. Here was a man who loved his mother and delighted in doing things for her. As for the china, Susanna wondered how the Colonel could worry about it being broken when it was his wife's heart that would be broken if his actions with Rita were discovered. Still, Mrs. Northam had been kind to Susanna and Daddy, so this was one small way she could pay the lady back.

"Just exactly where do you plan to do this operation?" She pictured bringing the crates into the house and spreading the china out on the long dining room table. They would need to add the extra leaves, and there would be a mess to clean up afterward with all of that straw packing—

"In the barn. We don't want anybody to know about it. My brothers and all the hands will be out herding cattle or working in the fields all morning, but we'll still have to be quick about it."

"Harrumph." Daddy glared at Nate. "Young man, do you mean to say you're going to be in the barn behind closed doors alone with my daughter?"

Surprised by his concerns, Susanna held back a laugh. "But, Daddy—"

"Oh." Nate's face turned red beneath his tan. "I didn't even think how that would look. Would you approve if Zack worked with us? He's the only person who knows the secret other than the Colonel and me." His eagerness to do the job added to his already dangerous appeal. He was nothing if not persistent, another admirable quality to add to the list Susanna was trying not to compose in her mind.

Daddy's expression changed from a scowl to a smile quicker than a blink. "Why, that would do just fine, Nate. You have my approval."

Nate's grin broadened. "Thank you, sir." He focused on Susanna. "Will you help?"

She couldn't keep from smiling at his boyish enthusiasm. "Of course I will."

An hour later, after Rosamond and Mrs. Northam had left, she followed Nate's instructions on going to the barn. She left the house by the front door and meandered around the grassy yard smelling the roses and checking on the columbines. Some of the transplanted flowers had wilted or lost blooms, but none looked as if they wouldn't make it. She next wandered toward one of the corrals, where several horses munched on a pile of hay. Several barn cats called out to her, and she took a moment to pet them. Then, following Nate's instructions on how to avoid being seen from the kitchen window, just in case Angela looked out, she found a door on the far side of the barn and quickly entered.

A medium-size black-and-white dog wandered out of a stall and eyed her curiously, tail wagging. Susanna bent down to pet her and noticed a litter of four or more puppies amid the straw and burlap on the stall floor. Her heart melting at the adorable creatures, she rubbed behind the mother's ears. "Hello, little girl. What's your name?"

"That's Bess." Nate sauntered over. "She's been keeping to the barn since having her pups, but I expect her to get out more as time goes on."

"Will she let me hold one?" Despite a strong urge to cuddle a puppy, she didn't want to upset the mother.

"Sure." Speaking to Bess in soothing tones, Nate

picked up one of the pups and set it in Susanna's waiting arms. "This little girl is the runt of the litter, but she's pretty healthy.

"Oh, how sweet." Susanna held her up to one cheek and received a good lick. "My, you're friendly."

Bess danced around as if worried, so Susanna set the puppy back among the others. "I must have one of them, Nate, unless they're all promised."

"I think we can work that out once they're weaned." Nate walked toward the specially rigged wagon where Zack stood awaiting orders. "Let's get started." He grabbed a crowbar and started to pry open one of the crates.

"Now, you just hold on a minute, Mr. Nate Northam." Susanna marched over to the wagon, suddenly feeling the weight of responsibility for this endeavor. "Just exactly where do you plan to lay out the pieces as you unpack them?"

The two men exchanged a look.

"Um…" Nate looked around the barn as if he'd never seen it before.

Zack pushed his hat back and scratched his head. "Well, I'll be. Hadn't thought of that."

"What did you do when you inspected the shipment at Pueblo?" She glanced around, not sure what she was looking for. All she saw were stalls, bales of hay, harnesses and other items used for the care of horses.

"The trading post owner's wife let us use her dining room." He and Zack traded a look and a laugh. "I think that man's going to have a hard time when his next anniversary comes around."

"Well, he should." Susanna fully understood the <u>la</u>dy's feelings. Mama had always expected something special to celebrate her wedding anniversary and always gave Daddy something special in return. "Do you have some blankets we can lay out?"

The two men scrambled to pull out several large blankets used for horses in the winter. After shaking out the dust, they laid them on the flat dirt floor.

"Don't know what we would have done without you." Nate gave Susanna that charming grin of his, and she couldn't help but smile back.

He opened one crate, removed a handful of straw and lifted out a plain oak chest. "As you can see, it's all in smaller boxes." Inside the box were four crystal goblets, each safely nestled in its own flannel-lined compartment.

"This is like a treasure hunt." Susanna couldn't wait to see what the next box held. "My brother and I used to hunt pretend treasures." She wished back the words as soon as she said them. Would Nate think she was a "money-grubbing prospector," as his father had accused?

"My brothers and I did, too." Nate winked at her as he pulled out another box, and her heart warmed. Not for the first time did she consider how different he was from his father.

The box he held contained plates separated by flexible, flannel-covered dividers. All in all, they counted twenty-four place settings, plus numerous serving pieces. Platters, serving bowls, finger bowls, creamers, sugar bowls, all in the same blue, silver-rimmed Wedgwood pattern.

As they began to repack the items, Susanna felt close to tears. Not one piece was broken. Mrs. Northam would be so pleased, and she deserved this wonderful gift. Susanna could only pray that she would never know how her gift was tainted by an unfaithful husband.

"I can hardly believe nothing's broken. That's answered prayer." Nate tucked the inventory list into his shirt in case Mother returned early and asked about the fancy parchment paper he was carrying. "And once again, I have you to thank." He eyed Susanna, who was daintily dabbing her face with a handkerchief. "Sorry you had to work up a sweat, but this barn gets mighty hot during the summer." He tried to think of a clever comparison as to how hot it got, but nothing came to mind.

"Mr. Nate Northam!" She glared at him in that cute way of hers. "Ladies do not sweat. We perspire." She sniffed with mock indignation. "And you're very welcome about the china."

Zack snorted out a laugh at the lady's remark. "I should go, boss. The boys will wonder why I'm not out there working alongside 'em."

"The boys can wait. I need you here another minute." Nate wouldn't give Mr. Anders any cause to worry about his daughter's reputation. "Susanna, do you give your stamp of approval on the way we stored the boxes?"

"Now, wouldn't I have said so if I didn't?"

"Yes, indeed, I'm sure you would have." He loved it when she got sassy. It showed spirit and optimism, maybe even faith in the midst of her difficulties. Yet one small thing nagged at him. As they'd opened each of the boxes, she hadn't viewed their contents with the same covetous glint he'd seen in the eyes of the trading post owner's wife. In fact, Susanna had inspected the dishes with a critical, even knowledgeable approach, searching for possible blemishes. She appeared to be familiar with Wedgwood and named other china patterns made by the company.

Were the Anderses truly poor, as he'd assumed? Had they fallen from wealth into hard times? Was a patrician background the reason Susanna carried herself with such dignity? Did Mr. Anders want to seek his fortune in the San Juan silver fields so they could return to some former social status? Nate didn't dare ask Susanna these questions, for that would be the worst side of rude. Maybe it was time he got better acquainted with her father so he could disguise his questions as friendly interest.

He sent Susanna out first, then waited a few minutes while Zack shuffled his feet impatiently.

"Good work handling that china, Zack. You've been a big help with it all along."

The old cowboy grinned and shrugged. "My ma never had anything that fancy, but she did teach me how to treat nice things."

"Good, because I want you to meet me in the addition tomorrow morning first thing. There's nobody I can trust to help me finish it."

As expected, the other man rebuffed his praise. "I'll be glad to, boss. Now, I'd better head out."

As Zack left, Nate gave one last appraising look at the stall where he'd stored the boxes of china. The men, and even his brothers, knew better than to go poking around the barn, and the dust-and-straw-covered canvas on top of the boxes would keep anyone from prying.

He ambled out of the barn and headed toward the house to take the inventory list to the Colonel's office.

He didn't particularly want to see his father, but if he was in, Nate would have a chance to tell him how much Susanna had helped with the china…again.

Entering the house through the back door, he followed his nose to the kitchen. There he found Susanna up to her elbows in dishwater and Angela pulling bread pans from the oven.

"I sure did come in at the right time, didn't I?" Nate swallowed hard at the overwhelming aroma of the freshly baked bread.

Always accommodating, Angela dumped a loaf onto a cloth on the table and cut a large slice for him. "Butter, Señor Nate?" She brought a crock from the side table, then went back to her work.

Nate slathered butter on the slice and started to take a bite, then paused. Susanna hadn't spoken to him or even looked his way since he came into the room. That was taking their secret a bit too far. If she'd just look at him, he could give her a surreptitious wink. Since she didn't seem inclined to do so, he broke off a bite of bread, stepped over to her and put it up to her lips.

"Want a bite?"

She pulled back from him. "From those dirty hands?" She sniffed in her haughty way. "No, thank you."

Laughing, he popped the bite into his own mouth. This little gal got under his skin in the worst—or the best—way. What he wouldn't give to just consider courting her.

He whistled as he strode up the hall to the Colonel's office at the front of the house. Maybe his father would be out in the fields, although this summer he was spending less time working side by side with the hands than in previous years. If he wasn't in, Nate would tuck the inventory list in his desk drawer, where Mother never looked.

At his knock, the Colonel called, "Enter," in his gruff, commanding voice.

A sigh of disappointment escaped Nate as he obeyed the order. He crossed the room, removing the inventory paper from inside his shirt. "All there and in perfect condition."

"Hmm." The Colonel didn't look up from his ledger. "That was fast. You sure you didn't break anything?"

Clenching his teeth, Nate placed the paper on the desk. "If it hadn't been for Miss Anders, I could well have broken some. She made suggestions on how to go about it, then on how to store everything until the party."

At the mention of Susanna's name, the Colonel's head snapped up, and he glared at Nate. "She helped you, did she?"

"Yessir, she and Zack." Better get that information out there right away so the Colonel didn't assume they'd been alone. Yet at his father's harsh expression, rebellion kicked up inside Nate. "And by the way, I promised her one of Bess's pups."

The Colonel placed his knuckles on his desk, stood and leaned toward Nate. "They are not yours to promise. You know very well we're going to raise those dogs to herd cattle, and we need every one of them. Why do you think I sent for an expert dog handler all the way from Scotland? To train them, that's why."

Nate glared back at his father while a half dozen retorts came to mind. In the end, he just spun on his heel and strode from the room, not bothering to shut the door. He stormed out of the house and across the yard back to the barn. Up in the loft, he grabbed a pitchfork and started tossing down hay. Lots of hay. And when he'd tossed down more than the horses would need that evening, he climbed down and tossed some of it out the door into the attached corral, where the horses already had plenty to eat. Then he kicked a fence post. Which only served to send pain shooting up his leg. Now he had to move the extra hay back to the loft so the horses wouldn't overeat and get sick.

Court Susanna? What was he thinking? Two unchangeable things kept him from it. His father's vise grip on his life, and his own inability to manage his temper. That last one worried him most. He didn't really want to use that pitchfork on the Colonel, but someday he might just give in to the temptation to land a punch on his father's square, stubborn jaw.

Chapter Eleven

"Before coming here, I never ate anything made from chokecherries." Susanna stirred a bite of pancake into the dark red puddle on her plate. "This syrup is delicious."

"Just don't eat the berries raw." Nate sat across the kitchen table from her, his teasing smirk not getting in the way of his polishing off his griddle cakes. "There's a reason they're called *choke*cherries. Right, Angela?"

Working as usual at the stove, Angela nodded her agreement. "*Sí*. Never eat them without sugar or honey, or you will be sorry."

Seated next to Susanna, Rosamond ate her breakfast with the same enthusiasm as her brother. "Maybe you'll still be here in September when we gather the berries and help Angela put them up. Won't that be fun?"

"Oh, yes. I always loved—" she stopped before blurting out that she'd helped the family's cook put up jelly "—making blackberry jelly. I'm sure this will be just as enjoyable."

His mouth too full for speaking, Nate nodded and arched his eyebrows, as if he was saying he also hoped she would still be here. If it wasn't for the Colonel, Susanna could almost wish for the same thing.

As these few days had passed, it had become harder to remember all the reasons she'd been taught to hate Yankees. She found this family not just tolerable, but worthy of her friendship. Except for the Colonel, of course. A lady couldn't be expected to sit at the supper table every evening under his angry looks without feeling a bit uncharitable in return, especially knowing what she did about his treatment of young Rita. But otherwise, Susanna's days had been fairly pleasant as she basked in the hospitality of the rest of the family.

Still, she must keep Nate at arm's length and not let their friendship go any deeper. She'd always had her heart set on marrying a Southern gentleman just like Daddy and Edward Jr., and she must not lose sight of that dream. The South was her world, the place where she belonged, where she was welcomed by everyone. This small community could not compare to all she'd left behind.

But then there was Nate. No Southern gentleman had ever dug into her heart as he had begun to do. Perhaps the only way to keep a hold on her emotions was to treat all the Northam brothers the same. "Where are Rand and Tolley? I never see them except at supper."

Nate's brief scowl surprised her, but she had no time to examine his reaction.

"My brothers and I are out early for chores every day. They grab a bite to eat in the bunkhouse, then head out with the hands."

"But you don't?"

"Usually I do. Right now I'm building the addition." He shoveled in another bite.

"Oh, yes." She remembered what he'd said about the structure. "Your father's gift to your mother for their anniversary." She would wink at him if such a gesture wasn't unladylike.

"Yep." He kept his expression neutral.

"I must say I'm impressed to learn you're a builder." She was rewarded with his most attractive smile, and her uncontrollable emotions did somersaults inside her. Such feelings would not help her reach her dream of going home.

"Nate's had a hand in just about every building on this property." Rosamond's voice was filled with sisterly pride. "Not to mention the church and several barns for our neighbors."

"My, my." Susanna could not imagine her own brother doing such hard labor, but she'd grown very proud of Daddy for learning many manual skills on the trek west.

Nate stood and carried his plate to the dishpan by the sink. "Can't sit around jawing. Gotta get to work. What are you girls doing today?" He directed his question to Susanna, but Rosamond didn't seem to notice.

"Mother suggested that I take Susanna on a tour of the ranch." She began to clear the table but paused. "That is, if you'd like to go."

"I would indeed. That is, after I wash these dishes." Since Rita had been relieved of the duty, Susanna tried to step in as often as she could. She actually enjoyed the chore. She'd been surprised to see the indoor pump and sink like the one her family had back home. A pipe in the sink drained the water out through the floor and all the way to the kitchen garden.

"No, no, *señorita*." Angela clicked her tongue in a

maternal fashion. "You wash dishes yesterday. Today you go along with Señorita Rosamond." She set her stirring spoon on the table beside the stove and stepped toward the dishpan. "I will wash them."

"Please let me." Susanna blocked her as graciously as she could. "You all work so hard, and it would be silly for me to sit around with my hands folded in my lap."

Her words brought an approving smile from both Nate and Rosamond.

"Let her help, Angela." Nate spoke with a hint of gentle authority, and the housekeeper nodded her acceptance.

"*Sí,* Señor Nate."

"I'll help, too." Rosamond tied on an apron and offered one to Susanna.

"You ladies have a nice time." Nate disappeared through the kitchen door.

With some difficulty, Susanna turned her attention to the task at hand. Too bad Nate couldn't go with them on the tour of the ranch.

Once the chore was completed and she had checked to make sure Daddy had everything he needed, Susanna joined her hostess outside the back door. "Is Mrs. Northam well? I wondered why she wasn't in the kitchen for breakfast."

"She's very well, thank you." Rosamond beckoned to Susanna, and they began their walk toward the outbuildings. "This morning she's working on Father's anniversary present. It's a surprise, of course, so she always has to wait to work on it until he goes off on business or out to see how the men are managing things. Today he went to Alamosa and will be there overnight, so she'll have all day and evening."

"I see." Despite her dislike of the Colonel, Susanna felt that funny little tickle inside over helping to keep a secret. "Do you know what she's giving him?"

"Yes." Rosamond giggled. "And I know what he *thinks* she's giving him. She's making a quilt from scraps of all our clothes since we came to Colorado. It's for him to take on trail drives or other such trips. She has a Singer, so she should get much of it done today." She snickered. "Father knows about the quilt, but makes a big show of pretending not to know."

Fondly remembering her own parents' secrets at gift-giving time, Susanna laughed. "But that's not the real present?"

"Nope." Rosamond looped an arm around Susanna's and leaned close. "She's having a set of silver-and-turquoise spurs made for him by our blacksmith. Just the three of us know about it." Another giggle. "And now four. I can trust you not to tell Father, can't I?"

Susanna could barely keep from choking. No, she would not tell the Colonel about the spurs or anything else. She could hardly look at him without feeling a little sick. Forcing herself to recall his generous gift of china now hidden in the barn, she managed a smile. "Of course. I didn't realize your family employed a black-smith. And to think he's a silversmith, too."

"Bert's like everyone else around here. He has to do more than one job." She waved a hand in the direction of an outbuilding near the stable. "That's his work-shop." Above the weatherworn wooden structure, a gray stream of smoke drifted into the air. "We'll go there in a minute, but first I have something else to show you."

They had crossed the wide backyard to the barn, and Susanna surveyed the place with interest as if she'd never seen it before. When they went inside, she studiously kept from looking toward the stall where a deceptively dusty canvas covered the china crates. Fortunately, Rosamond's attention was on Bess, who bounded over to them, her tail wagging furiously.

Kneeling down, Susanna pretended not to have met the dog. As uncomfortable as it made her feel, she decided not telling all she knew was not the same as lying, especially when the secrets she was keeping were not hers to divulge.

"What a sweet dog." Susanna suffered Bess's affectionate licks with good grace. "And what adorable puppies." Which one would Nate give to her? Maybe the chubby little one who was pouncing boldly through the straw to join them. No, she'd much prefer the little runt she'd held on Monday. Right now the little female stayed in the back corner of the stall whimpering for her mother and melting Susanna's heart. She'd always felt a special affection for the underdog.

"Father and Mr. Eberly brought a trainer from Scotland to teach them how to herd cattle." Rosamond picked up the brave puppy and cuddled it. "Maisie gets to take care of the puppies' father. It's an experiment, so we'll see how it works out." She held it up with its nose to hers and murmured, "You're going to tell those great big steers what to do, aren't you?"

As Susanna tickled the runt's tummy, she noticed it had one underdeveloped rear paw. The puppy settled comfortably into her arms and promptly fell asleep. Susanna decided she would call her Lazy Daisy. "When do you think they'll be weaned?" She could hardly wait to make this little one her own.

"Usually before they're two months old, but we

won't rush it. Father wants to be sure they're happy and healthy before their training begins." Rosamond spoke of the Colonel with great affection, but never called him by his rank, as Nate did. Susanna hadn't noticed how Rand and Tolley referred to him.

After they had their fill of puppy affection, Rosamond took Susanna to the blacksmith shop and introduced her to Bert, a former slave. He showed them his handiwork, large silver plates fashioned to fit over the boot tops. Each was adorned with turquoise stones and delicate scrollwork. Even the leather bands and the spiked rowels had attractive etchings.

"Of course, Father won't wear them for work, just for dressing up," Rosamond said as they left the blacksmith to his work.

Susanna's mind spun with the contradictions she was seeing. So the Colonel employed a former slave, entrusting him with such an important job as blacksmithing. Many Southerners, including Daddy, had often condemned the North for freeing the slaves and then not providing a livelihood for them. Once off the plantation, countless former slaves wandered the South with no way to earn a living. For all of his evil ways, this former officer had at least given a job to one such freedman.

When her family had sold their plantation, Susanna had been too young to have learned much about the day-to-day operation of producing a cotton crop. Now with Rosamond as her guide, she could observe the many and varied activities on a ranch, and she began to comprehend all the work that went into producing any sellable product, whether cotton or beef.

"Until we get more businesses in the area, Four Stones Ranch has to be self-sustaining." Rosamond pointed to another structure beyond the blacksmith shop. "Besides Bert, we have Joe, who tans leather and makes anything from saddles to belts to boots. We won't go over there because it really stinks when he's tanning."

Susanna had noticed the pungent smell and wondered what it was. Today a warm breeze carried most of the stench away.

Rosamond now indicated a distant field, where green, knee-high alfalfa waved in the breeze. "Of course, we grow our own feed for the animals."

"And your own food," Susanna said. "I certainly do admire that kitchen garden."

"I noticed you liked the squash." Rosamond wrinkled her nose. "You and Nate are the only ones who do, other than Mother and Father."

Susanna felt another one of those emotional somersaults near her heart. As silly as it seemed, she was pleased to learn she and Nate liked some of the same things.

A high-pitched whinny sounded from a corral some distance from the barn, and both girls turned to investigate.

"Now, that's exciting," Rosamond said. "Looks like Rand's planning to teach Tolley how to break a new horse." She grabbed Susanna's hand and rushed her toward the scene. "Let's watch."

Her excitement was catching, so Susanna ran along beside her and copied her as she climbed on the lower rail of the corral and hung over the upper rail to get a better view.

Rand was as tall as Nate and their father, but not as broad in the chest. He still gave the impression of being able to handle any of the varied duties of a cowboy. Right now he was murmuring instructions to his younger, shorter, thinner brother, who stood beside a restless horse. Susanna couldn't hear their exact words, but Tolley seemed to chafe under Rand's cautionary tone.

"If you can do it, I can." Tolley turned away from his brother, slung a blanket on the horse's back and transferred a saddle from the fence to the animal.

Before he could reach under and grab the cinch, the horse sidestepped and bucked, throwing the saddle to the ground.

"Whoa." Rand, holding the bridle and reins, tried to apply a soothing touch, but the horse tossed its head and snorted angrily.

At least it sounded angry to Susanna. She glanced at Rosamond, who was chewing her lip. Sudden protectiveness for young Tolley filled Susanna's heart. She'd noticed a bit of acrimony among the brothers, but this was certainly not the time for these two to argue. Lifting a silent prayer for both to be safe, she tightened her grip on the rail.

"Hey!" Nate appeared on the scene and entered the corral through a gate. "What do you think you're doing?"

At his take-charge tone, relief swept through Susanna. She couldn't stand it if anything happened to young Tolley. Like her little puppy, he almost seemed like the runt of the litter.

Rand rolled his eyes, but Tolley appeared relieved to see his oldest brother.

"Rand keeps treating me like a kid." Tolley shot a glance toward Susanna and Rosamond, and his face reddened. "Why don't you two go make a cake or something?"

Rosamond laughed, clearly not concerned about her little brother. "Or I could break that horse for you."

Susanna had already stepped down from the fence, but she couldn't walk away until she saw how Nate handled the situation.

"Rand, you know the Colonel put me in charge of breaking these horses." Although his hands were bunched into fists, his voice was surprisingly calm.

His hands also fisted, Rand cast a quick glance toward Susanna, and the scowl he had aimed at Nate softened. "I know he did. He also told you to go all the way to Pueblo for supplies and build that addition and make sure the hands were kept busy." He shrugged and gave Nate a smirking grin. "With all you've got to do, I'm just trying to help you out, big brother."

"So you think Tolley getting his neck broken is helping?"

"Hey—" Tolley now scowled at Nate.

Nate waved a hand to silence him. "Both of you ride out and help Seamus and Wes check the fencing, especially in the south pasture. You know it needs to be checked every day." The brothers exchanged glowering looks all around. "Now!"

Tolley jumped at his command and hurried to exit the corral.

Rand lifted his hands in surrender. "All right. All right. Ladies." He tipped his hat to Susanna and Rosamond and sauntered toward the gate. Then he jerked his head toward the horse and gave Nate another smirk. "I'll leave you to take care of Spike."

"No." Nate took a step toward him. "You'll take care

of him and put away this saddle." He paused as if waiting to see whether Rand would obey him.

Rand glared, then shrugged and moved toward Spike. "Come on, you dumb beast. Back you go to your friends till the big boss here makes time for you in his busy schedule."

"And about tonight," Nate said, "just because the Colonel is away, don't get any ideas about going over to Del Norte with Seamus."

Spike snorted, and Rand laughed. "That about sums up what I think of that order."

As he led the horse out of the corral, Nate didn't respond. Susanna couldn't help but admire his self-control, even as she failed to comprehend why he and his brothers, especially Rand, seemed to have some sort of rivalry. She and Edward had always gotten along so well, despite his being six years older. A sudden ache to see her dear, protective brother swept through her. All the more reason to go back home.

"Did you ladies finish your tour?" Nate spoke so pleasantly one would never know he'd almost come to blows with his brother.

"Yep." Rosamond stepped down from the railing. "I guess it's about time to help Angela fix supper."

Nate came out of the corral, and the three of them walked toward the house.

"What did you like best, Susanna?"

Hoping to ignite some playful banter, she gave him a saucy smile. "Why, the puppies, of course. I fell in love with one in particular."

His responding frown sent a shard of worry through her. "Yep, they're heartbreakers. That's for sure." He kicked a stone in his path with unusual force.

Susanna's heart sank. Had he changed his mind about giving her the puppy? Or had she made a mistake by hinting at his promise while they were in Rosamond's company?

No matter the cause of his displeasure, one thing seemed apparent. She would not be getting Lazy Daisy for a pet. And that hurt more than she could have imagined.

Chapter Twelve

The next morning, Susanna approached the breakfast table with great hesitation. Nate's pleasant but subdued greeting confirmed her fears. He'd changed when she'd mentioned the puppies, so something had happened between his promise and that moment. From the cheerful way Mrs. Northam and Rosamond greeted her, she knew they were not the cause. It had to be the Colonel. While the three family members carried on their usual morning chitchat, she considered her options. Maybe the mean old bear of a colonel would sell her Lazy Daisy. She'd hand him a solid five-dollar gold piece and enjoy the shock on his face. That would show him she wasn't a poor little nobody who didn't even deserve common courtesy.

Having cheered herself, she looked across the table at Nate, trying to think of something clever to cheer him up, too. He chose that second to rise from the table and gather his plate and silver.

"Well, those rooms won't get finished if I sit here jawing." Now he gave Susanna a warm smile that held no reservations and punctuated it with a wink. "You ladies have a nice day."

As disappointed as she was that he was leaving, her heart still skipped pleasantly. Until she shushed it up with a reminder that he was not the Southern gentleman of her dreams, and Four Stones Ranch was not the home she'd always wanted.

"Rosamond, you may use the Singer today." Mrs. Northam stood and straightened her apron. "Angela and I will clean up the kitchen so you can get started on those shirts right away."

"Yes, ma'am." Rosamond finished her glass of milk. "Susanna, would you like to help?"

"Indeed, I would. For whom are you making shirts?"

"Just about every man on this ranch." Rosamond beckoned to her, and they proceeded up the back stairs.

"Oh, my. How many will that be?" The more, the better to Susanna's way of thinking. She loved to sew and should have brought Mama's Singer on the trip west. Of course, the horse thieves probably would have stolen or destroyed that, too.

"About eighteen or twenty." Rosamond headed toward her parents' bedroom at the far end of the hall. "Give or take a few. Some hands aren't as reliable as others, so Father and Mother aren't as eager to provide for them."

"That makes sense." She hesitated at the bedroom door, hoping they wouldn't be sewing in there.

"It'll take both of us to carry the machine downstairs." Rosamond's words set her mind at ease.

"Of course. Just a moment." After a quick hello to Daddy and reporting the happy news that she would be sewing today, she joined Rosamond in carrying the Singer downstairs to the sunny dining room. The heavy treadle machine, housed in an oak sewing cabinet, gave them more of a challenge than either one had expected. As usual, Susanna knew Mama would be shocked at how strong she had grown over these past months.

After they set the machine in front of the two wide windows, Rosamond stood back and breathed out a hearty, "Whoosh! Next time we'll get the men to move it."

Susanna laughed as she tried to catch her breath. "Sounds like a good idea."

The time had come for her to revise her opinion of Rosamond as a spoiled girl. She was as hardworking as her parents and brothers. Now she sorted through the heavy bolts of fabric Nate had brought over the mountains nestled among and cushioning the boxes of china.

"This green plaid will make a nice shirt for Nate, don't you think?" Rosamond nodded toward a bolt of bright cotton she'd set on the dining table. "Of course, there's enough to make shirts for Rand and Tolley, too. What do you think?"

Susanna guessed that her friend was baiting her, but she refused to bite. "I suppose. Do your brothers mind dressing like triplets?"

They both laughed, but Susanna did wonder how the three men—well, one boy and two men—would appreciate having that connection, considering their quarrels.

"They don't have much choice." Rosamond sat in front of the Singer and started pumping the treadle to wind thread onto a bobbin. "We girls often run into a twin at church because we can't let the material go to waste. Oh, here's Nate now."

"What about Nate?" As he entered the room, he gave his sister a suspicious frown. "What are you two up to?"

"Oh, nothing." Rosamond kept her eyes on the machine. "Susanna, would you hold that material up to him and see what you think? If it doesn't suit him, we'll use it for the cowpokes. Most of them don't care what color they wear."

Susanna did as she was told and was not in the least surprised when Nate's green eyes lit up like emeralds. This was a good color on him, all right, and her pulse started to race when he gazed down at her. Gracious, what was wrong with her?

"It'll do." She set the bolt back on the table and took up the sleeve pattern they had made earlier from newspaper. "Stick out your arm."

"Yes, ma'am." As he obeyed, he grinned at her with mischief in those green eyes. All of his reserve had disappeared, so maybe she was wrong about the puppy.

That happy thought swept away her fears. Or was it his increasingly intense gaze? She avoided looking at his eyes and concentrated on measuring the length of his arm. His very muscular arm. Trying not to touch him, she felt her insides shake like aspen leaves in the wind. No sense in denying that he was an attractive man, but she must not let him affect her this way.

"So, Mr. Nate Northam, what have you been up to the past hour?" She kept her tone as light as possible but still could hear her own breathiness. She gave his shoulder a shove so he'd turn his back to her for measuring.

"Like I said at breakfast, working on the addition." As he turned, he tilted his head toward the double sliding doors he'd just come through. "Just a few more finishing touches, then the carpenter can come in to do the fancy woodwork. That's going to be one very fine ballroom, not to mention the additional bedrooms upstairs."

"A ballroom!" Susanna couldn't have been more sur-

prised. "My, my." She held a piece of newspaper and
marked his size on it with a stubby pencil, then used
a tape measure to double-check her work. Gracious,
what a broad back. She wrote down the measurements
with a shaking hand. "Just imagine having a ballroom
way out here in the country." She laid the paper on the
table and took a deep, quiet breath to calm her nerves
while she cut it to shape.

"Mother loves to entertain." Rosamond's voice held
a hint of defensiveness. "Other than barns, nobody has
enough room for the whole community to come together, and she didn't want to leave anyone out of the
anniversary party."

Having intended her teasing remark for Nate, Susanna was appalled that she'd wounded Rosamond.
"Well, I think it's just grand. All the plantation houses
back home have ballrooms for entertaining." She
shouldn't have said that. Daddy wanted her to keep
their social prominence a secret. "I attended a ball
once." More than once, of course. Oh, she was making
a muddle of it all. "I think I hear Daddy calling." She
left the pattern pieces spread across the table and fled
the room, using the back stairs to avoid any possible
encounter with the Colonel.

Nate stared after Susanna until he noticed Rosamond
watching him. "Wonder what got into her." He shrugged
for effect before heading for the door.

"Yes. I wonder." Rosamond's laughter followed him
all the way into the kitchen.

She and Mother were getting a little obnoxious in
their subtle teasing about their houseguest. Didn't they
know the Colonel had other marriage plans for him?

Not that he'd go along with those plans, even if Susanna weren't here. But he sure wished they'd all leave him alone to decide what to do with his own life.

One thing he'd decided overnight was that he would keep his promise to Susanna about the puppy. He would tell the Colonel not to pay him next month's wages in exchange for it. That should impress his father with how serious he was. There would be other litters, but a promise was a promise, no matter what the Colonel thought about either Mr. Anders or Susanna. Nate would have to find out which one she'd fallen for so he could give it to her as a surprise, maybe with a big red bow around its neck.

Other than trying to figure out how she knew so much about Wedgwood china, he hadn't been too concerned about her past, but that comment about attending a ball rang true. While not one item he'd seen in the prairie schooner indicated Mr. Anders came from money, Nate got the impression they'd once been wealthy, maybe before the war. Of course, Susanna would have been a small child when the war ended, so that didn't answer his questions about her fine manners. He'd never known a poor person who behaved with such grace nor one with such knowledge of fine china.

He didn't care whether the Anderses had been poor. He just wanted, *needed,* to know more about them. If he decided to go to war with the Colonel over letting them stay until Mr. Anders healed, he didn't want any unpleasant surprises about them to come up later. Of course, his father would misunderstand his intentions and assume he was interested in Susanna, a luxury Nate couldn't afford until he'd settled on his own future. If she turned out not to be what she seemed, that would be the last straw in losing what little respect his father had for him. Not to mention the heartache he would bring upon himself, maybe even Mother and Rosamond. He'd visit Mr. Anders this afternoon and check up on him. If a few personal questions slipped out, all the better.

After dinner, he left Zack to finish painting the ballroom ceiling and made his way upstairs. Last week when he'd brought Susanna and her father to the ranch, he'd been more than willing to surrender his own bedroom to the injured man. Now seeing Mr. Anders's pale face and sunken cheeks reinforced his determination to keep him here until he regained his strength. He must make certain the Colonel didn't turn the old man out.

"How's it going?" Nate kept his tone cheerful as he pulled a chair up beside the bed.

"Can't complain." Mr. Anders tried to sit up but fell back with a grimace. "Not much, anyway." His deep chuckle brought another pained expression.

"Hush, now." Nate already felt guilty over his plans to interrogate the man, and now he'd caused him pain. "Have Angela and Zack been keeping you comfortable?" The room smelled surprisingly fresh for a sickroom.

"They have indeed." Gratitude shone from the invalid's eyes. "I just hope we're not putting you out too much."

"Not at all, sir." Nate waved a dismissive hand. "In fact, Susanna's been a big help around the house. She's helped with everything from cooking to sewing, not to mention working in the kitchen garden."

"That's good." The older man gave an approving nod. "She's like her mama, not wanting to sit idly by while others do the housework."

Nate scrambled to decipher that comment. Had her mother been able to choose whether or not to perform household chores?

Mr. Anders stared at him. "You want to ask me something?"

Feeling foolish over his suspicions, Nate shrugged. "Nothing in particular." Maybe Mr. Anders was one of those people a man could talk to with candor. Not like the Colonel, whose anger Nate was always trying to dodge. "Just thought it was about time we got better acquainted. Mind you, I don't mean to be nosy."

"Of course not." Mr. Anders's doubtful expression belied his words. "I understand your father doesn't think much of prospectors."

"Yessir." Nate appreciated the way this man took the bull by the horns. "And if Susanna told you that, she probably told you it's because of the freight drivers who left our cargo at Pueblo so they could go off prospecting." He didn't need to add that the Colonel didn't want prospectors to settle in the community because of their generally unreliable character.

"She did. That was downright dishonest of those men, especially if your father paid them in advance." He pressed a hand against his ribs and took a deep, raspy breath. "But I can't say I'm sorry they did quit the job. No telling how long we would have been up on that pass without help if you hadn't come along."

Nate chuckled. "And I wouldn't have come along if I hadn't gone to Pueblo. Yessir, I've thought of that." Probably wouldn't have met Susanna, either, an idea he didn't care to dwell on because it made his heart sink clear down to his belly. He really needed to stop that nonsense.

"Then rest your mind about it, Nate. It was God's plan all along." Mr. Anders stared at the wall, but didn't really focus. "The Lord's been leading me across the entire continent, so I have to trust that the robbery was part of His plan." His eyes closed briefly, then he gazed at Nate again. "About my prospecting, I'll know what I'm looking for when I find it." His eyes briefly flared with some emotion Nate couldn't define. Rage? Lust for riches? It sure was different from Susanna's detached viewing of the china.

Mr. Anders's face softened into a more peaceful expression, so much so that Nate wondered if he'd been mistaken. "After I find it, I'll go home." The old man's voice grew even raspier as he closed his eyes again and shuddered, as if the warm breeze coming through the window had chilled him.

"Yessir." Worry for Mr. Anders threaded through Nate, so he tugged the patchwork quilt up to the old man's chin. Lying still like this could give the man ague, so he'd better consult with Angela or Charlie Williams about the situation. "I'm praying you'll be back on your feet soon so you can start your search."

Not that he was in a hurry for them to leave. After this short talk, Nate felt certain Mr. Anders was a man of integrity, whatever his past, just as he was a man of faith. If he needed to restore his lost fortune for his family's sake, then that made him all the more admirable. And it made Nate all the more determined to get closer to Susanna before she left Four Stones.

Giving her the puppy would be just the beginning of what he would do for her.

Chapter Thirteen

Susanna helped the other ladies pack the large picnic baskets with sandwiches, cold coffee and baked goods. After three days of sewing, she was eager for a change, especially one that would take her out of doors. Today Mrs. Northam insisted she must help Rosamond carry the noon meal out to the men working in the field. While she endeavored to ignore the older lady's obvious matchmaking, she did look forward to seeing Nate. Having finished his work on the ballroom, he now worked with the men every day and took his breakfast in the bunkhouse. Susanna missed seeing him.

With their horses saddled and the packhorse laden with the baskets, they began their trek at a slow pace. Once again, Susanna rode sidesaddle on the agreeable little mare, Sadie, while Rosamond rode her bay gelding astride.

"How far do we have to go?" Better to ask that simple question rather than ask whether or not they might encounter the Indians again.

"Just under a mile, over in that field." Rosamond indicated the uncultivated land to the west. With her hat hanging on its strings down her back, she tossed her long, dark brown hair in the breeze. "Too far for the men to walk back to the house to eat, then walk back out to work."

"That makes sense." Not to mention it gave her a chance to see Nate.

With the sun beating down on her, Susanna longed to go bareheaded like her companion. But this worn straw bonnet had saved her complexion on the long journey west, so she must not toss it aside. With her lighter coloring, she might not fare as well as Rosamond, whose sun-browned skin looked surprisingly attractive, especially with her green eyes, so much like Nate's, sparkling like jewels in the bright day.

"There they are." Rosamond waved toward the men some fifty yards away. "They're digging irrigation ditches and... Oh, dear." She pulled her horses to a stop, and Susanna came up beside her. "Let's just wait here until they notice us."

"Why?" Susanna focused on the men briefly before quickly looking back at her friend. "'Oh, dear' indeed." Heat rushed to her cheeks.

"We mustn't blame them." Rosamond giggled. "Ditch digging can make a man terribly hot, not to mention ruin a good shirt."

Susanna bit her lower lip to keep from laughing. Mama had taught her all about modesty, and Mrs. Sweetwater had reemphasized those lessons. But on the wagon train, privacy had sometimes given way to expediency, leading to some awkward situations. Today, Susanna thanked the Lord they had not ridden closer to the working men and embarrassed them all.

A sharp whistle split the air, and they saw Nate with

his shirt back on and waving his brown hat. The other four men were also properly clothed.

"Let's go." Rosamond urged her horse forward using her knees, as Susanna had observed before. While she couldn't imagine riding astride, she could see how practical it was for this life. She gave Sadie a little tap with her riding crop, and the mare followed the other horse.

They neared the work party, and her heart began to race. Yes, indeed, it had been entirely too long since she'd seen Nate, and the sight of him made her happier than she could have imagined. My, he looked healthy. Due to his outdoor work, his cheeks had tanned even darker than before. Beneath his hat, his green eyes glinted in the sunlight, just like Rosamond's.

"It's about time." He wiped a red handkerchief over his face. "I hope you brought plenty."

The men crowded around the packhorse and wasted no time in removing the baskets.

Nate sauntered over to Susanna and tilted his hat back. "Will you girls join us?" He gave her that charmingly crooked grin of his, and her heart did its usual somersault, despite his smelling of hard work.

"Of course." Rosamond jumped down from her horse and hurried to the grassy spot where the men were laying out blankets and digging into the food. "Don't you men ever wash your hands?" One hand fisted at her waist, she pointed with the other to the nearby stream they were working to connect with the ditch. "Wash. Now."

Tolley was the first to obey, then Rand and the other two men joined him at the water. While they were occupied, Nate gripped Susanna's waist and helped her down from Sadie, and pleasant shivers shot up to her neck. "Will you stay and eat with us?" His hands still on her waist, he gazed down at her, not seeming to realize he'd already asked that question.

She had to take a deep breath before offering him a shaky "Yes, thank you." Gracious, would she ever feel this way about a Southern gentleman? Did that nice young minister from Virginia have a wife? Susanna hadn't noticed a lady at his side last Sunday.

"Why, Mr. Nate Northam." She stepped back to break his grip, but her breathiness refused to subside. Nor could she manage to inject the slightest bit of sassiness into her voice. "Shouldn't you go wash up? And pay particular attention to that dirt smudge on your nose or it just might end up in your dinner."

"Yes, ma'am." With a laugh, he wiped his handkerchief over his face again, then headed toward the stream.

Watching him walk away, Susanna could only admire his fine, manly form. In fact, she couldn't think of a single thing not to admire about either his physical presence or his character. *Oh, Mama, this is one thing you never taught me. I'm trying so hard not to fall in love with this Yankee, but my heart refuses to mind me. What am I supposed to do now?*

As he'd stared down into Susanna's sky-blue eyes, Nate had felt his pulse hammer wildly. He was glad to have an excuse to walk away from her before he did something foolish. Like tuck those loose blond curls back under her bonnet. Or tell her how pretty she looked. Or tell the boys he was taking the afternoon off so he could spend it with her. Now wouldn't that be something for the Colonel to hear about? And Rand might just be the one to tell him.

Just this morning, Nate had come to the decision that he would quit feeling so partial toward her. Oh, he'd still work a month to give her the puppy of her choice. He wouldn't break that promise. But until he could control his temper and get over his anger at the Colonel, it wouldn't be fair to her or any other lady to seek anything more than friendship.

Even so, he silently thanked Rosamond for bringing Susanna along to deliver dinner. He'd missed seeing her these past couple of days, missed her sassy, teasing ways. Now that his part of building the ballroom was finished, he had to leave the house every day before daylight and ride herd on his brothers and the hands. That meant he saw Susanna only at supper under the Colonel's watchful eyes. In fact, they hadn't had a private conversation in three days, if he could count that bit of teasing in front of Rosamond private.

Settling down on one of the blankets the girls had brought, he fished a ham sandwich out of the basket and took a bite. Just as Susanna finished setting out items on the other blanket, Seamus gave her an appraising look Nate didn't care for in the slightest.

"Will you join us, miss?" The Irishman spoke with that foreign brogue some women found so appealing.

"Well…" she began.

Nate felt heat rushing up his neck. "She's already accepted my invitation." He waved her over. "I've saved you a spot, Miss Anders." That should put Seamus in his place. Nate might not be able to court Susanna, but he wasn't about to let just any cowpoke sweet-talk her.

He had an obligation before the Lord to take care of her
while her father was laid up.

"I was going to say—" walking over to his blanket,
Susanna wore that cute, scolding look on her face "—
someone should say grace before anyone eats."

Nate felt a pinch of shame. As the foreman in charge,
he should have set an example for the men, especially
his brothers. "You're right. Let's pray." He offered up
a spoken prayer of gratitude for the food, for the hands
that prepared and brought it out to them, and for good
progress as they continued to work on the ditch that
afternoon. Once he said "amen," he silently prayed for
the Lord to give him guidance about Susanna. After
his hot reaction to Seamus's friendly invitation to her,
something any cowboy might say to a pretty girl, Nate
could not deny he was beginning to care deeply for her.
But it just wouldn't work out.

Now, if he could just make his foolish emotions accept that painful fact.

Susanna sat cross-legged on the blanket, one folded
knee only a foot away from Nate's. Mama would be
shocked by her posture, but Susanna had learned early
on the trip west that for the noon meal, it was either sit
like this or stand. She could tolerate the temporary ache
in her back so she could be near Nate. She'd appreciated
the way he'd set Seamus straight about where she was
going to eat. On the other hand, his protectiveness had
stirred up some unruly emotions she couldn't seem to
silence. She tried to think of some way to tease him,
but finally settled on a neutral topic.

"The ballroom is beautiful, Nate. You and Zack did
a fine job. The wallpaper is exquisite, and there's not

a wrinkle in it." She picked at the bread crumbs that had fallen on the blanket to avoid looking into those appealing eyes.

"You saw it? Nobody was supposed to go in there." He scowled at his sister. "The Colonel wants Mother to be the first one to see the finished room."

Rosamond returned a haughty sniff. "And just how are we supposed to make those velvet drapes if we don't go in and measure the windows?"

"Oh." He gave Susanna a sheepish grin. "You're helping make the curtains? That's real nice, but you don't have to do it."

Warmth spread through her chest at his appreciative gaze. "I enjoy sewing."

"Susanna is very good with velvet," Rosamond said. "It always slips for me, and I end up with puckers or uneven seams. And she refuses to give me her secret." She laughed along with her complaint, so it didn't give Susanna cause for worry.

"Can't give away family secrets, now, can I?"

"Well, I still say it's real nice."

As he gazed at her, Nate's expression softened in a way Susanna had never seen before, almost to a glow. With difficulty, she looked away, fighting the pleasant bonding of her heart to him. Did he feel the same way? Were his friendly feelings toward her growing into something more, as hers were toward him? And if they were, what could they do about it? She just couldn't marry a Yankee. If she did, she'd never be able to go home to Marietta. And surely Nate could never get his father's approval, for the Colonel not only disliked her, he obviously hated her.

"Have you and Mr. Anders had time to read any more of *Bleak House?*"

Lost in thought, Susanna jumped at Nate's question. "A little, yes." She scrambled to remember where they'd left off last night, but she'd fallen asleep right in the middle of reading. Daddy'd had to wake her up and send her off to bed. "I must say, there are so many characters and story lines, it's difficult to keep track. I was making a chart on our trip, but the horse thieves must have thrown it in the fire, because it's not anyplace in our wagon."

His eyes darkened a little at the mention of the thieves, but then he grinned. "A chart, eh? Have you figured out who the villain is yet?"

"Daddy and I disagree, so we're having a little contest to see who's right. It makes our traveling more fun. If he wins, I'll have to shine his shoes, and if I win, he'll have to wash dishes. That is, once we're back on the trail."

"That's a nice way to pass the time." Nate's soft gaze lingered on her, making it hard for her to swallow. Was he hoping, as she was, that it would be some time before she and Daddy would be back on the trail?

After all those months of traveling, surely she could rest for a while longer and enjoy the fellowship of this community. In spite of the Colonel, she really wanted to attend the anniversary party. Or any party, for that matter, if anyone happened to throw one.

Her hopes were realized two days later when Maisie rode over from the Eberly ranch with an invitation to her family's barn raising the following week. Joining the ladies in the kitchen, she announced, "After the work's done, we're having a big shindig to celebrate Independence Day." Shrugging, she added, "And my birthday."

"You don't have to tell me twice." Rosamond gave her a sly smile. "We already have your present." She winked at Susanna. The two of them had made a new shirtwaist for Maisie, and both looked forward to giving it to her. At Susanna's insistence, it had many more frills than Maisie's usual shirts.

"Why, Maisie," Mrs. Northam said, "I'd forgotten that you share your birthday with our United States. Of course we'll be there. What can we bring?"

"Cook's gonna roast a side of beef and a whole pig over open pits, so any side fixings will be good. And Ma said to tell you to bring your special lemon cake."

While the other ladies discussed what their neighbors might bring, Susanna scrambled to think of something she could prepare. Not that they would need her efforts, but she'd still like to participate. If Angela had the right ingredients, Susanna could impress Nate…well, *everyone,* with her special dessert.

Maisie chuckled. "Anybody want to make a guess what Mrs. Halstead will bring?"

"No need to guess." Rosamond pinched her nose as if smelling something bad. "Sauerkraut."

As Mrs. Northam laughed at their banter, Susanna glanced around the kitchen searching for the ingredients for her special recipe. Her heart skipped when she located molasses, pecans and even vanilla. She couldn't wait to ask Angela to help her. Yet even as she planned, she chided herself. Her growing desire to please Nate in every way only added to her slippery hold on her heart.

Chapter Fourteen

"Don't forget the barn raising at the Eberly place this coming Thursday," Reverend Thomas announced as he stepped down from the podium after his sermon. "Not that I think any of you will." Chuckling, he walked up the aisle toward the door. "Some people will do any kind of work to chow down at one of Joe's barbecue feasts."

Nate laughed along with the rest of the congregation as they all stood to leave the church. Although he didn't think any cook in the San Luis Valley could compete with Angela, he did agree that Joe ranked right near Pam Williams as second best. Remembering his discussion with Susanna while they were out on the trail, he leaned against her lightly in the pew.

"Maybe you'll fix one of your family recipes." He gave her his most charming grin and wiggled his eyebrows. "I seem to recall your bragging about them."

"Nate Northam." She sniffed with artificial haughtiness. "I never did any such thing." Her pretty face creased into a cute, teasing smirk. "But you just wait and see. You're the one who'll be bragging that you know me." She peered around him, and her smile vanished as she scooted out of the pew.

Nate didn't have to turn to know the Colonel was responsible for the change in her. As much as he didn't want to look at his father, his head swiveled involuntarily. He lifted his hat from the pew and gave the Colonel a curt nod. "Nice sermon."

"Glad you were listening." His father's eyes darted briefly toward the door, where Susanna stood in line waiting to chat with Reverend Thomas. "Maybe you'll take heed."

For a moment, Nate couldn't grasp his meaning. Then some of the passages the preacher read from Proverbs came to mind, and he could barely resist slamming his fist into his father's stubborn jaw. If Susanna heard his insulting remark, the Colonel deserved nothing less.

Lord, forgive me. Here I am in Your house, and I'm thinking such sinful thoughts. But what am I supposed to do, to feel, *when the Colonel is so unfair and judgmental against someone so sweet and innocent? Someone I can't help but care for? Help me, Lord, 'cause it's a sure thing I can't help myself.*

He moved out of the pew and followed the rest of the congregation toward the door. Susanna had stepped out onto the front stoop and stood shaking hands with the preacher.

"Daddy would be so pleased if you could come visit, Reverend Thomas." She gazed up at the preacher with a sweet, guileless smile that would charm a grizzly bear.

A wave of jealously swept over Nate, almost knocking him off his feet. Reverend Thomas was a bachelor, just like Seamus, who'd flirted with Susanna earlier in the week. Only the minister wasn't some free-ranging cowpoke, but a godly, upright man. Rebellion kicked up inside Nate. Maybe the preacher could marry Maisie. That would show the Colonel. It would also set Nate free to court Susanna. *Court!* There was that word again, one that increasingly sprang up in his mind like the pesky cowlick on the back of his head.

Conviction struck hard on the heels of those thoughts. Anger. Jealousy. Rebellion. Right here in God's house. Nate mentally slammed a fist into his own square jaw, a replica of his father's he stared at every morning when he shaved. Until he dealt with those faults, those *sins,* he wasn't fit to court—or marry—anybody.

After overhearing the Colonel's insulting words, clearly aimed at her, Susanna appreciated the warm firmness of Reverend Thomas's grip as he shook her hand. She thrust aside all unpleasant thoughts and gave her full attention to the minister. In his eyes, she noticed a brief spark that hinted at something beyond pastoral interest. Nothing improper, of course. Merely the look of an unmarried gentleman appraising an unmarried lady. A Southern gentleman, she reminded herself, and therefore a prime candidate for the fulfillment of her lifelong dreams. But she doubted he would want to leave his church and go back to the South. And as she returned his gaze, no emotions somersaulted through her chest. No giddy sentiments caused her hand to tremble. Instead, she felt just plain comfortable, as she did with her kindly old minister back home.

"I'll be happy to visit your father, Miss Anders," Reverend Thomas said. "You just name the day and time."

"Why not today, Reverend?" Mrs. Northam came up

beside Susanna and put her arm around her waist. "It's been too long since you've been out to the ranch for Sunday dinner, and we'd be delighted if you'd come. It would give us an excuse to cook something special on a Sunday instead of eating leftovers. I know my boys would appreciate it."

The joy that surged through Susanna and brought tears to her eyes had nothing to do with romantic feelings. Mrs. Northam's kind touch reminded her of Mama's loving embraces. More than that, her hospitality to this fine minister would mean he could talk with Daddy this very day, maybe encourage him and help them find another place to live.

If the Colonel thought she hadn't heard his despicable comment to Nate, he was sadly mistaken. Or perhaps he'd meant for her to hear. Either way, she just had to get away from his wicked judgments.

She might not be a perfect Christian, but she wasn't like the immoral woman in Proverbs, not in any way. All her life, Mama had set an example of being a godly Proverbs 31 woman. And all Susanna's life, that was exactly what she'd also striven to be, as did every Southern lady she knew. But what would a Yankee colonel know of such things? The way General Sherman and his troops had swept through the South, murdering and pillaging as they went, they'd never honored Southern women nor cared whether they lived or died. How hypocritical of the Colonel to cast aspersions on her character when his own moral behavior was reprehensible.

Once they all arrived at the ranch, Susanna offered to help in the kitchen because it was Angela and Rita's day off. Last week, the family had eaten sandwiches and spent the day resting. With Reverend Thomas as their guest, however, Mrs. Northam insisted upon a more formal meal. While the ladies cooked, Nate kindly offered to take the minister upstairs to meet Daddy.

"I don't know what I'd do without you." Mrs. Northam patted Susanna's arm as she peeled potatoes. "On the rare Sunday when we have company, Rosamond and I always have to rush around to get the meal on the table. It's so nice to have an extra pair of helping hands."

"You're very welcome, ma'am." Susanna put on her best, brightest smile, but her heart ached. Was this dear lady so blind to her husband's faults that she couldn't see how he treated their unwilling guest?

Rosamond stoked the fire in the cast-iron stove, placed a large skillet on top and lay flour-covered pieces of chicken into the bacon grease left from breakfast. Soon the aromas mingled into a mouthwatering scent that filled the room and probably the rest of the house.

Trying to ignore her growling stomach, Susanna decided she would take her own dinner upstairs to eat with Daddy so she could avoid the Colonel. Maybe Reverend Thomas would eat with them. No, of course not. He'd accepted Mrs. Northam's invitation, so he would dine with the family. At least the minister was with Daddy now. She would pray Daddy would inquire about another place to live, but last night he seemed more than content to stay at Four Stones. Of course, hidden away in Nate's bedroom, he didn't have to put up with the Colonel's constant censure. What would he think if she told him about the Colonel's insinuation this morning? She couldn't tell him, of course, for it would only grieve him that he was unable to protect her.

Tolley burst through the kitchen door, his black Sunday suit changed for a blue shirt and denim trousers. "I'm starved. How soon will dinner be ready?"

Susanna found his youthful brashness a welcome interruption to her unhappy thoughts, but she couldn't help but wish his oldest brother would come to the kitchen, too.

"If you set the table, it'll be ready a lot sooner." Mrs. Northam put a pan of bread into the oven, then brushed strands of frizzy gray-brown hair from her face with the back of her hand.

"That's women's work." Tolley sauntered over to the sideboard and snatched up a leftover biscuit from breakfast.

Turning chicken over in the skillet, Rosamond snorted in a rather unladylike way.

"Humph." Mrs. Northam nudged her son with her elbow. "Then get out of my kitchen so we can finish our *women's work.*"

"What women's work?" Nate breezed through the door, and Susanna's heart did its usual somersault. "How can I help?" He gave Tolley a meaningful look. What a good example he set for his youngest brother. There went her heart again.

Tolley grimaced and put the half-eaten biscuit on the sideboard. "We can set the table." He moved to the cabinet where his mother kept her best china.

Soon to be second-best china, Susanna thought as a tiny bolt of happiness shot through her. How could she possibly leave before seeing this kind lady receive her extraordinary gift from her extraordinarily wicked husband? That meant Susanna would have to endure another three weeks in this house. Even then, how could she drag Daddy away when Zack and Angela took such good care of him? Unless he healed faster than he had in the past week, she would have to manage everything all by herself, an impossible task. She was stuck like a possum in a pot of tar, no question about it.

Once they'd prepared the food, Susanna found the tray Angela used to carry up Daddy's meals and loaded it with enough for two people. Laying a linen towel over the tray, she headed for the back stairs.

"Think your father can eat all of that?" Nate cut her off and peeked under the towel, then gave her a dubious grin. "May I carry it up for you?"

"My, you're full of questions, Nate Northam." As much as her silly emotions had improved when he'd come to the kitchen, she'd hoped to make her escape without attracting his notice. But he'd been entirely too helpful in the meal preparations, maybe enjoying her presence as much as she enjoyed his. "I can manage very well, thank you."

"I have no doubt you can." His gentle tone and soft gaze soothed her bruised soul like a healing balm. Did he realize she'd heard his father's cruel insinuations and want to make up for them? "But I'd still like to help."

Her eyes began to burn, so she clicked her tongue dramatically and shook her head. "Land sakes, do let me get on with it before the mashed potatoes get cold." If he didn't let her go right this second, she'd break down and cry. How could this man be so different from his father?

Nate stepped back to let Susanna pass, and she scurried out of the room almost as if she was afraid. Not of him, but of something. That confirmed his worst suspicions. He'd come to the kitchen on the pretext of helping so he could see how she was doing. While she still had a bit of sass in her, her crestfallen posture and overly bright comments to Mother and Rosamond had made it clear she'd heard the Colonel's remarks.

That tears it. This afternoon after Reverend Thomas left, Nate would confront the Colonel in his office and insist that he quit insulting Susanna and start treating her with proper respect. In the meantime, when they all sat down to dinner, he couldn't even look at his father, only stare at the empty chair across the table where Susanna should be sitting.

"A very fine sermon, Reverend." The Colonel sounded as if he was awarding a medal to one of his soldiers. At least that was how it sounded to Nate.

While Mother and Rosamond added their agreement, Rand and Tolley were busy stuffing their faces. Nate wished they would pay attention. Several things the preacher had said would apply to one or both of them. Yet when Nate looked at the Colonel, he was staring straight at him, as though he was some reprobate sinner. Not that he didn't struggle with his anger, but that wasn't what his father referred to. Yes, they'd have a talk this afternoon, and if he lost his temper, so be it.

"Thank you, sir." Like everyone else in the area, the preacher seemed to stand in awe of the Colonel, if his modest shrug was any indication. "I've been studying the Book of Proverbs for some time now and find its wisdom useful for the spiritual growth of an individual or a community."

"Hmm." The Colonel nodded thoughtfully. "An interesting insight. I look forward to seeing how you develop this series."

A whole series on Proverbs? How had Nate failed to hear that bit of information? Maybe instead of talking to the Colonel, he should take Rand aside, give him a firm shake and warn him to listen next Sunday instead of dozing off.

Or, maybe instead of doing either one, he would take Susanna out for a walk and try to make up for the way his father treated her. That would be a much better way to spend a Sunday afternoon.

"So *Alamosa* is Spanish for *grove of cottonwoods?*" Susanna walked with her arm looped through Nate's. Although she wasn't concerned about stumbling over the roots and rocks on the uneven path, she did enjoy holding on to his muscular forearm. The last time she'd walked arm in arm with a gentleman was last Christmas, when a would-be suitor tried to talk her out of coming west. Even though she hadn't wanted to leave her hometown, her promise to Mama that she would take care of Daddy defeated the arguments of every friend who wanted to keep her there. And now, of course, she found Nate's company far more enjoyable than that of any other man she'd ever met. Even though he was a Yankee.

"That's right." Nate looked up toward the cottonwood branches swaying in the warm summer breeze. "You've noticed we have lots of Spanish names around here."

"I recall you said so the day we met." Had it been only nine days since he'd saved Daddy and her on that mountain pass? It seemed a lifetime ago. "But your ranch's name isn't Spanish. How did your folks come up with Four Stones?" She guessed it had something to do with the family's four children.

Nate glanced at the house with obvious pride and affection. "The day we finished clearing this plot, the Colonel asked Mother how big she wanted her new home to be. She told each of us children to pick up a stone and mark out the four corners." He chuckled at the memory. "I don't think the Colonel expected us to make it so big because he walked away mumbling to himself. Of course, he eventually granted Mother's wishes, saying the ranch would be officially named Four Stones."

Susanna laughed with him, and it felt good deep inside. She needed to keep this conversation light before her foolish heart did something, well, foolish. "What do you think your town will be named?"

Nate shrugged one shoulder. "Don't have any idea." He stopped and gazed down at her, his green eyes bright in the daylight. "Don't know how to say this in Spanish, but I'd like to call it *the place where I hope Susanna settles down*."

She should answer with something saucy. Should laugh and walk away. Instead, she breathed out, "Oh, Nate, what a lovely thing to say."

She had no idea how long they stood staring at each other. Yet she felt no embarrassment or awkwardness, just very much at home. Distant sounds reached her ears. Birds sang. Cattle bawled. Bess barked. None shattered the wrapped-in-cotton feeling that surrounded her. Against everything Mama had taught her, against her own sense of right and wrong, she longed for him to kiss her right here and now. She also hoped he would not. That was a bridge they must not cross, not now or ever.

"I just wanted you to know—" He hesitated, shook his head, then took her hand to resume their walk. After several moments, he added, "I'm getting used to having you around." The deep tremor of emotion in his voice said far more than his words.

Was he experiencing the same hopelessness about their...*friendship* as she was? Did he realize, as she did, that they had no hope of happiness together? If only she could forget that fact, maybe she could enjoy this day, this hour. Tomorrow a new week would begin and—

A happy little jolt reversed the downward spiral of her emotions and sent them bubbling upward. Tomorrow she would discover whether Angela would mind her using the ingredients for her special dessert. If she didn't mind, Susanna would give Nate a delicious treat he'd never forget.

Chapter Fifteen

Nate stood in a row with a dozen other men, each of them gripping a rope. At George Eberly's shout, they all pulled, and the wall frame of the barn slowly rose to an upright position. Other men scrambled to pound in nails to join this section to the adjacent raised wall, while more workers removed the ropes and attached them to the opposite frame. With each successful part of the work done, a cheer went up from the crew.

The needs of the Eberlys' livestock had outgrown the original barn, so George had torn it down to build the new one. The barn raising had begun before first light, with George's cook, Joe, providing breakfast to everyone who came early. By midmorning, close to fifty men, all of them the Colonel's handpicked settlers of the community, had joined in the work. The air was filled with the aroma of Joe's side of beef and a whole pig roasting over open pits, so everyone labored with enthusiasm as they looked forward to their reward at the end of the day.

Nate never felt more content than when he was working with his friends on a community project, whether it was a barn, the church, a home for a newcomer or a building to house a business. Each success inspired the next one and fostered a sense of community among the settlers. He had to admit the Colonel had a gift for gathering his troops, so to speak, and motivating them to do great things. Nate would be foolish to leave all of this, even though his father's constant criticism was hard to deal with, not to mention his groundless disapproval of Susanna and Mr. Anders.

Thoughts of Susanna drew his attention across the barnyard to where she and the other ladies were preparing the noon meal in the shade of several elm trees. To his surprise, she was looking his way, so he gave her a little wave. She was by far the prettiest girl there, even prettier than the five Eberly sisters, all of them too young for him. Rosamond wasn't bad-looking, but as his sister, she didn't count. Nor did any of the married ladies. No, Susanna had them all beat. For the past four days, she'd been holed up in the kitchen with Angela, and they'd refused to let him in. Since she'd accepted his challenge, he couldn't wait to see what she'd concocted for today. In fact, he'd better be close to the front of the line, or her dessert might be all gone by the time he reached it. Even if it didn't measure up to Angela's desserts, he would say it was the best he'd ever eaten.

"Watch out, Nate." Wes caught a board that had fallen from the frame and nearly hit Nate on the head. "What are you thinking about?" He glanced toward the ladies. "Never mind. It's obvious."

"Thanks, pal." Nate gave him a friendly shove. "But mind your own business."

And he'd better mind this business of building, or the next loose board might just knock him senseless. Not that he wasn't already senseless when it came to Susanna.

* * *

With a gasp, Susanna caught the empty platter before it hit the hard-packed ground. She'd been watching Nate and had seen his close call, so it took a moment to regain her composure. Thank the Lord one of the other men—Wes, if she wasn't mistaken—had caught that board just in time. When she started to return Nate's wave, he'd already gone back to work. Maybe it was best that he not look her way again.

"Here, honey, just lay these sandwiches out on that platter." Mrs. Eberly, a rounder version of Maisie and her four sisters, set a large basket on the cloth-covered plank table beside Susanna. "Do you think we'll have enough to feed everyone?"

Her question was aimed more toward the older ladies who'd busied themselves with food preparations. Several spoke up, some certain they'd have no trouble feeding this army, others just as certain they needed to go inside and cook more food.

Glad not to be in charge, Susanna arranged the square sandwiches in a random fashion so they would be easy to pick up, then spread a linen towel over the platter to keep the flies away. She looked around for another task, but the other ladies seemed to have everything in hand. Her dessert lay tucked away in the Northams' wagon, ready to be brought out when she was certain Nate would get a healthy serving. Because of all the time she'd spent in the kitchen, she'd had to tell Mrs. Northam her secret. Of course, she hadn't mentioned that Nate's teasing had motivated her, so her kind hostess kept complimenting her willingness to contribute to the feast.

With nothing to do, Susanna wandered in the shade watching the hum of activity. Countless workers buzzed about like a hive of bees, everyone seeming to know just what to do in building the massive barn. Even some of the children who were too young for such strenuous work carried water or lemonade to the men.

"Susanna, come over here," Rosamond called from the back porch of the large, two-story house. Beside her stood Maisie and two of her sisters.

Pleased to be included in whatever was happening, Susanna had to force herself not to run. Even in this informal setting, she could not forget Mrs. Sweetwater's teaching, *Ladies do not run. Ever.*

"What are you all doing?" Treasuring the generous way they'd accepted her, she climbed the two steps onto the wide, covered porch.

Rosamond giggled. "I just couldn't wait until this evening to give Maisie her present. Is that all right with you?"

"Oh, yes." Susanna had delighted in making the white shirtwaist, especially when Mrs. Northam had produced some lace from her sewing supplies.

Giggling as they went, the five girls scurried inside the house and upstairs to Maisie's bedroom, which she shared with one of her four sisters. On her bed lay the brown paper package tied with red grosgrain ribbon.

With no ceremony whatsoever, Maisie tore into the package and pulled out the shirtwaist. And stared at it as if she had no idea what it was. "Oh. How nice."

Susanna and Rosamond exchanged a worried look.

Maisie's sisters, on the other hand, squealed with delight and reached out to touch the cotton garment.

"It's beautiful. Can I borrow it?" Grace asked.

"Me, too," Beryl said.

"You don't like it." Rosamond seemed near to tears.

"Oh, no." Maisie flung her arms around her friend, squeezing the blouse between them. "It truly is beautiful. I really will wear it." Her eyes reddened, too. "Someplace."

"Maybe church," one sister volunteered.

"Yes. Of course." Maisie gave Rosamond a weak smile. "Church."

Susanna felt like backing out of the room and disappearing. She'd insisted on the lace and frills, and now she understood her mistake. Here in this very nice, very plain bedroom, she could not see a single other frilly item. Maisie was a cowgirl, not a debutante, and had no use for such fripperies. The shirts she and her sisters wore with their split skirts looked just like men's shirts, and they wore the same style to church with plain skirts. Even their boots didn't have a single feminine design etched into the leather. Having no sons, Mr. Eberly must be training his daughters to run the ranch.

"Well." Rosamond dabbed at her eyes with a handkerchief. "That's that. At least now we have one fancy shirtwaist among us, so if anyone needs something a bit more elegant than our usual clothes, they can borrow it."

The other girls laughed rather boisterously, as if they wanted to help her smooth over the awkward situation.

"It's about time to eat." Maisie tossed the shirtwaist onto her bed. "Let's see how we can help."

While the other girls dashed from the room and thundered down the staircase to the back door, Susanna stifled a sigh and descended the stairs at a more ladylike pace. To Rosamond's credit, she did not blame Susanna for the gift, and it would be pointless to claim responsibility now. Maybe later she could explain it all to Maisie. These girls were younger and less genteel than she was, but they had good hearts, and she despaired of ruining their budding friendship.

Nate lined up with the other men to clean up at the washtubs, then made his way to the food lines. After his near accident, he'd lost track of Susanna, but now saw her behind one of the tables serving food. He could always tell when she was sad or depressed. Although her posture never sagged, he could see the smallest difference in the tilt of her head or the turn of her shoulders. If the Colonel had said something to hurt her feelings, today of all days when she was working as hard as any of the ladies, he'd have to find a way to make it up to her when he reached her spot.

"Won't you have one of Mrs. Barkley's pickles?" She poked a fork into a Mason jar and pulled out a plump one that carried a powerful briny smell.

In the corner of his eye, he saw Mrs. Barkley nearby, so he smiled at Susanna. "Yes, thank you." With memories of how the older lady's pickles tasted, he decided he could bury it later when nobody was watching. "When do I get some of that dessert you made?" He waggled his eyebrows in the hope that she would give him one of her sassy responses.

She didn't even look directly at him, didn't even smile. "Mrs. Eberly said dessert will be served in the middle of the afternoon. That way nobody will get too full and not be able to go back to work."

"Good idea."

He touched the brim of his hat and moved on. Something had caused her sadness, and he intended to find out what it was. Once work resumed, he'd look for an opportunity to come back to ask her. But after he finished eating and returned to the rhythm of working on the walls side by side with the other men, no such opportunity arose.

In midafternoon, a one-horse buggy rolled onto the property. The driver, a youngish-looking man in a black suit, clearly wasn't looking to be a part of the work crew. When Nate noticed the Colonel and George Eberly striding toward the newcomer, curiosity got the better of him. He turned his job of toting siding boards over to another man and followed his father.

"Dr. Henshaw." The Colonel greeted him with an outstretched hand. "Welcome. Let's secure your horse away from the work area, and then I'll introduce you around. This is George Eberly."

While they talked, Nate ambled up as though just passing by. "Can I take care of your rig for you?" So this was the doctor the Colonel had summoned to serve their community, the son of the doctor who'd been his company's physician in the army.

"Why, thank you." He wrapped the reins around the brake and took great care in climbing down. Once on the ground, he straightened his jacket and bow tie.

Dandy. The word popped into Nate's mind before he could stop it. It wouldn't do to judge this man too hastily.

"Doc, this is my oldest boy, Nate." The Colonel jerked his head in Nate's direction. "How's your father?"

"He is well, thank you." The doctor removed leather gloves to reveal soft, pale hands. Even Preacher Thomas had a workingman's hands and had labored all day beside the others on the barn. "He said to give you his regards." The doc chuckled. "And his thanks for getting me out of his hair."

"Sounds just like him." The Colonel snorted out a laugh. "I guess he did all his bragging about you when he wrote to me." He clapped the other man on the shoulder. "Let me introduce you to the folks you'll be taking care of."

The three of them walked away while Nate led the horse to a corral by a shady stand of cottonwoods. There he unhitched him to graze with the other carriage horses. Nate would send one of the younger boys with water for all of the animals, but now he needed to get back to work.

Boy. That was what the Colonel had called him to this fellow who couldn't be more than a year or two older than Nate. And he'd shown more respect for the doctor than he'd ever shown Nate. He wouldn't fault the doc. That wouldn't do any good. But it soured in his belly like one of Mrs. Barkley's pickles to practically run Four Stones Ranch for his father and yet still be called a boy.

Would he get more respect if he became a doctor? A preacher? An army officer? He'd never know, because the Lord sure hadn't called him to any other profession than ranching. If his father had so little regard for that occupation, why on earth had he ever come west?

Susanna joined the other girls in washing dishes so the older ladies could rest before starting supper preparations. Several large washtubs were set on benches, and the stronger girls carried hot water from a cauldron over an open fire.

Despairing of ever having soft, white hands again,

Susanna plunged into the task with all the energy she could muster. Before leaving home, she'd never had a callus on her palms or sunburn on the backs of her hands. But complaining or feeling sorry for herself wouldn't help, so she tried to join in the good humor of the other girls. All of them were as brown as berries and didn't seem to mind at all.

"Why, Miss Northam." Maisie held up a sopping dishcloth and moved toward Rosamond. "I do believe you have a smudge on you cheek. Do allow me to get it off."

"Ha." Rosamond laughed. "I know your game." Before Maisie could reach her, Rosamond splashed a handful of water on her.

Maisie squealed and returned a similar gesture. Soon all the girls had joined the fray, and Susanna had to back away to avoid a soaking. Maisie's curly red hair fell out of its pins and down her back in a fiery cascade. Rosamond managed to keep her head dry, but her skirt was dripping. She lifted a cupful of water from the tub and started to fling it.

"Wait." Maisie froze, her eyes focused on something near the half-built barn. "*Who* is that?"

All the girls followed her gaze.

"Oh, my," Rosamond said. "That's one fine-looking gentleman."

Giggling, the other girls made similar remarks. Except Maisie. She just stared, and her jaw hung loose. Susanna had the urge to reach over and lift her friend's chin.

Colonel Northam had gathered the men around the newcomer, and although they were some distance away, his voice carried across the wide yard. Susanna had never seen him so enthusiastic, especially in the way he clapped the young man around the shoulders.

"You all know how much we appreciate Charlie Williams for taking care of our broken bones and sicknesses these past few years." He gave a nod in Charlie's direction, and everyone applauded. "To help him out a bit, I've brought John Henshaw from Boston. Now, he's a new doctor, so I'm sure Charlie will need to teach him a lot of things."

The crowd laughed, especially when Charlie declared his immediate retirement from doctoring. Susanna could see no one took the declaration seriously.

She searched for Nate among the men and found him leaning against a corral railing, his hat tipped back and his arms crossed. His bemused expression wrung her heart. The Colonel was behaving like a proud father toward the newcomer, something she'd never seen in his treatment of Nate.

After several minutes, Colonel Northam and Mr. Eberly walked toward the ladies with the well-dressed younger man in tow. Maisie squeaked like a mouse and spun away, dashing toward the house.

Susanna touched Rosamond's arm. "Should we see if she's all right?"

Rosamond gave her a doubtful frown. "Well—"

"Rosamond." The Colonel beckoned to his daughter. "Come meet the son of an old friend."

Susanna had never even seen him smile, but this was more than a smile. More like when she and Daddy had set out from home. Daddy's face had been lit with hope and, for lack of a better word, joy. Anybody looking on could easily see that the Colonel planned to play matchmaker for his daughter and this handsome doctor.

To avoid any possible awkwardness, such as the Colonel not bothering to introduce her to the man, Susanna ducked away and hid among the other ladies. Still worried about Maisie, she decided it was best simply to pray for her. If her sisters or Rosamond weren't concerned, Susanna would let the matter rest.

Nate, on the other hand, was one person she could encourage. Making her way through the wagons and buggies parked in a nearby field, she found the Northams' wagon and retrieved her basket from under the driver's seat. When she returned to the tables, the other ladies were spreading out cakes, pies, cookies and other assorted desserts, and the men had lined up to partake. All except Nate. He still stood by the corral, arms crossed, staring down at the ground.

She had to dodge several men, Rand and Tolley in particular, who'd heard about her special dessert, but at last she reached Nate. His hangdog expression broke her heart. She'd refused to let him cheer her up earlier, so she owed him some teasing.

"Well, Mr. Nate Northam." She sauntered up next to him, hugging the basket like a treasure. "Here I thought you'd be storming the castle to get some of my dessert, but you don't even seem half-interested." She glanced over her shoulder. "Guess I'll just surrender it to Tolley. He almost snatched it right out of my hands."

Nate's gloomy expression slowly gave way to a smile, but she could see his heart wasn't in it. "Don't you dare give it to that boy. He'll eat it all in one sitting, then end up sick."

"All right, then." She held up the basket and opened the lid. "Help yourself." All of a sudden, her pulse sped up. What if he didn't like her best recipe?

He peered into the basket, then gave her a questioning look. "What is it?" His green eyes twinkled just a bit. "Is it edible?"

"The very idea!" She snapped the basket lid closed and spun away. "I'll offer it to someone who'll appreciate—"

Before she could take two steps, he gripped her arm and gently tugged her back.

"Oh, come on, now." He put on a pitying frown. "I'll save you from embarrassment and eat one."

"Don't do me any favors." She could hardly keep from laughing. This was her Nate, teasing in his lighthearted way. *Her* Nate? Not really. But hers to enjoy just for now.

He reached into the basket, lifted out one of the soft, light brown squares and bit into it. His eyes grew round, and he grinned as he chewed. "What are these? I like pecans a whole heap, but I've never tasted them done up this way. They're delicious." He made a grab for the basket, but she held on tight. "Can I have another one? Please?"

"They're pralines." She gave him a smug look. "And you'd better not eat any more. As you mentioned, too many sweets will make you sick."

"Oh, I doubt that." He gripped the basket. "Let's see how many I can tolerate."

"There are two kinds of pralines." Somehow she felt the need to explain. "Some are hard like candy. These are creamier because they're made with cream and molasses. The pecans are the best part." She permitted him to take one more, then firmly retrieved the container. Remembering the look on his face when she offered him

Mrs. Barkley's pickles, she had a pinch of doubt about his sincerity. "Do you really like them?"

"Mmm-hmm." He nodded vigorously as he chewed. "Never tasted anything as good as these."

The glint in those green eyes convinced her that he spoke the truth. How good it felt to give this noble man a reward for all his kindnesses to her and Daddy.

"Well, I'd better go find Tolley. If I don't save him one of these, he'll never speak to me again." She turned to walk away.

Again, Nate caught her arm and tugged her back to stand in front of him. "Thank you, Susanna." His rich, warm voice, accompanied by his soulful, puppy-dog look, sent a pleasant feeling skittering through her insides. He wasn't talking about pralines.

"Thank you, Nate." Now she really had to walk away. If his father thought they were sparking, he'd make life impossible for both of them.

Sure enough, across the barnyard, the Colonel stood staring at them, hands fisted at his waist, thunder riding on his brow. *Lord, have mercy.*

Because she had a feeling that if the Colonel set himself against either her or Nate, God's mercy was the only thing that would save them.

Chapter Sixteen

"I can't thank you enough for all your help." George Eberly stood in the center of his newly completed barn, with the entire community of workers standing around him or seated on bales of hay.

"We can't thank you enough for all that food," a man called from the crowd.

Nate joined in the laughter ringing to the rafters. He hadn't been this exhausted since the trail drive last year, but it was a good, rewarding tiredness. Both his spirits and his stomach were fully satisfied. Maybe even his heart. His short visit with Susanna had gone a long way to heal his bruised feelings about the Colonel's partiality toward the new doctor. She'd also introduced him to those remarkable pralines, his new favorite dessert. He'd have to make sure she knew he wasn't just being polite when he complimented her cooking.

"Well, with Colorado winters so harsh, our barns have to go up in the summer," George continued, "so I appreciate your generous gift of time when you all could be building on your own land. Just give me a holler if you need my help on anything." He surveyed the group.

"Today we made it through without too many injuries, and our new doc has taken care of those."

Even Nate had consulted the doctor about a splinter, one he could have removed himself. But he'd wanted to take the man's measure, and he found the doc to be a decent sort. Friendly, humble, glad to be part of the new community. Nate couldn't let the Colonel's partiality toward John Henshaw influence his own feelings about him.

George settled his gaze on Nate's parents. "Now, I've already apologized to Colonel and Mrs. Northam for stealing their thunder and having a big shindig just three weeks before their special anniversary party."

"Except ours will be a lot fancier, so wear your Sunday best," the Colonel called out. "And you won't have to work for your supper."

More laughter filled the barn.

"All right, all right." George waved a dismissive hand at the Colonel. "Folks, it's still early enough for us to have a little bit of dancing before our Independence Day fireworks. But we have one more thing to celebrate. Maisie, get on over here." He looked toward the door, where only four of the Eberly sisters stood with Susanna and Rosamond. "Where's Maisie?"

"Here, Pa." Maisie poked her head around the barn door, and several people gasped, Nate among them.

Was this the same little gal who'd engaged in mud and water fights with his sister and could outride most men he knew? Indeed it was, but the former tomboy had suddenly transformed into a lady. She wore a bright blue skirt instead of her usual riding getup. Pearl earrings dangled against her clean-scrubbed, freckled cheeks. Her bright red hair was piled up on her head in a tidy, fancy do, and she wore an equally fancy white shirt-waist. If Nate wasn't mistaken, that was the one Susanna and Rosamond had made for her. Across the way, the Colonel eyed him and tilted his head toward Maisie. Nate just shrugged. While he had to admit she made a fine picture, she still wasn't the girl for him.

George called his daughter over and announced that this was her eighteenth birthday. While everyone shouted birthday wishes, the Colonel motioned Nate toward Maisie. Nate's heart plummeted to his stomach. How could he make his father understand he had no desire to court Maisie, much less marry her? *Lord, help me, 'cause You know I won't marry that sweet little gal.* Not when Susanna stood right there beside Maisie, outshining her in every way, despite her wilted clothes and unkempt hair.

Fiddles, guitars and an accordion were brought out, and the musicians struck up "Old Dan Tucker." While couples took to the floor for a lively jig, Susanna moved closer to Rosamond and squeezed her hand. "Maisie looks beautiful, but is she just trying to make us feel better by wearing the shirtwaist?"

"I don't know for sure." Rosamond shook her head. "But I have a suspicion. Look."

Across the way, Maisie whispered something to her father, and he led her over to the new doctor. Instead of her usual boldness, she seemed almost demure. Almost. The dear girl obviously didn't know the meaning of the word, for she gripped his hand and shook it as if she was pumping water. Even so, Doc Henshaw gave her a big smile and waved his free hand toward the dance floor.

"Oh, my." Susanna laughed softly. "That's a surprise. A very nice surprise." She wasn't sure Maisie and the doctor would make a good match, but from the smile on Rosamond's face, jealousy over the newcomer would not come between the two friends. For her part, Susanna would look for the first opportunity to ask him to visit Daddy.

"Yes, a surprise indeed." Rosamond had just enough time to agree with her before Wes approached and asked her to dance. From the corner of her eye, Susanna saw Seamus, the Irishman, moving in her direction. Although her feet itched to be out there with the other merrymakers, she'd much prefer a different partner.

"Miss Anders." Seamus gave her an elaborate bow and a wink. "I'd be pleased and proud if you would honor me with this dance." If she wasn't mistaken, he was intensifying his Irish brogue for effect. Though he failed to charm her, she still couldn't turn him down. All these cowboys deserved a dance or two for all of their hard work.

"Thank you." She took his offered hand and walked with him to the center of the hard-packed barn floor. Too late she saw Nate headed in her direction. He waggled a scolding finger at her, but she stifled a laugh at his antics. No doubt he'd be waiting to claim the next dance with her.

Sure enough, when the fast-paced music ended, she managed to graciously decline Seamus's request for another dance and move right into Nate's waiting arms.

"I was about to get jealous." He put his hand at her waist as the three-four rhythm of "Sweet Betsy from Pike" began.

"And why would that be, Nate Northam?" Hadn't he seen his father's earlier scowl? "At best, you and I are just friends. Besides, Seamus, being Irish, outshines any other cowboy when it comes to a lively jig."

"Is that so?" Not missing a step in guiding her around the floor, he shrugged and laughed. "Anything else in particular that you prefer about him?"

"Well, you can't beat that brogue for charming." Susanna easily followed Nate as he raised their joined hands and guided her into a turn beneath his arm. Anyone watching might think they'd danced together for years. How good it felt to be on a dance floor again, even a hard-packed dirt one, with this particular partner.

"On the other hand, I did see him step on your toes more than once." He shrugged again. "Of course, I couldn't tell if it was your fault or his."

"His, of course." She gazed up at him, enjoying his firm grasp on her waist. Where had he learned to lead a dance partner so skillfully? Maybe that year he spent in Boston. "And you were watching us the whole time?"

"Only now and then." He looked particularly appealing when he put on his smug face. "With so many pretty girls here, it's hard to pay attention to just one." And yet his eyes hadn't left hers since they'd begun dancing.

"So remind me of why you were jealous when Seamus was my partner."

"Ha!" He tossed his head back. "You caught me." He guided her into another elaborate spin, perhaps to avoid saying more.

The music ended, and he led her to the refreshment table, somehow managing to politely rebuff several men who approached to ask her to dance. "You've been on your feet all day. Don't want you to get tired out."

"Tsk." She sniffed indignantly. "As if I can't keep up with the likes of you."

Handing her a glass of lemonade, he again gazed down at her with an intense look that sent her heart into a spin. "You can indeed, Miss Anders. That's one of the things I like about you."

The moment he used her false last name, her heart stopped spinning. How she longed to reveal her real one to him, to tell him she came from money, the same as he did. Daddy still insisted they keep quiet about their past. What would happen if Nate knew they were social equals and should be able to court if they felt so inclined? A quick glance beyond him answered that question. His Yankee colonel father stood across the barn glaring at the two of them as if they'd just shot Lincoln. For her part, if she surrendered her heart to Nate, she could never go home to Marietta. What would he risk if he fell in love with her?

Nate didn't have to look behind him to know why Susanna's smile disappeared. No doubt the Colonel was scowling at them the way he had this afternoon. And yet his father appeared not to have noticed that Rand had slipped out the back door about ten minutes ago, glass of punch in hand. If the Colonel expected this community to keep liquor out, he should start watching his own favorite son a bit more closely.

"Let's go out and get some fresh air." Nate set down his glass and started to guide her toward the door.

"Why, Nate Northam." She didn't move. "What kind of a girl do you think I am?"

"Uh-oh." Nate felt like a steer on locoweed. No lady would accept an invitation like that. "Should have thought it through a bit more." He grimaced. "Please excuse me, but I need to check on something."

"Never you mind, Nate." She gave him one of her saucy smiles. "I can take care of myself." She glanced around the barn as if looking for another partner.

Nate stewed on that for a moment, hating to leave her so some other man could stake a claim on her while he was tending to family business. Pretty selfish, considering he couldn't court her. Anyway, if she went with him, he'd be showing her the worst side of his family. She probably thought the Colonel was the worst.

Spying Tolley, he beckoned to him. When the boy arrived, he clapped a hand on his shoulder. "You see what a homely pup my little brother is," he said to Susanna. "Would you do us all a favor and dance with him?"

Tolley ignored Nate's insult. "Miss Susanna, would you do me the honor?"

"I'd be delighted."

She took his arm without a backward glance at Nate, but he didn't have time to worry about that now. As they lined up next to Rosamond and others for the Virginia reel, he headed out the back door.

He found Rand and Seamus, along with several other hands from various ranches, kneeling around a low plank, where playing cards and coins were spread, illuminated by lantern light. His back to Nate, Rand didn't see him approach.

A cowboy slapped his cards on the makeshift table, faceup. "Read 'em, boys. A full house." While he raked in the pot, the other men threw down their cards, grumbling.

"We'll do better next time, friends." Rand tossed a coin on the table. "I'm in."

Nate snorted. The gambler's eternal trap. Quickly forget the loss and believe he'd win the next time. "Say, little brother." He gripped Rand's shoulder. "There's a lot of pretty young ladies inside without partners. Why not join the dancing?" Never mind that the cowboys actually outnumbered the ladies. If he could get his brother to his feet, he could smell his breath for liquor.

"Maybe you're right." Rand stood and shoved the coin back into his pocket, blowing out a long sigh. "Sorry, boys. This just isn't my night."

Relief, not the stink of liquor, almost knocked Nate over. Here he'd expected the worst, but all he could smell on Rand was lemonade and sweat. Not that gambling wasn't pure evil, but he'd tackle one of his brother's faults at a time.

While the Colonel drove, Mrs. Northam next to him on the driver's bench, Susanna sat beside Nate on a cushion in the back of the wagon as they wended their way home. Above them, thousands of stars sparkled against the black sky, while the moon was only a sliver of light. To keep the wagon safely on the rough road, Seamus and Wes rode ahead with lanterns held high. On the other side of the wagon bed, Tolley slept against Rosamond's shoulder while Rand shuffled a deck of cards.

After Nate had enticed his brother back inside the Eberlys' barn, he'd watched over him, as Edward had always watched over Susanna. She could see his affection for Rand and his worry about his bad habits. She didn't know why she was surprised to see such fraternal concern in a Yankee family. She supposed it was from a lifetime of prejudices being poured into her. As each day passed, she was learning that many of those prejudices were groundless when it came to a man like Nate. Now, his father was an entirely different story.

The Colonel reinforced every one of her opinions about the North.

"Did you like the fireworks?" Nate leaned toward her to whisper, probably to keep his father from hearing him. As it was, a strong breeze blew from the east, so she doubted his words would reach the front bench. That didn't keep Nate's warm breath from sending a pleasant shiver down her spine.

"Yes, I did. They were a bit loud, but it was exciting to see the sky all lit up like that." Susanna felt a great deal of satisfaction over participating in the barn raising, but she almost hadn't been able to come. The Colonel hadn't been pleased to see her approach the wagon early this morning, but Mrs. Northam's gracious insistence that Susanna was needed to help the womenfolk had won out over her husband's objections. So naturally, every time Susanna turned around today, the Colonel was scowling at her. Didn't he have anything better to do?

"Did you have Independence Day fireworks back home?" As soon as Nate asked the question, he leaned back and seemed to frown, although she couldn't quite be sure in the dark.

How could she answer? Due to the war, many folks back home wanted no part in celebrating the signing of the Declaration of Independence. Others insisted the South had as much right to claim that great document as the North because it had set all of the former colonies free from England.

"Some." Daddy always hated the fireworks because they reminded him of being in the thick of battle. Every time a cannon thundered or a rocket exploded, he ducked, then got embarrassed. But Susanna couldn't

very well say that to Nate. Although it could be her
imagination, they both seemed to avoid talking about
the war.

Nate nodded as if he understood her brief answer.
"Well, I know one thing." His voice took on the teasing tone she loved so much. "You may have attended
only one ball in your short life, but you did manage to
learn how to dance fairly well. Why, you almost kept
up with me."

Rosamond snickered. "Say, Nate, did you ever get
around to dancing with Maisie?"

He didn't even look at his sister. "Who?" He leaned
close to Susanna again, and his breath smelled of sugar
and pecans. So he'd eaten that last praline she'd tucked
away for a bedtime snack. He must like them as much
as he'd claimed. "You hardly missed a dance. I'll be
surprised if you can even walk tomorrow."

Maybe it was that sliver of moonlight shining in his
green eyes. Maybe she was just too tired. But for some
reason, Susanna couldn't think of a single sassy reply.
She could only smile up at him and wish with all her
heart he would kiss her.

"Go ahead, Nate." Rosamond stretched out her foot
and kicked his boot. "Kiss her."

Susanna gasped softly as both she and Nate pulled
away from each other and shot worried glances toward
the Colonel.

Across the wagon, Rand and Rosamond laughed
softly as if they were in on a great secret. A secret Susanna refused to admit to herself. She would not fall in
love with Nate Northam. She would not!

Chapter Seventeen

"You can't take a girl for granted like that or some other man will snatch her up before you get your head on straight." The Colonel leaned back in his desk chair and eyed Nate. "Last night Maisie got all gussied up to show you how much she's grown up, and you didn't ask her to dance even once."

Nate couldn't remember the last time his father had invited him to sit on one of the expensive leather chairs in front of this desk, and he knew better than to sit without an invitation. That thought and his aching feet and back from yesterday's activities made him more than a little irritable.

"She seemed to be doing all right without me." He tried to keep the crossness out of his voice but could hear it nonetheless. "Your Doc Henshaw took to her right away." That wasn't the smartest thing to say.

The Colonel snorted. "John was just being polite because it was her birthday. He danced with Rosamond, too, and they make a fine-looking couple."

"You think so?" Nate couldn't keep the challenge from his voice.

"Yes, Mr. Knows-It-All, I think so." His father stood and leaned forward with his knuckles on his desk, as he always did when he was about to give orders. "You think I didn't notice you hanging all over that Anders girl? And her looking at you all moon-eyed? She's not our sort, Nathaniel, and you would do well to remember that. I don't want to see you spending any more time with her. Is that understood?"

"What—" His father hadn't taken a minute to get acquainted with Susanna. How could he know what *sort* she was?

"Seems to me that lazy father of hers has had enough time to get back on his feet. You go upstairs this morning and tell him I want them gone as soon as he can put one foot in front of the other."

"But—" Nate's head felt as if it would explode. He would not send an injured man out to fend for himself with only his daughter to take care of him. If Mr. Anders and Susanna had to leave, Nate would go with them.

"And as soon as you do that, ride out and check the south fence again. George says somebody tried to break through a section of his fencing, so we may have some cattle rustlers trying to get in." The anger in the Colonel's tone sounded as if it was directed more at Nate than any rustlers.

"No, sir." Nate's right hand fisted almost as if it had a mind of its own. He needed to get out of this room before he did something he would regret for the rest of his life.

"What?" The Colonel's eyes blazed. "What did you say to me?"

"I said 'no, sir.' If you want to throw Mr. Anders

and Susanna out, you'll do your own dirty work. If you want somebody to check that south fence, tell Rand to do it. He could do with having some responsibility around here."

"Now, you see here, boy." He thumped his fist on the desk.

"No." Nate shook from head to toe. "*You* see my back walking out the door." He spun around and strode from the room, with every step fighting the urge to go back and strike his father.

Snatching his hat from the front hall tree, he rushed down the center hallway toward the back door, ignoring Mother's call from the kitchen as he passed by. No one needed to see him like this. No one needed to hear the thoughts racing through his mind. *Anger* hardly seemed a strong enough word to describe his feelings. *Rage,* that was what it was.

Before he knew how he got there, he was on Victor and they were tearing up the road faster and harder than he'd ever ridden his stallion. With no idea where he was going, he just knew something in his life had to give way, had to break, or he wouldn't be able to go on.

At last his mount's labored breathing reached his awareness, and he gently tugged the reins, slowing Victor to a walk. The animal wheezed and snorted, tossing his head as if to ask what that had been all about.

"Sorry, boy." How foolish to punish Victor for his father's insufficiencies. Victor wasn't just any horse. He would sire Nate's string of cow ponies once he had his own place.

If he ever had his own place. Maybe after today the Colonel would disown him. In fact, maybe that would be best. One thing was certain. Nate needed to find a better way to deal with his anger before he did some real damage to some innocent person or beast. Riding a valuable horse into the ground was about the dumbest thing he'd ever done in his life. He'd always known that this strain of cow ponies wasn't bred for long, hard rides.

What would happen if he came right out and defied the Colonel, not just in the privacy of his office, but in front of everybody? Maybe his father was just waiting for him to do that. And what on earth had he meant by Mr. Knows-It-All? What a crazy thing to say.

Defiance, controlled defiance. That was the way to get out from under his father's thumb. Nate's first step would be to follow his heart and pursue a deeper relationship with Susanna. If everybody thought they were courting, so be it.

Anytime Susanna found herself in the kitchen with Mrs. Northam and Rosamond, she savored the easy camaraderie among them. It helped to ease the pain of missing her friends and family back home more than she could have imagined. How could she hate these Yankee ladies who treated her only with kindness? Or dear, warmhearted Angela, whose maternal ways reminded her of her childhood nurse. Did this wise woman know her own daughter rode into the settlement several times a week, days when the Colonel was also gone from the ranch house? If only Susanna could find a way to rescue Rita from his evil clutches. She stifled a sigh so the other ladies would not ask questions about her sudden depression.

Mercy, she'd done it again, dashed her own happy thoughts. She should be thinking about yesterday and how the whole community had come together to build that impressive barn. Should be thinking about dancing with Nate and the way he'd almost kissed her. Or the way she'd hoped he would, then been glad when he hadn't because of the trouble it could have caused. Oh, how she enjoyed his company. How she wished she were free to love him.

"Susanna, would you mind setting the table?" Mrs. Northam said. "We'll just be five for the noon meal."

"Yes, ma'am." As Susanna removed the mismatched everyday dishes from the cupboard, a happy thought silenced her concerns over eating with the Colonel. In a few weeks, Mrs. Northam would receive her Wedgwood china. What an exciting day that would be. Nate had told her other surprises awaited his mother, but she doubted he knew about the silver spurs for his father. Maybe that fine gift from his wife would shame the Colonel into improving his ways, spur him into good behavior, so to speak.

Chuckling at her own wordplay, she carried the plates and silverware to the dining room and set them around the linen-covered table. The Colonel always sat at the head, Mrs. Northam at the foot by the kitchen door, Rosamond to her left, Nate next to his sister and Susanna across from them. She retrieved freshly pressed linen napkins from the buffet just as the Colonel came through the door. He stared at her with his usual scowl. Her heart seemed to stop beating.

"We'll be only four at the table for dinner."

"Yes, sir." Barely giving him a glance, she put away one napkin and cleared one place setting, then made haste to return to the kitchen. She didn't need to be told twice that he didn't want her eating with the family. She, who had once dined with the governor of Georgia and attended balls at a senator's home, one of those plantation houses General Sherman had failed to burn down on his march to Atlanta.

Even if her own Southern heritage wasn't an impediment to her falling in love with Nate, the Colonel's rudeness toward her would always stand in the way of their happiness. She could not, must not surrender to her attraction to Nate.

Nate gave Victor his head, and the stallion trotted along the lane into the settlement right up to the hitching rail beneath the trees in front of the church.

"Whoa, boy." Nate leaned down to pat his neck. "This is Friday, not Sunday. What are we doing here?"

"Hello, Nate." Reverend Thomas came around the building, rolled-up shirtsleeves and dusty trousers indicating he'd been working in his garden. "Did you need to see me?"

Nate stared at him for a moment, then down at Victor. He grunted out a mirthless chuckle and dismounted. "I guess I do." Tying Victor's reins to the rail, he checked the horse's legs and breathing. After their hard run, he'd cooled him down with a long walk and given him a drink in the river, so he should be all right here in the shade.

"Come on into the house. We'll have some lemonade."

Nate followed him next door to the parsonage, a simple three-room edifice that would need to be enlarged if the young preacher married.

"Mrs. Eberly sent me home with some beef and pork, not to mention a whole basket load of other fine food."

After washing his hands in a dishpan on the kitchen table, Reverend Thomas lifted the lid on his small ice-box and pulled out a plate of sliced meat and other items. "This community not only builds fine barns for their neighbors, they know how to take care of their bachelors, too. Will you have dinner with me?"

The aroma of the beef started Nate's stomach growling, reminding him of his ill-timed departure from home. "Thank you. I will."

Soon they were seated at the table enjoying sandwiches and potato salad, washing it all down with tangy lemonade.

"How's everything out at the ranch?" Reverend Thomas had set some of Mrs. Barkley's pickles on a plate and now offered them to Nate. When Nate declined, the preacher took a big bite of one. "Mmm-mmm. That lady sure knows how to make fine pickles."

Being of a decidedly different opinion, Nate would not comment on them. But what should he say? Had the Lord led him here to seek counsel? Should he speak against his father to a man who owed the Colonel his current position, his very livelihood?

"You probably noticed when you were out there last Sunday how the crops are thriving. We finished digging the irrigation ditch to channel water from Cat Creek closer to the hay fields." He mentioned a few other improvements made around the place. "And I'm glad to say the new addition is almost completed. The carpenter from Denver arrived yesterday to do all the fancy woodwork in the ballroom."

"Very good. Everyone's talking about the anniversary party. It'll be quite an event." The minister ate the rest of his pickle, clearly enjoying it. But even the smell ruined Nate's appetite. "I don't have to tell you the Colonel not only has the respect of everyone hereabouts, he also has their affection. Very few of us would be here without his sponsorship."

Nate took a drink to avoid responding.

"Planning and building a community on biblical principles is nothing short of the Lord's work." Some of Reverend Thomas's Southern inflections reminded Nate of Susanna, but he wouldn't feel comfortable bringing her into the conversation, nor the Colonel's dislike of her and her father. "I'm not one to be a respecter of persons, but I believe the Lord's hand is surely on the Colonel."

Nate started. "You think so?"

The preacher blinked. "Why, yes."

If God was on the Colonel's side, where did that leave Nate? He stared at the lemon seeds in the bottom of his glass.

"In fact, I consider him a wise man." Reverend Thomas held out the plate of sandwiches, silently offering Nate another one, but he declined. "I wouldn't hesitate to seek his counsel if I needed it."

Nate's thoughts tumbled all over each other. The Colonel might be smart. But wise? "Now, that surprises me. You're the preacher here. People come to you for advice."

He chuckled ruefully. "They do. But unfortunately, a seminary degree only denotes knowledge, not wisdom." His words echoed Nate's thoughts. "That's why I've been studying the Book of Proverbs. That's why I look to older, godly men for guidance."

The preacher's humble attitude touched something deep inside Nate. What did this man see in the Colonel that Nate couldn't? Maybe it was a simple matter of perspective, like Mrs. Barkley's pickles. Some liked them and some didn't. Right now he didn't much like his father. But how would this man feel if the Colonel corrected everything he did? Criticized every sermon? Told him whom to marry? It was all well and good to admire a man who wasn't trying to control every minute of his life. Still, the near-reverence the minister exhibited toward the Colonel gave Nate something to consider. And to pray about.

"Well, I'd best be going." He stood and retrieved his hat. "Much obliged for the sandwich."

Reverend Thomas walked him to the door. "Did I miss something, Nate? Did you need to discuss anything?"

"Nope." Nate shook the preacher's hand. "I think we about covered it."

"Ah." Understanding crossed his face. "The Lord works in mysterious ways."

Indeed He did. Nate headed home, pondering the deeper meaning behind their conversation. The preacher had been concerned that he'd missed something, but it was Nate who still could not comprehend why anyone would think the Colonel was wise. If that was the case, why did he refuse to give Susanna and her father a chance to prove themselves, as he had every other decent person who'd come to the community? If his father was so wise, why couldn't the two of them have a simple conversation to discuss their differences? If he'd just treat Nate with a little respect, Nate wouldn't have to constantly remind him that he knew a thing or two about running a ranch.

Chapter Eighteen

Susanna helped Daddy to a sitting position and put several pillows behind him on the bed, then tucked a napkin into his nightshirt collar. "Chicken and dumplings, dearest. One of your favorites." She brought the tray to him and made sure it sat firmly on his lap before taking her own bowl in hand. "Not as good as Minerva's, of course, but still tasty." Even though Angela was an excellent cook, Susanna often longed for their former housekeeper's delicious cuisine.

After they said grace, he dipped his spoon into the broth and brought out a small, round dumpling. "I don't know about that, daughter. Miss Angela's a mighty fine cook, too. I've enjoyed all her meals."

Something in his tone gave her pause, but she quickly dismissed it. Of course Daddy would become fond of the servant who took such good care of him.

"A new doctor arrived at the barn raising yesterday." She wouldn't mention that the Colonel had summoned the man from Boston to tend the community's health needs, for that would give their unwilling host too much credit. "I asked him to come see you today."

"Gracious, girl." Daddy coughed, as he often had since being laid up. "I'll be fine. Why, Zack and Miss Angela are planning to get me on my feet this very afternoon."

"That's good news, but nevertheless, I want the doctor to look you over before you try to stand." Still stinging from the way the Colonel dismissed her from the dining room, she basked in Daddy's fond gaze. Poor Nate, having such a disagreeable father, who never showed such disapproval to his other children as he had to Nate all day at the Eberlys'. "Besides, that cough of yours worries me, so I want him to make sure you don't have pneumonia."

Securing his agreement to see the doctor, she went on to tell him about the barn raising, the food and the dance.

"Did he dance with you?" Daddy gave her a teasing grin.

"Who?" Had he guessed about her struggles not to become attached to Nate?

"Why, the doctor, of course." His eyes twinkled, but he was watching her closely. "Who else would I be talking about?"

"Oh, gracious, Daddy." She finished her dinner and set down her bowl. "That barn was overrun with cowboys. I danced until my feet ached." She brushed invisible lint from her borrowed skirt. "They still ache."

"I see."

Before he could further comment, a light tap sounded on the door. Susanna admitted Angela into the room.

"Eduardo," she began, then quickly added, "forgive me, Señor Anders, the doctor has arrived."

Susanna glanced between the two of them, but before she could question the housekeeper's use of the Spanish version of Daddy's first name, Zack and Dr. Henshaw entered.

Greetings were offered, introductions were made and then the doctor ushered Susanna and Angela out.

"The very idea! Why can't we stay?" Susanna huffed as they stood outside the closed door.

Angela frowned with equal displeasure, then shook her head. "He is in good hands."

"Yes, Dr. Henshaw does seem quite competent."

"No, *señorita,* it is the Lord's hands I speak of." She patted Susanna's shoulder. "Now I must prepare supper. With many people to feed, something must always be cooking, *si?*"

"I'll be glad to help." Susanna followed her down the back stairs. Maybe she would see Nate, if he hadn't already left the house after eating dinner. What had he thought about her absence at the table? Had he guessed his father was responsible?

They found Rosamond washing dishes in the kitchen. "There you are, Susanna. Where've you been? With you and Nate gone, I was left to entertain my parents during dinner."

"Nate was gone?"

"Yep." Rosamond squeezed out her dishrag and wiped it across the wooden counter. "Father said he told you Nate wouldn't be there, and since you didn't plan to eat with us, you should have set only three places."

Her thoughts in a whirl, Susanna busied herself pulling potatoes from the wooden vegetable bin and placing them on the table to peel. The Colonel hadn't been dismissing her, simply informing her that Nate wouldn't be at dinner. But she hardly could have asked him to clarify his terse statement. Although she felt somewhat embarrassed, she was mostly annoyed. He'd turned a misunderstanding into a criticism of the way she set the table. What an impossible man!

Seeing a slow-moving wagon ahead, Nate urged Victor to a trot and soon pulled beside the large, canvas-covered conveyance. "Howdy." He touched his hat brim. "You men headed to Four Stones Ranch?"

"Yep." The driver and his rifle-toting partner offered guarded greetings.

"I'm Nate Northam. Follow me."

Thus assured he wasn't out to rob them, they responded with more enthusiasm, no doubt eager to deliver their heavy load. What had the Colonel ordered this time? Nate was privy to only a few of his father's secrets about the anniversary, mainly how fancy the ballroom would be once all the furnishings arrived. And of course, the china.

Every time he thought about the china, he thanked the good Lord for using it to introduce him to Susanna. Wasn't the way they met sufficient proof that God smiled on his feelings for her? Maybe he should have asked Reverend Thomas about that.

Riding slightly in front of the four-horse team, Nate guided the lead animals around the worst of the holes in the rutted road. When they got to Four Stones Lane, he'd ride on ahead and suggest to Mother that she might want to go upstairs and work on her quilt. Whatever was in the wagon, she'd play her game of pretending not to notice its arrival. He sure did look forward to seeing her face when the Colonel gave her all those surprises. And for all of Nate's anger toward the man, he knew his father would make a big fuss about what a fine quilt she'd made, saying it was exactly what he'd always wanted. A man had to admire a couple who still loved each other so dearly after twenty-five years of marriage.

Which only added to Nate's confusion about the Colonel's insistence that he marry Maisie. Couldn't the old man see how important it was to marry a woman he loved? Nobody submitted to arranged marriages anymore.

When he arrived at the house, Mother dutifully decided it was time to head upstairs to get busy with her quilting. Nate had directed the men to deliver the wagon's contents to the veranda outside the ballroom. The three of them started to unload the first wooden carton, but it proved too heavy. Nate rounded up several more hands, including the carpenter, who was staining the ballroom's mahogany balustrade. The two large boxes sat safely inside just as the Colonel entered, crowbar in hand.

Nate braced himself for a confrontation, but his father's mood was nothing short of jubilant.

"Let's take a look." He nodded to the driver. "It didn't have a scratch when I checked it in Alamosa last week." Not giving the other man a chance to respond, he began to pry open the slats.

Nate pitched in to help, and they soon had the packing removed. At last, the Colonel slid off the heavy quilted cotton protecting the object and ran a hand over his purchase for inspection.

"A grand piano," Nate said in hushed tones. He guessed this large, rectangular instrument was the finest piano in the entire San Luis Valley. The shiny mahogany surface matched the newly installed woodwork.

"Let's get the base unpacked. Bring it over here by the staircase." The Colonel directed the men, and they soon had the body secured on the base, which boasted four elegantly carved legs. "I see some scratches." His shoulders hunched up like a grizzly bear's, and he sent a dark look toward the driver.

"Do not vorry, Herr Northam." The carpenter scurried over to inspect the damage, his toolbox in hand. "The damage, you vill never know it vas there."

The German craftsman proved true to his word. A bit of sandpaper, a touch of stain, and even a magnifying glass would not betray the spots. As he worked, Nate noticed the Colonel's shoulders relaxing. In those brief moments, he saw a side of his father he'd never before noticed. Or maybe hadn't given enough thought.

His generosity and protectiveness—to friends, to neighbors and especially to Mother—could not be denied. This was the better part of the man, the one people like Reverend Thomas saw and admired. Why did he not bestow any of those better feelings on Nate? Could he himself be the one in the wrong?

After paying the deliverymen and receiving their assurance that the rest of the furniture would be delivered the following week, the Colonel sent them on their way. Then he stood in the center of the room surveying every detail with a critical eye. "What do you think?"

Nate had to look around to be sure he was the person being addressed. "Looks good so far. With the rest of the furniture and the drapes Miss Anders is making, it'll be the finest ballroom in Colorado."

At the mention of Susanna's name, the Colonel cut him a sharp look. "What are you talking about? Rosamond is making the drapes."

Determined not to argue or even get angry, Nate shrugged. "Rosamond said she has trouble sewing velvet, but Susanna has a talent for keeping it from puckering."

The Colonel continued to glare at him as if it was his fault. "I'll be speaking to your sister about that." He stalked toward the interior door then turned back. "What are you doing for the rest of the day?" His tone was unusually genial, and his expression had softened.

Nate shrugged again. "Guess I'll ride out and check that south fencing."

The Colonel didn't turn away quite fast enough to hide his grin. For some odd reason, instead of irritating Nate, it stirred up a warm feeling in his chest. Maybe there was still hope for their relationship.

On Monday morning, Susanna made her way to Nate's room to check on Daddy. To her surprise, he and Nate stood beside the bed, with Daddy balancing himself with the crutch Zack had fashioned from a forked tree branch. A cushion, probably sewn on by Angela, covered the wood to spare his underarm. "Just look at you getting around on your own."

"Doc Henshaw gave his approval last Friday, and I've been practicing these past few days." He'd lost weight, but the color was returning to his cheeks. "It feels mighty good."

"And look at your new outfit." She sent a grateful glance toward Nate. Obviously, he'd loaned Daddy those denim trousers and that plaid shirt. If Mrs. Northam would sell her some of the material Nate had carted in with the china, Susanna could start sewing a new wardrobe for her father. "You look like a cowboy."

Daddy chuckled. "Maybe I'll go downstairs and take a turn around the property this afternoon."

"That's a good idea," Nate said. "I'll help you negotiate the stairs. In fact, why not come down for dinner?"

Daddy eyed him and frowned. "I don't want to put anybody out."

"Do you mean you don't want to run into the Colonel?" Nate gave him a rueful smile. "Never mind about that."

Daddy shrugged. "If you're certain, then I will. I'd enjoy sitting at a table again."

With the matter settled, they helped Daddy down the wide front staircase and out onto the shady front lawn. The effort tired him, so Susanna sat on a bench with him while Nate excused himself to do chores.

"The preacher asked about you yesterday." Susanna had thoroughly enjoyed the Sunday service, especially the singing. "He said he'll be out to visit you sometime this week."

"I'll be glad to see him again." Daddy gave her one of his long, speculative looks. "He's a real Southern gentleman and a handsome young man, don't you think?"

"Yes, he is." Susanna didn't try to hide her amusement. "I'd say between his looks and the doctor's, though, the doctor wins by a nose."

Daddy laughed, catching her joke about the doctor's most prominent facial feature. "But neither one can hold a candle to a certain cowboy."

Susanna released a long, weary sigh. No use trying to deny the obvious. Of course Daddy would have noticed her partiality for Nate, even tucked away in his bedroom all this time. In a way, though, it felt good to have her struggles out in the open. "Oh, well. He's a

Yankee, so that's that." Her tone didn't sound as dismissive as she would have liked.

Daddy gazed out over the western field, where sunflowers towered above half-grown corn. "The heart is an untamed beast, daughter. Sometimes it tries to take us where we know we shouldn't go."

"I know." Her spirits sank at his pronouncement. "The heart is deceitful above all things, and desperately wicked. Who can know it?"

Daddy started. "Whoa, daughter. I believe that verse in Jeremiah refers to matters of faith in the Lord, not a person you come to care about deeply." He ran a hand over the smooth wooden bench. "I don't believe it's wicked to love any person. It's what you do about it that matters."

"What if that person is a Yankee?" She held her breath waiting for his answer. If he granted her permission to care for Nate, she'd have no reason to deny her own heart's longing. And truly, in spite of all she'd told herself, in spite of her dreams to marry a Southern gentleman, she did care for Nate. Cared enough to stay right here in the San Luis Valley rather than return home to Georgia.

"What if that person is a—" He shook his head. "Well, look who's here."

Nate rounded the corner of the house, and Susanna's emotions did their usual turn. She'd seen him only a few minutes ago, yet one would think it had been a month of Sundays. Daddy greeted Nate like a long-lost friend, but she couldn't help but notice he'd failed to answer her question.

"Let's eat." Nate helped Daddy back into the house and down the center hallway to the dining room.

"Mr. Anders, I'm so pleased you're able to join us." Mrs. Northam's warm welcome almost overcame the chill emanating from the Colonel. Almost.

But Daddy, ever the Southern gentleman, comported himself with dignity and grace that would have made Mama proud.

That afternoon, after seeing Daddy safely back upstairs, Susanna joined Nate and Rosamond for an errand into the settlement. Mrs. Northam, busy with arranging food for the anniversary celebration, needed to know what to expect from their neighbors. Although Rosamond could have managed the errand alone, the Colonel sent Nate along, citing their run-in with the Utes two weeks ago. When they invited Susanna, she eagerly accepted.

As they neared the cluster of homes and businesses, she longed to direct Sadie down some of the lanes to see the varied architecture. Some of the houses appeared quite elegant, while others had a humbler look. Reining her horse nearer to Nate's, she asked, "Do you plan to name your town anytime soon?"

"That's a question I'd like answered myself. Seems like it's about time." He pointed to a lane, almost a street, which met their road at a right angle. "You can see the town's already been platted, but until we're incorporated, nobody wants to attach a name to it."

"When the railroad reaches us next year, we'll need to have a name." Rosamond gazed off thoughtfully. "I like Mountain View because whichever way you look, you can see mountains."

Susanna decided she could not improve on her friend's idea.

In the center of the settlement, they reached Miss Pam's café and dismounted.

"Now, you know she'll want us to have some pie," Nate said.

"That won't hurt my feelings." Susanna could just taste the delicious elderberry pie Miss Pam had served them when Nate had first brought her and Daddy through. Every time she saw the sweet lady, she thanked her again for the use of her boar-hair brush. One day she would repay her with more than words.

Soon the three of them were digging into their cream-covered pie and discussing what Miss Pam would bring to the anniversary party.

"My garden has an abundance of green beans," she said. "They'll be ripe for picking just in time."

Miss Pam also passed along several bits of benign gossip, such as the imminent arrival of a woman who would set up a mercantile next door to her café. "I've been waiting for a place nearby to go shopping since I left St. Louis nine years ago. I'm tired of getting my supplies over in Del Norte."

While they all enjoyed a good laugh over that, the news gave Susanna special delight. Not only would she be able to repay Miss Pam, but she would also be able to purchase material to replace Daddy's clothes that had been ruined by the thieves.

"Charlie's been hired to string the telegraph," Miss Pam said. "It'll be nice to have a faster way than letters to communicate with folks beyond the Valley."

Filled with pie and news, they took their leave and made the rounds of the town, gathering a list of food and beverages people would contribute to the party. Everyone seemed eager to participate.

Just beyond the church, Susanna noticed a pretty two-story Queen Anne home. "How lovely. Who lives there?" Outside the front fence, a vaguely familiar horse stood tied to a post under a shady elm.

"Mr. and Mrs. Foster," said Nate. "They knew the Colonel years ago, so when he invited them to be a part of this community, they couldn't resist. Mrs. Foster gives piano lessons and—" Strangely, he clamped his mouth shut. Maybe he'd come close to blurting out a secret about the party.

"If you haven't noticed—" Rosamond laughed "—our father has very strong persuasive powers."

Now Susanna clamped her mouth shut. She most certainly had noticed the Colonel's controlling ways. As they rode down the next street, she glanced back at the lovely home. To her shock, she saw Rita exiting the yard with an older lady. They embraced and shared a laugh, then Rita mounted the horse and rode away, while the lady went back inside.

"Do you mind?" Susanna turned Sadie around. "I haven't touched a piano since we left home." Never mind if they wondered how she could afford one. "Do you think Mrs. Foster would let me play just for a few minutes?"

Nate got that cute, surprised look on his face. "You play piano?" Why did he seem so happy about it?

"I think she'd love the company," Rosamond said. "Let's go."

As expected, the older woman graciously invited them in for a visit. When she learned Susanna played, she waved her to the piano stool. After a few arpeggios, with several missed notes due to a lack of practice, Susanna launched into "Brahms's Lullaby," then a few verses of "Amazing Grace," while the others joined in singing.

"How absolutely lovely. Another pianist in our community." Mrs. Foster, gray-haired and maternal, clasped her hands to her heart as if transported by the music. "And you play Brahms! I was just saying to young Rita that we must bring more classical music here. Colonel Northam was so wise to recognize her talent, and she's doing so well in her preparations for the anniversary party and— Oh, my." She put her hands to her cheeks in horror. "Have I spoiled the surprise? Surely not. You must know your father has arranged for Rita to learn how to play. She told me the piano arrived just the other day."

Rosamond smothered a laugh with her hand, while Nate cleared his throat. "Yes, ma'am. We know, but Mother doesn't. She's not allowed in the ballroom until their party. It's good of you to let Rita come and practice every day. She can't practice at home or Mother would hear her."

While they chattered away about the grand surprise, Susanna sat in stunned silence as the truth slammed into her. As sure as the sun did shine, God had arranged for her to see Rita leaving the piano teacher's house. The Lord, who knew every heart, knew she would seize the opportunity to find out what was going on. Which was not at all the evil she had imagined. Once again, the Colonel had found a way to please his wife. That was why he was so upset when Rita cut her hand. In the deepest part of her soul, Susanna knew not many Southern men would be so generous to a dark-skinned girl unless they had improper expectations.

Horrified, sickened even, by her own evil judgments

against the man, Susanna could only offer a weak smile and thank-you as they left Mrs. Foster's parlor. Colonel Northam certainly had more than a few redeeming qualities. That still didn't answer why he hated her and Daddy so much, but she would pray for him and try very hard to excuse his bad manners.

As they headed back toward the ranch, Nate and Rosamond chatted about their visit. "Too bad you didn't get to meet Mr. Foster," Rosamond said to Susanna. "He's been Father's friend since the war, when they both rode with General Sherman."

Nate shot a worried glance at Susanna. "Yes, well…"

Susanna almost gave vent to a bitter laugh. So much for her guilty feelings. She may have misjudged the Colonel regarding Rita. But there was no misjudging any soldier who rode with Sherman. Nor was there enough forgiveness in any Southerner worth his or her salt to pardon Sherman's troops for what they did to the South. And to her family in particular.

Chapter Nineteen

Nate blamed himself. He should have had a frank discussion with Susanna regarding the Colonel's war service. Still, he gave her several days to recover from her obvious shock over hearing that his father rode with Sherman. He regretted his failure to alert Rosamond about how such a careless comment might upset their guests.

The whole family knew the Anderses were from Georgia, one of the states to suffer greatly during Sherman's march to the sea. He and his siblings had grown up accepting the general's brutal drive as necessary to end the war, which had killed over a half million men and nearly destroyed the United States. Of course, Southerners would view the matter differently. Not all of them were like Reverend Thomas, who had said in one of his sermons how much he welcomed the reunification of the North and South into one country.

Nate should sit Susanna down for a discussion on the matter and sort it out in a sensible way. It was madness for their generation to continue fighting the war that ended thirteen years ago. But until the anniversary party next week, he had too many responsibilities to complete. In the meantime, he admired the way she kept working around the house and taking care of her father. As for Mr. Anders, he began taking long walks around the property using the crutch Zack had made for him. He enjoyed visits from Doc Henshaw and Reverend Thomas. He even spent some time with Joe, the tanner, helping with his leatherwork. So much for the Colonel's assertion that Mr. Anders was a lazy Southerner.

On Thursday, the rest of the ballroom furniture arrived: four velvet chairs, two brocade settees, six mahogany side tables, four lampstands and an exquisite crystal chandelier. Susanna completed the drapes and sent Rosamond to fetch Nate to help hang them. The whole time he worked on nailing up the curtain rods over the four wide windows and adjusting the finished product, Susanna kept her eyes on the thick green drapes, pulling and picking at them to make sure they hung just right. Not once did she trade a glance with Nate or even Rosamond.

"Excellent." The Colonel's voice boomed behind them, and they all turned to see him standing on the steps leading down into the ballroom. He strode across the space and examined the drapes more closely. "Miss Anders, I understand you are responsible for this fine work. I insist upon paying you. Name your wages."

Her eyes blazing, she lifted her chin. "Why, no, indeed, Colonel Northam. Your *hospitality* while my father recuperates is more than sufficient payment." The iciness in her tone was enough to freeze the sunshine right out of the room. She spun around and marched away, head held high.

Only then did Nate realize how deeply she hated his father. But had he lost his own chance to win her affection?

If she'd given him one look these past few days, one hint that she wanted to talk to him, he would go to her right now. Instead, Rosamond gave him a rueful frown and followed Susanna. That gave Nate a measure of peace. With the girls getting along so well, he had that one tiny thread of hope. It wasn't as though Susanna could go anyplace until her father was fully back on his feet.

"Very fine indeed." The Colonel acted as though nothing unpleasant had happened. Instead, he sauntered around the room inspecting every detail. From time to time, he sent an approving glance in Nate's direction.

Since the silent resolution of their argument last week, his father had been treating him with more respect. He'd even taken Nate's advice about giving Rand more responsibility in managing things around the ranch. Wanting to ensure their truce, Nate made a point of agreeing with—or at least deferring to—several of his father's decisions on things Nate usually handled.

"Mother will be overwhelmed." He moved up beside the Colonel as he studied the scalloped molding near the ceiling. "And happy."

His father gave him a curt nod, but he was smiling… almost. Nate's heart lifted unexpectedly. This was the way things had been when the two of them had shouldered the burden of moving the family across the country ten years ago. Somehow a bridge had been mended, and Nate couldn't be more pleased. Remembering Reverend Thomas's words, he tried to think of a way to reaffirm his trust in the Colonel's wisdom.

"Yessir, you sure do have some mighty fine ideas." Whether running a ranch, developing a community or honoring his wife.

His father eyed him with a hint of suspicion that

quickly dissolved. He clapped Nate on the shoulder. "I'm glad to hear you say that, son."

Nate felt a foolish grin spread across his face. He'd taken the first step to earning the right to persuade his father to accept Susanna. Now he had to find a way to convince Susanna they needed to forget the war and the Colonel's part in it and move on with their own lives.

Even as she longed to get out of this house, Susanna felt waves of nostalgia as she worked on various projects leading up to the party. At her parents' last anniversary together just over a year ago, Mama had been so beautiful in a rose-colored gown, and Daddy his most handsome in an elegant black suit. She would treasure those memories as long as she lived and would try to help make this anniversary as memorable for the Northams.

Despite loathing the Colonel, Susanna still could find no fault in Mrs. Northam. The lady had opened her home and provided for her and Daddy without a hint of reservation. What a stark contrast between her and her husband. Did the Colonel realize Susanna had it within her power to ruin all of his carefully planned surprises? That it was her Southern-bred honor that kept her mouth shut around those secrets? After the party, she would make sure he knew all about it.

Nor did she reveal to Daddy about the Colonel riding with Sherman. If she did, there was no telling what he'd do.

The week of the event arrived, and only a few more tasks required Susanna's assistance. Mrs. Northam instructed Nate to bring a large oak chest from the attic storeroom, and she opened it to reveal a tarnished silver tea service.

"Oh, my, these are exquisite, Mrs. Northam." She lifted out the creamer and sugar bowl to have a closer look at the etched designs. "Don't you think so?" Without thinking, she handed one of the pieces to Nate. At the touch of his hand on hers, a spark shot up her arm, and they shared a smile. He seemed particularly pleased to receive hers, if the sudden brightening of his green eyes was any indication. Oh, how she had missed their friendly banter, missed just being with him. Was it wrong to care so deeply for him when she could feel only loathing for his father?

"Bert gave me his secret baking-soda concoction to clean away the tarnish." Mrs. Northam rolled up her sleeves and lay a sheet out on the table. "Let's hope it works." From the sideboard, she took a small jar and several lengths of torn sheets.

"Please let me do it." Susanna would perform this one last kindness for her hostess. Right after the party, she and Daddy would be moving to a house Reverend Thomas had found for them, where they would stay until Daddy was able to travel to the silver fields. If he still wanted to go. "You have enough to do."

Mrs. Northam gave her a doubtful look. "Are you certain?"

"I can help." Nate removed the tea server from the box, then pulled out a large silver tray. The center boasted the monogram GEM in large script letters. The bottom of the piece was inscribed with the silversmith's name. "Paul Revere! Mother, why haven't I seen this before?"

She laughed. "I suppose because we haven't had a grand enough occasion."

"I'm duly impressed." Even living in the South, Susanna had learned of Revere's patriotic ride through Longfellow's 1861 poem.

"Well, your twenty-fifth anniversary is supposed to be the silver one," Nate said, "so I'd say that makes it grand enough. A Paul Revere silver service for a silver celebration."

"All right, then." Mrs. Northam eyed Susanna, then Nate. "I'll leave you to it. Don't have too much fun."

After she left, they sat at the table and began to work. Sure enough, Bert's secret formula, plus a strong dose of elbow grease, cut through the tarnish without scratching the silver.

"I've missed you." Nate kept his eyes on the creamer he was rubbing with a cloth.

She should say she'd been there all the time, eating with the family, answering when spoken to. But that wasn't what he meant. "I've—"

"Hey, Nate." Tolley burst through the door. "Seamus's got himself in a pickle with that mustang mare. Can you come help?"

Nate's shoulders slumped. "I'll be right there." He rubbed the black marks from his hand. "I'll come back as soon as I can."

After he left, the dining room felt more than empty. It felt bereft. Or maybe she was just thinking of how hard it would be to leave him behind.

She heard the thump of Daddy's crutch on the hallway floor. "Daddy? Come keep me company."

He poked his head through the open door. "I was just headed to the kitchen for a glass of water."

Susanna had noticed he made frequent such trips when Angela was busy cooking, but she wouldn't question him. "You can go through this way. Come see what I'm doing."

He limped toward the table, and his face contorted oddly.

"Daddy? What's wrong?"

"What do you have there, daughter?" His terse question was accompanied by eyes burning with anger.

"I-it's a silver tea service." What could be wrong? Daddy never got angry this way, even when the thieves had beaten and nearly killed him. "Paul Revere made it." Her words came out like an apology.

"I know who made it." He threw down his crutch and snatched up the half-cleaned tray. "Do you see this monogram?"

She nodded.

"GEM. Gabriel Edward MacAndrews." He traced the letters with a reverence that belied his rage. "Your great-great-grandfather."

"What?" Susanna scrambled to make sense of his words.

He pulled out the chair next to her and sat. "Listen, daughter." He ran a hand over his mouth, a nervous, angry gesture. "You thought I came to Colorado on a quest for silver, and you were right. But this—" he gently tapped the teapot "—this is the silver I've been searching for."

"Oh, Daddy." Tears filled her eyes, and she touched his arm. "This is Mama's silver service the Yankees took."

He nodded. "That's not all." He pulled on the chain around his neck and retrieved a locket from beneath his shirt. Inside was her parents' tiny tintype wedding portrait. "You know I wore this into battle, and you've seen the picture many times, but you've never asked about the necklace your mother is wearing."

She shook her head. Countless belongings had been stolen from their family during the war, but Mama had also sold some of her remaining valuables after the war to help Daddy start his business. Susanna had never wanted to bring up such a sensitive subject. "Tell me about it."

"Eleven sapphires, graduated in size and set in silver, an heirloom, like the tea service, this one from my mother's family." He winced when he mentioned Grandmama. Susanna knew he'd never quit grieving her death. "You were just six years old, so maybe you don't recall when these were taken." He stared off, a dark frown creasing his forehead. "I was away fighting when those Yankee cowards came. Your brother was twelve." He drew in a ragged breath. "You may wonder why Edward Junior is such a cautious man. He wasn't always that way. Why, when he saw the Yankees storming onto our property, he started shooting and wounded a couple of them before they caught him." Daddy trembled at the memory, and Susanna gripped his forearm. He covered her hand with his.

"He was just a boy." Daddy's voice shook. "But they would have hanged him to set an example for any other Southerner who dared to defy them if your mother hadn't intervened. She promised a treasure to their commanding officer in return for Edward's life. She would have given them anything, everything, including her own life, to save either one of you. As it was, that officer was satisfied with this silver service and the sapphire necklace. She told them where she'd buried the items, and they helped themselves."

Daddy slumped wearily against the table. "In spite of that, the officer ordered your brother's guns, *my* guns, taken, too. He also ordered the house to be burned down with everything else in it. Then he ordered Edward's arms to be broken."

Bile rose into Susanna's throat. She vaguely remembered the grand plantation house and how her childhood nurse had hurried her away from the scene on Mama's orders. She knew the Yankees had hurt Edward, who'd never regained full use of his arms. And, as Daddy said, he'd become a cautious man. Almost fearful. As more memories flooded her mind, one currently familiar face came into focus. "Colonel Northam." She spat out the name.

"Colonel Northam." Daddy straightened. "Now you know everything. The Yankees recorded the names of every person who resisted them, so ours went on their list. That's why I changed our name when we came west. Why I didn't want them to know about our social standing back home. The best way to defeat an adversary is to keep him ignorant about who you are and what you plan to do."

"We have to go." Susanna rubbed tarnish from her hands and stood. "We have to leave this place right away."

Daddy gripped her arm and tugged her back down on the chair. "Don't be hasty, daughter."

She questioned him with a look.

"When I learned the name of the officer who brutalized and robbed my family, I knew I couldn't let it rest. I wrote letters and found out exactly where Frank Northam had settled. Before your mama died, I promised her I would settle the score, and the Lord led us here as surely as He led Moses to the Promised Land."

Susanna's hair seemed to stand on end. Was there

more to Mama's dying plea for her to take care of Daddy? Had she thought Susanna could somehow stop his quest for revenge? As for his biblical reference, she would not remind him that Moses hadn't been permitted to enter Israel's new home because he'd failed to honor God in an important matter. But what would the Lord have her do in this situation?

"Only the Almighty could have arranged our meeting with Nate." Daddy chuckled. "Of course, I wish He'd found a less painful way. But then we wouldn't be in this house, wouldn't have had our silver put right into our hands."

Queasiness swept through Susanna. "What do you plan to do?"

His expression grew wily. "We don't have your mama's necklace, but we have this silver service, and it belongs to you. Go ahead and shine it with pride. When we leave, we'll take it with us."

"But that's stealing, Daddy. It would make us no better than the Colonel."

"That so?" Daddy gripped her shoulders. "Do you remember your grandmama's death? No, of course not. Your mama would have shielded you. *My* mama died of apoplexy right after that raid. Right out in the field as she watched the Yankees ride off and a fire destroy the home where she'd spent her entire married life and widowhood." His eyes shining with some undefinable emotion, he picked up a cloth and began to reverently rub away the tarnish from the silver platter.

While they worked in silence, Susanna considered all he'd said. Her conclusions came down to one question. How could she take these valuable items from this house when she and Daddy were beholden to Nate for their very lives and to Mrs. Northam for her extraordinary hospitality? Lying about their name and social standing was one thing; stealing, another.

On the other hand, all her life she'd heard friends and neighbors railing against the North for their invasion. Every person she knew considered it his or her duty to despise any and every Yankee. Had she betrayed her Southern heritage by falling in love with this family, with Nate? For indeed she did love him. There was no way she could deny it.

As Susanna was growing up, Mama hadn't talked much about the day when blue-coated soldiers invaded their home, had never discussed the way Grandmama died, preferring to help her family move on with their lives. But Susanna had heard frightening stories from other people. How far would Daddy go to take his revenge? Would he kill the Colonel and be hanged for it?

Voices sounded from the kitchen, meaning Angela and Mrs. Northam would soon need her help with supper. Before anyone else entered the room, she had to get the matter settled.

"Promise me one thing," she whispered.

He gave her a long look. "Depends on what it is."

She let out a long sigh. "Promise me you won't try to kill the Colonel, and I'll help you take the silver."

He didn't answer right away, then at last gave her a brief nod. But the hatred she saw in his eyes generated more than a little concern. Until this moment, her always-truthful father hadn't told her the real reason for their journey west. What made her think he wasn't still withholding the truth?

Chapter Twenty

Nate had one last strategy to try to recapture the friendship he and Susanna had forged before she knew about the Colonel and Sherman. Surely, by saving her father's life up on La Veta Pass, he'd won her trust, but he wouldn't try to manipulate her by bringing it up.

Instead, after breakfast the morning of the party, he asked her to take a look at the columbines to be sure they were presentable for their guests. With noticeable reluctance, she accompanied him out the back door, but refused his hand when descending the steps. Nor did she offer even a hint of a smile as they walked toward the flower bed.

"They'll look nicer if you trim off the wilted parts." She gave a dismissive wave of her hand and turned back to the house.

Disappointed that she hadn't teased him about such an obvious solution, he gently gripped her upper arm. "Wait. That's not all." The angry set of her jaw threatened to defeat him, but he wouldn't give up so easily. "Bess's pups are weaned. Do you still want that cute little runt?"

Surprise and a hint of joy spread over her face, reminding him of how beautiful she was. "W-well…" She stared down at the ground and bit her lip, as if thinking the matter over. At last she looked up at him with determination in those bright blue eyes. "Yes, but I plan to pay you for her."

He laughed. "Nobody pays for a dog. Not out here."

Her eyes narrowed, changing the brightness to ice. "I'll pay or not take her at all."

Take her? Did that mean she planned to leave? "Well, let's go give her the good news."

She glanced toward the barn, then back at the house. "I promised Mrs. Northam I would help in the kitchen."

"It'll just take a minute." He remembered the day they unpacked the china and addressed an obvious concern. "Wes is out there mucking out stalls, so we won't be alone."

Her eyes softened a bit. "All right."

Instead of the leisurely stroll he'd hoped for, she strode across the barnyard as if she was on a forced march. Once inside the barn, however, she stopped outside the stall where the puppies were sleeping one on top of another. All except the runt, who was curled up with one of the barn kittens, a tiny gray one just about the same age.

"Oh, how adorable." She sank down onto her knees beside them and began to stroke their fur. Awakened, both climbed into her lap and returned some of that affection. Susanna giggled like a child. "Oh, you silly things."

While she babbled cute little nonsense words to the animals, Nate felt a bittersweet pang in his chest. He hadn't heard her laugh in so many days, he couldn't count them. "Well, looks like you'll be adopting two critters instead of one."

She held up the kitten, its nose to her nose, and shushed its tiny mewing. "There, there, sweet thing. Don't cry. I'll take care of you."

Another pang struck deep in Nate's chest. How he longed to say *I'll take care of you* to Susanna. Yet until he made peace between the Colonel and Susanna, it was a promise he couldn't make. If he could never bring them together, even in an uneasy truce, would he have to choose his father over the woman he loved? He did love her, no doubt about it, and he believed she loved him. Why must a long-over war have to keep them from declaring what was in their hearts?

Susanna choked back tears, disguising her emotions by talking gibberish to the darling little animals she could soon call her own. With Nate so close beside her, she longed, *ached* to throw away all she'd ever known and tell him how deeply she cared for him. But to what end? They could never marry, for she refused to be a part of Colonel Northam's family. Imagine having children who would adore such an evil man and call him Grandpapa! She would never permit it.

Setting the puppy and kitten down with one last caress, she couldn't keep from looking straight into Nate's green eyes. She'd avoided his longing gazes for days, but now good manners obliged her to speak.

"Thank you. As you can see, I've fallen completely in love." She gasped. "With them, I mean."

"You can tell they return the sentiment." His eyes twinkled, and one side of his lips lifted in that heart-stopping grin.

"See you, boss." Pushing the filled wheelbarrow through the open barn door, Wes disappeared. How good of Nate to arrange for him to chaperone them for these few moments.

"I'd better go." Susanna couldn't stop staring into Nate's eyes.

"Right." He didn't seem in any hurry to leave, either. After an endless, agonizing moment, his gaze drifted to her lips, and he leaned toward her.

Longing welled up inside her to accept his kiss, her very first ever. But a memory flashed into her mind's eye. The scene of a raging fire her nurse had not been able to completely shield her from. Her family home deliberately destroyed by Nate's father. The fiery image consumed her tender yearning. She spun away from him and dashed from the barn back to the house. Finding Daddy resting in Nate's room, she flung herself into his arms, at last giving vent to her tears of hopelessness.

"Shh, daughter." He caressed her hair and placed a kiss on her forehead. "Everything will work out."

"How?" She moved back, pulled a handkerchief from her pocket and brushed away her foolish tears.

"The Lord hasn't brought us this far to leave us." His gaze hardened. "He'll show us what to do."

Vengeance is Mine; I will repay, saith the Lord. The verse from Romans sprang to the tip of her tongue, but Daddy shushed her.

"You get all dressed up fancy and enjoy the party tonight. I'll be there sitting in a corner. I'm not in any hurry to make my plans."

Susanna dutifully obeyed, completing the chores she'd promised to do for Mrs. Northam and then going to Rosamond's room to prepare for the evening. With all the enthusiasm she could muster, she helped the dear girl dress and arrange her hair, and accepted the same help in return. Flowers in their hair and fans at their wrists, they were ready to go.

"We're quite the picture, aren't we?" Rosamond looped her arm in Susanna's and directed her gaze into the dressing-table mirror. "You're so beautiful. You should always wear pink."

Susanna nodded. "Permit me to return the compliment." She could not despise this generous girl, who'd shared everything with her, even her clothes, since she'd arrived. This was the sister she'd always longed for.

Rosamond gripped Susanna's shoulders and stared into her eyes. "Listen, I don't know what happened between you and Nate, but I want you to fix it."

Susanna choked out a soft laugh. Like Maisie, Rosamond had no idea about subtlety. She shook her head. "Some things can't be fixed."

"Humph. Is my brother being stubborn about something? He can be pretty pigheaded, you know."

Susanna grasped her friend's hands. "I believe the Lord has it all under control."

"Oh." Rosamond blinked. "Of course. Well, then, let's go down to the party."

Pleased to be free of her questioning, Susanna lifted a silent prayer for the day when this precious girl fell in love, entreating the Lord that no complications would threaten her happiness.

Arm in arm, they descended the front staircase. They waved to Pedro, a relative of Angela's hired to serve at the party, whose job was to greet guests at the front door and direct them to the parlor. There, dressed in their Sunday best, Nate and Tolley stood as sentinels outside the ballroom's closed double doors.

The look in Nate's eyes and his enthusiastic "Wow"

confirmed Rosamond's compliment about Susanna's appearance. Yet what good did it do? She had no plans to dance with him or even to accept a glass of punch from him. If her feet betrayed her and insisted upon dancing, she would ask Tolley to be her partner.

But that wasn't likely to happen. Ever since Daddy told her about the day their valuables had been stolen, dark memories had emerged from the distant past, things her nurse and Mama had tried to shield her from, tried to make her forget. But she'd been six years of age, old enough to comprehend the terrifying events. And she would never let herself forget them again.

"Ladies, please step this way." The brothers slid open the double doors and waved them inside.

"Allow me." Nate offered his arm to Susanna, but she pulled up her fan and waved it before her face.

"Thank you. I can manage." She slid past him and stepped through the doorway, taking hold of the mahogany banister as she descended the five steps into the ballroom. As he'd promised, Daddy sat in the corner on a settee, and he waved her over. "I don't think I can do this," she whispered.

He squeezed her hand. "Yes, you can. Just sit here with me. The evening will pass quickly enough."

Rita entered, along with the three musicians who had played at the barn raising, and they formed an orchestra beside the piano. As the others played, Rita joined in softly so their instruments would cover the sound. Across the room, a photographer had set up his camera in front of one window, closing the drapes for a background for the pictures he would take.

Despite her reservations, Susanna found the fully decorated ballroom enchanting. The scent of roses wafted down from floral garlands hung from the scalloped molding some eight inches from the ceiling. The oak flooring had been polished to a sheen, then lightly dusted with chalk to keep dancers from slipping. Rosamond had stationed herself beside the silver tea service, which sat on a table. Susanna didn't see the china anywhere in the room. If she'd planned the party, she would have it all set out so Mrs. Northam would see it right away. Maybe the Colonel was afraid some of it would break during the dancing. But why on earth did she bother to think about his concerns?

The room filled with neighbors Susanna had met at the barn raising and church, and each one came to meet Daddy and welcome him to the community. When he didn't correct them and say he was a prospector, Susanna experienced no little relief. Reverend Thomas and Dr. Henshaw paid their respects to him and Susanna, with the doctor asking her to save him a dance. Pedro's two brothers passed among the guests offering refreshments from wooden trays.

"Good evening and welcome, everyone." The Colonel's voice boomed throughout the room as he and Mrs. Northam made a grand entrance and stood at the top of the staircase. The entire assembly applauded, and numerous whistles sounded above the noise. The sight of the Colonel, handsome to a fault in his blue army uniform, medals gleaming on his chest, caused Susanna to gasp in horror. Even Daddy jolted beside her, and a deep growl emanated from his throat. But Susanna's eyes quickly moved to Mrs. Northam, resplendent in a blue satin gown, with Mama's brilliant sapphire necklace sparkling around her neck. In an instant, every good or kind or admiring thought Susanna had toward Mrs. Northam vanished.

If Daddy hadn't held Susanna's hand in a vise grip, she would have dashed across the room and snatched the heirloom jewels right off the woman. How could she not know they belonged to another lady? How could she boldly wear the spoils of war? Susanna's gaze darted to the silver set, and a terrible truth dawned in her mind. With the monogram clearly etched on that silver tray, Mrs. Northam had to know these were stolen vessels. How could she serve beverages to these other church friends, knowing another lady was bereft of her valuable heirlooms? Did this Yankee woman have no shame?

Apparently not, for she stood gazing about the room, laughing and exclaiming over every beautiful adornment, especially the piano. The crowd laughed with her, as did her pompous husband. How clever he must feel, Susanna thought. Giving his wife gifts that cost another woman so dearly.

"Mrs. Northam, may I have this dance?" The Colonel sketched an elaborate bow before his wife.

Rita launched into a Strauss waltz, and the anniversary couple took to the floor. After they made a few turns, others joined in. Seated beside Daddy, Susanna declined each gentleman who invited her to dance. When Nate approached, she focused on her father and refused to look at him.

"I couldn't bear to be in his arms, Daddy," she whispered after he indicated Nate had gone.

Daddy nodded his understanding. His own gaze hadn't left Mrs. Northam since she entered the room. Was he thinking about the last time Mama wore that lovely necklace so many years ago?

Across the room, Nate spoke to Tolley and pointed his chin in her direction. Tolley questioned him, then shrugged. He fetched two glasses of punch and, with his usual puppy-dog eyes, ambled their way. "Thought you might be thirsty." He set the cups in their hands, then moved away before they could object.

"Thank you," Susanna said too late for him to hear her. Her eyes stung, both over his kindness and her own bad manners, which would shame Mama.

"Nate keeps looking out for us, doesn't he?" Daddy's eyes were a bit moist, too.

The party went on and on, yet even the lively accordion music did not tempt Susanna to stand up with any of the gentlemen who continued to approach her. She did take some pleasure in watching Maisie and Dr. Henshaw dance together. If she wasn't mistaken, they already had a romance under way. In church last Sunday, they had sat together and shared a hymnal, along with many warm smiles. Apparently, he found her tomboy ways a part of her charm.

At last a buffet supper was announced, and Reverend Thomas offered grace. Guests took turns wandering into the dining room to retrieve plates of beef, chicken and pork, with countless side dishes and fixings. Susanna managed to sneak full plates for herself and Daddy without any unpleasant encounters, but her lack of appetite caused her to leave half of hers uneaten.

When everyone reassembled in the ballroom, the Colonel took his wife's elbow and gave Nate a nod. Nate in turn signaled to his brothers, who stood just inside the door. Like a line of marching soldiers, they and their cowhands carried in wooden boxes and set them on a table hastily moved to the center of the room. The few children not outside playing were warned to stay with their parents, then a hush came over the assembly.

"Charlotte," the Colonel said, "in honor of the best twenty-five years of my life, a life that just keeps getting better and better because you are my wife, I'd like to present you with a small token of my affection."

Mrs. Northam began to open the boxes and exclaimed over and over how beautiful the china was, how clever and good her husband was, how she'd thought this beautiful ballroom was her gift, which was far more than she'd hoped for, and on and on. She then surprised him with the exquisite silver spurs. Everyone in the crowd laughed at the Colonel's genuine shock and his artificial disappointment over not receiving the quilt he'd been expecting. George Eberly quipped that it was about time somebody outwitted the Colonel. Again the crowd erupted in laughter until Susanna's ears began to hurt from the sound of it.

The couple's mutual adoration stung her heart. Daddy and Mama had also loved each other with the same kind of deep devotion. What would these evil people think if some man stole this china and gave it to another woman? But Susanna did like Mr. Eberly's remark. Soon she and Daddy would also be *outwitting* the Colonel, and she could hardly wait for that day.

After many toasts and speeches by neighbors proclaiming all that the Colonel and Mrs. Northam had done to create a wonderful, vibrant community, Mr. Eberly announced that a vote had been taken. Everyone agreed the best name for their growing town was Northam City, or just plain Northam.

As if he already knew about their scheme, the Colonel modestly accepted the honor, declaring that he would prefer the name Mountain View, or the Spanish version, Monte Vista. "But who am I to argue with popular opinion?"

With that matter settled, he beckoned to Nate and Maisie. "Come on over, you two."

Nate's face turned a darker shade of tan, and Maisie glanced up at Dr. Henshaw with nothing short of bewilderment. They slowly approached the Colonel, and he took his place between them, imprisoning them with his long arms around their shoulders.

"I'm sure this young couple has been hiding their good news so as not to overshadow tonight's little celebration."

His face now a deep red, Nate tried to pull back from his father, but the Colonel held on tight. "Ever since George and I settled this land side by side, we've looked forward to the day when we could expand our holdings to benefit both of us. Now that Maisie is all grown up—" he gave her a tighter hug "—it's time to announce the joining of our properties through her marriage to Nate. As my eldest son, he will inherit..."

He continued talking, but Susanna no longer heard his words. Wide-eyed, she stared at Daddy while her heart twisted inside her chest. So all this time, Nate had only been flirting with her. He'd never intended to court her. Never intended to do anything other than play with her emotions with all of his sweet talk and outward courtesies. He was just like the rest of his family. A Yankee through and through, with every bad quality that name indicated.

"Well, that settles that." Daddy squeezed her hand. "I'm sorry, daughter. In spite of everything, I hoped you and Nate—"

She couldn't listen to another word. She hastily wended her way through the crowd and up the stairs to the parlor. There she collided with Dr. Henshaw, who was claiming his hat from Pedro.

"It seems I'm not the only one shocked by the news." He tipped the hat to her and strode toward the front hall and out the door.

Turning the other way, Susanna ran up the stairs to Rosamond's room, where she slammed and locked the door. Facedown on the bed, she sobbed bitterly. To think this very afternoon Nate had tried to steal a kiss from her. He was more like his father than she'd ever imagined.

"But, Colonel." Maisie twisted free of his hold and almost shouted her protest. "I don't want to marry Nate. He's like a brother to me." She fisted her hands at her waist. "Didn't you know I'm sweet on the doc? And he's sweet on me?" She cast a look of exasperation toward the door he'd just exited.

Even as relief flooded Nate, he saw the color rising up the Colonel's neck. Maisie's short speech may have set him free from his father's plan, but it also threatened to shame the Colonel before the entire community, maybe beyond repair. No matter how angry his father had made him, he couldn't let that happen. "Yep, Colonel, I should have told you." He let his posture droop with apparent disappointment. "Once you brought that Harvard-educated doctor to the community, I lost out."

The Colonel's confusion quickly cleared, and he grasped the lifeline Nate offered. "Well, I'll be a Christmas goose. How's a man supposed to keep up with such goings-on?"

Maisie seemed to catch on, because she patted the

Colonel's shoulder in a comforting gesture. "It's not your fault, sir. You know how fickle we women can be. I took one look at Doc, and all these cowpokes disappeared." She cast an apologetic grin over the assembly, and everyone laughed.

At that moment, Nate wanted to give her a big, brotherly kiss, but that would ruin everything. Across the room, George Eberly scratched his head in confusion. For the first time, Nate doubted Maisie's father had even been aware of the Colonel's plans.

"Well, time's a-wasting." Maisie strode toward the steps. "I got me a doctor to catch." More boisterous laughter rang throughout the room.

Nate made a split-second decision, not caring how it looked. "Hang on, Maisie. I'll help you catch him." Behind him, the good-natured laughter continued in the ballroom as he followed her all the way to the front door. "Do you need me?"

"Naw." She thumped her fist against his shoulder. "I expect you need to do some catching yourself." With that, she dashed outside.

"*Señor,* if it is the other young lady you seek." Pedro pointed toward the staircase.

"*Gracias.*" Nate took the steps three at a time. Hearing Susanna's sobs through the door of Rosamond's room, he knocked softly. "Susanna, open up. Please let me explain." How he ached to comfort her and explain it all away. Yet in an odd way, he also felt a bit encouraged. She wouldn't be crying about his supposed engagement if she didn't care for him.

Chapter Twenty-One

"That was some party." Nate lingered in the kitchen after breakfast in hopes of seeing Susanna, but only Rosamond joined him at the kitchen table. It was still dark outside, but he'd already done his early chores, then came back for some of Angela's griddle cakes.

"Yes, it was." Rosamond wore an uncharacteristic frown, which put Nate on alert. "Mother's sleeping. When she gets up, we're going to take some of the leftover food from last night to needy folks in the neighborhood."

"Good." Nate took a sip of coffee. "Maybe Susanna can go with you." If he didn't have work to do that couldn't be postponed, including helping Tolley break his first mustang, he'd spend the day wooing her like a lovesick Romeo. Restless all night, he'd fallen asleep only after deciding to tell the Colonel of his feelings for her and face whatever came after that.

But life on a ranch didn't wait on either courting or confrontation, so he'd have to bide his time and wait until he was free to take care of both matters. He assumed Rosamond's downcast mood concerned Susanna. If she'd just come downstairs, he could at least see whether he had a chance with her or whether he should resign himself to being miserable for the rest of his life.

He finished his griddle cakes and carried his empty plate to Rita, who was up to her elbows in the dishpan. "That was some fine music last night, Rita. I hope you'll keep up your playing."

"*Sí,* Señor Nate. Señor Colonel says I must learn everything Mrs. Foster can teach me." Beside her, Angela beamed with maternal pride.

He headed toward the back door, considering his strategy for teaching his youngest brother the fine art of taming a wild horse. Before he could put his hand on the doorknob, the Colonel burst in looking oddly wild-eyed. Nate hadn't spoken with him since the embarrassing incident at the party, so a wave of apprehension surged through him.

"Where's Rand?" Desperation colored his father's tone, something Nate had only seen once before when his middle brother had suffered a bad fall from the roof.

"Rand? I don't know."

"What do you mean you don't know?" This was the old Colonel, worried about his favorite son.

"I mean—" Nate forced the rancor from his voice "—well, he was up before me, so I assumed he rode out with the boys to cut the calves for branding." He couldn't keep from adding, "Like you ordered him to do."

"Did you see him after the party last night? See him in bed?"

Nate frowned. "Now that you mention it, no, sir. I didn't see him. Maybe he slept in the bunkhouse."

The Colonel slammed his hand against the doorjamb. "Just as I suspected. He and that no-good Seamus have ridden over to Del Norte on a gambling binge. Saddle up. We're going after him."

An odd feeling washed through Nate. The Colonel usually let Rand get over his binges himself, after which his brother, like the biblical Prodigal Son, dragged himself home, where his sins were never even mentioned. Never before had the Colonel chased after him. Maybe he'd shake some sense into Rand. *Maybe* Nate's prayers were getting through at last.

Susanna stayed in bed as long as she could, but hunger finally drove her to get up and dress. After checking on Daddy, she descended the back stairs fully aware that she would have to face Rosamond. She'd rebuffed the younger girl's attempts at conversation both at bedtime and early this morning. Rosamond's wounded tone of voice had revealed her hurt, and now Susanna tried without success to dismiss her guilty feelings. It wasn't Rosamond's fault her parents had stolen Mama's valuables. Not Rand's nor Tolley's and certainly not Nate's. She constantly had to remind herself that Nate had saved Daddy's life, and hers, too. Of course, that didn't obligate him to love her, not when he'd been promised to Maisie.

Mama always said there was no excuse for bad manners, and Susanna wouldn't excuse herself this time. The only way to apologize would be to put on a cheerful face and continue to help around the house. Only now she would assume the attitude of a servant, maybe even stop taking meals with the family so she didn't have to sit down with the Colonel and Mrs. Northam. If Daddy still wanted to eat with them, that was his business.

"Good morning." She entered the kitchen only to find Rosamond wasn't there. Nevertheless, she gave the room's sole occupant a bright smile, despite the disturbance it caused in her stomach.

"Susanna." Mrs. Northam rose from the table and embraced her. "Good morning. I'm so glad to see you. Did you sleep well?"

Susanna couldn't keep from stiffening, but she kept her artificial smile in place. "Why, yes, indeed, I did, thank you. Did you sleep well after all that celebrating last night?" She almost gagged on the question. After the plantation house burned, had Mama lain awake at night fearing the Yankees would return?

Mrs. Northam laughed as she returned to her seat. "After all the months of planning, I have to confess it's a relief to have it all over and done with."

"My, my." Susanna knew she needed to keep her mouth shut before some of her bitterness leaked out. With no choice but to sit down with this woman, she went to the stove and served herself some bacon, eggs and griddle cakes. What she wouldn't give for a bowl of grits and molasses right about now.

"I will confess, however," Mrs. Northam said, "it will be hard to get back to normal, whatever normal is on a ranch. Seems like something out of the ordinary is always happening."

"Mmm." Now seated, Susanna busied herself with devouring her breakfast. Once she convinced Daddy they needed to leave, she would cut several five-dollar gold pieces from her old petticoat to pay for the food they'd eaten and the two animals Nate had sold her. Of course, they'd need horses, too, so maybe Nate would sell them a team. She hadn't worn the petticoat since arriving, hiding it in the back of a drawer and using Rosamond's outgrown clothes instead. Maybe she would buy some of those to wear until she could make her own.

Biting into a crisp piece of bacon, she looked up to see Mrs. Northam watching her thoughtfully. She questioned the woman with a single raised eyebrow, although Mama would not approve of such a gesture, especially when Susanna's mouth was full.

"Is something wrong, dear?"

Susanna swallowed. "No, ma'am. Everything's fine." A wild thought crossed her mind. "I heard you tell Colonel Northam you're working on a new shirt for him. Can I help you do that today?"

"Why, thank you. You're a gifted seamstress. Rosamond tells me you made the ballroom drapes. I've never had success sewing with velvet. You must teach us how to do it."

"I'd be pleased to. Why don't we start right after breakfast?"

"Oh, didn't Rosamond tell you? Today we wanted you to go with us while we take some leftover food to our needy neighbors."

Susanna scrambled for a reason to stay home and settled on Daddy. "My father didn't look particularly well this morning, so I'd best stay home with him. I'd love to make use of my time and work on that shirt while you're gone."

Mrs. Northam opened her mouth, probably to object, then nodded. "That would be lovely. After you finish eating, we'll go up to my room and I'll show you what I've done so far."

"Oh, my." Susanna almost laughed. Going to the master bedroom was exactly what she'd hoped to do. Only one problem presented itself. "Why, Miz Northam—" she poured on her thickest Southern pronunciations "—I would be mortified if the Colonel showed up and I was in your bedroom. Why, what would he think of me?" Not that she cared.

Mrs. Northam had the grace to look abashed. "You're right, of course. I hadn't thought of that. But my husband isn't home today. He and Nate had to…" She frowned and released a weary sigh. "They had to ride over to Del Norte." She tilted her head toward the west. "Rand and his friend Seamus may have gotten into a little mischief. They may need some help getting out of it." She let out another sigh. "In any event, they won't be home until late this afternoon."

Susanna could see the woman's embarrassment, and her heart softened. From what she'd seen, Rand wasn't wicked, just prone to tomfoolery. "I'll pray they bring him safely home." The words were out before she could stop them, but she would keep the promise for Rand's *and* Nate's sakes.

Mrs. Northam's eyes reddened. "Thank you, Susanna. I pray without ceasing for each of my children, but Rand's always needed a double dose." She laughed softly. "We mothers want only to see our children happy and healthy." After dabbing her eyes with her napkin, she stood. "Shall we go up?"

"I should wash my dishes first."

"You go," Rita said. "As you can see, I am washing dishes again. The Colonel, he says it is permissible after the anniversary playing."

With that, Susanna and her hostess made their way to

the upstairs chamber. The room was grandly decorated with wallpaper, brass sconces, draperies, a stone fireplace with brass andirons and elegant mahogany furniture. Under the west window sat the sewing machine.

"You can work right here. Then, if you see the men returning up the lane, you can leave." She tapped her chin thoughtfully. "In fact, why don't we bring your father in to keep you company, maybe read you the latest newspaper from back east as you work? He'll be comfortable on the chaise longue, don't you think?"

"Yes, ma'am." Everything was working out just as Susanna had hoped. Beside the tall mahogany wardrobe stood a matching dressing table. On it, next to the usual hand mirror and brush, lay a black velvet jewel box, maybe containing Mama's sapphires. Her heart skipped a beat. "That will be just fine."

After Mrs. Northam showed her the half-completed shirt, she sat comfortably before the Singer and began to pin and sew the sleeves to the rest of the shirt. When Rosamond entered the room, Susanna managed a cheery greeting she really meant. It would be nothing short of wickedness to blame the children for their father's sins. Besides, sewing always relaxed her, so this would be a good day.

Before leaving on their charitable mission, the two ladies escorted Daddy from Nate's room and settled him on the chaise, a blanket, a newspaper and *Bleak House* on his lap.

"Angela or Rita will be up to check on you from time to time," Mrs. Northam said as they exited the bedroom.

When Susanna saw their carriage driving up the lane, she huffed out a sigh. "I thought they'd never leave." She dashed to the dressing table and picked up the faded black velvet box. Although it had been brushed to clean the fabric, she could still see some deeply embedded gray soil. Her heart ached to think of Mama having to bury this box, only to have those Yankees dig it up and steal it.

"What do you have there, daughter?" Daddy peered at her over the edge of the *Boston Globe.*

Not opening the box, she moved to the edge of the chaise. "What do you think?"

He took it reverently in hand as though he, too, noticed the imbedded soil from home. Slowly lifting the lid to reveal the glimmering silver and sparkling sapphires, he blinked as tears rolled down his cheeks. "Oh, Belle," he choked out. "What I wouldn't give to see you wear these again."

Susanna swallowed her own tears. Mama had never desired jewels or fancy clothes. Despite her frightening experiences during the war, or maybe because of them, all she'd ever wanted was for her family to be happy and healthy. Like Mrs. Northam. The thought came unbidden, and Susanna thrust it away, along with the guilt that tried to seize her. This was Mama's necklace, and it was high time to reclaim it and the other valuables. "I know where the tea service is kept."

Daddy's eyes brightened. "And?"

"We need to take our belongings and leave. Today." She studied his face and reassured herself that his color was good. He could travel without a relapse. "The Northams are away and won't be home until evening. We can buy another team of horses right here. Nate's told me they always have some for sale, and Wes or one of the other hands would know which ones are best for pulling the prairie schooner." Mentioning Nate's name brought a sharp pain to her heart, but she would not dwell on it. "The wagon is in the barn, and when I checked the other day, no one had opened the secret compartment. Our gold is still there."

"Today?" Daddy stared off thoughtfully, but she could see he liked the idea.

"Yes, today." As her excitement mounted, she laughed and cried at the same time. "This is what you came for." She took the open jewel box in hand, seeing for the first time the countless number of tiny diamonds circling each sapphire. "Forget living in this community. Now we can go back home to Marietta."

He drew back with a frown. "Marietta?"

She stared at him. "What ails you, Daddy? Yes, Marietta. You know, that finest of Southern cities in the state where we were both born and bred? Where our family and friends will welcome us back with open arms and scold us for ever leaving?" She punctuated her speech with a laugh, but when he continued to frown, she closed and set down the jewel box and gripped his hands. "What is it, Daddy?"

His expression was a study in cautious happiness. "I can't go back to Marietta. Can't go back to anyplace in Georgia."

"What? What are you talking about?" Clearly, the thought did not dismay him as it did her.

He pulled one hand from her grip and touched her cheek. "Please listen to me with an open heart, daughter." At her nod, he continued, "You know I loved your mama. Still do. But she's with the Lord now, and I'm still here." He grimaced, as if he feared to continue. Susanna squeezed his hand to encourage him. "All these weeks we've been here, Miss Angela has taken mighty good care of me. It was always proper, mind you, with Zack always around to help with things she shouldn't do. We've had some wonderful talks and, well, I've fallen in love with her, daughter. I plan to marry her."

"You've fallen in love with Angela?" Susanna liked the woman very much, but—

"Now, I know what you're going to say. She's a Mexican." He breathed out a long sigh. "I no longer care about such things. She's a good, sweet Christian lady. But you know as well as I do that the folks back home will never accept her as my wife, no matter how strong a Christian she is. I won't leave her behind, and I won't dishonor her by asking her to go with me under any arrangement other than marriage."

"But—" Susanna couldn't quite sort it out. Daddy falling in love again? At his age? "I can't stay here loving Nate as I do and knowing he's obligated to marry Maisie."

"Marry Maisie?" Daddy chuckled. "I forgot to tell you—"

"Ah, there you are, Señor Anders." Angela entered the room, her face aglow. Did that mean she loved Daddy in return? "May I bring dinner up for you and Señorita Susanna, or would you like to go down to the dining room?"

Daddy reached out a hand and tugged her down to the nearby chair. "I've told her, sweetheart."

Angela gasped and turned a hopeful look in Susanna's direction. "You are not angry?"

Susanna's bothersome tears started again. "Not in the least. I'm thankful to you for bringing joy to my father. I wish you both great happiness." Now that Angela would be taking care of him, Susanna would no longer need to keep her promise to Mama. "I-is there some way I can go back home?" Oddly, the thought of returning to Marietta without him seemed painfully unacceptable. The thought of never seeing Nate again pained her even more. But why? Even if he wasn't promised to Maisie, she would never consider marrying into his family.

"But no, *señorita*." Angela glanced at Daddy. "You must stay and live with us. Many people here love you." She exchanged another look with Daddy. "Tell her."

Stunned, Susanna could only stare at them. Finally, she lightly smacked Daddy's hand. "Where was I when all of this was going on?"

"Why, if I'm not mistaken, you were involved with affairs of the heart yourself."

She snorted in a most unladylike way. "And you saw last night how well that turned out."

"Ah," Angela said. "She does not know this."

"What else don't I know?" Susanna had experienced just about all the surprises she needed for a while.

"Why," Daddy said, "that fool of a Colonel thought he could force Nate to marry Maisie, but she told the whole community she's in love with the doc, and he with her." Daddy threw back his head and laughed. "You should have seen what a fool that man made of himself. And Nate rescued him by claiming he was disappointed in Maisie's choice."

"Yes, well, he's pretty good at rescuing people, isn't he?" Relief poured over Susanna. Nate was free to marry whom he chose. An odd bit of hope skittered through her, but she quickly dashed it. She refused to be a part of the Colonel's family, so seeing Nate again would only cause her grief. A sense of urgency filled her. "We need to get the silver and leave while they're gone. Now."

"Eduardo?" Angela gave Daddy a chiding frown.

"Now, honey, I've told you all about that. Those things belong to us. The Colonel stole them from my wife during the war."

The older woman sighed and bowed her head. "Oh, Dios, what is Your will? Give us guidance that we might not sin against You." She looked at Daddy. "All my life, many of my belongings have been stolen by bandits until I come here. I would like to have my things back again, but that will never be. I will go with you, and we will take your stolen things. But please remember, no matter what they did to you, the Northams have been kind and protected my daughter and me."

He gave her a decisive nod. "I understand."

"And!" She held up a scolding forefinger, and he smothered a grin. "You will not seek any other revenge against the Colonel. I have already seen one husband hanged by our enemies. This Colonel Northam is too powerful to cross. You will promise, or I will not marry you."

Daddy considered her words for a moment, then nodded. "I don't want to see you grieved again, Miss Angela, so I'll do as you say." He brushed a hand over her cheek. "But I'll never forgive him, never forget what he and the North did to my family." Carefully moving his injured leg over the side of the couch, he positioned his crutch so he could stand. "All right, let's get packed up."

"Yes, sir." Susanna's heart leaped into her throat as she and Angela helped him to his feet. "Instead of taking the house the preacher found for us, let's go back toward Alamosa or down south to Angela's relatives."

Daddy chuckled. "Daughter, do you think you're the only one who's been making plans? I've already sent the money to Reverend Thomas to buy that plot of land where the three of us can live in peace."

Susanna's jaw dropped. "What? You want to stay in a community named for Colonel Northam?"

He shrugged. "What better place to settle? Here I can be a burr in the saddle of that arrogant Yankee."

"Why, you rascal." This was her old daddy, and she couldn't be more pleased. "And you did all of that without me?"

He shrugged. "A man's got to make plans, daughter. Now, you go find Zack or Wes and see about those horses. If they'll sell them to us, have them bring out the wagon."

Susanna traded a look with Angela.

"You best do as he says." The amusement in Angela's eyes tickled Susanna's insides.

Now, if they could just make their escape before any of the Northam family came back home. Angela assured them the family wouldn't miss the silver items because they would assume she'd stored them. But if they did realize they were gone, Susanna knew Nate would be terribly disappointed in her, perhaps even hate her.

And maybe that was best.

Chapter Twenty-Two

Nate followed the Colonel into the Shady Lady saloon north of Del Norte. In the middle of the day, even a Saturday, he hadn't expected to see so many patrons gambling and imbibing. To his surprise, nearly every table was filled, and the rank smell of liquor hung in the air. He couldn't see Rand, but when a couple of the women called out to him, Nate quit searching and focused on his father. If one of those foolish girls got friendly with him, he'd just tell her to go to church and make friends with God.

"Good morning, Colonel Northam." The bartender no doubt made it his business to know the important people in the surrounding area. "Come for your son?"

The Colonel stormed up to the bar, casting an uneasy glance toward the steps leading upstairs. "Where is he?"

The man had the audacity to laugh, but his tone held no mockery. "Why, over at the jail, of course. He—"

The Colonel spun on his heel and marched back through the swinging doors. They rode in silence to the center of town, where the sheriff's office was located. Leaving their horses at the hitching rail, they entered the two-story wood-frame building.

"Dad!" Rand broke from a group of men near the jail cells and strode across the wide room. "Am I glad to see you. Wait till you hear—"

"I don't need to hear anything you have to say." The Colonel brushed past him and approached the sheriff. "What do I owe you for his bail?"

"Owe me?" The sheriff gave him a long look. "It's what we owe him we need to talk about."

"What?" The Colonel barked out the question in a way that usually made two of his sons cower.

As usual, Rand just laughed. "Wait till you hear this, Dad. Tell him, Sheriff."

Nate swallowed his disgust at Rand's brashness. Once again his brother would get off without punishment.

"Why, these two boys—" the sheriff beckoned to Seamus, who sheepishly joined the group "—these two *men* are responsible for rounding up a couple of the mangiest, lowdown horse thieves I've ever seen. Outdrew them and shot one in the leg. The other one's over at the undertaker's."

In a flash, pride in his brother's heroism cooled Nate's anger, and he sent Rand an approving glance. Then he peered around the sheriff to see a dark-suited man, probably a doctor, tending a scruffy fellow in the cell. A chill went up his spine. The scar-faced wounded man fit the description Mr. Anders had given of one of the thieves who'd beaten him. If Susanna hadn't been fetching water, Nate shuddered to think what the surly thief would have done to her. As it was, he wanted to pummel the man who'd nearly killed her father. His old temper threatened to carry him over to the cell to do just that, so he turned his attention back to the sheriff.

"I've been trying to catch those two varmints for over a year. They had gold from the sale of the horses they've stolen, and they were loco enough to go over to the Shady Lady to gamble it away. That's where they encountered your son and Seamus." The middle-aged sheriff beamed at them with paternal approval. "He was just telling me how he came to know they were thieves."

Rand shuffled his feet and stared down at the floor. "It didn't take much. After a few drinks, they were bragging about killing some old man up on La Veta Pass and making off with his horses. That one—" he jerked a thumb toward the cell "—even bragged about giving his girlfriend some fancy duds he found in the prairie schooner." He grimaced as he looked at Nate. "I knew right away he was talking about Mr. Anders and Susanna. Thank the Lord the old man didn't die, or this one would be up for hanging."

"Horse stealing's a hanging offense, too," the sheriff said. "The circuit judge will be riding through soon. Then we'll see this one's taken care of." He seemed to relish the idea. "Now, what am I gonna do for you boys? O'course the money you won from 'em at cards is yours, but there's also a reward for their capture, dead or alive."

"Aw, I don't care about the money." Rand stared down at his feet. "In fact, I feel a little sick to my stomach over the whole matter. I've got a lot to sort out." He traded a look with Seamus, who gave him a firm nod. "One thing's for sure. I'm done with gambling. Give the money to charity."

Seamus echoed his vow, and Nate could see by the relief in his eyes that he meant it. He also had a suspicion that Rand had been dragging Seamus along on his escapades just to have some company.

Rand looked at the Colonel. "Dad, I can't say I'm proud to have killed a man, but they gave us no choice. Once I called them on the robbery, they went for their guns. Please forgive me for shaming your name by consorting with such evil men."

Nate started to protest that he'd done the right thing, but the Colonel beat him to it. "Son, I had to do some things during the war that still eat at my soul. But just as God helped David kill Goliath, this was a righteous killing. You can check with Reverend Thomas, but I believe God's forgiven you for it. As for the gambling, I have. Any shame connected with it will be canceled out by righteous living from now on. But—" he held a finger up to Rand's face "—I expect you to be accountable to me from now on for everything you do."

"Thanks, Dad." Rand's eyes reddened. "I'll do that."

Nate could feel a bit of dust in his own eyes. "Colonel?" He wished he could feel comfortable calling him Dad. "Some of that money ought to go to Mr. Anders for the sale of his horses and for the other stolen things. I know they could use it." He wouldn't even think about reclaiming Susanna's dresses after some saloon girl had worn them.

Rand chimed in with his agreement, and they settled on three hundred dollars, sixty for each horse and sixty for the other belongings. The sheriff insisted that Rand and Seamus should split the five-hundred-dollar reward, and at the Colonel's urging, they accepted it.

As they rode back home, Nate felt a strange mixture of emotions. Most of all he felt pride in Rand's courage and, best of all, his repentance. But he was also disappointed when their jubilant chatter as they traveled kept him from telling his father he planned to court Susanna. A smidgen of anxiety also colored his thoughts. What if she didn't accept his courtship?

Anyway, this was Rand's day and a time to celebrate. Of course, most days were Rand's days, but somehow that awareness didn't depress Nate as it usually did. He was just glad his brother was all right. Further, he couldn't deny his relationship with the Colonel had greatly improved. Just the fact that his father had insisted he come along to rescue Rand bolstered Nate's confidence that one day soon he'd feel comfortable addressing the man as Dad.

"Oh, Mamá," Rita cried. "I am happy for you, but I am not yet ready to manage the kitchen by myself."

"Of course you are, my little one. When I was your age, I alone managed my father's house because *madre mia* was with the Lord." Angela embraced her daughter while Susanna and Daddy finished packing the prairie schooner. "You know we would be pleased if you went with us, but as we decided, Colonel and Mrs. Northam have been so good to you and me, *si?* We must not leave them without a cook. Just remember all I have taught you. If you have *problema,* you come to my new home on the day of your piano lessons." The pride in her voice when mentioning her *new home* moved Susanna almost to tears. Every woman, no matter what her culture, longed for a place to call her own.

Zack had chosen four sturdy horses from those available for sale and hitched them to the wagon. Once he'd driven it around to the front of the house, Susanna surreptitiously checked the stash of gold and found it still safely tucked into the secret compartment. What a wonder that the thieves hadn't found it. Perhaps they were too busy beating Daddy and destroying their supplies and clothing to search too diligently. How wise of Daddy to insist that they wear rough clothing and use only paper money so no one would suspect they had gold.

She'd decided not to take a single item from Rosamond's wardrobe, for that truly would be stealing. Instead, she now wore her old brown wool skirt and mended shirtwaist. She missed the pleasant feeling of being nicely dressed.

"Come along, daughter." Daddy scurried around with such excitement, Susanna began to worry about his health. Angela reassured her that he would be all right.

"Will you come with us?" Daddy placed a hand on Zack's shoulder. "I could use your help, and I'll pay you well."

Zack tipped his hat back and scratched at his forehead. "Well, sir, you give me something to think about. Since Nate's been the foreman, he hasn't let me do what I used to on account of a few broken bones over the years. Treats me like an old man." He studied Daddy up and down. "Tell you what. If you put me to work and let me decide how much I can do, I'll feel worth my salt more than I do here."

"It's a bargain." Daddy held out his hand, and they shook on it.

As glad as Susanna was that Daddy would have a man to help him, she couldn't help but admire the way Nate had looked out for Zack, just as he had her and Daddy. Swallowing the tears that kept threatening to slow her down, she busied herself arranging the contents of the wagon.

With the last of their few possessions packed and the retrieved valuables safely hidden beneath Angela's clothes and blankets, the party began to climb aboard. Taking one last look around, Susanna saw Bess and two of her pups near the barn.

"Wait. I forgot Lazy Daisy and Shadow."

"What on earth?" Daddy called from the driver's bench. "Daughter, we need to leave."

"I'll just be a moment." She dashed across the wide barnyard and into the structure. "Come, my little ones." Already weaned, neither seemed to mind being taken from its mother. At least she hoped not.

She hurried back across the yard just in time to see the Northam men turn down the lane. Breathless now, she paused at the back of the wagon and handed the tiny pets to Angela, who was already settled inside.

"Here, Rita." She pulled a gold piece from her pocket and handed it to the girl. "Tell Colonel Northam this is for the animals. Nate said I could have them."

Before she could climb in, the men arrived in a cloud of dust. Nate was the first one to dismount, with the others right behind him. Seeing the Colonel's hunched-up shoulders, Susanna swallowed a lump of fear. His posture had been just like that when they'd arrived. Surely, now he should be glad to see them gone.

"You're leaving?" Nate's wounded tone cut deep into her heart. "But I wanted—"

"Let 'em go."

For once, the Colonel's snapped response didn't silence Nate.

"Look." Standing by the wagon, he pulled from his

pocket a leather bag that jingled as he held it up to Daddy. "Rand and Seamus found the thieves. I'm sorry to say your horses were already sold, but here's the money for them." His brief explanation of their trip to Del Norte astounded Susanna, and she could see Daddy's shock, as well. "Don't you want to stay until the trial so you can be a witness? The circuit judge will be here in the next month or so."

"Oh, we'll still be around." Daddy spoke to Nate in a loud enough voice for the Colonel to hear. "Got me a little place up on the Rio Grande." He accepted the bag from Nate. "This'll help pay expenses. Thank you, Nate. Not just for this but for all you've done."

Susanna hated that he wanted to maintain their pose of poverty. Why couldn't they just tell them all who they were and be done with it?

"Zack." The Colonel was the only one who hadn't dismounted. Susanna suspected he wanted to maintain a more intimidating position. "I'm assuming you'll be returning my horses once you park these people someplace far away from here."

Zack started to answer, but Daddy held up a hand to silence him.

"Colonel Northam." His voice cut through the air like steel rapier, something Susanna had rarely heard from her mellow father. "I paid for these horses, a fact to which both your man Wes and my man Zack will attest. You'll find your money in young Rita's care, and I have the bill of sale right here." He patted his tattered jacket right above the pocket.

Thunder rode across the Colonel's brow. "*Your* man Zack?"

Zack cleared his throat. "Um, yessir. I've decided to go to work for Mr. Anders."

Colonel Northam snorted out his disgust. "So much for your loyalty to me."

His arrogant remark must have stung Zack because he spat over the side of the wagon and pulled his hat lower on his forehead.

"But where will you go?" Nate reached for Susanna's hand, and a pleasant shiver went up her arm. Oh, they really must leave before his protectiveness undid her.

"As Daddy said, we have a place." She refused to look into his eyes, even when he tugged on her hand.

"Where? When can I come see you?" He looked up at Daddy, then briefly at the Colonel.

"Let them go, son." The Colonel dismounted and handed his horse off to Rand, then gripped Nate's shoulder. "We're well rid of them."

"No, we're not. I—"

Puppy yips from inside the wagon interrupted him, and he gave her his lopsided grin.

"I'm glad you didn't forget her. Did you take the kitten, too?" His sweet look tore at Susanna's heart. It was all she could do not to throw herself into his arms.

"I told you," the Colonel barked, "she can't have that dog." He marched to the back of the wagon and lowered the tailgate. "Angela, what are you doing here? Are you deserting us, too?"

Nate started. "What's going on?" This time he spoke to Daddy.

"Well, son, Miss Angela and I have decided to get married."

Susanna broke away from Nate and hurried to the Colonel. "This puppy is the runt of the litter and has a bum leg, so she won't do you any good for herding cattle. And I paid for her. Ask Rita." She waved a hand toward the girl, whose round eyes revealed her anxiety and who quickly held up the gold coin.

"What else did you *buy?*" The Colonel began to fling aside the blankets. "Well, well, well. Nate, get over here, boy. Take a look at what your sweetheart and her thieving father decided to carry off along with some of my employees."

Nate heard Mother's buggy arrive, but Tolley had just come over from the barn. He'd have to take care of helping her down. Nate walked to the back of the prairie schooner on wooden legs, terrified of what he would see. Casting a glance at Susanna, he noted that her chin jutted out and defiance blazed in her eyes.

"Now, don't those boxes look familiar?" The Colonel reached in and pulled one crate onto the lowered tailgate. He lifted the lid to reveal Mother's silver tea service. "See anything amiss here, son?"

Nate couldn't speak for the sick feeling clogging his throat. Nor could he look at Susanna. What a fool he'd been. While Mr. Anders's injuries had been real, everything else Nate had believed about the two of them was surely a lie.

"What's happening here?" Mother joined them, with Rosamond and Rand right behind her. She first saw Angela and started to address her. Then, seeing the silver set, she gasped. "Susanna, what have you done?" Mother reached out to touch Susanna, but Susanna jerked away.

"What have I done?" She moved toward the front

of the wagon. "Why don't you ask your husband what he has done?"

"Now, wait just a minute." Nate could feel his temper rising at her angry tone of voice. Standing here with his family, he knew where his loyalties lay.

"No. *You* wait just a minute." Susanna glanced up at her father. "Am I going to tell them, or are you?"

"Well, daughter, you were there when it happened, so you go right ahead."

At the old man's smug look, Nate wanted to plant his fist on his jaw. "Dad, why don't we just send for the sheriff and be done with it?" He was gratified to see his father didn't correct the way he addressed him.

"You can do what you like, Nate." The curl of Susanna's lips shouted her disgust. "But first you and your whole family will hear what I have to say." She pointed an accusing finger at the Colonel. "This fine, upstanding leader of your community is nothing but a thief and a murderer."

"Now, just a minute," Nate repeated. Every good thing he'd ever thought about her now made him sick to his stomach.

"Quiet, son." The Colonel crossed his arms and narrowed his eyes. "Go on, girl."

She faltered for a moment and, oddly, Nate wanted to help her. What a foolish, lovesick puppy he was. No wonder his father had wanted him to listen to Reverend Thomas's sermon on Proverbs. This truly was one deceitful woman in front of him now.

"First of all, our name isn't Anders. It's MacAndrews." She gave the Colonel a piercing look. "Does that sound familiar, Colonel? You should know it seeing as how you tried to wipe it off the face of this earth."

His glare softened, replaced by a look Nate couldn't identify. Worry? Shame?

"Y'all are so proud that Colonel Northam rode with General Sherman," Susanna said. "Well, I'm going to tell you something you don't know about that little excursion. On November 29, 1864, he and his troops rode onto my father's plantation. Daddy was away fighting, so of course those coward Yankees took great pleasure in terrifying the women and children he'd left behind. When my brother, just twelve years old, tried to stop them, this *heroic* soldier ordered him hanged. Hang a twelve-year-old! If my mama hadn't given him the buried silver tea service and her own sapphire necklace—*our* family heirlooms—he would have murdered a mere boy who was just trying to protect his mama and baby sister." She went to the back of the wagon and returned with a black jewel box, then held it in front of Mother. "Look. You can still see Georgia soil imbedded deep in the velvet."

"Oh, Frank." Mother held a hand up to her lips, and her eyes filled with tears.

Nate still felt sick to his stomach, but for a different reason. Why wasn't the Colonel denying these charges? Instead, his face had gone pale, almost ashen, and his arms dropped to his sides.

"As if that wasn't enough." Susanna's eyes also filled, "this brave officer ordered my brother's arms broken and the house burned down with everything in it. His men killed our livestock and even our pets." Her voice shook, but she seemed to force herself to continue, "My sweet old widowed grandmama died of apoplexy right out in the field while those coward Yankees rode away laughing." She looked around at each member of Nate's family, her accusing gaze settling at last on him.

He quickly turned to his father, whose face bore no denial of her charges.

"Frank, is this true?" Mother dabbed at her tears with a handkerchief.

"MacAndrews. Yes, I remember the place." The Colonel eyed Susanna's father and studied him briefly. "I remember." His shoulders slumped, and he walked to his horse, mounted and rode south.

As the hoofbeats died away, quiet settled over the front yard. The rest of the family stared around at each other.

Mother stood to her full height of five feet nothing and marched to the wagon. "Mr. Anders, I should say, Mr. MacAndrews, I never would have worn that necklace or used that lovely tea service if I'd known they were spoils of war. I thought my husband bought them in New York on his way home from the war." The pain in her voice sent shards of remorse through Nate for the way he'd spoken to brave Susanna. "Please keep your heirlooms with my blessings. You will have no trouble from anyone named Northam on this account." She looked at Nate, Rand, Rosamond and Tolley, silently ordering each of them to obey as only Mother could.

Mr. MacAndrews tipped his hat to her. "Ma'am, I can see you're entirely innocent in this matter. And now, please accept my humble gratitude for taking such good care of my daughter and me in our ill fortune. I don't know what we would have done if Nate hadn't come along." He spared Nate a smile and a nod. "We'll be eternally grateful."

Thumbs hooked on his gun belt, Nate shrugged and

scuffed the toe of his boot across a piece of driveway gravel. He noticed Susanna struggling to lift the tailgate and hurried over to help her. Just brushing his arm against hers sent a bittersweet pang through his chest. Wordlessly, he helped her into the wagon beside Angela, then secured the gate. Through no fault of their own, their love was doomed never to blossom. This must be the way Romeo and Juliet felt when their families' feud kept them apart.

With no little difficulty, he walked around to the front of the wagon. "Ready to go, sir."

"Thank you, my boy." Mr. MacAndrews touched the brim of his hat. "Shall we go, Miss Angela?" he said over his shoulder. "We have an appointment with the preacher, and we don't want to keep him waiting."

As they drove away, Susanna peered out at Nate just as she had weeks ago while they'd crossed the Valley in their separate wagons. Only now, instead of her cheerful smiles and friendly waves, her lovely face exuded the same sense of desolation weighing on his chest like a one-ton bull. And with her went every hope he'd ever had for happiness.

Chapter Twenty-Three

Susanna and Zack stood up with Daddy and Angela for their wedding ceremony in the church. Afterward, as they all sat in Reverend Thomas's small parlor sipping coffee and eating the cake Angela had cleverly brought along, Daddy retold their story.

The minister listened with great interest. "As a Southerner, I understand how you must feel, Mr. MacAndrews. My father fought for the Confederacy, but his brother chose the Union. They still don't speak to each other. Some of that same animosity still runs deep in the South, especially with the failure of Reconstruction." He accepted Angela's offer of more cake and dug into it before continuing.

"Like everyone else growing up in a divided family, I've had to sort out my own opinions about the war. In truth, I'm glad the Confederacy failed. I'm thankful to the Lord for bringing us back together as a country. After growing up in Virginia, then attending seminary in Massachusetts, I just couldn't go back to a town where President Lincoln's assassination is still celebrated. That's why I accepted Colonel Northam's invitation to serve this community as their pastor. Maybe out here in the West, we can put all of that behind us and start doing the Lord's work in earnest."

He smiled at the newlyweds, then focused on Daddy. "I can see you've already set aside some of your old ideas."

"Reverend, we will say no more about those old ideas." Daddy took Angela's hand and gazed at her fondly. "Miss Angela is a gift from the Almighty, a light in my dark, lonely world."

Susanna watched them through tear-filled eyes. The minister was right, of course. They needed to leave the past behind and find out what the Lord wanted for their future. While Susanna had no hope of ever marrying Nate, she couldn't help but be happy for Daddy. Even Mama wouldn't want Daddy to be alone the rest of his life, but what would she think of his marriage to a Mexican lady? Then again, Mama was in heaven, so it didn't matter. That thought shocked Susanna, but it also rang true deep in her soul.

Now she had to figure out her own opinions. She already liked Angela and had enjoyed working side by side with her in the kitchen. Her generosity and faith in God set an example, especially considering all that she'd suffered. And although she'd been a servant, she knew how to manage Daddy. That alone was an admirable feat.

"Daughter?" Daddy touched her hand and winked. He must have noticed her preoccupation. "What have you decided to call your new stepmama?"

Susanna saw the lady's apprehensive smile, and her heart warmed with the desire to reassure her. For a Southerner, that meant only one thing.

"Why, if it's all right with both of you, I believe I'd like to call her *Miss* Angela."

* * *

Nate settled uneasily back into his old room. Oddly, not a trace of Mr. Anders—MacAndrews—remained, not a single gray hair or scent of liniment. Either Angela had cleaned it before they left, or Rita was eager to show the family she could manage all of the housekeeping chores. Still, Nate missed sitting at the bedside chatting with the old man. He'd felt closer to him than he ever had the Colonel.

That wasn't true. During those long months ten years ago as the family had traveled across the country, first by train, then by wagon train, he and his father had worked side by side taking care of the others. He'd been only thirteen years old when they started out, but the Colonel had treated him with respect and depended on him as if he were a grown man. Sometime after they arrived in the San Luis Valley and began to build their ranch, his father changed. He gave Rand his head, ignored Tolley, doted on Rosamond and just barked orders at Nate. Nate still had no idea what had happened to bring about that change.

Now the Colonel had changed again. He did his work and showed up for supper every evening, but his eyes bore a haunted look, and he took no interest in conversation. That was the final proof Nate needed to believe everything Susanna had said. No wonder she hated his father.

Although Nate had been shocked to learn of the connection between his family and hers, he couldn't condemn the Colonel. He and Sherman and Grant had done what they had to do to end the war and preserve the Union. From the way the Colonel had reacted to Susanna's story, he no doubt felt a hefty measure of guilt for some of his actions. Nate just hoped his father took up the matter with the Lord before his guilty feelings made him sick. He also hoped never to go to war himself, but a man had to go when duty called.

Nate already felt pretty sick about losing Susanna. As much as he wanted to ride up to the settlement and find where she lived, maybe go see how she and her father were doing, he had responsibilities on the ranch that couldn't be put off. In the next week, he and some of the hands would ride up into the hills where the largest part of their cattle herd had grazed all summer. They'd round them up, drive them down to the ranch, check them for disease and injuries, brand any calves that had been born and then send the healthy ones off to market before winter snows closed all of the passes.

All that was left to him was to pray for Susanna to find peace. And maybe remember him from time to time. He knew he'd never forget her. Only one bright thought cheered him. Her father had bought property and wouldn't be likely to leave it. When Nate came home from roundup, he couldn't think of a single thing to prevent him from going to see her. Whether she wanted to see him was an entirely different matter.

"You silly puppy." Susanna removed Lazy Daisy from the burlap bag beside her on the ground. The pesky pup seemed determined to dig out every potato Susanna placed in it. With Shadow, the dog's favorite playmate, back at the house, she was doing her best to get into mischief while Susanna worked.

Bending over to retrieve the scattered potatoes, Susanna straightened carefully, holding one hand against her aching back. Several yards away, Miss Angela hummed as she plunged a pitchfork into the ground beside a withered plant, pressed down on the handle and pushed the round, red potatoes to the surface. No matter how much she watched her stepmother, Susanna could not figure out how she could work so hard without hurting her back or complaining. With her example and Mama's before her, Susanna tried to maintain a cheerful attitude, even as her heart cried for Nate. If he'd truly cared for her, wouldn't he come see her? Or had his father forbidden him?

The season's first hard frost had come early, setting the sugars in the fruit and berries, and signaling harvest time for the potatoes and other produce. Today Zack had driven them in the prairie schooner to a farm north of their new home, just across the Rio Grande, where for a small fee the farmers allowed people to dig their own supply of potatoes. These vegetables were not Susanna's favorite, but they were an important staple to keep on hand. She did look forward to enjoying the corn they'd already picked and dried. The widow who'd sold Daddy the property left behind some chickens and a hog, and Zack located a milk cow. These provisions, along with what they could purchase at Winsted's General Store, just opened beside Williams's Café, would see them through the winter.

Like the Northams' house, the foundation, fireplaces and chimneys of her new home were built of stones gathered from the surrounding fields. Zack explained that the man who'd built the house had wisely chosen a rocky bluff above the flood plain to lay his foundation. There in the shade of cottonwood, elm and pine trees, they could enjoy the river flowing beside their property without worrying about spring floods wash-

ing them away. They could also add to their larder all
the trout Daddy and Zack could catch. Susanna and
Angela put up elderberry and chokecherry preserves
and dried slices of the plump green apples from the
tree beside the house.

While they worked, Susanna questioned Miss Angela about her life. What began as a means of forgetting Nate ended up as an education.

"In 1840, the government of Mexico gave my father a land grant north of Mount Blanca. After the war
between Mexico and the United States, the Treaty of
Guadalupe Hidalgo said we must leave. My father had
been a wealthy man, and he put all of his money into
his ranch. When his land was taken without payment,
he would not leave my mother's grave. He stayed in
the San Luis Valley, working as a horse trainer for the
American man who was given our land."

Susanna felt a chill go up her spine. Miss Angela's
family had suffered at the hands of a conqueror just
as hers had. "How can you speak so casually about it?
Seems as if you would despise all Americans."

Miss Angela shrugged. "The Indians, whose land
was stolen in the first place, have tried to drive us all
out since the days of the *conquistadores,* but they, too,
fight among themselves. Even now the Utes try to in-
timidate the whites into leaving. But there are too many
for them to drive out. If they go to war, what good will it
do? No good at all, only death, only grief for everyone.
To have peace in here—" she tapped her chest above
her heart "—it is better to forgive. Better to see others
through the eyes of Dios." She tightened the cord around
the mouth of the bag of potatoes she'd just filled. "Better to find the place where Dios wants you to be, better

to become the person He wants you to be. That alone brings true peace inside you."

Peace. How Susanna longed for it. Forgiveness did seem a better path to finding it, a better attitude than bitterness, so she would try to follow Miss Angela's example in regards to Colonel Northam. The entire North, in fact. She'd seen Daddy struggle with it, and now he seemed at peace. Miss Angela was a good influence on him, and maybe having Mama's valuables had helped to settle the matter for him. At least now Susanna and Miss Angela didn't have to worry about his taking revenge and possibly getting hanged.

"Dios wants us to have joy," Miss Angela said. "Sometimes He wants us to be with a special person." She gave Susanna a teasing grin. "I know this one young *vaquero guapo,* very kind, very strong, very handsome. Maybe Dios wants you to be with him?"

While Susanna appreciated her wise advice, her frequent hints about Nate didn't help in the slightest. Yes, he was all the things she said, but if he wasn't willing to go against his father, they had no future together.

Shading her eyes, she surveyed the section of field they'd just harvested for any missed potatoes. Lazy Daisy scampered across the field, and Susanna chased after her, catching her before she reached the edge. In the distance, across the river, she saw a familiar form of man on a horse, and her heart skipped. Nate! Before she could wave, he turned his horse southward and rode away. Had he been watching over her all this time? Maybe he was working up the courage to visit her.

In the days that followed, however, he didn't come. Nor did she encounter any of the other Northam family members in the burgeoning settlement. On Sundays, to avoid possible unpleasantness, Daddy took his household to the community church in Del Norte.

With each passing week, Susanna grew more and more resigned to her loss. Maybe when spring arrived, she should return to Marietta as she'd planned, marry a Southern gentleman and forget all about a certain cowboy.

But that thought no longer satisfied her daydreams. In fact, it didn't sit well with her at all.

Chapter Twenty-Four

Even though Nate had only seen Susanna at a distance, he relished the memory of watching her in the field. He'd laughed at the puppy's antics as Susanna tried to work, but he hadn't had time to cross the river and talk to her. In a hurry to get back home from doing an errand for Mother, he'd consoled himself that he would see her at church on his last Sunday before roundup. When the MacAndrewses hadn't shown up, he had a hard time listening to Reverend Thomas's sermon. Every time he heard feet shuffling behind him, he'd turned to see if they were coming through the door.

On the ranch, once the Colonel had returned, no one spoke of the incident with the MacAndrewses. Thus, nothing much had changed for the Northam family, except for the gaping hole Nate felt without Susanna in the house. He sort of suspected Rosamond and Mother missed her, too, and of course they all missed Angela.

Now up in the hills to bring down the herd, Nate lingered by the chuck wagon to eat his supper to avoid joining the Colonel, Rand and the other boys around the campfire. Why his father had felt it necessary to come on this roundup was beyond him. Once again the Colonel was managing everything. He seemed so pleased with Rand's repentance over his gambling and his staying awake in church that he barely noticed Nate's constancy. Nor did he spend any time with Tolley. At fifteen, the boy had no friends his own age with whom to release his boyish foolishness, so one of these days he might do something rash to get the Colonel's attention. Nate tried to commend his youngest brother at every opportunity, but the boy's hangdog glances at their father showed whose approval he really wanted. Nate understood how he felt.

After turning his tin plate and fork over to Cookie after supper, he sat on his bedroll and leaned back against his saddle to gaze at the sky, just as he and Susanna had done the first night after they met back in June. The countless number of stars strewn across the night sky reminded him of the tiny diamonds on the necklace Susanna had reclaimed. Of course, everything reminded him of something about Susanna. Further, he still missed his chats with Mr. MacAndrews. Now, there was an attentive father, a man who set an example Nate wanted to follow when and if he ever had children of his own. Not that the old man was perfect. Nate would never drag a daughter halfway across the continent just to reclaim some stolen valuables. Of course, if Mr. MacAndrews hadn't done so, Nate never would have met Susanna, a depressing thought.

Words from Reverend Thomas's Sunday sermon came to mind. Speaking on the story of the Prodigal Son, he'd said, *Only God can be the perfect Father.* Nate couldn't argue with that.

He eyed the Colonel, whom he'd not called Dad again

since that fateful day weeks ago in Del Norte. His father's face, never in the least bit fleshy, now had a thin, haggard look. Did he struggle with guilt over the incident at the MacAndrews plantation? If not that, something was eating at him, and for once Nate felt sorry for him. Too bad he didn't have a close friend to confide in, somebody like Mr. Foster, who'd served with him in the war and would understand his struggles.

One thing Nate was sure about. He was tired of being angry and bitter. The preacher's sermon had spoken to him, and he'd vowed that day he wouldn't be like the Prodigal Son's bitter older brother. Holding on to a grudge was like holding a rattler to his chest, just waiting for it to bite. *Lord, I'm letting go. You take over.*

No matter what the Colonel did or didn't do, he would show him respect, real, honest respect. As for Rand, Nate would keep on praying he'd never go back to gambling. And Tolley? Well, he'd watch over the kid like the Colonel should be doing. In only one matter would Nate stand up to his father. When they returned to the ranch, he would announce his plans to ask Mr. MacAndrews if he could court Susanna. If the Colonel said no, Nate would seek the Lord's guidance for the next step. If God told him to move out and move on, he'd do that.

"I sent Rand out to see about those calves we branded today." The Colonel eased himself down beside Nate.

Lost in thought, he hadn't noticed his father's approach. Here was his first chance to keep his vow. "Good idea." Any one of the men could have done it. Maybe his father wanted to give Rand more responsibility, as Nate had suggested.

"You doing all right?" his father said.

Where had that come from? It was a question his father never asked him.

"Yessir." He had the strange notion he was being tested, but whether by God or the Colonel, he didn't know. He sent up a quick prayer for wisdom.

"I've been thinking." His father looked up at the sky and released a long, weary sigh. "A man who steals from helpless women and children is no better than those thieves who stole MacAndrews's horses."

Nate's spine tingled. Yes, this was a test, but not what he'd expected. The Colonel was confiding in him, something he'd never anticipated. Could he be the friend his father needed? He searched for a response to the Colonel's declaration, but no words would come.

"We did what we had to do. We got the job done. We scorched the South and won the war. The slaves were freed, the Union saved."

Right about now, Nate thought he should say, *Praise the Lord,* but he couldn't speak. So he continued his silent prayer.

"But that doesn't stop the guilt."

Nate longed to tell his father he had no cause to feel guilty, but the words stuck in his throat. He didn't believe it, anyway. War or not, he'd done wrong.

"I've been burying my memories all these years. It feels good to have them out in the open. Now I can face what I did and confess it to the Lord."

Nate nodded, still unable to speak. By now he was pretty sure he wasn't supposed to.

"That boy, Rand." The Colonel grunted. "He reminds me of my little brother, the one who ran away to join the army and died at Gettysburg. Our father was always pretty harsh with him. I think that's why he ran away. I never wanted to make that mistake with Rand."

Nate swallowed hard. So all this time, the Colonel had been acting out of fear, not favoritism for his middle son. Now that Nate thought on it, the favoritism had begun after Rand disobeyed their father's orders while they were building the ranch house and suffered that bad fall from the roof.

"Not like you." The Colonel clapped Nate on the shoulder. "I could always trust you to do the right thing." He chuckled. "Of course, you've always been Mr. Knows-It-All, but I'm glad to see you've listened to the preacher's talk on Proverbs. Knowledge isn't worth much if it's not accompanied by wisdom." He grunted again. "But your attitude isn't a surprise. You remind me of a young lieutenant I used to know."

From his rueful grin, Nate guessed he was talking about himself. Still, the knows-it-all charge was valid. Nate had always been proud of his ability to tackle any job and do it well. He was good at figuring things out, sometimes even better than his father. However, such talents were gifts from the Lord and didn't give him the right to be boastful. He'd be wise to keep thinking on that.

"Get some sleep." The Colonel stood and ambled toward his own bedroll. "You have the next watch."

Nate started to say, *I know that.* He caught the words just in time. "Good night, Dad."

The Colonel looked his way and gave him a slight smile. "Good night, son."

Nate couldn't begin to describe the feeling of peace flooding his soul. He knew only that his relationship with his father would be all right from now on. And now he realized his father hadn't been referring to Susanna

as the strange woman in Proverbs, hadn't been thinking about her at all. So maybe, just maybe, he could
persuade Dad to revise his opinion of Susanna, who'd
never done him any harm.

Susanna double-checked the contents of the prairie
schooner. Miss Angela's special corn bread, potato salad,
ham sandwiches, green beans, one plain cake for serving
right away, a second fancier cake for a cakewalk prize.
And, of course, Susanna's pralines. Trepidation and excitement vied for control of her emotions as the family
packed for their journey into the settlement. The entire
community would be meeting for their annual Harvest
Home in the field next to the church and across the road
from Williams's Café and Winsted's General Store. They
would have speeches, horse races, games for grown-ups,
games for the children, singing, dancing and far more
food than all of them put together could consume.

She would see Nate today, and the thought made her
insides flutter. After learning two weeks ago he'd gone
on a roundup, she'd realized he hadn't been ignoring her.
Even so, she had no idea how she would behave when
she saw him. If Miss Angela was right, Nate would be
eager to see her, but Susanna wouldn't count on it. If
his loyalties lay with his father, he'd probably done his
best to forget her.

As for her view of the Colonel, she'd taken Miss
Angela's advice to heart and concentrated on forgiv-
ing him. His plundering of the plantation hadn't been
a personal attack against her family. Even Daddy admitted to being troubled by his own actions during the
war, so how could she hate a Yankee officer who was
doing his duty, however evil that duty might be? She'd

probably never like the Colonel, but she could show him God's love, just as Miss Angela had taught her. On the other hand, if she and Nate did mend their fences and marry, she would resign herself to his father's dislike. Back home, her poor brother, Edward, never did anything right, according to his mother-in-law.

The five-mile trip to the settlement seemed to take forever. At last, the church spire came into view, then the larger homes and, last of all, the two-story general store. Zack drove the wagon into the field and found a spot where the horses could graze. Susanna jumped down from the driver's bench and helped Miss Angela and Daddy carry their food to plank tables set up beneath the cottonwoods.

Their arrival was noticed right away by the other ladies. While many called out greetings, Mrs. Northam offered a wary smile. Rosamond hurried around the table and pulled Susanna into a tight embrace, nearly knocking her over. "I've missed you so much."

"I've missed you, too." Susanna's voice broke, and tears sprang to her eyes. *Oh, bother.* She had promised herself she wouldn't cry.

To cover their heightened emotions, both girls began to rearrange various bowls and plates on the table, chattering along with the other ladies about the abundant harvest. Across the way, Susanna caught sight of the Colonel and gasped softly to herself. In the few short weeks since she'd last seen him, he appeared to have aged ten years. The lines of his face had deepened considerably, and his dark brown hair was streaked with gray. Even his posture, always military straight, was now slightly bowed. To her surprise, he approached Daddy.

"MacAndrews, may I have a minute of your time?"

His voice lacked its usual booming authority. "Will you accompany me to a more private location?" He waved a hand toward the church.

For a moment, Daddy stared up at the taller man with a calm regard. Then he gave a curt nod. When Miss Angela tried to follow, Daddy whispered something to her, and she let them go.

Susanna tried to busy herself, but her hands were shaking.

"They'll be all right." Nate's words, spoken softly near her ear, sent a shiver of surprise and happiness down her neck.

She looked up to see his charming, lopsided grin and those bright green eyes. Her heart did a dozen somersaults, and she found it hard to breathe. With some difficulty, she managed to say, "La-di-da, Mr. Nate Northam, I'm sure they *will* be just fine." But it all came out on a sigh, not at all the saucy tone she'd intended.

His gaze intensified, and his smile disappeared. "May I speak to you privately over by your wagon?" Worry lines appeared on his forehead and around his eyes.

"Yes." Rosamond gave Susanna a shove. "Go."

Even Miss Angela tilted her head in that direction, granting both permission and her blessing.

"Very well." Susanna took Nate's offered arm and walked with him to the site.

When they arrived, he lifted her up onto the lowered tailgate and leaned against its side. "We have a lot of things to sort out." He gave her a doubtful look. "That is, if you're interested."

Every pert answer she might have given him fled from her mind. "I'm interested. Go on."

"Your father…" He looked out across the field and chewed his lower lip. "I mean, my father…"

"Nate." She set a hand on his arm. "This isn't about their quarrel or about the war or about anything else. This is about you and me."

"You're right. It is." His worried expression cleared. "I've already told Dad I'm going to ask your father if I can court you, but considering the circumstances, I thought I'd—"

"Wait." She held up one hand to punctuate her interruption. "You're asking me whether you can ask my father to ask me whether I want to court." She burst into an uncontrollable giggle that almost pitched her off the tailgate. Surely, her giddiness came from relief and joy.

Nate laughed, too. Then he guffawed, a sound that lifted Susanna's heart clear up to the top of the nearby cottonwoods. "Yep. That's about right."

As soon as she could control herself, she forced a sober tone into her voice. "Well, I don't know, Nate Northam. If you'll kindly recall, you did call me a thief." She challenged him with a hard stare.

He blinked and frowned. "Yes, I guess I did." He crossed his arms and gave her a sidelong look. "I still say you're a thief."

Her jaw fell open, and she had a hard time closing it. "Why, Nate Northam. How dare you?" All her hopes exploded in a painful burst.

She started to jump to the ground, but he swung around in front of her and placed his hands on the tailgate on either side of her.

"Now, don't deny it." There went that grin again. "You stole my heart."

"Oh, you!" She smacked his hand while joy and relief

flooded back into her chest. "Yes, I want you to speak to Daddy. Yes, you may court me." She shook a scolding finger in his face. "Just don't plan on a long courtship, you hear me?"

He offered a mock salute. "Yes, ma'am. Whatever you say."

"Oh, Nate." She touched his cheek, enjoying the gentle scratch of his late-morning stubble.

"Oh, Susanna," he sang in his slightly off-pitch way. "Oh, won't you marry me?"

Her heart still giddy with joy, she giggled again. Mama would be appalled at her lack of self-control. No, under the circumstances, Mama would be laughing, too.

"Young man." Daddy marched toward the wagon, followed by the Colonel. "You have not asked my permission to court my daughter."

Not doubting his approval for a moment, Susanna gave Nate a mock-worried frown. "Oh, my. What are you going to do now?"

"Mr. MacAndrews, sir." Nate straightened and stepped over to Daddy. "May I court your daughter?"

"You may." His eyes dancing, Daddy shook Nate's hand. Then he glanced over his shoulder at the Colonel. "I assume you have no objections."

The Colonel's expression was less than cheerful, but he shook his head. "None that I can think of right off."

"Well, I do." Susanna jumped down from the wagon and marched to the center of the little group. "I object to you two being enemies. I want to see you shake hands right now." They traded a look but made no move to mind her.

Somewhere in the back of her mind, she became aware of a crowd gathering around them, but she persisted in her mission.

"You'd better listen to me." She shook a schoolmarm finger in each of their faces. "If you two don't put aside the past, as Nate and I have done, I'll never let either of you see your grandchildren. I won't have the war refought on my front porch for the rest of your lives."

"That's the way to tell 'em, Susanna," Miss Pam called from the crowd.

"The war's over," someone else cried. "No more fighting."

"That's why we came out west," Reverend Thomas added.

Other folks chimed in with their agreement.

"Well, Colonel," Daddy said, "seems like the residents of Northamville, or Northam Town or Northampton or whatever you plan to call this place, have spoken. I'll go along with them. What do you say?"

The Colonel wiped a hand down the side of his face. "I had a short speech prepared for later, but I may as well deliver it now, since you're all right here." He cleared his throat and surveyed the gathering. "We can't change what happened in the past or our opinions about the war, but we can move forward and make a better future for our children and grandchildren. As to the name of our town, I'm honored that you voted to name it for my family, for me. But I'm declining that honor."

Groans and protests arose from the crowd, but he lifted his hands in a placating gesture. "Let's choose something that shows just what we've been talking about. We've all come west in hopes of making a new life, a new *way* of life. Does anyone object to New Hope?"

"Or—" Daddy moved in front of the Colonel and faced the crowd "—in keeping with the local custom of using Spanish names, how about the Spanish word for *hope, Esperanza?*" He sent Miss Angela a smile. "Esperanza, Colorado."

"I like it," Miss Pam called out.

To a person, all agreed. With that matter settled, everyone returned to their activities.

Nate pulled Susanna aside into the shadow of the prairie schooner. Holding her in a gentle embrace, he caressed her cheek. "I love you, Susanna. I have since that moment on La Veta Pass when I looked up to see you holding a Winchester on me. You're brave and beautiful and sweet and sassy. I admire the fact that you know your own mind and, most of all, that you're a woman of faith. Will you marry me?"

"La-di-da, Mr. Nate Northam." She couldn't resist teasing him. With all, or most, of their problems solved, she could now relax and have some fun with this Yankee boy. Yankee *gentleman,* she amended. "When I said I wanted a short courtship, I didn't mean only fifteen minutes."

He threw back his head and laughed. "Well, how about if I ask you again after dinner?" He pointed his chin to the tables, where folks had lined up to fill their plates.

"That might do just fine."

Without so much as a by-your-leave, Nate bent and kissed her. Just a quick peck, so she couldn't object too much, although she noticed one older lady watching them with a scowl.

On the other hand, there stood Daddy and the Colonel talking quietly like old friends, although Susanna noticed a familiar gleam in her father's eyes. Just as he'd overrode the Colonel's will in naming the town, she was certain he had every intention of challenging everything the Colonel did from here on out.

Chapter Twenty-Five

Back home in Georgia, September and October weather could be counted on for warm, sunny days and gradually cooler nights. Nonetheless, Susanna found the frosty autumn weather of the San Luis Valley very much to her liking. Of course, part of her happy sentiments were due to her upcoming wedding.

After conferring with Miss Angela and Mrs. Northam, she decided to make a white wedding dress, no matter how impractical it seemed for a dress worn only once. However, such a gown could be made with wide seams and a deep hem so it could be passed down to future Northam brides who might grow taller and wider than Susanna. Mrs. Winsted must have expected to supply just such needs, for her new general store stocked several large bolts of white silk and plenty of lace.

While the ladies split their time between wedding preparations and preserving the winter's supply of food, the men had their own duties. The Colonel had chosen Rand as his trail boss, and most of the cowhands had gone with him to drive the cattle to market. That meant

Nate had to shoulder much of the responsibility around the ranch, so Susanna didn't see him often enough to suit her. He did continue the Northam family custom of resting on Sundays, only now he spent those days at the MacAndrews house.

"Angela, I've missed your cooking something fierce," he said over dinner one Sunday after church. "Maybe after the wedding, I'll just move up here to live with you folks."

Daddy and Miss Angela laughed, while Zack shook his head.

"Why, Nate Northam." Susanna sniffed with artificial displeasure. "I'll have you know I'll be doing the cooking for you and me." Not only was Miss Angela a gifted cook, she was also an excellent teacher. Susanna had perfected many dishes under her guidance. But she wouldn't undermine Rita and insist upon cooking for the rest of the Northams, for she doubted she could ever please the Colonel.

"But, darlin'." Nate leaned back in his chair and mimicked Zack's cowboy dialect. "As tasty as your pralines are, a man can't live on 'em."

She shook her fork at him. "Just for that, no dessert for you today."

Of course, Miss Angela served him two slices of apple pie with a heavy dose of cream poured over them. Only after he'd praised the flavor did Susanna admit she'd made it.

"Well, then, I guess you'll do." He shoveled in the last bite with a flourish and gave her a wink. "At least when it comes to desserts."

Later, after Susanna and Miss Angela cleaned up the

kitchen and he'd had his weekly chat with Daddy, they walked hand in hand down to the river.

"I can't imagine what takes all of your time." Susanna couldn't bear being parted from him for another week. "Now that the herd's off to market, what on earth do you do out there on the ranch all day?"

His bright green eyes sparkled in the sunshine, and he puckered away a smile. "Oh, you have no idea. Got horses to tend, fences to mend, hay to harvest and store."

She got the feeling he was hiding something from her, but Mama, and now Miss Angela, had warned her against being a nag.

Instead, they talked about their future, about both of them wanting a large family, about the day they'd have their own house and, most of all, about the extraordinary way the Lord had brought them together.

"Say, did you and your father ever finish reading *Bleak House?*"

"We did." She sat on a fallen pine tree beside the river. "It was long and sometimes tedious, but there's a lesson to be learned about being honest and not keeping secrets from those we love. I also liked the ending. Even though the lawsuit destroyed several lives, good, sweet Esther ended up the happy mistress of her own house, married to a wonderful man who loved her."

"Hmm." He sat beside her and put an arm around her waist. She leaned against his sturdy shoulder, relishing his strength. "It occurs to me that our fathers could have gone to court over your silver. Some people regard spoils of war an honest way to acquire property. It would all depend upon the judge how it would turn out."

She shuddered. "Thank the Lord for their reconciliation."

He chuckled "And thank Him for my mother's interference. After finding out how my father got those things, she wouldn't have kept them even if Mr. Lincoln himself had handed them to her."

She gazed up at him, her heart bursting with joy and love. "Like Esther, now I get to be the happy mistress of my own home. But with all the teasing we like to do, it will be anything but a *bleak* house."

Now he laughed out loud, a sound she dearly loved. Unlike his singing, his laughter was decidedly musical. She could listen to it all day, and soon she would be able to.

Nate stood beside Dad and Reverend Thomas at the front of the church. The ladies had been keeping secrets lately, so he had an idea Susanna's wedding getup was something to behold. Rita started playing the "Wedding March" on the small pump organ, and Rosamond walked slowly down the aisle. When she reached the front of the church, Susanna entered on her father's arm, and sure enough, she was a vision like nothing Nate had ever seen.

"Steady, son." Dad put a hand on Nate's shoulder. "Breathe."

Nate did as he was told, gasping in a breath.

Mr. MacAndrews still limped a little, so it was hard to tell who was leaning on whom as they moved toward the front. Before Nate knew what had happened, he was saying "I do," and Reverend Thomas gave him permission to kiss the bride.

Mindful of the watching crowd, he bent down and placed a quick peck on Susanna's pretty pink lips. To his surprise, she gave him one of her cute little scolding looks.

"Is that all I get?" She grabbed the front of his shirt, stood on her tiptoes and taught him a thing or two about kissing.

Goose bumps shot through his entire body, and he was all but certain his toes curled up right inside his boots.

"There." Susanna put on her smug look. "Now we're honestly and truly married."

Before Nate could answer, Dad cleared his throat. "Son, may I speak to your bride?"

All humor left her face, but here in front of the entire community, how could he say no? He gave a quick nod.

"Susanna," Dad said, "we got off on the wrong foot, and I'm entirely to blame. You are a lovely young woman, and I'm proud you've chosen to marry my son. Welcome to the Northam family."

Nate held his breath. Every time he'd brought up his father's inhospitality or his actions against her family during the war, she'd changed the subject. Did she realize how much was riding on her response?

Susanna's eyes burned as she blinked away tears. What would Mama have her do? In the past weeks, she'd had more memories of that last fateful day on the plantation. She saw brave Mama facing this same man, who'd never had the courtesy to even dismount from his horse while ordering the livestock killed and the house set on fire. Susanna blinked again, and the tears rushed down her cheeks. She cast a pleading glance at Miss Angela, who tapped her chest above her heart, and the answer came clear and fast. She had to make peace with this man before moving back into his house, this time permanently.

She stepped past Nate and reached up to place a kiss on her father-in-law's cheek. "Thank you, Father Northam. I'm pleased as punch to be a member of your family."

Applause erupted from the congregation, along with a few cheers.

"Let's eat," somebody called out.

They all adjourned to the field next door, where linen-covered plank tables held a grand wedding feast. For over an hour as folks ate and danced, Susanna and Nate suffered the usual teasing about newlyweds. She overheard Zack and another cowboy whispering about a shivaree, and she cast a worried glance at Nate.

Grabbing her hand, he put one finger to his lips. "Shh. Let's go."

He led her around to the back of the church, where Mother Northam's buggy stood hitched and ready to go. "Let's hope nobody misses us."

Taking a long road around the settlement to avoid being seen, Nate drove them at last down the long road to the ranch. But when they came to the stone archway, he kept on going.

"Mr. Nate Northam, just where do you think you're taking me?"

"Just wait and see." A quarter mile from the Four Stones archway, he turned down a newly smoothed road and up to a pretty white house with a stone foundation and chimney.

"What do you think?" Filled with a worried look, Nate's green eyes had never been so appealing. "Would you like to live here?"

For a moment she couldn't speak. All this time, he hadn't been neglecting her. He'd been building their own home. She wouldn't have to live with her in-laws after all. "Oh, Nate, it's beautiful."

He jumped down from the buggy, lifted her in his arms and carried her right through the front door. "Welcome home, Mrs. Nate Northam." He set her down and waved one arm to take in the sizable parlor, a hallway on one side no doubt leading to the bedrooms, and the dining room and kitchen off to the other side. "Make yourself at home."

"Why, *Mr.* Nate Northam." She flung herself into his arms. "I believe I'll do just that."

* * * * *

**"I... What did you say your surname was?"
she asked in a choked voice.**

"Hopkins," Will replied. The girl's face went deathly white.

She pulled her satchel up onto her lap and started sorting through her things. Finally she pulled out a paper and handed it to him. It was the ad his mother had created to find him a housekeeper. The ad Miss Stewart had answered. But did that mean... No, it couldn't be. The woman in front of him, who looked as if she might give in to tears at any moment, *couldn't* be Abigail Stewart.

"You're...you're Miss Stewart?" Will said incredulously.

Tommy poked his brother. "She's our new house?"

"House*keeper*," Willy hissed.

She straightened her back and tilted her chin up to look the boys' father straight in the eye. "Yes."

Any answer Will might have given was interrupted by Tommy's response. Throwing his arms around the woman's waist, he squeezed tight while yelling out, "You're our Auntie House!"